"You can st..."
Ellie said.

"Like what?"

"Like you're feeling sorry for the poor little foster girl playing make-believe. I did just fine."

"I never said otherwise," Matt said gruffly.

"You didn't have to say a word. I can see what you're thinking clear as day. I've seen pity plenty of times. But I've done just fine," Ellie insisted, lifting her chin. "And I don't care what you think about me, Harte."

"Good. Then it won't bother you when I tell you I think about you all the time. Or," he finished quietly, "when I tell you that I think you're just about the prettiest thing I've ever seen standing in my barn."

Ellie's jaw sagged open, and she stared at him, wide-eyed.

"Close your mouth, Doc," he murmured wryly.

She snapped it shut, knowing exactly what he was going to do...

RaeAnne Thayne finds inspiration in the beautiful northern Utah mountains, where the *New York Times* and *USA TODAY* bestselling author lives with her husband and three children. Her books have won numerous honors, including RITA® Award nominations from Romance Writers of America and a Career Achievement Award from *RT Book Reviews*. RaeAnne loves to hear from readers and can be contacted through her website, raeannethayne.com.

Linda Goodnight, a *New York Times* bestselling author and winner of a RITA® Award in Inspirational Fiction, has appeared on the Christian bestseller list. Her novels have been translated into more than a dozen languages. Active in orphan ministry, Linda enjoys writing fiction that carries a message of hope in a sometimes-dark world. She and her husband live in Oklahoma. Visit her website, lindagoodnight.com, for more information.

STAR VALLEY WINTER

NEW YORK TIMES **BESTSELLING AUTHOR**
RaeAnne Thayne

H Harlequin

BESTSELLING AUTHOR COLLECTION

Harlequin®
BESTSELLING
AUTHOR
COLLECTION

Recycling programs
for this product may
not exist in your area.

ISBN-13: 978-1-335-01624-9

Star Valley Winter
First published as The Valentine Two-Step in 2002.
This edition published in 2025.
Copyright © 2002 by RaeAnne Thayne

To Protect His Children
First published in 2021. This edition published in 2025.
Copyright © 2021 by Linda Goodnight

Harlequin Enterprises ULC
22 Adelaide St. West, 41st Floor
Toronto, Ontario M5H 4E3, Canada
www.Harlequin.com

Printed in U.S.A.

CONTENTS

STAR VALLEY WINTER   7
RaeAnne Thayne

TO PROTECT HIS CHILDREN   271
Linda Goodnight

Also by RaeAnne Thayne

HQN

Sleigh Bells Ring
The Path to Sunshine Cove
Christmas at Holiday House
The Sea Glass Cottage
Coming Home for Christmas
The Cliff House
Season of Wonder

Harlequin Special Edition

The Cowboys of Cold Creek

Starstruck
Light the Stars
Dancing in the Moonlight
Dalton's Undoing
The Cowboy's Christmas Miracle
A Cold Creek Homecoming

Visit her Author Profile page at Harlequin.com,
or raeannethayne.com, for more titles!

STAR VALLEY WINTER

RaeAnne Thayne

To Lyndsey Thomas, for saving my life and my sanity more times than I can count! Special thanks to Dr. Ronald Hamm, DVM, animal healer extraordinaire, for sharing so generously of his expertise.

Prologue

"It's absolutely perfect." Dylan Webster held her hands out imploringly to her best friend, Lucy Harte. "Don't you see? It's the only way!"

Lucy frowned in that serious way of hers, her gray eyes troubled. In the dim, dusty light inside their secret place—a hollowed-out hideaway behind the stacked hay bales of the Diamond Harte barn loft—her forehead looked all wrinkly. Kind of like a shar-pei puppy Dylan had seen once at her mom's office back in California.

"I don't know…" she began.

"Come on, Luce. You said it yourself. We should have been sisters, not just best friends. We were born on exactly the same day, we both love horses and despise long division and we both want to be vets like my mom when we grow up, right?"

"Well, yes, but…"

"If my mom married your dad, we really *would* be sisters. It would be like having a sleepover all the time. I could ride the school bus with you and everything, and I just know my mom would let me have my own horse if we lived out here on the ranch."

Lucy nibbled her lip. "But, Dylan…"

"You want a mom of your own as much as I want a dad, don't you? Even though you have your aunt Cassie to look after you, it's not the same. You know it's not."

It was exactly the right button to push, and she knew it. Before her very eyes, Lucy sighed, and her expression went all dreamy. Dylan felt a little pinch of guilt at using her best friend's most cherished dream to her own advantage, but she worked hard to ignore it.

Her plan would never work if she couldn't convince Lucy how brilliant it was. Both of them had to be one-hundred-percent behind it. "We'd be sisters, Luce," she said. "Sisters for real. Wouldn't it be awesome?"

"Sisters." Lucy burrowed deeper into the hay, her gray eyes closed as if, like Dylan, she was imagining family vacations and noisy Christmas mornings and never again having to miss a daddy-daughter party at school. Or in Lucy's case, a mother-daughter party.

"It *would* be awesome." That shar-pei look suddenly came back to her forehead, and she sat up. "But, Dylan, why would they ever get married? I don't think they even like each other very much."

"Who?"

"My dad and your mom."

Doubt came galloping back like one of Lucy's dad's horses after a stray dogie. Lucy was absolutely right. They *didn't* like each other much. Just the other day, she heard her mom tell SueAnn that Matt Harte was a stubborn old man in a younger man's body.

"But what a body it is," her mom's assistant at the clinic had replied, with a rumbly laugh like grown-ups make when they're talking about sexy stuff. "Matt Harte and his brother have always been the most gorgeous men in town."

Her mom had laughed, too, and she'd even turned a little bit pink, like a strawberry shake. "Shame on you. You're a happily married woman, Sue."

"Married doesn't mean dead. Or crazy, for that matter."

Her mom had scrunched up her face. "Even if he is… attractive…in a macho kind of way, a great body doesn't make up for having the personality of an ornery bull."

Dylan winced, remembering. Okay, so Lucy's dad and her mom hadn't exactly gotten along since the Websters moved to Star Valley. Still, her mom thought he was good-looking and had a great body. That had to count for something.

Dylan gave Lucy what she hoped was a reassuring smile. "They just haven't had a chance to get to know each other."

Lucy looked doubtful. "My dad told Aunt Cassie just last week he wouldn't let that city quack near any of his livestock. I think he meant your mom."

Dylan narrowed her eyes. "My mom's not a quack."

"I know she's not. I think your mom's just about the greatest vet around. I'm only telling you what he said."

"We just have to change his mind. We have to figure out some way to push them together. Once they get to know each other, they'll have to see that they belong together."

"I'm not so sure."

Dylan blew out a breath that made her auburn bangs flutter. Lucy was the best friend anybody could ask for—the best friend she'd ever had. These last three months since they'd moved here had been so great. Staying overnight at the ranch, riding Lucy's horses, trading secrets and dreams here behind the hay bales.

They were beyond best, best, best friends, and Dylan loved her to death, but sometimes Lucy worried too much. Like about spelling tests and missing the bus and letting her desk get too messy.

She just had to convince her the idea would work. It would be so totally cool if they could pull this off. She wanted a dad in the worst way, and she figured Matt Harte—with his big hands and slow smile and kind eyes—would be absolutely perfect. Having Lucy for a sister would be like the biggest bonus she could think of.

Dylan would just have to try harder.

"It's going to work. Trust me. I know it's going to work." She grabbed Lucy's hand and squeezed it tightly. "Before you know it, we'll be walking down the aisle wearing flowers in our hair and me and my mom will be living here all the time. See, I have this plan...."

Chapter 1

"They did *what*?"

Ellie Webster and the big, gruff rancher seated beside her spoke in unison. She spared a glance at Matt Harte and saw he looked like he'd just been smacked upside the head with a two-by-four.

"Oh, dear. I was afraid of this." Sarah McKenzie gave a tiny, apologetic smile to both of them.

With her long blond hair and soft, wary brown eyes, her daughter's teacher always made Ellie think of a skittish palomino colt, ready to lunge away at the first provocation. Now, though, she was effectively hobbled into place behind her big wooden schoolteacher's desk. "You're telling me you both *didn't* agree to serve on the committee for the Valentine's Day carnival?"

"Hell no." Matt Harte looked completely horrified by the very idea of volunteering for a Valentine's Day carnival committee—as astonished as Ellie imagined he'd be if Ms. McKenzie had just asked him to stick one of her perfectly sharpened number-two pencils in his eye.

"I've never even heard of the Valentine's Day carnival until just now," Ellie offered.

"Well, this does present a problem." Ms. McKenzie folded her hands together on top of what looked like a grade book, slim and black and ominous.

Ellie had always hated those grade books.

Despite the fact that she couldn't imagine any two people being more different, Ellie had a brief, unpleasant image of her own fourth-grade teacher. Prissy mouth, hair scraped back into a tight bun. Complete intolerance for a scared little girl who hid her bewildered loneliness behind defiant anger.

She pushed the unwelcome image aside.

"The girls told me you both would cochair the committee," the teacher said. "They were most insistent that you wanted to do it."

"You've got to be joking. They said we *wanted* to do it? I don't know where the he—heck Lucy could have come up with such a harebrained idea." Matt Harte sent one brief, disparaging glare in Ellie's direction, and she stiffened. She could just imagine what he was thinking. *If my perfect little Lucy has a harebrained idea in her perfect little head, it must have come from you and your flighty daughter, with your wacky California ways.*

He had made it perfectly clear he couldn't understand the instant bond their two daughters had formed when she and Dylan moved here at the beginning of the school year three months earlier. He had also made no secret of the fact that he didn't trust her or her veterinary methods anywhere near his stock.

The really depressing thing was, Harte's attitude seemed to be the rule, not the exception, among the local ranching community. After three months, she was no closer to breaking into their tight circle than she'd been that very first day.

"It does seem odd," Ms. McKenzie said, and Ellie chided herself for letting her mind wander.

Right now she needed to concentrate on Dylan and this latest scrape her daughter had found herself in. Not on the past or on the big, ugly pile of bills that needed to be paid, regardless of whether or not she had any patients.

"I thought it was rather out of character for both of you," the quiet, pretty teacher went on. "That's why I called you both and asked you to come in this evening, so we all could try to get to the bottom of this."

"Why would they lie about it?" Ellie asked. "I don't understand why on earth the girls would say we volunteered for something I've never even heard of before now."

The teacher shifted toward her and shrugged her shoulders inside her lacy white blouse. She made the motion look so delicate and airy that Ellie felt about as feminine as a teamster in her work jeans and flannel shirt.

"I have no idea," she said. "I was hoping you could shed some light on it."

"You sure it was our girls who signed up?"

Ms. McKenzie turned to the rancher with a small smile. "Absolutely positive. I don't think I could possibly mix that pair up with any of my other students."

"Well, there's obviously been a mistake," Matt said gruffly.

Ms. McKenzie was silent for a few moments, then she sighed. "That's what I was afraid you would say. Still, the fact remains that I need two parents to cochair the committee, and your daughters obviously want you to do it. Would the two of you at least consider it?"

The rancher snorted. "You've got the wrong guy."

"I don't think so," the teacher answered gently, as if chiding a wayward student, and Ellie wondered how she could appear to be so completely immune to the potent impact of Matt Harte.

Even with that aggravated frown over this latest scheme their daughters had cooked up, he radiated raw male appeal, with rugged, rugged-hewn features, piercing blue eyes and broad shoulders. Ellie couldn't even sit next to him without feeling the power in those leashed muscles.

But Sarah McKenzie appeared oblivious to it. She treated him with the same patience and kindness she showed the fourth graders in her class.

"I think you'd both do a wonderful job," the teacher continued. "Since this is my first year at the school, I haven't been to the carnival myself but I understand attendance has substantially dropped off the last two years. I'm sure I don't have to tell you what a problem this is."

"No," the rancher said solemnly, and Ellie fought the urge to raise her hand and ask somebody to explain the gravity of the situation to her. It certainly didn't seem like a big deal to her that some of the good people of Salt River decided to celebrate Valentine's Day somewhere other than the elementary school gymnasium. Come to think of it, so far most of the people she'd met in Salt River didn't seem the types to celebrate Valentine's Day at all.

"This is a really important fund-raiser," Ms. McKenzie said. "All the money goes to the school library, which is desperately in need of new books. We need to do something to generate more interest in the carnival, infuse it with fresh ideas. New blood, if you will. I think the two of you are just the ones to do that."

There was silence for a moment, then the rancher sat forward, that frown still marring his handsome features. "I'm sorry, Miz McKenzie. I'd like to help you out, honest. I'm all in favor of getting more books for the library and I'd be happy to give you a sizable donation if that will help at all. But I'm way out of my league here. I wouldn't know the first thing about putting together something like that."

"I'm afraid this sort of thing isn't exactly my strong point, either," Ellie admitted, which was a bit like saying the nearby Teton Mountain Range had a couple of pretty little hills.

"Whatever their reasons, it seemed very important to your daughters that you help." She shifted toward Matt again. "Mr. Harte, has Lucy ever asked you to volunteer for anything in school before? Reading time, lunch duty, anything?"

The rancher's frown deepened. "No," he finally answered the teacher. "Not that I can think of."

"All of her previous teachers describe Lucy as a shy mouse of a girl who spoke in whispers and broke into tears if they called on her. I have to tell you, that is not the same girl I've come to know this year."

"No?"

"Since Dylan's arrival, Lucy participates much more

in class. She is a sweet little girl with a wonderfully cre-
ative mind."

"That's good, right?"

"Very good. But despite the improvements, Lucy still
seems to prefer staying in the background. She rarely
ventures an opinion of her own. I think it would be
wonderful for her to help plan the carnival under your
supervision. It might even provide her with some of the
confidence she still seems to be lacking."

"I'm a very busy man, Miz McKenzie—"

"I understand that. And I know Dr. Webster is also
very busy trying to establish her practice here in Star
Valley."

You don't know the half of it, Ellie thought grimly.

"But I think it would help both girls. Dylan, as well,"
the teacher said, shifting toward her. "I've spoken with
you before with some of my concerns about your daughter. She's a very bright girl and a natural leader among
the other children, but she hasn't shown much enthusiasm for anything in the classroom until now."

The teacher paused, her hands still folded serenely
on her desk, and gave them both a steady look that had
Ellie squirming just like she'd been caught chewing
gum in class. "It's obvious neither of you wants to do
this. I certainly understand your sentiments. But I have
to tell you, I would recommend you put your own misgivings aside and think instead about your daughters
and what they want."

Oh, she was good. *Pour on the parental guilt, sister.
Gets 'em every time.*

Out of the corner of her gaze Ellie could see Harte
fighting through the same internal struggle.

How could she possibly do this? The last thing on

earth she wanted was to be saddled with the responsibility for planning a Valentine's Day carnival. Valentine's Day, for heaven's sake. A time for sweethearts and romance, hearts and flowers. Things she had absolutely no experience with.

Beyond that, right now she was so busy trying to salvage her floundering practice that she had no time for anything but falling into her bed at the end of the day.

Still, Dylan wanted her to do this. For whatever reasons, this was important to her daughter. Ellie had already uprooted her from the only life she'd known to bring her here, to an alien world of wide-open spaces and steep, imposing mountains.

If being involved in this stupid carnival would make Dylan happy, didn't she owe it to her to try?

And maybe, just maybe, a selfish little voice whispered, *this might just be the ticket to help you pile drive your way into the closed circle that is the Star Valley community.*

If she could show the other parents she was willing to volunteer to help out the school, they might begin to accept her into their ranks. Lord knows, she had to do something or she would end up being the proud owner of the only veterinary practice in Wyoming without a single patient to its name.

"I suppose I'm game," she said, before she could talk herself out of it. "What about you, Harte?"

"It's a Valentine's Day carnival. What the hell do I know about Valentine's Day?"

She snickered at his baffled tone. She couldn't help herself. The man just rubbed her wrong. He had gone out of his way to antagonize her since she arrived in town. Not only had he taken his own business elsewhere, but she knew he'd convinced several other ranchers to do the same. It hurt her pride both professionally and personally that he made no secret of his disdain for some of her more unconventional methods.

"You mean nobody's sent you one of those cute little pink cards lately? With that sweet disposition of yours, I'd have thought you would have women crawling out of the woodwork to send you valentines."

She regretted the snippy comment as soon as she said it. Whatever her views about him, she should at least try to be civil.

Still, she felt herself bristle when he glowered at her, which seemed to be his favorite expression. It was a shame, really. The man could be drop-dead gorgeous when he wasn't looking like he just planted his butt on a cactus. How such a sweet little girl like Lucy could have such a sour apple of a father was beyond her.

Before he could answer in kind, the schoolteacher stepped in to keep the peace with the same quiet diplomacy she probably used to break up schoolyard brawls. "There's no reason you have to make a decision today. It's only mid-November, so we still have plenty of time before Valentine's Day. Why don't both of you take a few days to think it over, and I'll talk to you about it next week."

Ms. McKenzie rose from behind her desk. "Thank you both for coming in at such short notice," she said, in clear dismissal. "I'll be in touch with you next week."

Left with no alternative, Ellie rose, as well, and shrugged into her coat. Beside her, Lucy's father did the same.

"Sorry about the mix-up," he said, reaching out to shake hands with Ms. McKenzie. Ellie observed with

curiosity that for the first time the other woman looked
uncomfortable, even nervous. Again she thought of that
skittish colt ready to bolt. There was an awkward pause
while he stood there with his hand out, then with a
quick, jerky movement, the teacher gripped his hand
before abruptly dropping it.

"I'll be in touch," she said again.

What was that all about? Matt wondered as he followed the city vet out of the brightly decorated classroom into the hall. Why did Miz McKenzie act like
he'd up and slapped her when all he wanted to do was
shake her hand? Come to think of it, she'd behaved the
same way when he came in a month earlier for parent-
teacher conferences.

She and Ellie Webster ought to just form a club, since
it was obvious the lady vet wasn't crazy about him, either. Matt Harte Haters of America.

He didn't have time to dwell on it before they reached
the outside door of the school. The vet gave him a funny
look when he opened the door for her, but she said nothing, just moved past him. Before he could stop himself,
he caught a whiff of her hair as her coat brushed his
arm. It smelled clean and fresh, kind of like that heavenly lemon cream pie they served over at the diner.

He had absolutely no business sniffing the city vet's
hair, Matt reminded himself harshly. Or noticing the
way those freckles trailed across that little nose of hers
like the Big Dipper or how the fluorescent lights inside the school had turned that sweet-smelling hair a
fiery red, like an August sunset after an afternoon of
thunderstorms.

He pushed the unwanted thoughts away and followed

Ellie Webster out into the frigid night. An icy wind slapped at them, and he hunched his shoulders inside his lined denim coat.

It was much colder than normal for mid-November. The sky hung heavy and ugly overhead, and the twilight had that expectant hush it took on right before a big storm. Looked like they were in for a nasty one. He dug already cold fingers into his pockets.

When he drove into town earlier, the weatherman on the radio had said to expect at least a foot of snow. Just what he needed. With that Arctic Express chugging down out of Canada, they were sure to have below-zero temperatures tonight. Add to that the windchill and he'd be up the whole damn night just trying to keep his cattle alive.

The city vet seemed to read his mind. "By the looks of that storm, I imagine we'll both have a busy night."

"You, too?"

"I do still have a few patients."

He'd never paid much mind to what a vet did when the weather was nasty. Or what a vet did any other time, for that matter. They showed up at his place, did what he needed them to do, then moved on to their next appointment.

He tried to imagine her muscling an ornery cow into a pen and came up completely blank. Hell, she looked hardly big enough to wrestle a day-old calf. He'd had the same thought the first day he met her, back in August when she rode into town with her little girl and all that attitude.

She barely came up to his chin, and her wrists were delicate and bony, like a kitten that had been too long without food. Why would a scrawny city girl from California want to come out to the wilds of Wyoming and wrestle cattle? He couldn't even begin to guess.

There were only two vehicles in the school parking lot, the brand spankin' new dually crew cab he drove off the lot last week and her battered old Ford truck. He knew it was hers by the magnetized sign on the side reading Salt River Veterinary Clinic.

Miz McKenzie must have walked, since the little house she rented from Bob Jimenez was just a couple blocks from the school. Maybe he ought to offer her a ride home. It was too damn cold to be walking very far tonight.

Before he could turn around and go back into the school to make the offer, he saw Ellie Webster pull her keys out of her pocket and fight to open her truck door for several seconds without success.

"Can I help you there, ma'am?" he finally asked.

She grunted as she worked the key. "The lock seems to be stuck...."

Wasn't that just like a city girl to go to all the trouble to lock the door of a rusty old pickup nobody would want to steal anyway? "You know, most of us around here don't lock our vehicles. Not much need."

She gave him a scorcher of a look. "And most of you think karaoke is a girl you went to high school with."

His mouth twitched, but he refused to let himself smile. Instead, he yanked off a glove and stuck his bare thumb over the lock.

In the pale lavender twilight, she watched him with a confused frown. "What are you doing?"

"Just trying to warm up your lock. I imagine it's frozen and that's why you can't get the key to turn. I guess you don't have much trouble with that kind of thing in California, do you?"

"Not much, no. I guess it's another exciting feature unique to Wyoming. Like jackalopes and perpetual road construction."

"When we've had a cold wet rain like we did this afternoon, moisture can get down in the lock. After the sun goes down, it doesn't take long to freeze."

"I'll remember that."

"There. That ought to do it." He pulled his hand away and took the key from her, then shoved it into the lock. The mechanism slid apart now like a knife through soft wax, and he couldn't resist pulling the door open for her with an exaggerated flourish.

She gave him a disgruntled look then climbed into her pickup. "Thank you."

"You're welcome." He shoved his hand into his lined pocket, grateful for the cozy warmth. "Next time you might want to think twice before you lock your door so it doesn't happen again. Nobody's going to steal anything around here."

She didn't look like she appreciated his advice. "You do things your way, I'll do things mine, Harte."

She turned the key, and the truck started with a smooth purr that defied its dilapidated exterior. "If you decide you're man enough to help me with this stupid carnival, I suppose we'll have to start organizing it soon."

His attention snagged on the first part of her sentence. "If I'm man enough?" he growled.

She grinned at him, her silvery-green eyes sparkling, and he fought hard to ignore the kick of awareness in his stomach. "Do you think you've got the guts to go through with this?"

"It's not a matter of guts," he snapped. "It's a matter of having the time to waste putting together some silly carnival."

"If you say so."

"I'm a very busy man, Dr. Webster."

It was apparently exactly the wrong thing to say. Her grin slid away, and she stiffened like a coil of frozen rope, slicing him to pieces with a glare. "And I have nothing better to do than sit around cutting out pink and white hearts to decorate the school gymnasium with, right? That's what you think, isn't it? Lord knows, I don't have much of a practice thanks to you and all the other stubborn old men around here."

He set his jaw. He wasn't going to get into this with her standing out here in the school parking lot while the windchill dipped down into single digits. "That's not what I meant," he muttered.

"I know exactly what you meant. I know just what you think of me, Mr. Harte."

He sincerely doubted it. Did she know he thought about her a lot more than he damn well knew he ought to and that he couldn't get her green eyes or her sassy little mouth out of his mind?

"Our daughters want us to do this," she said. "I don't know what little scheme they're cooking up—and to tell you the truth, I'm not sure I want to know—but it seems to be important to Dylan, and that's enough for me. Let me know what you decide."

She closed the door, barely missing his fingers, then shoved the truck into gear and spun out of the parking lot, leaving him in a cloud of exhaust.

Chapter 2

Matt drove his pickup under the arch proclaiming Diamond Harte Ranch—Choice Simmentals and Quarter Horses with a carved version of the brand that had belonged to the Harte family for four generations.

He paused for just a moment like he always did to savor the view before him. The rolling, sage-covered hills, the neat row of fence line stretching out as far as the eye could see, the barns and outbuildings with their vivid red paint contrasting so boldly with the snow.

And standing guard over it all at the end of the long gravel drive was the weathered log and stone house his grandfather had built—with the sprawling addition he had helped his father construct the year he turned twelve.

Home.

He loved it fiercely, from the birthing sheds to the maze of pens to the row of Douglas fir lining the drive.

He knew every single inch of its twenty thousand acres, as well as the names and bloodlines of each of the three dozen cutting horses on the ranch and the medical history of all six hundred of the ranch's cattle.

Maybe he loved it too much. Reverend Whitaker's sermon last week had been a fiery diatribe on the sin of excess pride, the warning in Proverbs about how pride goeth before destruction.

Matt had squirmed in the hard pew for a minute, then decided the Lord would forgive him for it, especially if He could look down through the clouds and see the Diamond Harte like Matt saw it. As close to heaven as any place else on earth.

Besides, didn't the Bible also say the sleep of a laboring man was sweet? His father's favorite scripture had been in Genesis, something about how a man should eat bread only by the sweat of his face.

Well, he'd worked plenty hard for the Diamond Harte. He'd poured every last ounce of his sweat into the ranch since he was twenty-two years old, into taking the legacy his parents had left their three children so suddenly and prematurely and building it into the powerful ranch it had become.

He had given up everything for the ranch. All his time and energy. The college degree in ag economy he was sixteen credits away from earning when his parents had died in that rollover accident. Even his wife, who had hated the ranch with a passion and had begged him to leave every day of their miserable marriage.

Melanie. The woman he had loved with a quicksilver passion that had turned just as quickly to bitter, ferocious hate. His wife, who had cheated on him and lied to him and eventually left him when Lucy wasn't even three months old.

She'd been a city girl, too, fascinated by silly, romantic dreams of the West. The reality of living on a ranch wasn't romantic at all, as Melanie had discovered all too soon. It was hard work and merciless weather. Cattle that didn't always smell so great, a cash flow that was never dependable. Flies in the summer and snowstorms in the winter that could trap you for days.

Melanie had never even made an effort to belong. She had been lost. He could see that now. Bitterly unhappy and desperate for something she could never find.

She thought he should have sold the ranch, pocketed the five or six million it was probably worth and taken her somewhere a whole lot more glitzy than Salt River, Wyoming. And when he refused to give in to her constant pleading, she had made his life hell.

What was this thing he had for women who didn't belong out here? He thought of his fascination with the California vet. It wasn't attraction. He refused to call it attraction. She was just different from what he was used to, that's all. Annoying, opinionated, argumentative. That's the only reason his pulse rate jumped whenever she was around.

A particularly strong gust of wind blew out of the canyon suddenly, rattling the pickup. He sent a quick look at the digital clock on the sleek dashboard, grateful for the distraction from thoughts of a woman he had no business thinking about.

Almost six. Cassie would have dinner on soon, and then he would get to spend the rest of the night trying to keep his stock warm. He eased his foot off the brake and quickly drove the rest of the way to the house, parking in his usual spot next to his sister's Cherokee.

Inside, the big house was toasty, welcoming. His stomach growled and his mouth watered at the delectable smells coming from the kitchen—mashed potatoes and Cassie's amazing meat loaf, if he wasn't mistaken. He hung his hat on the row of pegs by the door, then made his way to the kitchen. He found his baby sister stirring gravy in a pan on the wide professional stove she'd insisted he install last year.

She looked up at his entrance and gave him a quick smile. "Dinner's almost ready."

"Smells good." He stood watching her for a moment, familiar guilt curling in his gut. She ought to be in her own house, making dinner for her own husband and a whole kitchen full of rug rats, instead of wasting her life away taking care of him and Lucy.

If it hadn't been for the disastrous choices he made with Melanie, that's exactly where she would have been.

It wasn't a new thought. He'd had plenty of chances in the last ten years to wish things could be different, to regret that he had become so blasted dependent on everything Cassie did for them after Melanie ran off.

She ought to go to college—or at least to cooking school somewhere, since she loved it so much. But every time they talked about it, about her plans for the future, she insisted she was exactly where she wanted to be, doing exactly what she wanted to be doing.

How could he convince her otherwise when he still wasn't completely sure he could handle things on his own? He didn't know how he could do a proper job of raising Lucy by himself and handle the demands of the ranch at the same time.

Maybe if Jesse was around more, things might be different. He could have given his younger brother some of the responsibilities of the ranch, leaving more time to take care of things on the home front. But Jess had never been content on the Diamond Harte. He had other dreams, of catching the bad guys and saving the world, and Matt couldn't begrudge him those.

"Where's Lucy?" he asked.

"Up in her room fretting, I imagine. She's been a basket case waiting for you to get back from the school. She broke two glasses while she was setting the table, and spent more time looking out the window for your truck than she did on her math homework."

"She ought to be nervous," he growled, grateful for the renewed aggravation that was strong enough to push the guilt aside.

Cassie glanced up at his tone. "Uh-oh. That bad? What did she do?"

"You wouldn't believe it if I told you," he muttered and headed toward the stairs. "Give me five minutes to talk to her, and then we'll be down."

He knocked swiftly on her door and heard a muffled, "Come in." Inside, he found his daughter sitting on her bed, gnawing her bottom lip so hard it looked like she had chewed away every last drop of blood.

Through that curtain of long, dark hair, he saw that her eyes were wide and nervous. As they damn well ought to be after the little stunt she pulled. He let her stew in it for a minute.

"Hey, squirt."

"Hi," she whispered. With hands that trembled just a little, she picked up Sigmund, the chubby calico cat she'd raised from a kitten, and plopped him in her lap.

"So I just got back from talking with Miz McKenzie."

Lucy peered at him between the cat's ears. She cleared her throat. "Um, what did she say?"

"I think you know exactly what she said, don't you?"

She nodded, the big gray eyes she'd inherited from her mother wide with apprehension. As usual, he hoped to heaven that was the only thing Melanie had passed on to their daughter.

"You want to tell me what this is all about?"

She appeared to think it over, then shook her head swiftly. He bit his cheek to keep a rueful grin from creeping out at that particular piece of honesty. "Tough. Tell me anyway."

"I don't know."

"Come on, Luce. What were you thinking, to sign me up for this Valentine's carnival without at least talking to me first?"

"It was Dylan's idea," Lucy mumbled.

Big surprise there. Dylan Webster was a miniature version of her wacky mother. "Why?"

"She thought you'd be good at it, since you're so important around here and can get people to do whatever you want. At least that's what her mom says."

He could picture Ellie Webster saying exactly that, with her pert little nose turned up in the air.

"And," Lucy added, the tension easing from her shoulders a little as she stroked the purring cat, "we both thought it would be fun. You know, planning the carnival and stuff. You and me and Dylan and her mom, doing it all together. A bonding thing."

A bonding thing? The last thing he needed to do was *bond* with Ellie Webster, under any circumstances.

"What do you know about bonding? Don't tell me that's something they teach you in school."

Lucy shrugged. "Dylan says we're in our formative preteen years and need positive parental influence now more than ever. She thought this would be a good opportunity for us to develop some leadership skills."

Great. Now Ellie Webster's kid had his daughter spouting psychobabble. He blew out a breath. "What about you?"

She blinked at him. "Me?"

"You're pretty knowledgeable about Dylan's views, but what about your own? Why did you go along with it?"

Lucy suddenly seemed extremely interested in a little spot on the cat's fur. "I don't know," she mumbled.

"Come on. You can do better than that."

She chewed her lip again, then looked at the cat. "We never do anything together."

He rocked back on his heels, baffled by her. "What are you talking about? We do plenty of things together. Just last Saturday you spent the whole day with me in Idaho Falls."

She rolled her eyes. "Shopping for a new truck. Big whoop. I thought it would be fun to do something completely different together. Something that doesn't have to do with the ranch or with cattle or horses." She paused, then added in a quiet voice, "Something just for me."

Ah, more guilt. Just what he needed. The kid wasn't even ten years old and she was already an expert at it. He sighed. Did females come out of the box with some built-in guilt mechanism they could turn off and on at will?

The hell of it was, she was absolutely right, and he

knew it. He didn't spend nearly enough time with her. He tried, he really did, but between the horses and the cattle, his time seemed to be in as short supply as sunshine in January.

His baby girl was growing up. He could see it every day. Used to be a day spent with him would be enough for her no matter what they did together. Even if it was only shopping for a new truck. Now she wanted more, and he wasn't sure he knew how to provide it.

"Wouldn't it have been easier to tell me all this *before* you signed me up? Then we could have at least talked it over without me getting such a shock like this."

She fidgeted with Sigmund, who finally must have grown tired of being messed with. He let out an offended mewl of protest and rolled away from her, then leaped from the bed gracefully and stalked out the door.

Lucy watched until his tail disappeared down the end of the hall before she answered him in that same low, ashamed voice. "Dylan said you'd both say no if we asked. We thought it might be harder for you to back out if Ms. McKenzie thought you'd already agreed to it."

"That wasn't very fair, to me or to Dr. Webster, was it?" He tried to come up with an analogy that might make sense to her. "How would you like it if I signed you up to show one of the horses in the 4-H competition without talking to you first?"

She shuddered, as he knew she would. Her shyness made her uncomfortable being the center of attention, so she had always avoided the limelight, even when she was little. In that respect, Miz McKenzie was right— Dylan Webster had been good for her and had brought her out of her shell, at least a little.

"I wouldn't like it at all."

"And I don't like what you did any better. I ought to just back out of this whole crazy thing right now."

"Oh, Dad, you *can't*!" she wailed. "You'll ruin *everything*."

He studied her distress for several seconds, then sighed. He loved his daughter fiercely. She was the biggest joy in his life, more important than a hundred ranches. If she felt like she came in second to the Diamond Harte, he obviously wasn't trying hard enough.

Lucy finally broke the silence. "Are you really, really, really mad at me?" she asked in a small voice.

"Maybe just one really." He gave her a lopsided smile. "But don't worry. I'll get you back. You'll be sorry you ever heard of this carnival by the time I get through with you."

Her eyes went wide again, this time with excitement. "Does that mean you'll do it?"

"I guess. I think we're both going to be sorry."

But he couldn't have too many regrets, at least not right now. Not when his daughter jumped from her bed with a squeal and threw her arms tightly around his waist.

"Oh, thank you, Daddy. Thank you, thank you, thank you. You're the best."

For that moment, at least, he felt like it.

"No way is Matthew Harte going to go through with it. Mark my words, if you agree to do this, you're going to be stuck planning the whole carnival by yourself."

In the middle of sorting through the day's allotment of depressing mail, Ellie grimaced at SueAnn Clayton, her assistant. She had really come to hate that phrase. *Mark my words, you're not cut out to be a large ani-*

mal vet. Mark my words, you're going to regret leaving California. Mark my words, you won't last six months in Wyoming.

Just once, she wished everybody would keep their words—and unsolicited advice—to themselves.

In this case, though, she was very much afraid SueAnn was right. There was about as much likelihood of Matt Harte helping her plan the carnival as there was that he'd be the next one walking through the door with a couple of his prize cutting horses for her to treat.

She sighed and set the stack of bills on SueAnn's desk. "If he chickens out, I'll find somebody else to help me." She grinned at her friend. "You, for instance."

SueAnn made a rude noise. "Forget it. I chaired the Halloween Howl committee three years in a row and was PTA president twice. I've more than done my share for Salt River Elementary."

"Come on, SueAnn," she teased. "Are you forgetting who pays your salary?"

The other woman rolled her eyes. "You pay me to take your phone calls, to send out your bill reminders and to hold down the occasional unlucky animal while you give him a shot. Last I checked, planning a Valentine's Day carnival is nowhere in my job description."

"We could always change your job description. How about while we're at it, we'll include mucking out the stalls?"

"You're not going to blackmail me. That's what you pay Dylan the big bucks for. Speaking of the little rascal, how did you punish her, anyway? Ground her to her room for the rest of the month?"

That's what she should have done. It was no less than Dylan deserved for lying to her teacher. But she'd chosen a more fitting punishment. "She's grounded from playing with Lucy after school for the rest of the week *and* she has to finish reading all of *Little Women* and I'm going to make sure she does a lot of the work of this carnival, since it was her great idea."

"The carnival she ought to be okay with, but which is she going to hate more, reading the book or not playing with her other half?"

"Doesn't matter. She has to face the music."

SueAnn laughed, and Ellie smiled back. What would she have done without the other woman to keep her grounded and sane these last few months? She shuddered just thinking about it.

She winced whenever she remembered how tempted she'd been to fire her that first week. SueAnn was competent enough—eerily so, sometimes—but she also didn't have the first clue how to mind her own business. Ellie had really struggled with it at first. Coming from California where avoiding eye contact when at all possible could sometimes be a matter of survival, dealing with a terminal busybody for an assistant had been wearing.

She was thirty-two years old and wasn't used to being mothered. Even when she'd *had* a mother, she hadn't had much practice at it. And she had been completely baffled by how to handle SueAnn, who made it a point to have her favorite grind of coffee waiting every morning, who tried to set her up with every single guy in town between the ages of eighteen and sixty, and who brought in Tupperware containers several times a week brimming with homemade soups and casseroles and mouthwatering desserts.

Now that she'd had a little practice, she couldn't believe she had been so fortunate to find not only the best assistant she could ask for but also a wonderful friend.

"What's on the agenda this morning?" Ellie asked.

"You're not going to believe this, but you actually have two patients waiting."

"What, are we going for some kind of record?"

SueAnn snickered and held two charts out with a flourish. "In exam room one, we have Sasha, Mary Lou McGilvery's husky."

"What's wrong with her?"

"Him. Sasha, oddly enough, is a him. He's scratching like crazy, and Mary Lou is afraid he has fleas."

"Highly doubtful around here, especially this time of year. It's too cold."

"That's what I tried to tell her. She's convinced that you need to take a look at him, though."

Dogs weren't exactly her specialty, since she was a large animal veterinarian, but she knew enough about them to deal with a skin condition. She nodded to SueAnn. "And patient number two?"

Her assistant cleared her throat ominously. "Cleo."

"Cleo?"

"Jeb Thacker's Nubian goat. She has a bit of a personality disorder."

"What does that mean?"

"Well, let's put it this way. Ben used to say that if she'd been human, she'd have been sent to death row a long time ago."

Ellie grinned, picturing the old codger who had sold her the practice saying exactly that. Ben Nichols was a real character. They had formed an instant friendship the first time they met at a conference several years ago. It was that same bond that had prompted him to make all her dreams come true by offering her his practice at a bargain basement price when he decided to retire, to her shock and delight. He and his wife were now thoroughly enjoying retirement in Arizona.

"What's Cleo in for?"

"Jeb didn't know, precisely. The poor man 'bout had a panic attack right there when I tried to get him to specify on the paperwork. Blushed brighter than one of his tomatoes and said he thought it was some kind of female trouble."

A homicidal goat with female trouble. And here she thought she was in for another slow morning. "Where's Jeb?"

"He had to go into Afton to the hardware store. Said he'd be back later to pick her up."

"In that case, let's take care of the dog first since Mary Lou's waiting," she decided. She could save the worst for last.

It only took a few moments for her to diagnose that Sasha had a bad case of psoriasis. She gave Mary Lou a bottle of medicated shampoo she thought would do the trick, ordered her to wash his bedding frequently and scheduled a checkup in six months.

That done, she put on her coat and braved the cold, walking to the pens behind the clinic to deal with the cantankerous goat. Cleo looked docile enough. The brown-and-white goat was standing in one of the smaller pens gnawing the top rail on the fence.

Ellie stood near the fence and spoke softly to her for a moment, trying to earn the animal's trust. Cleo turned and gave her what Ellie could swear was a look of sheer disdain out of big, long-fringed brown eyes, then turned back to the rail.

Slowly, cautiously, she entered the pen and approached the goat, still crooning softly to her. When she was still several feet away, she stopped for a cursory look. Although she would need to do a physical exam to be certain, she thought she could see the problem—one of Cleo's udders looked engorged and red. She probably had mastitis.

Since Cleo wasn't paying her any mind, Ellie inched closer. "You're a sweet girl, aren't you?" she murmured. "Everybody's wrong about you." She reached a hand to touch the animal, but before her hand could connect, Cleo whirled like a bronco with a burr under her saddle. Ellie didn't have time to move away before the goat butted her in the stomach with enough force to knock her on her rear end, right into a puddle of what she fervently hoped was water.

With a ma-aaa of amusement, the goat turned back to the fence rail.

"Didn't anybody warn you about Cleo?" a deep male voice asked.

Just what she needed, a witness to her humiliation. From her ignominious position on the ground, she took a moment to force air into her lungs. When she could breathe again, she glanced toward the direction of the voice. Her gaze landed first on a pair of well-worn boots just outside the fence, then traveled up a mile-long length of blue jeans to a tooled silver buckle with the swirled insignia of the NCHA—National Cutting Horse Association.

She knew that buckle.

She'd seen it a day earlier on none other than the lean hips of her nemesis. Sure enough, Matt Harte stood there just on the other side of the pen—broad shoulders, blue eyes, wavy dark hair and all.

She closed her eyes tightly, wishing the mud would open up underneath her and suck her down. Of all the people in the world who might have been here to watch her get knocked to her butt, why did it have to be him?

Chapter 3

Matt let himself into the pen, careful to keep a safe distance between his own rear end and Jeb Thacker's notoriously lousy-tempered goat, who had retreated to the other side of the pen.

"Here, let me help you." He reached a hand down to the city vet, still sprawled in the mud.

"I can do it," she muttered. Instead of taking his hand, she climbed gingerly to her feet by herself, then surreptitiously rubbed a hand against her seat.

Matt cleared his throat. "You okay?"

"I've had better mornings, but I'll live."

"You hit the ground pretty hard. You sure nothing's busted?"

"I don't think so. Just bruised. Especially my pride," she said wryly. She paused for a minute, then smiled reluctantly. "I imagine it looked pretty funny watching me get tackled by a goat."

She must not take herself too seriously if she could laugh about what had just happened. He found himself liking her for it. He gazed at her, at the way her red hair had slipped from its braid thingy and the little smudge of dirt on her cheek. Her eyes sparkled with laughter, and she was just about the prettiest thing he'd seen in a long time.

When he said nothing, a blush spread over her cheeks and she reached a hand to tuck her stray hair back. "Did you need something, Mr. Harte?"

He was staring at her, he realized, like some hayseed who'd never seen a pretty girl before. He flushed, astounded at himself, at this completely unexpected surge of attraction. "You might as well call me Matt, especially since it looks like we'll be working on this stupid school thing together."

Her big green eyes that always made him think of new aspen leaves just uncurling in springtime widened even more. "You're going to do it?"

"I said so, didn't I?" he muttered.

She grinned. "And you sound so enthusiastic about it."

"You want enthusiasm, you'll have to find somebody else to help you."

"What made you change your mind?"

He didn't know how to answer that, and besides, it wasn't any of her business. He said he'd do it, didn't he? What more did she need? But somehow the sharp retort he started to make changed into something else.

"Miz McKenzie's right," he finally said. "Lucy's done better in school this year than she ever has. She never would have wanted to organize something like this last year. I don't want to ruin the improvement she's made. Besides, she usually doesn't ask for much. It's a small price to pay if it's going to make her happy."

Ellie Webster cocked her head and looked at him like she'd just encountered a kind of animal she'd never seen before.

"What?" he asked, annoyed at himself for feeling so defensive.

"Nothing. You're just full of surprises, Mr. Harte."

"Matt," he muttered. "I said you should call me Matt."

"Matt." She smiled suddenly, the most genuine smile she'd ever given him. He stared at it, at her, feeling like he'd just spent a few hours out in the hard sun without his hat.

"Is that why you stopped?" she asked. "To tell me you decided to help with the carnival?"

He shrugged and ordered his heartbeat to behave itself. "I had to drop by the post office next door anyway. I thought maybe if you had a second this morning, we could get a cup of coffee over at the diner and come up with a game plan. At least figure out where to start."

Again, she looked surprised, but she nodded. "That's a good idea. But if you're just looking for coffee, SueAnn makes the best cup this side of the Rockies. We can talk in my office."

"That would be fine. I've already had breakfast. You, ah, need to get cleaned up or anything?"

She glanced down at her muddy jeans, then at the goat with a grimace. "Can you wait ten minutes? Since I'm already muddy, I might as well take a look at Cleo now."

He thought of the million-and-one things he had to do at the ranch after he ran to the parts store in Idaho Falls—the buyers he had coming in later in the afternoon, the three horses waiting for the farrier, the inevitable paperwork always confronting him.

He should just take a rain check, but for some reason that completely baffled him, he nodded. "Sure, I can wait." His next question surprised him even more. "Need me to give you a hand?"

She smiled again, that sweet, friendly smile. "That would be great. I'm afraid Cleo isn't too crazy about her visit to the vet."

The next fifteen minutes were a real education. With his help, Ellie miraculously finessed the ornery goat into holding still long enough for an exam. She murmured soft words—nonsense, really—while her hands moved gently and carefully over the now docile goat.

"Okay, you can let go now," she finally said. He obeyed, and the goat ambled away from them.

"What's the verdict?" he asked.

She looked up from scribbling some notes on a chart. "Just as I suspected. Mastitis. She has a plugged milk duct. I'll run a culture to be sure, but I think a round of antibiotics ought to take care of her."

"Just like a cow, huh?"

"Just like. Same plumbing involved."

"Cleo's a hell of a lot uglier than any of my ladies."

She grinned at him again. "Beauty's in the eye of the beholder, Harte. I imagine Jeb Thacker wouldn't agree. Anyway, thanks for your help."

She led the way inside the small building where she worked. While she went in the back to change her clothes, he shot the breeze with SueAnn, who went to high school with him and whose husband ran the local nursery in town.

In a surprisingly short time, Ellie returned wearing

a pair of surgical scrubs. He figured she probably was supposed to look cool and professional in the scrubs, but instead they made her look not much older than one of Lucy's friends on her way to a sleepover, especially with her auburn hair pulled back in that ponytail.

"Sorry to keep you waiting," she said, sounding a little out of breath.

"No problem."

SueAnn hopped up and poured a cup of coffee for Ellie. "Here you go, sugar."

"Thanks. We'll be in my office if you need me."

"Take your time."

Matt didn't miss the not-so-subtle wink SueAnn sent the vet or the quick frown Ellie volleyed back. Before he could analyze the currents going on here, she walked into a cluttered office with books and papers everywhere. Dominating one wall was a window framing a beautiful view of the Salt River mountain range that gave the town its name. On the other was a big print of a horse—a Tennessee walker, if he wasn't mistaken—running across a field of wildflowers, all grace and power and beauty.

"Thanks again for helping me with Cleo," Ellie said as soon as he was seated.

"No problem. It was interesting to see you working on her."

She raised an eyebrow. "Interesting in what way?"

He shrugged. "I kept waiting for you to pull out the needles or whatever it is you use for that stuff you do."

"That stuff I do?"

There were suddenly as many icicles in her voice as he had hanging from his barn. "You know, that acupuncture stuff. You don't do that all the time, then?"

Whatever friendliness might have been in her expression faded away, and she became guarded once more. "Just when the situation calls for it."

"And this one didn't?"

Her smile was paper-thin. "See that diploma on the wall? I'm a board-certified vet with several years' experience in traditional veterinary medicine. The acupuncture stuff, as you call it, was just extra training to supplement my regular skills. I only use it as an alternative when some of the more orthodox treatments have failed or aren't appropriate."

"And when would that be?"

"A lecture on veterinary acupuncture is not the reason you stopped by, Mr. Harte."

"I'm curious about what you do."

She hesitated for a moment before answering. "Animals I treat most often are horses with performance problems, like short stepping or mysterious lameness. I've treated moon blindness successfully and also older horses with degenerative conditions like arthritis or joint disease. You'd be surprised at how effective acupuncture can be."

He didn't doubt that. He didn't want to sound too skeptical, not when they were going to have to work together for the next few months, but he thought the whole thing was a bunch of hooey. Her California crowd might buy all this New Age crap, but folks in Wyoming looked at things like this a little differently.

For a minute, he thought about keeping his mouth shut and changing the subject, but she and her kid had been good for his daughter. He didn't want to see her practice go under, since Lucy would just about wither away if Dylan moved.

He cleared his throat. "Don't take this the wrong way, Dr. Webster, but it seems to me you might be better off focusing on those more traditional things you were talking about and leave the rest of that, er, stuff back in California."

She pursed her lips together tightly. "Thank you for the advice," she said, in a tone that left him in no doubt of her real feelings. And they probably didn't include gratitude.

He should have stopped right there, but something made him push the issue harder. "Look, it's no secret around town that you've lost a lot of customers in the last few months to Steve Nichols, Ben's nephew. Hell, I've been using him myself. A lot of people don't understand why Ben sold his practice to you in the first place instead of to Steve. Anyway, I'm pretty sure you could lure some of those folks back if you didn't focus so much on the acupuncture side of things in your ads and all."

"I don't tell you how to run your ranch," she said quietly, folding her hands tightly on the desk. "So please don't tell me how to operate my practice."

He sat back in the chair, aware he sounded like an idiot. Bossy and arrogant, just like Cassie always accused him of being. "Sorry," he muttered. "It's none of my business what you do. Just thought you should know that out here we tend to prefer the things we know, the way we've always done things, the way they've been done for generations. Especially when it comes to our stock."

"Tell me about it."

"Sorry if I offended you."

She shrugged. "You're only saying to my face what

I'm sure everyone else has been saying behind my back. I appreciate your frankness. Now can we talk about the carnival?"

"Uh, sure." Who would have dreamed twenty-four hours ago that he would consider a Valentine's Day carnival a safe topic of conversation?

"So I was thinking about calling it A Fair to Remember," she said. "What do you think?"

He scratched his cheek, not quite sure where she was going with this.

"From the movie. You know, Deborah Kerr, Cary Grant. Empire State Building. The one Meg Ryan bawled about in *Sleepless in Seattle*."

At his continued blank look, she shrugged. "Never mind. We can talk about it later. We have ten weeks to work out all the details."

Ten weeks working closely with Ellie Webster, with her green eyes and her wisecracks and her shampoo that smelled like lemon pie. He knew damn well the idea shouldn't appeal to him so much.

Chapter 4

"So we're agreed then," Ellie said fifteen minutes later. "Given our mutual lack of experience, we need to delegate as much as humanly possible. Our first step is to set up committees for booths, decorations, refreshments and publicity. Once we get some other willing victims, er, parents on board, we can go from there."

Matt scratched the back of his neck. "I guess. You know as much about this as I do. I just hope we can pull this off without making complete fools of ourselves. Or having the whole thing go down in history as the worst carnival ever."

He looked so completely uncomfortable at the task ahead of them that Ellie had to smile. He must love Lucy very much to be willing to put himself through it despite his obvious misgivings. Not many men she knew would be willing to take on such a project for their nine-year-old daughters, and she felt herself softening toward him even more.

"I can talk to Sarah this afternoon if you'd like and tell her we've both agreed to do it," she said.

"I'd appreciate that. I've got to run over to Idaho Falls to pick up a part for the loader, and it might be late before I get back in." He unkinked his considerable length from the low chair and rose, fingering his hat.

He was so tall she had to crane her neck to look into those startling blue eyes. Just how did the man manage to make her little office shrink to about the size of a rabbit hutch by his presence? The awareness simmering through her didn't help matters one bit.

"Sure you're not too busy to talk to Miz McKenzie?" he asked.

"I should be able to carve out a few moments," she murmured dryly. Her appointment schedule for the rest of the day was woefully empty, as she was fairly certain he must realize.

Sure enough, he looked even more ill at ease. After a moment, he cleared his throat. "Think about what I said before, would you? About folks around here being more comfortable with what they know. Your business might pick up if you keep that in mind. You never know."

Any soft feelings she might have been harboring toward him fluttered away like migrating birds. Before she could snap at him again to mind his own business, he shoved his hat on his head and walked out of her office with that long, ground-swallowing stride.

She might be annoyed with him, but that couldn't keep her from wandering out of her office to the reception area to watch through the window as he climbed into a shiny new pickup that probably cost as much as her entire practice.

He drove out of the parking lot with deliberate care, as she was sure he did everything.

She had a sudden wild desire to know if he would kiss a woman that way. Thoroughly. Studiously. Carefully exploring every single inch of her lips with that hard mouth until he memorized each curve, each hollow. Until her knees turned to jelly and her body ached with need....

"Dreamy, isn't he?"

Ellie whirled and found SueAnn watching her, mouth twitching with amusement. She swallowed hard and fought the urge to press a hand to her suddenly trembling stomach. "I don't know what you're talking about," she lied.

SueAnn just laughed. "Right. Whatever you say. You want me to pick that tongue off the floor for you?"

She snapped said tongue firmly back into her mouth. "Don't you have some work to do?"

"Oh, watching you go weak in the knees is much more fun."

"Sorry to ruin your entertainment, but one of us *does* have some work waiting. If you need me, I'll be in my office."

"No problem. Looks like we'll see plenty of Matt Harte between now and Valentine's Day."

That's exactly what she was afraid of. She sighed and headed for her office. She had only been at her desk for a few moments when the cowbell on the door jangled suddenly. From her vantage point, she couldn't see who came in, but she could watch SueAnn's ready smile slide away and her expression chill by several degrees.

Curious as to who might have earned such a frosty glare from the woman who invented congeniality, Ellie rose and walked to the door of her office for a better look.

Steve Nichols, her main competition in town and the nephew of the vet who had sold her the practice, was just closing the door behind him.

She should have known. SueAnn had a good word to say about everybody in town except for Ben's nephew. When it came to Steve, she was as intractable as Jeb Thacker's goat.

Ellie couldn't understand her animosity. From the day she arrived, Steve had gone out of his way to make her feel welcome in Salt River—treating her as a friend and respected colleague, not as a business rival who had bought his uncle's practice out from under him.

"Steve." She greeted him warmly to compensate for SueAnn's noticeable lack of enthusiasm.

His mouth twisted into a smile underneath his bushy blond mustache, then he gestured toward the parking lot. "Was that Matt Harte I just saw driving out of here?"

For no earthly reason she could figure out, she felt a blush soak her cheeks. "Er, yes."

"Is there a problem with one of his animals? Anything I should know about?"

"Oh, no. Nothing like that." She would have left it at that, but Steve continued to study her expectantly. Finally, she had to say something. "Our girls are in the same class and we're working on a school project together," she finally said. "We were just discussing some of the details."

"Really? What kind of project?"

She didn't understand this strange reluctance to divulge

any information—maybe she was just embarrassed—but couldn't bring herself to answer.

"They're cochairs for the annual Valentine's Day carnival." SueAnn finally broke the silence, her voice clipped and her expression still cool.

His mouth sagged open, then a laugh gurgled out. "You've got to be kidding me. Matt Harte planning a school carnival? That's the most ridiculous thing I've ever heard. Next thing I know, you're going to tell me he's opening up a beauty salon in town."

Steve's reaction matched her own when she had first heard about the carnival, so why did she feel so annoyed at him for it? And so protective of a bossy, arrogant rancher who couldn't seem to keep his nose out of her business?

"He's doing it for his daughter," she said with a coolness to match SueAnn's. "What's so ridiculous about that?"

"It just doesn't seem like his thing. Matt's not exactly the PTA type, you know what I mean?"

She didn't want to get into this with him, so she abruptly changed the subject. "Was there something you needed, Steve?"

He shrugged, letting the matter drop. "Do I need a reason to stop by and visit my favorite vet?"

Behind him, SueAnn made a rude noise that she quickly camouflaged behind a cough. Ellie didn't need to phone a psychic hot line to read her mind. She was fairly sure SueAnn thought Steve's favorite vet looked back at him in the mirror each morning.

The other woman opened her mouth to say something snide along those lines, Ellie imagined. She quickly gave her a warning glare. To her relief, after a moment SueAnn clamped her lips tightly shut.

"You don't need a reason to visit, Steve. You know that." Ellie spoke quickly to head off any more trouble. "You're always welcome here. But surely you wouldn't have dropped by during the middle of your busy time of day just to chat, right?"

He sent her that boyishly charming smile of his. "You caught me. Actually, I did have an ulterior motive for dropping by. I'm in a bit of a bind. I ran out of brucellosis vaccine this morning and I'm scheduled to inoculate the herd at Paul Blanchard's ranch in an hour."

Paul Blanchard! He was another of her regular clients, one of the few who had stayed with the clinic after she took over from Ben. Ellie's heart sank. Another deserter. They were dropping like flies.

SueAnn sent her a speaking glance, but before she could answer, Steve went on. "I've ordered a rush job on more but it won't be here until tomorrow. You wouldn't happen to have a few doses to tide me over until the shipment arrives, would you?"

"You want me to loan you some of my brucellosis vaccine for Paul Blanchard's stock?"

Steve seemed completely oblivious to the sheer audacity of asking a favor for an account he had just appropriated. He gave her a pleading smile. "If it's not too much of a bother. You won't need any before tomorrow, will you?"

She might have, if she had been the one treating Blanchard cattle. As it was, it looked as if she would have vaccine to spare. She ground her teeth in frustration. Her first instinct was to say no, absolutely not. He could find his own damn vaccine. But in her heart she knew it wasn't really Steve's fault her practice was struggling.

She also couldn't blame him for setting up his own competing clinic after Ben unexpectedly sold this one to her. If their roles had been reversed and she'd been the one left out in the cold by a relative, she would have done exactly the same thing. And probably wouldn't have treated the usurper with nearly the kindness Steve had shown her.

She forced a smile. "I'll go check my supply."

Trying hard not to mutter to herself, she pushed through the swinging doors that separated the front office and waiting room from the treatment area.

The refrigerator in the back was well-stocked, and she found a case immediately. For one moment, she debated telling him she couldn't find any but she knew that was petty and small-minded so she picked it up and shouldered her way through the swinging doors again.

Steve wasn't where she left him by the front desk, and she lifted a curious eyebrow at SueAnn, who scowled and jerked her head toward Ellie's office. Steve was sitting behind her desk, browsing through her planner where she meticulously recorded appointments and scheduled treatments.

With great effort, she swallowed her irritation. "Here you go," she said loudly. His gaze flew to hers, and he didn't seem at all embarrassed to be caught nosing around in her office.

"Thanks, Ellie. I really appreciate this." His mustache twitched again with his smile.

"Glad to help," she lied, and was immediately ashamed of herself for the ugly knot of resentment curdling in her stomach. "Read anything interesting in there?" she asked pointedly.

"Sorry. Professional curiosity. You don't mind, do you? I'm intrigued by the improvement you've noted here in that thoroughbred of Jack Martin's. I thought nothing would cure her. She's a beauty of a horse, and it would have been a real shame to have to put her down, but I thought she would always be lame."

"She's responded well to a combination of treatments. Jack and I are both pleased."

"So are things picking up?"

Not with you stealing my clients one by one, she thought. "Actually, it's been a pretty busy day."

"Have you given any more thought to my offer?"

She blew out a breath. She absolutely did not want to go into this with him today. "I have. The answer is still no, Steve. Just like it's been for the last month."

He rose from the chair and walked around to the other side of the desk. "Come on, Ellie. Think about it. If we combined our practices, we could each save tens of thousands a year on overhead. And pooling our workload would ease the burden on each of us."

What burden? She would kill for a little workload to complain about. Ellie sighed. His offer made common sense and, heaven knows, would help boost her meager income, but it also held about as much appeal to her as being knocked on her rear end by a hundred goats.

She didn't want to be partners, not with Steve or with anyone else. She wanted to stand on her own, to make her own decisions and be responsible for the consequences.

She had spent her entire adult life working for others, from volunteering in clinics while she was still in high school to the last seven years working for an equine vet in Monterey.

She was tired of it, of having to play by others' rules. Constantly having someone else tell her what animals she could treat and how she should treat them had been draining the life out of her, stealing all her satisfaction and joy in the career she loved.

It went deeper than that, though. If she were honest, her ferocious need for independence had probably been rooted in her childhood, watching her mother drink herself to an early grave because of a man and then being shuttled here and there in the foster care system.

She learned early she would never be able to please the endless parade of busybody social workers and foster parents who marched through her life. She couldn't please them, and she couldn't depend on them. Too often, the moment she began to care for a family, she was capriciously yanked out and sent to another one. Eventually, she learned not to care, to carefully construct a hard shell around her heart. The only one she could truly count on was herself.

This was her chance. Hers and Dylan's. The opportunity to build the life she had dreamed of since those early days cleaning cages.

She wasn't ready to give up that dream, patients or none.

Besides that, she had SueAnn to consider. With the animosity between the two, she and Steve would never be able to work together, and she didn't want to lose her as a friend or as an assistant.

"I'm not going to change my mind, Steve," she finally said. "It's a good offer and I appreciate it, really I do, but I'm just not interested right now."

If Dylan had given her that same look, Ellie would have called it a pout. After only a moment of sulking, Steve's expression became amiable again. "I'll keep working on you. Eventually I'll wear you down, just watch."

He picked up the case of vaccine and headed for the door. "Thanks again for the loan. I'll drop my shipment off tomorrow, if that's all right with you."

"That would be fine," she said.

At the door he paused and looked at her with a grin. "And have fun working with Matt Harte. The man can be tough as a sow's snout, but he's a damn hard worker. He's single-handedly built the Diamond Harte into a force to be reckoned with around here. I'm not sure that will help when it comes to planning a school carnival, but it ought to make things interesting."

Interesting. She had a feeling the word would be a vast understatement.

He was hiding out, no denying it.

Like a desperado trying frantically to stay two steps ahead of a hangin' party and a noose with his name on it.

A week after visiting Ellie at her clinic, Matt sat trapped in his office at the ranch house, trying to concentrate on the whir and click of the computer in front of him instead of the soft murmur of women's voices coming from the kitchen at the end of the hall.

As usual, he had a hundred and one better things to occupy his time than sit here gazing at a blasted screen, but he didn't dare leave the sanctuary of his office.

She was out there.

Ellie Webster. The city vet who had sneaked her way

into his dreams for a week, with that fiery hair and her silvery-green eyes and that determined little chin.

He thought she was only driving out to the Diamond Harte to drop her kid off for a sleepover with Lucy. She was supposed to be here ten minutes, tops, and wouldn't even have to know he was in here.

Things didn't go according to plan. He had a feeling they rarely would, where Ellie Webster was concerned. Instead of driving away like she should have done, she had apparently plopped down on one of the straight-backed kitchen chairs, and now he could hear her and Cassie talking and laughing like they'd been best friends for life.

They'd been at it for the last half hour, and he'd just about had enough.

He wasn't getting a damn thing done. Every time he tried to focus on getting the hang of the new livestock-tracking software, her voice would creep under the door like a sultry, devious wisp of smoke, and his concentration would be shot all to hell and back.

Why did it bug him so much to have her invading his space with that low laugh of hers? He felt itchy and bothered having her here, like a mustang with a tail full of cockleburs.

It wasn't right. He would have to get a handle on this awareness if he was going to be able to work on the school thing with her for the next few months. As to how, he didn't have the first idea. It had been a long time since he'd been so tangled up over a woman.

Maybe he should ask her out.

The idea scared him worse than kicking a mountain lion. He wasn't much of a lady's man. Maybe he used to be when he was younger—he'd enjoyed his share of buckle bunnies when he rodeoed in college, he wouldn't deny it—but things had changed after Melanie.

He had tried to date a few times after he was finally granted a divorce in absentia after her desertion, but every attempt left him feeling restless and awkward.

After a while he just quit trying, figuring it was better to wake up lonely in his own bed than in a stranger's.

He wasn't lonely, he corrected the thought quickly. He had Lucy and Jess and Cassidy and the ranch hands. He sure as hell didn't need another woman messing things up.

He cleared his throat. The action made him realize how thirsty he was. Parched, like he'd been riding through a desert for days.

The kitchen had water. Plenty of it, cold, pure mountain spring water right out of the tap. He could walk right in there and pour himself a big glass and nobody could do a damn thing about it.

Except then he'd have to face *her*.

He heaved a sigh and turned to the computer until the next wisp of laughter curled under the door.

That was it. He was going in. He shoved back from the desk and headed toward the door. He lived here, dammit. A man ought to be able to walk into his own kitchen for a drink if it suited him. She had no right to come into his house and tangle him up like this.

No right whatsoever.

Chapter 5

As soon as he walked into the big, warm kitchen, he regretted it.

He felt like the big, bad wolf walking in on a coop full of chickens. All four of them—Ellie, Cass and both of the girls—looked up, their cutoff laughter hanging in the air along with the sweet, intoxicating smell of chocolate chip cookies baking in the oven.

"Sorry. Didn't mean to interrupt," he muttered. "I, uh, just needed a drink of water and then I'll get out of your way."

"You didn't interrupt," Cassie said. "Sit down. The cookies will be done in a minute, and I know how much you love eating them right out of the oven."

Information his baby sister didn't need to be sharing with the whole damn world, thank you very much. Made him sound like a seven-year-old boy snitching goodies after school. "I've got things to do," he muttered.

"They can wait five minutes, can't they?"

His jaw worked as he tried to come up with a decent-sounding excuse to escape without seeming rude. How was a man supposed to think straight when he had four females watching him so expectantly?

Finally, he muttered a curse under his breath and pulled out a chair. "Just five minutes, though."

Like a tractor with a couple bad cylinders, the conversation limped along for a moment, and he squirmed on the hard chair, wishing he were absolutely anywhere but here. He was just about to jump up and rush back to the relative safety of his office—excuse or none—when Lucy ambushed him.

She touched his arm with green-painted fingernails—now where did she get those? he wondered—and gazed at him out of those big gray eyes. "Daddy, Dylan and her mom aren't going anywhere for Thanksgiving dinner since they don't have any family around here. Isn't that sad?"

Keeping his gaze firmly averted from Ellie's, he made a noncommittal sound.

"Do you think they might be able to come here and share our family's dinner?"

Despite his best efforts, his gaze slid toward Ellie just in time to catch her mouth drop and her eyes go wide—with what, he couldn't say for sure, but it sure looked like she was as horrified as he was by the very idea.

"I don't know, honey—" he began.

"That's a great idea," Cassie said at the same time. "There's always room at the table for a few more, and plenty of food."

"Oh, no. That's okay," Ellie said quickly. "We'll be fine, won't we, Dylan?"

Dylan put on a pleading expression. "Come on, Mom. It would be so cool. Lucy's aunt Cassie is a great cook. I bet she never burns the stuffing like you do."

Ellie made a face at her daughter, and Matt had to fight a chuckle. And he thought *Cass and Lucy* were bad at spilling family secrets.

"Be that as it may," Ellie said, her cheeks tinged slightly pink, "I'm sure the Hartes have a lovely family dinner planned. They don't need to be saddled with two more."

"It's no problem," Cassie said. "We'd love to have you come. Wouldn't we, Matt?"

He cleared his throat. Again, he couldn't seem to make his brain work fast enough to come up with an excuse. "Uh, sure."

Ellie raised an eyebrow at his less-than-enthusiastic response. He obviously didn't want to invite her for Thanksgiving any more than she wanted to accept.

"Good. It's settled," Cassie said, oblivious to their objections. "It's usually really casual. Just family—Matt, Lucy, our brother Jess and whichever of the ranch hands stick around for the holidays. We eat around two but you're welcome to come out any time before then, especially if you're into watching football with the guys."

What she knew about football would fit into a salt-shaker. Ellie sighed heavily. And what she knew about big rowdy Thanksgiving family dinners wouldn't even fit on a grain of salt.

It looked like she was going to be stuck with both things. So much for her good intentions about having as little as possible to do with the man who somehow managed to jumble up her insides every time she was around him.

What choice did she have, though? She didn't want to hurt his daughter's or sister's feelings by refusing the invitation. Lucy was a dear, sweet and quiet and polite. Exactly Dylan's opposite! It was a wonder they were friends, but somehow the two of them meshed perfectly. They brought out the best in each other.

To her surprise, she and Cassie had also immediately hit it off. Unlike Matt, his sister was bubbly and friendly and went out of her way to make her feel welcomed.

She would sound churlish and rude if she refused to share their holiday simply because the alpha male in the family made her as edgy as a hen on a hot griddle and sent her hormones whirling around like a Texas dust storm.

"Can I bring something?" she finally asked, trying to accept the invitation as gracefully as she could manage.

"Do you have a specialty?" Cassie asked.

Did macaroni and cheese count as a specialty? She doubted it. "No. I'm afraid not."

"Sure you do, Mom." Dylan spoke up. "What about that pie you make sometimes?"

She made pecan pie exactly twice, but Dylan had never forgotten it. Hope apparently springs eternal in a nine-year-old's heart that someday she would bake it again. "I don't know if I'd call that a specialty."

"Why don't you bring it anyway?" Cassie suggested. "Or if you'd rather make something else, that would be fine."

I'd rather just stay home and have our usual quiet dinner for two, she thought. But one look at Dylan revealed her daughter was ecstatic about the invitation.

Her eyes shone, and her funny little face had the same kind of expectancy it usually wore just before walking downstairs on Christmas morning.

She looked so excited that Ellie instantly was awash in guilt for all the years they had done just that—stayed home alone with their precooked turkey and instant mashed potatoes instead of accepting other invitations from friends and colleagues.

Why had she never realized her daughter had been missing a big, noisy celebration? Dylan was usually so vocal about what she wanted and thought she needed. Why had she never said anything about this?

"Whatever you want to bring is fine," Cassie assured her. "Really, though, you don't have to bring anything but yourselves. Like I said, there's always plenty of food."

"I'll bring the pecan pie," she said, hoping her reluctance didn't filter into her voice.

"Great. I usually make a pumpkin and maybe an apple so we'll have several to choose from. Knowing my brothers, I doubt any of them will last long."

She looked at Matt out of the corner of her eyes and found him watching her. What was he thinking? That she was an interloper who had suddenly barged her way in to yet another facet of his life when he had plainly made it clear she wasn't welcome? She couldn't tell by the unreadable expression in those startling blue eyes.

The timer suddenly went off on the oven.

"That would be the cookies." Cassie jumped up and opened the oven door, releasing even more of the heavenly aroma.

A smell so evocative of hearth and home that Ellie's heart broke a little for all the homemade cookies she never had time to bake for her daughter. She had shed her last tear a long time ago for all the missing cookies in her own childhood.

Cassie quickly transferred at least half a dozen of the warm, gooey treats onto a plate for Matt, then poured him a glass of milk from the industrial-size refrigerator.

She set both in front of him, and he quickly grabbed them and stood up. Ellie smiled a little at the blatant relief evident in every line of his big, rangy body.

"Thanks," he mumbled to his sister. "I'll let you ladies get back to whatever you were talking about before I interrupted you."

The girls' giggles at being called ladies trailed after him as Matt made his escape from the kitchen.

"Wow, Mom. You look really great," Dylan said for about the fifth time as they made their way up the walk to the sprawling Diamond Harte ranch house.

Ellie fought her self-consciousness. Matt's sister said Thanksgiving dinner would be casual, but she didn't think her usual winter attire of jeans and denim work shirts was quite appropriate.

Instead, she had worn her slim wool skirt over soft black leather boots and a matching dove-gray sweater— one of her few dressy outfits that only saw the light of day when she went to professional meetings. Was she hideously overdressed? She hoped not. She was nervous enough about this as it was without adding unsuitable clothes to the mix.

She shouldn't be this nervous. It was only dinner, nothing to twist her stomach into knots over or turn her mouth as dry as a riverbed in August.

She cleared her throat, angry with herself, at the

knowledge that only part of her edginess had to do with sharing a meal with Matt Harte and his blue eyes and powerful shoulders.

That might be the main reason, but the rest had more to do with the holiday itself. She had too many less-than-pleasant memories of other years, other holidays. Always being the outsider, the one who didn't belong. Of spending the day trying to fit in during someone else's family celebration in foster home after foster home.

This wasn't the same. She had a family now—Dylan. All she could ever want or need. Her funny, imaginative, spunky little daughter who filled her heart with constant joy. She was now a confident, self-assured woman, content with life and her place in it.

So why did she feel like an awkward, gawky child again, standing here on the doorstep, hoping this time the people inside would like her?

Dylan, heedless of her mother's nerves, rushed up the remaining steps and buzzed hard on the doorbell, and Ellie forced herself to focus on something other than her own angst.

She looked around her, admiring the view. In the lightly falling snow, the ranch was beautiful. Matt kept a clean, well-ordered operation, she could say that for him. The outbuildings all wore fresh paint, the fences were all in good repair, the animals looked well cared for.

Some outfits looked as cluttered as garbage dumps, with great hulking piles of rusty machinery set about like other people displayed decorative plates or thimble collections. Here on the Diamond Harte, though, she couldn't see so much as a spare part lying around.

It looked like a home, deeply loved and nurtured.

What must it have been like to grow up in such a place? To feel warm dirt and sharp blades of grass under your bare feet in the summertime and jump into big piles of raked leaves in the fall and sled down that gently sloping hill behind the barn in winter?

To know without question that you belonged just here, with people who loved you?

She pushed the thoughts away, angry at herself for dredging up things she had resolved long ago. It was only the holiday that brought everything back. That made her once more feel small and unwanted.

To her relief, the door opened before she could feel any sorrier for herself, sending out a blast of warmth and a jumble of delectable smells, as well as a small figure who launched herself at Dylan with a shriek of excitement.

"You're here! Finally!"

"We're early, aren't we?" Ellie asked anxiously. "Didn't your aunt say you were eating at two? It's only half past one."

"I don't know what time it is. I've just been *dying* for you to get here. Dylan, you have *got* to come up to my room. Uncle Jess bought me the new NSYNC CD and it's so totally awesome."

Before Ellie could say anything else, both girls rushed up the stairs, leaving her standing in the two-story entry alone, holding her pecan pie and feeling extremely foolish.

Okay. Now what did she do? She'd been in the huge, rambling ranch house a few times before to pick up Lucy or drop off Dylan for some activity or other, but she had always entered through the back door leading straight into the kitchen. She had no idea how to get there from the front door, and it seemed extremely rude to go wandering through a strange house on her own.

She could always go back and ring the doorbell again, she supposed. But that would probably lead to awkward questions about why her daughter was already upstairs while she lingered by the door as if ready to bolt any moment.

She was still standing there, paralyzed by indecision, when she heard loud male groans at something from a room down the hall, then the game shifted to a commercial—somebody hawking razor blades.

"You want another beer?" she heard Matt's deep voice ask someone else—his brother, she presumed, or perhaps one of the ranch hands. The deep timbre of it sent those knots in her stomach unraveling to quiver like plucked fiddle strings.

Seconds later—before she could come up with a decent place to hide—he walked out in the hall wearing tan jeans and a forest-green fisherman's sweater. She was still ordering her heart to start beating again when he turned and caught sight of her standing there like an idiot.

"Doc!" he exclaimed.

"Hi," she mumbled.

"Why are you just standing out here? Come in."

She thought about explaining how the girls had abandoned her for their favorite boy band, then decided she would sound even more ridiculous if she tried. She held up the pie instead. "Where's the best place for this?"

"Probably in the kitchen. I was just heading there myself, I can show you the way. Here. Let me take your coat first."

She tensed as he came up behind her and pulled her coat from her shoulders while she transferred the pie from hand to hand. Despite her best efforts, she was intensely aware of him, his heat and strength and the leathery smell of his aftershave.

After he hung her coat in a small closet off the entry, he took off down the hall. She followed him, trying fiercely not to notice the snug fit of his jeans or those impossibly broad shoulders under the weave of his sweater. Something was different about him today. It took her a moment to figure out what. He wasn't wearing the black Stetson that seemed so much a part of him, nor was his hair flattened from it.

The dark waves looked soft and thick. They would probably be like silk under her fingers, she thought. The impulse to reach out and see for herself was so strong, she even lifted a hand a few inches from her side, then dropped it quickly in mortification.

It was much safer to look around her. This part of the house was one she hadn't seen before, but it had the same warmth of the rest of the house, with family pictures grouped together on one wall and a huge log cabin quilt in dark greens and blues hanging on the other.

As they neared the kitchen, the smells of roasting turkey and vegetables grew stronger, and her stomach gave a loud, long rumble. She pressed a hand to it, hoping no one else could hear but her.

When she looked up, though, she found Matt giving her a lopsided grin, and she flushed.

"Oh, Ellie! You made it!" Matt's sister looked pretty and flustered as she stirred something on the stove with one hand while she pulled a pan of golden dinner rolls out of the oven with the other. "When it started to snow, I was afraid you'd decide not to make the drive."

"It's not bad out there. A few flurries, that's all. Just enough to make everything look like a magic fairyland."

"Wait until you've lived here for a few years. You won't describe the snow quite so romantically. Oh, is that your famous pie? Does it need to go in the refrigerator?"

"No. I don't think so."

"Good. I'm not sure I could find room for it." Cassie blew out a breath and tucked a stray strand of hair behind her ear just as the timers on the stove and microwave went off at the same time. The frazzled look in her eyes started to border on panic.

"Uh, anything I can do to help?" Matt asked suddenly.

His sister sent him a grateful look. "Actually, there is. Can you finish chopping the raw vegetables to go with that dip you like? Oh, rats," she exclaimed suddenly. "I forgot to bring up the cranberry sauce from the storeroom. Ellie, would you mind stirring this gravy for me? I think most of the lumps are out of it—just make sure it doesn't burn on the bottom."

"Uh, sure."

She set her pie on the only bare patch of countertop she could find and took the wooden spoon from Cassie, who rushed from the room, leaving her and Matt alone.

He immediately went to work on the vegetables. The cutting surface was on a work island in the middle of the kitchen with only a few feet separating it from the stove, forcing them to stand side by side but facing opposite directions.

Again she felt that sizzle of awareness but she sternly

tried to suppress it. They lapsed into an awkward silence while they did their appointed jobs.

"Everything smells divine," she finally said.

He seized on the topic. "Yeah, Cassidy's a great cook. I've always thought she should have her own restaurant."

"I didn't know Cassie was short for Cassidy." She paused, remembering something SueAnn had told her about the middle brother, the Salt River chief of police. "Let me get this straight, you have a brother named Jesse James and a sister named Cassidy?"

His low, rueful laugh sent the hairs on the back of her neck prickling. "Our dad was what I guess you'd call a history buff. One of his ancestors, Matt Warner, was a member of Butch Cassidy's Wild Bunch, and Dad grew up hearing stories about him handed down throughout the years. Dad was always fascinated by outlaws and lawmen of the Old West. The romanticism and the adventure and the history of it, I guess."

"So you're named after this scofflaw of an ancestor?"

"Yeah." His voice sounded rueful again. "Matthew Warner Harte. When the others came along, I guess he just decided to stick with the same theme."

A Wild West outlaw. Why didn't it surprise her that he had that blood churning through his veins? "And how did your mother handle having her own little wild bunch?"

His shrug brushed his shoulder into hers, and the subtle movement sent a shiver rippling down her spine. "My parents adored each other," he answered. "Mom probably wouldn't have complained even if Dad wanted to name us Larry, Moe and Curly."

He sent her another lopsided grin, and she was helpless to prevent herself from returning it. They gazed at each other for a moment, side by side across shoulders, both smiling. Suddenly everything seemed louder, more intense—the slurp and burble of the gravy in the pan, the chink of the knife hitting the cutting board, the slow whir of the ceiling fan overhead.

His gaze dropped to her mouth for an instant, just enough for heat to flare there as if he'd touched her, then his eyes flashed to hers once more before he turned abruptly, guiltily, back to the vegetables.

Now *that* was interesting.

She was still trying to come up with something to say in the midst of the sudden tension—not to mention trying to remind her lungs what they were there for—when their daughters burst into the kitchen in mid-giggle.

They both stopped short in the doorway when they saw their parents working side-by-side. Ellie opened her mouth to greet them but shut it again when two pairs of eyes shifted rapidly between her and Matt, then widened.

The girls looked at each other with small, secretive smiles that sent the fear of God into her. They were definitely up to something. And she was very much afraid she was beginning to suspect what it might be.

Chapter 6

"So tell us what brings a pretty California beach girl like yourself to our desolate Wyoming wilderness."

Matt sat forward so he could hear Ellie's answer across the table. If *he* had asked that question, he grumped to himself, she probably would have snapped at him to mind his own business. But it didn't seem to bother her at all that his brother wanted to nose around through her past.

Instead, she smiled at Jesse, seated to her left. "I'm afraid there weren't too many beaches around Bakersfield."

"Bakersfield? Is that where you're from?" Cassie asked.

If he hadn't been watching her so intently, Matt would have missed the way her smile slid away and the barest shadow of old pain flickered in her green eyes for just a moment before she shifted her gaze to the full plate in front of her. "Until I was seven. After that, I moved around a lot."

What happened when she was seven? he wondered. And why did she phrase it that way? *I moved around a lot*, not *My family moved around a lot*?

Before he could ask, Jesse spoke. "Even if you're not a beach girl, you're still the best-looking thing to share our Thanksgiving dinner since I can remember."

She laughed, rolling her eyes a little at the compliment, while Matt battled a powerful urge to casually reach over and shove his brother's face into his mashed potatoes.

He didn't want to admit it bugged the hell out of him the way Jesse flirted with her all through dinner, hanging on her every word and making sure her glass was always full.

Ellie didn't seem to mind. She teased him right back, smiling and laughing at him like she'd never done with Matt.

Not that he cared. He was just worried about her getting a broken heart, that's all. Maybe somebody ought to warn her about Jesse. His little brother wasn't a bad sort. Not really. In fact, for being such a wild, out-of-control son of a gun after their parents died, Jess turned out pretty okay.

Matt would be the first one to admit the kid did a fine job protecting the good people of Salt River as the chief of police, a whole hell of a lot better than the last chief, who'd spent more time lining his own pockets than he did fighting crime.

But Jess still had a well-earned reputation with the ladies as a love 'em and leave 'em type. He rarely dated a woman longer than a few weeks, and when he did, she was usually the kind of girl their mother would have described as "faster than she ought to be."

'Course, it was none of his business if Ellie Webster wanted to make a fool of herself over a charmer like Jesse James Harte, he reminded himself.

"So what brought you out here?" the charmer in question asked her again.

"My mom always wanted to move to the mountains and be a cowgirl," Ellie's daughter offered, helping herself to more candied yams.

A delicate pink tinged the doc's cheeks. "Thanks for sharing that, sweetheart."

"What?" Dylan asked, all innocence. "That's what you said, isn't it?"

She laughed ruefully. "You're right. I did. The truth is, I've always wanted to live and work in the Rockies. I met Ben Nichols when I was giving a lecture a few years ago. Afterward, when he told me about Star Valley and his practice here, I told him how much I envied him and casually mentioned I had always dreamed of living out here. I never imagined he would offer to sell his practice to me when he retired."

So that explained what brought her to Wyoming. What interested him was why a tiny little thing like her would choose such a physically demanding job as a large-animal vet in the first place. If she wanted to be a vet, she would have been better off with little things like dogs and cats instead of having to muscle a half-ton of steer into a chute.

He didn't think she'd appreciate the question, so he asked another one. "Where were you working before?"

She shifted her gaze across the table to him as if she'd forgotten he was sitting there. "I worked at a clinic in the

Monterey area. That's on the central coast of California—so I guess you were right, Jesse. Technically I suppose you could call me a beach girl, although I rarely had a chance to see it."

"I've heard that's a beautiful area," Cassie said.

"It is. Pebble Beach is just south of it, and Carmel-by-the-Sea."

"How many cattle operations did you find in the middle of all those golf courses and tourist traps?" he asked abruptly, earning a curious look from Cassie.

"Not many, although there are a few farther inland. My clients were mostly horses—thoroughbreds and jumpers and pleasure horses."

The conversation turned then to the physical differences between working horses and riding horses and then, with much prompting by Dylan, onto the best choice for a pleasure horse for a nine-year-old girl. Matt contented himself listening to the conversation and watching Ellie interact with his family.

Even after three years of marriage, Melanie had never fit in half as well. He felt vaguely guilty for the thought, but it was nothing less than the truth. She and Cassie had fought like cats and dogs from the beginning, and Jess had despised her.

So much for his grand plan to give his younger siblings more of a stable home environment by bringing home a wife.

He should have known from the first night he brought her home after their whirlwind courtship and marriage at the national stock show in Denver that he had made a disastrous mistake. She spent the entire evening bickering with Cassie and completely ignoring Jess.

But by then it was too late, they were already married. It took him three more years of the situation going from bad to worse for him to admit to himself how very stupid he had been.

He wouldn't make that mistake again.

He hated thinking about it, about what a fool he had been, so he yanked his mind off the topic. "Everything tastes great, as usual," he said instead to Cassie.

She grinned suddenly. "Remember that first year after Mom and Daddy died when you tried to cook Thanksgiving dinner?"

Jess turned his attention long enough from Ellie to shudder and add his own jab. "I remember it. My stomach still hasn't forgiven me. The turkey was tougher than roasted armadillo."

"And the yams could have been used to tar the barn roof."

He rolled his eyes as the girls giggled. Jess and Cassie teased him mercilessly about that dinner. Usually it didn't bother him—but then again, usually he didn't have Ellie Webster sitting across from him listening to the conversation with that intrigued look in her green eyes.

"Give me a break," he muttered. "I did my best. You're lucky you got anything but cold cereal and frozen pizza."

He'd been twenty-two when their parents died in a rollover on a slippery mountain road. That first year had been the toughest time of his life. Grieving for his parents and their sudden death, trying to comfort Cassie, who had been a lost and frightened thirteen-year-old, doing his damnedest to keep Jess out of juvenile detention.

Trying to keep the ranch and the family together when he didn't know what the hell he was doing.

It had been a rough few years, but they had survived and were closer for it.

"At least we had to only go through Matt's attempts to poison us for a while." Jess grinned. "Then Cassie decided to save us all and learned to cook."

"I had no choice," she retorted. "It was a matter of survival. I figured one of us had to learn unless we wanted to die of food poisoning or starve to death. Matt was too busy with the ranch and you were too busy raising hell. That left me."

Jesse immediately bristled, gearing up for a sharp retort, and Matt gave a resigned sigh. Cassie always knew how to punch his buttons. Jesse's wild, hard-drinking days after their parents died were still a sore point with him, but that never stopped Cass from rubbing his nose in it.

Before he could step in to head trouble off, Ellie did it for him. "Well, you learned to cook very well," she assured Cassie, with an anxious look toward Jess's glare. "You'll have to give me the recipe for your stuffing. I tend to over-cook it. Is that sausage I taste in there?"

She prattled on in a way that seemed completely unlike her, and it was only after she had successfully turned the conversation completely away from any trouble spots that he realized she had stepped in to play peacemaker as smoothly as if she'd been doing it all her life.

Had she done it on purpose? He wondered again about her background. She hadn't mentioned brothers or sisters, but that didn't mean she had none. What had happened when she was seven, the year after which she said she'd moved around so much?

He wanted badly to know, just as he was discovering he wanted to know everything about her.

"Come on, Ellie. It's our turn to watch football."

She looked at the dishes scattered across the table. "I can help clean up...."

"No way. The men get to do it—it's tradition. That's why I try to make the kitchen extra messy for them." She smiled sweetly at her brothers. "I think I used just about every single dish in the house."

Matt and Jesse groaned in unison. Unmoved, Cassie stood up. "Have fun, boys."

With guilt tweaking her, Ellie let Matt's sister drag her from the dining room, Dylan and Lucy following behind.

Cassie led her into a huge great room dominated by a towering river-rock fireplace. A big-screen TV and a pair of couches took up one corner, and a pool table and a couple of video games jostled for space in the other. As large as the room was, though, it was comfortable. Lived in, with warm-toned furniture and shelves full of books.

The girls immediately rushed to the pool table, and Cassidy plopped down on one of the plump, tweedy couches. "Boy, it feels good to sit down. I had to get up at four to put the turkey in, and I haven't stopped since."

"I'm sorry if I made extra work for you."

"Are you kidding? I didn't do anything I wouldn't have done anyway, and it's wonderful to have somebody else without a Y chromosome at the table besides Lucy!"

Cassie picked up the remote. "So which game do you want to watch? We have blue against red—" she flipped the channel "—or black against silver."

"I'm not crazy about football," she confessed.

The other woman sent her a conspiratorial grin. "Me, neither. I hate it, actually. When you spend your whole life around macho men, you don't really need to waste your time watching them on TV. Let's see if we can find something better until the boys come in and start growling at us to change it back."

She flipped the remote, making funny comments about every station she passed until stumbling on an old Alfred Hitchcock film with Jimmy Stewart.

"Here we go. *Rear Window.* This is what I call real entertainment. Could Grace Kelly dress or what?"

Ellie settled on the couch, the seductive warmth from the fireplace combining with the turkey put her into a pleasant haze.

She couldn't remember enjoying a meal more. The food had been delicious. And with the exception of the strange tension between her and Matt, the company had been great, too.

Their banter and teasing and memories of other holidays had been a revelation. This was what a family was all about, and if she closed her eyes, she could almost pretend she was a part of it.

One strange thing, though. For all their reminiscing, they hadn't brought up Lucy's mother one single time. It was almost as if the woman had never existed. Come to think of it, nobody had ever mentioned the mystery woman to Ellie.

"What happened to Lucy's mother?"

She didn't realize she had asked the blunt question out loud until Cassidy's relaxed smile froze, and she shot a quick glance at her niece. Ellie winced, appalled at herself. When would she ever learn to think before she opened her big mouth? At least neither of the girls was paying any attention to them, Ellie saw with relief.

"I'm so sorry," she said quickly. "That was terribly rude of me. It just slipped out. It's none of my business, really. You don't have to answer."

"No. It's just a…a raw subject." She looked at her niece again, and Ellie thought she saw guilt flicker in her blue eyes, then she flashed a bitter smile. She lowered her voice so the girls couldn't hear. "Melanie ran off with my…with one of our ranch hands. Lucy wasn't even three months old."

Ellie's jaw dropped. She tried to picture Matt in the role of abandoned husband and couldn't. Her heart twisted with sympathy when she imagined him taking care of a newborn on his own—late-night feedings, teething and all.

What kind of woman could simply abandon her own child like that? She thought of those first few months after Dylan was born, when she had been on her own and so very frightened about what the future might hold for the two of them.

Despite her fear, she had been completely in awe of the precious gift she'd been handed. Some nights she would lie awake in that grimy two-room apartment, just staring at Dylan's tiny, squishy features, listening to her breathe and wondering what she had done to deserve such a miracle.

She couldn't even comprehend a woman who would walk away from something so amazing.

Or from a man like Matt Harte.

"I'm so sorry," she said, knowing the words were terribly inadequate.

Cassidy shrugged and looked toward the girls. From

the raw emotion exposed on her features like a winter-bare tree branch, Ellie had the odd suspicion there was more to the story than losing a sister-in-law.

"It was a long time ago," Cassie said quietly. "Anyway, Matt's much better off without her. He'd be the first to tell you that. Melanie hated it here. She hated the ranch, she hated Wyoming, she hated being a mother. I was amazed she stuck around as long as she did."

Why on earth would he marry a woman who hated ranch life? Ellie wondered. For a man like Matt who so obviously belonged here—on this land he loved so much—it must have been a bitter rejection seeing it scorned by the woman he married.

She must have been very beautiful for him to marry her in the first place and bring her here. Ellie didn't even want to think about why the thought depressed her so much.

Cassie quickly turned the conversation to the Hitchcock movie, but even after Ellie tried to shift her attention to the television, her mind refused to leave thoughts of Matt and the wife who had deserted him with a tiny daughter.

As much as she hated bringing up such an obviously painful topic, she had to admit she was grateful for the insight it provided into a man she was discovering she wanted to understand.

No wonder he sometimes seemed so gruff, so cold. Had he always been that way or had his wife's desertion hardened him? Had he once been like Jesse, all charm and flirtatiousness? She couldn't imagine it. Good grief, the man was devastating enough with his habitual scowl!

After a moment, Cassie turned the tables. "What

about Dylan's father?" she asked suddenly. "Is he still in the picture?"

"He was never *in* the picture. Not really," Ellie answered calmly. After so many years the scab over her heart had completely healed. "Our relationship ended when Kurt saw that plus sign on the pregnancy test."

He had been so furious at her for being stupid enough to get pregnant, as if it were entirely her fault the protection they used had failed. He could lose his job over this, he had hissed at her, that handsome, intelligent face dark with anger. Professors who impregnated their star students tended to be passed over when tenures were being tossed around. Didn't she understand what this could do to him?

It had always been about him. Always. She had only come to understand that immutable fact through the filter of time and experience. In the midst of their relationship, she had been so amazed that someone of Kurt's charisma—not to mention professional standing—would deign to take her under his wing, first as a mentor and adviser, then as a friend, then as a lover during her final year of undergraduate work.

She might have seen him more clearly had she not been seduced by the one thing she had needed so desperately those days—approbation. He had told her she had talent, that she would be a brilliant, dedicated doctor of veterinary medicine one day.

No one else had believed in her. She had fought so hard every step of the way, and he was the only one who seemed to think she could do it. She had lapped up his carefully doled-out praise like a puppy starving for attention.

She thought she had loved him passionately and had

given him everything she had, while to him she had been one more in a long string of silly, awestruck students.

It was a hard lesson, but her hurt and betrayal had lasted only until Dylan was born. As she held her child in her arms—hers alone—she realized she didn't care anymore what had led her to that moment; she was only amazed at the unconditional love she felt for her baby.

"So you raised Dylan completely on your own while you were finishing vet school?" Cassie asked.

She nodded. "I took her to class half the time because I couldn't find a sitter, but somehow we did it."

Cassie shook her head in sympathetic disgust. "Men are pigs, aren't they?" she muttered, just as Jesse entered the great room.

He plopped next to Ellie on the couch, scowling at his sister. "Hey, I resent that. Especially since it just took two of us the better part of an hour to clean up the mess *you* made in the kitchen."

"I meant that figuratively," she retorted. "When it comes to knowing what a woman needs and wants out of a relationship, most of you have about as much sense as a bucket of spit."

"Don't listen to her, Doc. My baby sister has always been far too cynical for her own good."

Jesse grabbed Ellie's hand, and for one horrified second she thought he was going to bring it to his lips. To her vast relief, he just squeezed it, looking deep into her eyes. "Not all men are pigs. I, for one, always give a woman exactly what she wants. And what she needs."

His knowing smile fell just a few inches short of a leer, and she felt hot color crawl across her cheekbones at finding herself on the receiving end of it, especially from a man as dangerously attractive as Jesse James Harte.

Before she could come up with a reply, his little sister gave an inelegant snort. "See? What did I tell you? A bucket of spit."

Ellie smiled, charmed beyond words by both of them and their easy acceptance of her. Before she could answer, she felt the heat of someone's gaze on her. She turned around and found Matt standing in the doorway, arms crossed and shoulder propped against the jamb as he watched his brother's flirting with an unreadable look in those vivid blue eyes.

The heated blush Jesse had sparked spread even higher, until she thought her face must look as bright as the autumn leaves in his sister's centerpiece.

What was it about that single look that sent her nerves lurching and tumbling to her stomach, that affected her a thousand times more intensely than Jesse's teasing?

His daughter spotted him at almost the same time she did. "Daddy, come play with us," she demanded from the pool table.

He shifted his gaze from Ellie to the girls, his mouth twisting into a soft smile that did funny, twirly things to her insides. "I will in a bit, Lucy Goose. I have to go out and check on Mystic first, okay?"

"Mystic?" Ellie's question came out as a squeak that nobody but her seemed to notice.

"One of our mares," Matt answered.

"Mystic Mountain Moon," Lucy said. "That's her full name."

"She's pregnant with her first foal and she's tried to lose it a couple times," Matt said.

"She's a real beauty." Cassie joined in. "Moon Ranger

out of Mystic Diamond Lil. One heck of a great cutting horse. Matt tried her out in a few local rodeos last summer, and she blew everybody away."

"Her foal's going to be a winner, too," Matt said. "If she can hang on to it for a few more months, anyway."

He paused and looked at Ellie again. "You, uh, wouldn't want to come out and check on her with me, would you?"

She stared at him, astonished at the awkward invitation, an offer she sensed surprised him as much as it had her. She opened her mouth to answer just as he shook his head. "I guess you're not really dressed to go mucking around in the barn. Forget it."

"No," she said quickly. "These boots are sturdier than they look. I would love to." She suddenly discovered she wanted fiercely to go with him, to see more of the Diamond Harte and his beauty of a mare.

"Let me just grab my coat." She jumped up before he could rescind the invitation. Whatever impulse had prompted him to ask her to accompany him, she sensed he was offering her more than just a visit to his barn. He was inviting her into this part of his life, lowering at least some of the walls between them.

She wasn't about to blow it.

"Okay then." He cast his eyes around the room for a moment as if trying to figure out what to do next, then his gaze stopped on his daughter, pool cue in her hand.

"We shouldn't be long," he said. "I promise I'll be back in just a little while to whup both of your behinds."

The girls barely heard him, Ellie saw, too busy sharing another one of those conspiratorial looks that were really beginning to make her nervous. "You two take your time, Dad," Lucy said in an exaggerated voice. "Really, we can use all the practice we can get."

He looked vaguely startled by her insistence, then gave her another one of those soft smiles before turning to Ellie. "I'll go get your coat."

A few moments later, he returned wearing that black Stetson and a heavy ranch jacket and holding out her coat. He helped her into it and then led the way into the snow that still fluttered down halfheartedly.

Though it was still technically afternoon, she had discovered night came early this time of year in Wyoming. The sun had already begun to sink behind the Salt River mountains, and the dying light was the same color as lilac blossoms in the spring.

Her chest ached at the loveliness of it, at the play of light on the skiff of snow and the rosy glow of his outbuildings in the twilight. There was a quiet reverence here as night descended on the mountains. As if no one else existed but the two of them and the snow and the night.

He seemed as reluctant as she to break the hushed beauty of the scene. They walked in silence toward the huge red barn a few hundred yards from the house. When he finally spoke, it was in a low voice to match the magic of the evening. "Mystic likes to be outside, even as cold as it's been. I'll check to see if she's still in the pasture before we go inside the barn. You can wait here if you want."

"No. I'll come with you," she said in that same hushed voice.

They crunched through snow to the other side, with Matt just a few steps ahead of her. She was looking at her feet so she didn't fall in the slick snow when he growled a harsh oath.

She jerked her gaze up. "What is it? What's wrong?"

He pointed to the pasture. For a moment, she couldn't figure out what had upset him, then her gaze sharpened and she saw it.

Bright red bloodstains speckled the snow in a vivid, ugly trail leading to the barn.

Chapter 7

Dread clutched at her stomach. "Do you think it was a coyote?"

"I doubt it," he said tersely. "Not this close to the house and not in the middle of the day. They tend to stay away from the horses, anyway."

"What, then?"

"Mystic, I'd guess. She's probably lost the foal. Damn."

If the mare was hemorrhaging already, it was probably too late to save the foal, and Matt obviously knew it as well as she did. He jumped the fence easily and followed the trail of blood. Without a moment's hesitation, she hiked her skirt above her knees and climbed over the snow-slicked rails as well, then quickly caught up with him.

With that frown and his jaw set, he looked hard and dangerous, like the Wild West outlaw he was named after.

"I'm sorry," she offered softly.

He blew out a breath. "It happens. Probably nothing we can do at this point. I had high hopes for Mystic's foal, though. The sire is one hell of a cutter, just like—"

Before he could finish the sentence, they heard a high, distressed whinny from inside the barn, and both picked up their pace to a run. He beat her inside, but she followed just a few seconds later. She had a quick impression of a clean, well-lit stall, then her attention immediately shifted to the misty-gray quarter horse pacing restlessly in the small space.

A quick visual check told her the blood they saw in the snow was from a large cut on the horse's belly, probably from kicking at herself in an attempt to rid her body of what she thought was bothering her—the foal.

It relieved her mind some, but not much. "She hasn't lost it yet," she said.

Matt looked distracted as he ran his hands over the horse. "She's going to, though, isn't she?"

"Probably. I'm sorry," she said again. She had seen the signs before. The sweat soaking the withers, the distress, the bared teeth as pain racked the mare.

All her professional instincts screamed at her to do something, not just stand here helplessly. To soothe, to heal. But Mystic wasn't hers to care for, and her owner didn't trust Ellie or her methods.

Still, she had to try. "Will you let me examine her?"

She held her breath as he studied her from across the stall, praying he would consent. The reluctance in his eyes shouldn't have hurt her. He had made no secret of his opinions. But she still had to dig her fingers into the wood rail at the deep, slicing pain.

He blew out a breath. "I don't know...."

"I'm a good vet, Matt. Please. Just let me look at her. I won't do anything against your wishes."

His hard, masculine face tense and worried, he studied Ellie for several seconds until Mystic broke away from him with another long, frantic whinny.

"Okay," Matt said finally. "Do what you can for her."

"My bag's in the pickup. It will just take me a minute to get it."

Her heart pounding, she ran as fast as she dared out of the barn and across the snow toward the house, cursing the constricting skirt as she went. This was exactly why she preferred to stick to jeans and work shirts. Of course she had to choose today, of all days, to go outside her comfort zone just for vanity's sake.

She slipped on a hidden patch of ice under the bare, spreading branches of a huge elm, and her legs almost went out from under her. At the last minute, she steadied herself on the trunk of the tree and paused for just an instant to catch her breath before hurrying on, anxious for the frightened little mare.

She hated seeing any animal in distress, always had. That was her first concern and the thought uppermost in her head. At the same time, on a smaller, purely selfish level that shamed her to admit it to herself, part of her wanted Matt to see firsthand that she knew what she was doing, that she would try anything in her power to save that foal.

At last she reached her truck, fumbled with the handle, then fought the urge to bang her head against it several times. Locked. Rats! And her keys were in her purse, inside the house.

With another oath at herself for not learning her lesson the night he had to thaw out her locks, she hurried up the porch steps and through the front door. She was rifling through her purse on the hall table, conscious that with every second of delay the foal's chances grew ever more dim, when Cassie walked out of the family room.

Matt's sister stopped short, frowning. "What is it? Is something wrong?"

"Mystic," Ellie answered grimly. "She's losing the foal. I'm just after my bag in the truck. Naturally, it's locked."

"Oh, no. What a relief that you're here, though! Can you save it?"

As she usually did before treating an animal, Ellie felt the heavy weight of responsibility settle on her shoulders. "I don't know. I'm going to try. Listen, we might be a while. Is Dylan okay in here without me?"

"Sure. She and Lucy have ganged up on Jess at the pool table. They haven't even noticed you've been gone. Is there anything I can do to help?"

Pray your stubborn brother will let me do more than look. Ellie kept the thought to herself and shook her head. "Just don't let Dylan eat too much pie."

She rushed out the door and down the steps to her truck and quickly unlocked it. Her leather backpack was behind the seat and, on impulse, she also picked up the bag with her sensors and acupuncture needles, then ran to the horse barn.

Matt had taken off his hat and ranch coat, she saw when her eyes once more adjusted to the dim light inside the barn, and he was doing his best to soothe the increasingly frantic animal.

The worry shadowing his eyes warmed her, even in the midst of her own tension. Matt Harte obviously cared deeply for the horse—all of his horses, judging by the modern, clean facilities he stabled them in—and her opinion of him went up another notch.

"Sorry it took so long." She immediately went to the sink to scrub. "Anything new happen while I was gone?"

"No. She's just as upset as she was before."

She snapped on a sterile pair of latex gloves and was pleased he had the sense to open the stall for her so she could keep them clean.

"What do you need me to do?" he asked, his voice pitched low to avoid upsetting the horse more than she already was.

"Can you hold her head for me?"

He nodded and obeyed, then scrutinized her closely as she approached the animal slowly, murmuring nonsense words as she went. Mystic, though still frantic at the tumult churning her insides, calmed enough to let Ellie examine her.

What she found heartened her. Although she could feel contractions rock the horse's belly, the foal hadn't begun to move through the birth canal. She pressed her stethoscope to the mare's side and heard the foal's heart beating loud and strong, if a little too fast.

"Can you tell what's going on?" Matt asked in that same low, soothing voice he used for the mare.

She spared a quick glance toward him. "My best guess is maybe she got into some mold or something and it's making her body try to flush itself of the fetus."

He clamped his teeth together, resignation in his eyes. "Can you give her something to ease the pain, then? Just until she delivers?"

"I could." She drew in a deep breath, her nerves kicking. "Or I can calm her down and try to save the foal."

He frowned. "How? I've been around horses all my life, certainly long enough to know there's not a damn thing you can do once a mare decides a foal has to go."

"Not with traditional Western medicine, you're right. But I've treated similar situations before, Matt. And saved several foals. I can't make any guarantees but I'd like to try."

His jaw tightened. "With your needles? No way."

She wanted to smack him for his old-school stubbornness. "I took an oath as a veterinarian. That I'll first do no harm, just like every other kind of medical doctor. I take it very seriously. It won't hurt her, I promise. And it might help save the foal's life where nothing else will."

Objections swamped his throat like spring runoff. He liked Ellie well enough as a person—too much, if he were completely honest with himself about it—but he wasn't too sure about her as a vet.

Her heart seemed to be in the right place, but the idea of her turning one of his horses into a pincushion didn't appeal to him whatsoever.

"If she's going to lose the foal anyway, what can it hurt to try?" she asked.

Across Mystic's withers, he gazed at Ellie and realized for the first time that she still wore the soft, pretty skirt she'd had on at dinner and those fancy leather boots. The boots were covered in who-knew-what, and a six-inch-wide bloodstain slashed across her skirt where she must have brushed up against Mystic's belly during the exam.

Ellie didn't seem to care a bit about her clothes,

though. All her attention was focused on his mare. She genuinely thought she could save the foal—he could see the conviction blazing out of those sparkly green eyes—and that was the only thing that mattered to her right now.

Her confidence had him wavering. Like she said, what could it hurt to let her try?

A week ago he wouldn't have allowed it under any circumstances, would have still been convinced the whole acupuncture thing was a bunch of hooey. But he'd done a little reading up on the Internet lately and discovered the practice wasn't nearly as weird as he thought. Even the American Veterinary Association considered acupuncture an accepted method of care.

Mystic suddenly jerked hard against the bit and threw her head back, eyes wild with pain.

"Please, Matt. Just let me try."

What other choice did he have? The foal was going to die, and there was a chance Mystic would, too. He blew out a breath. "Be careful," he said gruffly. "She's a damn fine mare, and I don't want her hurt."

He watched carefully while she ran her hands over the animal one more time, then placed her finger at certain points, speaking quietly to both of them as she went.

"According to traditional Chinese veterinary acupuncture, each animal's body—and yours, too—has a network of meridians, with acupoints along that meridian that communicate with a specific organ," she said softly as she worked. "When a particular organ is out of balance, the related acupoints may become tender or show some other abnormality. That's what I'm looking for."

Mystic had a dozen or so needles in various places when Ellie inserted one more and gave it a little twist. Mystic jumped and shuddered.

He was just about to call the whole blasted thing off and tell Ellie to get away from his horse when the mare's straining, panting sides suddenly went completely still.

After a moment, the horse blew out a snorting breath then pulled away from him. With the needles in her flesh still quivering like porcupine quills, she calmly ambled to her water trough and indulged in a long drink of water.

He stared after her, dumbfounded at how quickly she transformed from panic-stricken to tranquil. What the hell just happened here?

Ellie didn't seem nearly as astonished. She followed the horse and began removing the needles one by one, discarding them in a special plastic container she pulled out of her bag. When they were all collected, she cleaned and dressed the self-inflicted wounds on Mystic's belly, then ran her hands over the horse one last time before joining Matt on the other side of the stall.

"Is that it?" he asked, unable to keep the shock out of his voice.

Her mouth twisted into a smile. "What did you expect?"

"I don't know." He shook his head in amazement. "I've got to tell you, Doc, that was just about the damnedest thing I've ever seen."

Despite the circumstances, her low laugh sent heat flashing to his gut. "I had the same reaction the first time I saw an animal treated with acupuncture. Some animals respond so instantly it seems nothing short of a miracle. Not all do, but the first horse I saw responded exactly like Mystic just did."

"Was she another pregnant mare?"

"No. It was a racehorse that had suddenly gone lame. For the life of me, I couldn't figure out what was wrong. I tried everything I could think of to help him and nothing worked. He just got worse and worse. Finally, as a last-ditch effort before putting him down, the owners decided against my advice to call in another vet who practiced acupuncture.

"I thought they were completely nuts, but I decided to watch. One minute the vet was sticking in the needles, the next he opened the door and Galaxy took off into the pasture like a yearling, with no sign whatsoever of the lameness that had nearly ended his life. I called up and registered for the training course the next day."

Her face glowed when she talked about her work. Somehow it seemed to light up from the inside. She looked so pretty and passionate it was all he could do to keep from reaching across the few feet that separated them and drawing her into his arms.

"How does it work?" he asked, trying to distract himself from that soft smile and those sparkling eyes and the need suddenly pulsing through him.

"The Chinese believe health and energy are like a stream flowing downhill—if something blocks that flow, upsetting the body's natural balance, energy can dam up behind the blockage, causing illness and pain. The needles help guide the energy a different way, restoring the balance and allowing healing to begin."

"And you buy all that?"

She sent him a sidelong look, smiling a little at his skeptical voice. "It worked for Mystic, didn't it?"

He couldn't argue with that. The mare was happily munching grain from her feed bag.

"I'm not a zealot, Matt. I don't use acupuncture as a treatment in every situation. Sometimes traditional Western medicine without question is the best course of action. But sometimes a situation calls for something different. Something more."

"But doesn't it conflict with what you know of regular medicine? All that talk about energy and flow?"

"Sometimes. It was hard at first for me to reconcile the two. But I've since learned it's a balance. Like life."

She smiled again. "I can't explain it. I just know acupuncture has been practiced for six thousand years—on people as well as animals—and sometimes it works beautifully. One of my instructors used to say that if the only tool in your toolbox is a hammer, the whole world looks like a nail. I want to have as many tools in my toolbox as I possibly can."

"You love being a vet, don't you?"

She nodded. "It's all I've ever wanted."

"Why?" He was surprised to find he genuinely wanted to know. "What made you become one?"

She said nothing for several moments, her face pensive as she worked out an answer. He didn't mind, strangely content just watching her and listening to the low, soothing sounds of the barn.

Finally she broke the comfortable silence between them. "I wanted to help animals and I discovered I was good at it. Animals are uncomplicated. They give their love freely and without conditions. I was drawn to that."

Who in her life had put conditions on loving her? Dylan's father? He longed to ask but reminded himself it was none of his business.

"Did you overrun your house with pets when you were a kid?" he asked instead.

Her laugh sounded oddly hollow. "No. My mother never wanted the bother or the mess."

She was quiet for a moment, gazing at Mystic, who was resting quietly in the stall. He had the feeling Ellie was miles away, somewhere he couldn't even guess at.

"I take that back," she said slowly. "I had a dog once when I was ten. Sparky. A mongrel. Well, he wasn't really mine, he belonged to a kid at one of the…"

She looked at him suddenly, as if she'd forgotten he was there.

"At one of the foster homes I lived in," she continued stubbornly, her cheeks tinted a dusky rose. "But that didn't stop me from pretending he was mine."

Her defiant declaration broke his heart and helped a lot of things about her finally make sense. "You lived in many foster homes?"

"One is too many. And yeah, I did."

She was quiet again, and he thought for a moment she was done with the subject. And then she spoke in a quiet, unemotional voice that somehow affected him far more than tears or regrets would have.

"My dad was a long-haul trucker who took a load of artichokes to Florida when I was five and decided to stay. Without bothering to leave a forwarding address, of course. My mother was devastated. She couldn't even make a decision about what shampoo to use without a man in her life, so she climbed into a bottle and never climbed back out. I stayed with her for about a year and then child-protective services stepped in." She paused. "And you can stop looking at me like that."

"Like what?"

"Like you're feeling sorry for the poor little foster girl playing make-believe with some other kid's dog." She lifted her chin. "I did just fine."

He didn't like this fragile tenderness twisting around inside him like a morning glory vine making itself at home where it wasn't wanted. Did not like it one single bit.

"I never said otherwise," he said gruffly.

"You didn't have to say a word. I can see what you're thinking clear as day in those big baby blues of yours. I've seen pity plenty of times—that's why I generally keep my mouth shut about my childhood. But I did just fine," she said again, more vehemently this time. "I've got a beautiful daughter, a job I love fiercely and now I get to live in one of the most beautiful places on earth. Not bad for a white-trash foster kid. I turned out okay."

"Which one of us are you trying to convince?"

Her glare would have melted plastic. "Neither. I know exactly where I've been and where I'm going. I'm very happy with my life and I really don't care what you think about me, Harte."

"Good. Then it won't bother you when I tell you I think about you all the time. Or that I'm overwhelmed that you'd be willing to wade through blood and muck in your best clothes to save one of my horses. Or—" he finished quietly "—when I tell you that I think you're just about the prettiest thing I've ever seen standing in my barn."

Somewhere in the middle of his speech her jaw sagged open and she stared at him, wide-eyed.

"Close your mouth, Doc," he murmured wryly.

She snapped it shut with a pop that echoed in the

barn, and he gave a resigned sigh, knowing exactly what he was going to do.

He had a minute to think that this was about the stupidest thing he'd ever done, then his lips found hers and he stopped thinking, lost in the slick, warm welcome of her mouth.

For a moment after his mouth captured hers, Ellie could only stand motionless and stare at him, his face a breath away and those long, thick eyelashes shielding his glittering eyes from her view.

Matt Harte was kissing her! She wouldn't have been more shocked if all the horses in the stable had suddenly reared up and started singing Broadway show tunes as one.

And what a kiss it was. His mouth was hot and spicy, flavored with cinnamon and nutmeg. Pumpkin-pie sweet. He must have snuck a taste in the kitchen when he was cleaning up.

That was the last coherent thought she had before he slowly slid his mouth over hers, carefully, thoroughly, as if he didn't want to miss a single square inch.

Ellie completely forgot how to breathe. Liquid heat surged to her stomach, pooled there, then rushed through the rest of her body on a raging, storm-swollen river of desire.

Completely focused on his mouth and the incredible things the man knew what to do with it, she wasn't aware of her hands sliding to his chest until her fingers curled into the soft fabric of his sweater. Through the thick cotton, steel-hard muscles rippled and bunched beneath her hands, and she splayed them, fascinated by the leashed power there.

He groaned and pulled her more tightly against him,

and his mouth shifted from leisurely exploring hers to conquering it, to searing his taste and touch on her senses.

His tongue dipped inside, and she welcomed it as his lean, muscular body pressed her against the stall. His heat warmed her, wrapped around and through her from the outside in, and she leaned against him.

How long had it been since she'd been held by a man like this, had hard male arms wrapped around her, snugging her against a broad male chest? Since she'd been made to feel small and feminine and *wanted*?

It shocked her that she couldn't remember, that every other kiss seemed to have faded into some distant corner of her mind, leaving only Matt Harte and his mouth and his hands.

Even if she *had* been able to recall any other kisses, she had a feeling they would pale into nothingness anyway compared to this. She certainly would have remembered something that made her feel as if she were riding a horse on a steep mountain trail with only air between her and heaven, as if the slightest false step would send her tumbling over the edge.

She'd been right.

The thought whispered through her dazed and jumbled mind, and she sighed. She had wondered that day in her office how Matt would go about kissing a woman and now she knew—slowly, carefully, completely absorbed in what he was doing, as if the fate of the entire world hinged on him kissing her exactly right.

Until she didn't have a thought left in her head except *more*.

She had no idea how long they stood there locked to-

gether. Time slowed to a crawl, then speeded up again
in a whirling, mad rush.

She would have stayed there all night, lost in the
amazing wonder of his mouth and his hands and his
strength amid the rustle of hay and the low murmuring
of horses—if she had her way, they would have stayed
there until Christmas.

But just as she twisted her arms around the strong,
tanned column of his neck to pull him even closer, her
subconscious registered a sound that didn't belong.
Girls' voices and high-pitched laughter outside the barn,
then the rusty-hinged squeak of a door opening.

For one second they froze, still tightly entwined together, then Matt jerked away from her, his breathing ragged and harsh, just as both of their daughters
rounded the corner of a stall bundled up like Eskimos
against the cold.

"Hi." The girls chirped the word together.

Ellie thought she must have made some sound but she
was too busy trying to grab hold of her wildly scrambled thoughts to know what it might have been.

"We came out to see if you might need any help,"
Lucy said.

Ellie darted a quick look at Matt and saw that he
looked every bit as stunned as she felt, as if he'd just
run smack up against one of those wood supports holding the roof in place.

"Is something wrong?" Dylan's brows furrowed as
she studied them closely. "Did…did something happen to the foal?"

She'd forgotten all about Mystic. What kind of a
veterinarian was she to completely abandon her duties
while she tangled mouths with a man like Matt Harte?

She jerked her gaze to the stall and was relieved to find the pregnant mare sleeping, her sides moving slowly and steadily with each breath. In a quick visual check, Ellie could see no outward sign of her earlier distress.

She rubbed her hands down her skirt—filthy beyond redemption, she feared—and forced a smile through the clutter of emotions tumbling through her. "I think she's going to be okay."

"And her foal, too?" Lucy asked, features creased with worry.

"And her foal, too."

Matt cleared his throat, looking at the girls and not at her. "Yeah, the crisis seems to be over, thanks to Doc Webster here."

"She's amazing, isn't she, Dad?" Lucy said. Awe that Ellie knew perfectly well she didn't deserve in his daughter's voice and shining in her soft powder-gray eyes.

Finally Matt met her gaze, and Ellie would have given a week's salary to know what he was thinking. The blasted man could hide his emotions better than a dog burying a soup bone. His features looked carved in granite, all blunt angles and rough planes.

After a few moments of that unnerving scrutiny, he turned to his daughter. "I'm beginning to think so," he murmured.

Nonplussed by the undercurrents of meaning in his voice, Ellie couldn't come up with an answer. She flashed him a quick look, and he returned it impassively.

"Are you sure you don't need our help?" Dylan asked.

She wavered for a moment, suddenly desperate for the buffer they provided between her and Matt. But it was cowardly to use them that way, and she knew it.

"No," she murmured. "I'd just like to stick around a little longer out here and make sure everything's all right. Both of you should go on back to the house where you can stay warm."

"Save us a piece of pie," Matt commanded.

Lucy grinned at her father. "Which kind? I think there are about ten different pies in there."

He appeared to give the matter serious thought, then smiled at her. "How about one of each?"

"Sure." She snickered. "And then I'll bring in a wheelbarrow to cart you around in since you'll be too full to move."

"Deal. Go on, then. It's chilly out here."

Dylan sent her mother another long, searching look, and Ellie pasted on what she hoped was a reassuring smile for her daughter. "It was sweet of you both to come out and check on Mystic, but what she really needs now is quiet and rest."

"Okay."

"But—" Lucy began, then her voice faltered as Dylan sent her a meaningful look.

"Come on. Let's go back inside," she said, in that funny voice she'd been using lately. She grabbed Lucy's arm and urged her toward the door, leaving Ellie alone with Matt and the memory of the kiss that had left her feeling as if the whole world had just gone crazy.

Dylan clutched her glee to her chest only until they were outside the barn and she had carefully shut the door behind them, then she grabbed Lucy's coat, nearly toppling her into the snow. She pulled her into a tight hug and hopped them both around in wild circles. "Did you see that? Did you see it?"

"What? Mystic? She looked fine, like nothing had happened. Your mom is really something."

She gave Lucy a little shake. "No, silly! Didn't you see them? My mom and your dad?"

"Well, yeah. We just talked to them two seconds ago." Lucy looked at her as if her brain had slid out.

"Don't you get it, Lucy? This is huge. It's working! I know it's working! I think he kissed her!"

"Eww." Lucy's mouth twisted in disgust like Dylan had just made her eat an earwig.

"Come on, Luce. Grow up. They have to get mushy! It's part of the plan."

Her mouth dropped open like she'd never even considered the possibility. For a moment she stared at Dylan, then snapped her jaws shut. "How do you know? What makes you think they were kissing? They seemed just like normal."

Dylan thought of her mother's pink cheeks and the way Lucy's dad kept sneaking looks at Ellie when he didn't think any of them were watching him. "I don't know. I just think they were."

She wanted to yell and jump up and down and twirl around in circles with her arms wide until she got too dizzy and had to stop. A funny, sparkling excitement filled her chest, and she almost couldn't breathe around it. She was going to have a father, just like everybody else!

"I can't believe it. Our brilliant plan is working! Your dad likes her. I told you he would. He just needed the chance to get to know her."

She pulled Lucy toward her for another hug. "If your dad likes my mom enough to kiss her, it won't be long before he likes her enough to marry her. We're going to be sisters, Luce. I just know we are."

Lucy still couldn't seem to get over the kissing. Her face still looked all squishy and funny. "Now what?"

"I guess we keep doing what we're doing. Trying everything we can think of to push them together. Why mess with it when everything seems to be working out just like we planned?"

As soon as the girls left the barn, Ellie wished fiercely that she could slither out behind them. Or hide away among the hay bales. Or crawl into the nearest stall and bury her head in her hands.

Anything so she wouldn't have to face the tight-lipped man in front of her. Or so she wouldn't have to face herself and the weakness for soft-spoken, hard-eyed cowboys that had apparently been lurking inside her all this time without her knowledge.

And why was he glowering, anyway, like the whole bloody thing was her fault? He was the one who kissed *her.* She was an innocent victim, just standing here minding her own business.

And lusting over him, like she'd been doing for weeks.

The thought made her cringe inwardly. So she was attracted to him. So what? Who wouldn't be? The man was gorgeous. Big and masculine and gorgeous.

Anyway, it wasn't like she had begged him to kiss her. No, he'd done that all on his own. One minute they had been talking, the next thing she knew he pulled her into his arms without any advance warning and covered her mouth with his.

She shivered, remembering. The man kissed like

he meant it. Her knees started to feel all wobbly again, but she sternly ordered them to behave. She had better things to do then go weak-kneed over a gruff, distrustful rancher who seemed content to remain mired in a rut of tradition.

Still, he *had* unbent enough to let her treat Mystic, despite his obvious misgivings. He deserved points for that, at least. Of course, then he had completely distracted her with a fiery kiss that washed all thoughts of her patient out of her head.

But no more. She took a deep breath. She had a job to do here. The mare wasn't out of the woods yet, and she needed to make sure Mystic didn't lose her foal. To do it, she needed to focus only on the horse and not on her owner.

"I'd better take another look at Mystic to make sure the contractions have completely stopped."

"You think she still might be in danger?"

"Like I told the girls, it's too early to say. We'll have to wait and see."

With a great deal of effort, she turned her back on him and focused on the horse again. Somehow she managed to put thoughts of that kiss out of her head enough to concentrate on what she was doing.

She was working so hard at it, centering all her energy on the horse, that she didn't hear Matt come up behind her until she turned to pick her stethoscope out of her bag and bumped into hard, immovable man.

She backed up until she butted against the horse and clutched her chest. "Oh. You startled me."

A muscle worked in his jaw. "Look, Doc. I owe you an apology. I had no business doing that."

She deliberately misconstrued his meaning. "Startling me? Don't worry about it. Just make a little more noise next time."

"No," he snapped impatiently. "You know that's not what I mean. I'm talking about before. About what happened before the girls came in."

Heat soaked her cheekbones. "You don't have to worry about that, either."

He pressed doggedly forward. "I shouldn't have kissed you. It was crazy. Completely crazy. I, uh, don't know what came over me."

Uncontrollable lust? She seriously doubted it. Still, it wasn't very flattering for him to look as astounded at his own actions as a pup did when he found out his new best friend was a porcupine.

"You shouldn't have," she said as curtly, hoping he would let the whole thing drop.

Out of the corner of her gaze, she watched that muscle twitch along his jaw again, but the blasted man plodded forward stubbornly. "I apologize," he repeated. "It won't happen again."

"Good. Then let's get back to business."

"I just don't want what happened here to affect our working relationship."

"We don't have a working relationship, Matt. Not really. We're running a school carnival together, but that will be over in a few months. Then we can go back to ignoring each other."

"I'd like us to. Have a working relationship, I mean. And not just with the stupid Valentine's carnival, either." He paused. "The thing is, I was impressed by what you did for Mystic. Hell, who wouldn't have been impressed? It was amazing."

Okay, she could forgive him for calling their kiss

crazy, she decided, as warmth rushed through her at the praise.

He rubbed a hand along Mystic's withers, avoiding her gaze. "If you're interested, I'd like to contract with you to treat the rest of my horses."

She stared at him, stunned by the offer. "All of them?"

"Yeah. We generally have anywhere from twenty to thirty, depending on the time of the year. The ranch hands usually have at least a couple each in their remudas, and I usually pay for their care, too."

She was flabbergasted and couldn't seem to think straight. How could the man kiss her one minute, then calmly talk business the next while her hormones still lurched and bucked? It wasn't fair. She could barely keep a thought in her head, even ten minutes later. How was she supposed to have a coherent conversation about this?

"What about Steve?" she finally asked.

"Nichols is a competent vet." He paused, as if trying to figure out just the right words. "He's competent, but not passionate. Not like Ben. Or like you.

"Don't get me wrong," he added. "Steve does a good job with the cattle. But to be honest, I'm looking for a little more when it comes to my horses. I can't expect somebody to spend thirty thousand and up for a competition-quality cutter that's not completely healthy."

He smiled suddenly, and she felt as if she'd just been thrown off one of those champion cutters of his. "I'd like to have a veterinarian on staff who's not content with only one tool in her toolbox. What do you think?"

She blew out a breath, trying to process the twists and turns the day had taken. The chance to be the Diamond Harte's veterinarian was an opportunity she'd never even dared dream about. She couldn't pass it up, even if it meant working even more closely with Matt.

"Only your horses?" she asked warily. "Not the cattle?"

He shrugged. "Like I said, Steve seems to be handling that end of things all right."

Steve. She gave an inward wince. What would he think when she took the lucrative Diamond Harte contract from him? It would probably sting his pride, at the very least.

On the other hand, he had no qualms about doing the same thing to her countless times since she arrived in Star Valley. If she was going to run her own practice, she needed to start thinking like a businesswoman. They were friends but they were also competitors.

"Do we have a deal?" Matt asked.

How could she pass it up? This is what she wanted to do, why she'd traveled fifteen hundred miles and uprooted her daughter and risked everything she had. For chances like this. She nodded. "Sure. Sounds great. When do you want me to start?"

"Maybe you could come out sometime after the holiday weekend and get acquainted with the herd and their medical histories."

"Okay. Monday would work for me."

"We can work out the details then." He paused for a moment, then cleared his throat. "And, uh, if you're at all concerned about what happened here today, I swear it won't happen again. I was completely out of line—a line I won't be crossing again. You have my word on that."

She nodded and turned to Mystic, not wanting to dwell on all the reasons his declaration made her feel this pang of loss in her stomach.

Chapter 8

Hours later, Matt sat in his favorite leather wing chair in the darkened great room of the Diamond Harte, listening to the tired creaking of the old log walls and the crackle and hiss of the fire while he watched fat snowflakes drift lazily down outside the wide, uncurtained windows.

He loved this time of the night, when the house was quiet and he could finally have a moment to himself to think, without the phone ringing or Lucy asking for help with her math homework or Cassie hounding him about something or other.

Ellie Webster would probably call what he was doing something crazy and far-out, like meditating. He wouldn't go that far. His brain just seemed to work better when he didn't have a thousand things begging for attention.

When the weather was warm, he liked to sit on the

wide front porch, breathing the evening air and watching the stars come out one by one—either that or take one of the horses for a late-night ride along the trails that wound through the thousands of acres of Forest Service land above the ranch.

Most of his problems—both with the ranch and in his personal life—had been solved on the porch, on the back of a horse or in this very chair by the fire.

And he had plenty of problems to occupy his mind tonight.

Ellie and her daughter had gone home hours ago, but he swore if he breathed deeply enough he could still smell that sweet, citrusy scent of her   like lemons and sunshine—clinging subtly to his skin.

She had tasted the same way. Like a summer morning, all fresh and sweet and intoxicating. He thought of how she had felt in his arms, of the way her mouth had softened under his and the way her body melted into him like sherbet spilled on a hot sidewalk.

He only meant to kiss her for an instant. Just a brief experiment to satisfy his curiosity, to determine if the reality of kissing her could come anywhere close to his subconscious yearnings.

So much for good intentions.

He might have been content with only a taste—as tantalizing as it had been—but then she murmured his name when he kissed her.

He didn't think she was even aware of it, but he had heard it clearly. Just that hushed whisper against his mouth had sent need exploding through his system like a match set to a keg of gunpowder, and he had been lost.

What the hell had he been thinking? He wasn't the kind of guy to go around stealing kisses from women, especially prickly city vets who made it abundantly clear they weren't interested.

He'd been just as shocked as she was when he pulled her into his arms. And even more shocked when she responded to him, when she'd kissed him back and leaned into him for more.

He sipped at his drink and gazed out the window again. What was it about Ellie Webster that turned him inside out? She was beautiful, sure, with that fiery hair and those startling green eyes rimmed with silver.

It was more than that, though. He thought of the way she had talked so calmly and without emotion about her childhood, about being abandoned by both her parents and then spending the rest of her youth in foster homes.

She was a survivor.

He thought of his own childhood, of his dad teaching him to rope and his mom welcoming him home with a kiss on his cheek after school every day and bickering with Jess and Cassie over who got the biggest cookie.

Ellie had missed all that, and his chest ached when he thought of it and when he realized how she'd still managed to make a comfortable, happy life for her and her daughter.

Despite his earlier misconceptions, he was discovering that he actually liked her.

It had been a long time since he had genuinely liked a woman who wasn't related to him. Ellie was different, and that scared the hell out of him.

But any way he looked at it, kissing her had still been a damn fool thing to do.

He must be temporarily insane. A rational man would have run like the devil himself was riding his heels after being twisted into knots like that by a woman he shouldn't want and couldn't have.

But what did he do instead? Contract with her to take care of his horses, guaranteeing he'd see plenty of her in the coming weeks, even if it hadn't been for the stupid Valentine's carnival their girls had roped them into.

It was bound to be awkward. Wondering if she was thinking about their kiss, trying to put the blasted thing out of his own mind. He was a grown man, though, wasn't he? He could handle a little awkwardness, especially if it would benefit his horses.

And it would definitely do that. He'd meant it when he told her he'd never seen anything like what she'd done to Mystic. He never would have believed it if he hadn't seen it for himself. *Something* had happened in that barn while she was working on the horse. He wasn't the sort of man who believed in magic—in his own humble opinion, magic came from sweat and hard work—but what she had done with Mystic had been nothing short of miraculous.

Maybe that was one of the reasons for this confounded attraction he had for her—her wholehearted dedication to her job, to the animals she worked with. He respected it. If not for that, he probably wouldn't have decided to go with his gut and offer her the contract to care for all of his horses.

He had given up plenty of things for the good of the ranch in the years since his folks died. It shouldn't be that hard to put aside this strange attraction for a smart-mouthed little redhead with big green eyes and a stubborn streak a mile wide.

Especially since he knew nothing could ever come of it anyway.

The room suddenly seemed colder, somehow. Darker. Lonely.

Just the fire burning itself out, he told himself. He jumped up to throw another log onto it, then stood for a moment to watch the flames curl and seethe around it. It was an intoxicating thing, a fire on a snowy night. Almost as intoxicating as Ellie Webster's mouth.

Disgusted with himself for harping on a subject better left behind, he sighed heavily.

"Uh-oh. That sounded ominous."

He turned toward his sister's voice. She stood in the doorway, still dressed in her jeans and sweater. "You're up late," she said.

He shrugged. "Just enjoying the night. What about you? I thought you turned in hours ago."

"Forgot I left a load of towels in the washing machine this morning. I just came down to throw them in the dryer."

"I can do that for you. Go on to bed."

"I already did it. I was just on my way back upstairs."

She stood half in, half out of the room, her fingers drumming softly on the door frame. He sensed an odd restlessness in her tonight. Like a mare sniffing out greener pastures somewhere in the big wide world.

In another woman he might have called it melancholy, but Cassie had always been the calm one. The levelheaded one. The soft April rain to Jesse's wild, raging thunderstorm.

Tonight she practically radiated nervous energy, and it made him uneasy—made him want to stay out of her way until she worked out whatever was bothering her.

He couldn't do that, though. He loved her too much,

owed her too much. If something was bugging her, he had an obligation to ferret it out then try to fix it.

"Why don't you come in and keep me company?" he invited.

"I don't want to bother you."

"No bother. Seems like we're always so busy I hardly ever get a chance to talk to you anymore."

She studied him for a moment, then moved into the room and took a seat on the couch, curling her long legs under her. "What were you thinking about when I came in that put that cranky look on your face?"

It wasn't tough for him to remember, since that stolen kiss in the barn with Ellie Webster had taken center stage in his brain for the last six hours. For one crazy moment, he debated telling Cassie about it. But he couldn't quite picture himself chatting about his love life—or lack thereof—with his little sister.

"Nothing important," he lied, and forced his features into a smile. Knowing how bullheaded she could be about some things—a lot like a certain redhead he didn't want to think about—he decided he'd better distract her. "What did Wade Lowry want when he called earlier?"

Cassie picked at the nubby fabric of the couch. "He wanted me to go cross-country skiing with him tomorrow into Yellowstone."

Could that be what had her so edgy? "Sounds like fun. What time are you leaving?"

He didn't miss the way her mouth pressed into a tight line or the way she avoided his gaze. "I'm not. I told him we had family plans tomorrow."

He frowned. "What plans? I don't know of any plans."

In the flickering light of the fire, he watched heat

crawl up her cheekbones. "I thought I'd help you work with Gypsy Rose tomorrow," she mumbled. "Didn't you say you were going to start training her in the morning? You'll need another pair of hands."

And he could have used any one of the ranch hands, like he usually did. No, there was more to this than a desire to help him out with the horses.

"What's wrong with Lowry? He's not a bad guy. Goes to church, serves on the library board, is good with kids. The other ladies seem to like him well enough. And he seems to make a pretty good living with that guest ranch of his. He charges an arm and leg to the tourists who come to stay there, anyway. You could do a whole lot worse."

She made a face, like she used to do when Jess yanked on her hair. "Nothing's wrong with him. I just didn't feel like going with him tomorrow. Since when was it a crime to want to help your family?"

"It's not. But it's also not a crime to get out and do something fun for a change."

"I do plenty of fun things."

"Like what?"

"Cooking dinner today. That was fun. And going out on roundup with you. I love that. And taking care of Lucy. What greater joy could I find? My whole life is fun."

Every one of the things she mentioned had been for someone else. His hands curved around his glass as tension and guilt curled through him, just like they always did when it came to his baby sister and the sacrifices he had let her make. She needed more than cooking and cleaning for him and for Lucy.

"You can't give everything to us, Cass," he said quietly. "Save some part for yourself."

She sniffed. "I don't know what you're talking about."

She did, and they both knew it. They'd had this very conversation many times before. Just like always, he was left frustrated, knowing nothing he said would make her budge.

He opted for silence instead, and they sat quietly, listening to the fire and the night and the echo of words unsaid.

She was the first to break the silence. "Do you ever wonder if they're still together?" she said after several moments.

He peered at her over the rim of his glass. "If who are together?"

She made a frustrated sound. "Who do you think? Melanie and Slater."

His wife and her fiancé, who had run off together the week before Cassie's wedding. A whole host of emotions knifed through him. Betrayal. Guilt. Most of all sharp heartache for the sweet, deliriously happy girl his little sister had been before Melanie and that bastard Slater had shattered her life.

They rarely talked about that summer. About how they had both been shell-shocked for months, just going about the constant, grinding struggle to take care of the ranch and a tiny, helpless Lucy.

About how that love-struck young woman on the edge of a whole world full of possibilities had withdrawn from life, burying herself on the ranch to take care of her family.

"I don't waste energy thinking about it," he lied. "You shouldn't, either."

He didn't mean to make it sound like an order, but it must have. Cassie flashed him an angry glare. "You can't control everything, big brother, as much as you might like to. I'll think about them if I want to think about them, and there's not a damn thing you can do about it."

"Aw, Cass. Why torture yourself? It'll be ten years this summer."

She stared stonily ahead. "*Get over it.* Is that what you mean?"

Was it? Had he gotten over Melanie? Whatever love he might have once thought he felt for her had shriveled into something bitter and ugly long before she left him. But he wasn't sure he could honestly say her desertion hadn't affected him, hadn't destroyed something vital and profound inside of him.

Maybe that was why he was so appalled to find himself kissing a city girl like Ellie Webster and for craving the taste of her mouth again so powerfully he couldn't think around it.

He looked at his sister, at her pretty blue eyes and the brown hair she kept ruthlessly short now and the hands that were always busy cooking and cleaning in her brother's house. He wanted so much more for her.

"You've got to let go, Cassie. You can't spend the rest of your life poking and prodding at the part of you that son of a bitch hurt. If you keep messing at it, it will never be able to heal. Not completely."

"I don't poke and prod," she snapped. "I hardly even think about Slater anymore. But I'm not like you, Matt. I'm sorry, but I can't just shove away my feelings and act like they never existed."

He drew in a breath at the sharp jab, and Cassie immediately lifted a hand to her mouth, her eyes horrified. "Oh, Matt. I'm sorry. I shouldn't have said that. I should never have brought them up. Let's just drop it, okay?"

"Which brings us back to Wade Lowry. You need to go out more, Cass, meet more people. Give some other lucky guy a chance to steal you away from us."

She snorted. "Oh, you're a fine one to talk. When was the last time you went out on a date?"

She had him there. What would his sister say if she knew he'd stolen a kiss from the vet earlier in the barn? And that his body still churned and ached with need for her hours later? He took a sip of his drink, willing Ellie out of his mind once more.

Cassie suddenly sent him a sly look. "You know who would be really great for you? Ellie Webster."

He sputtered and coughed on his drink. "What?"

"Seriously. She's pretty, she's smart, she's funny. I really like her."

So did he, entirely too much.

"I think the two of you would be perfect together," Cassie said.

He refused to let his baser self think about exactly how perfect they might be together at least in one area of a relationship, judging by the way she had melted into his arms.

"Thanks for the romantic advice," he said gruffly, "but I think I'll stick to what I know. The ranch and the stock and Lucy. I don't have time for anything else."

She was quiet for a moment, then she grabbed his hand. "We're a sorry pair, aren't we? You're the one who told me not to put my life on hold. If I go skiing with Wade Lowry tomorrow, will you at least think about taking Ellie out somewhere? Maybe to dinner in Jackson or something?"

"Sure," he answered. "If you'll go skiing with Wade and promise to have a good time, I'll think about taking Doc Webster to dinner."

But thinking about it was absolutely the only thing he would do about it.

"So I'm off. I'll see you in the morning."

Ellie glanced up from her computer and found SueAnn in the doorway bundled into her coat and hat with that big, slouchy bag that was roomy enough to hide a heifer slung over her shoulder.

She blinked, trying to force her eyes to focus. "Is it six already?"

"Quarter past. Aren't you supposed to be heading out to the Diamond Harte pretty soon?"

"The carnival committee meeting doesn't start until seven. I should still have a little more time before I have to leave. I'm taking advantage of the quiet without Dylan to try to finish as much as I can of this journal article."

"She's with Lucy again?"

"Where else?"

Dylan had begged to ride the school bus home with her friend again. And since Ellie knew she would be able to pick her up when she went out to the ranch later in the evening, she gave in.

"I've got to turn this in by the end of the week if I want to have it considered for the next issue, and I'm way behind."

"I imagine you haven't had much time these last few weeks for much of anything but your patients, have you?"

Ellie knew her grin could have lit up the whole town of Salt River. "Isn't it something?"

"Amazing. We haven't had a spare second around here since Thanksgiving."

Christmas was only a few weeks away. The towns scattered throughout Star Valley gleamed and glittered. Everybody seemed to get into the spirit of the holiday— just about every ranch had some kind of decorations, from stars of Bethlehem on barn roofs to crèches in hay sheds to fir wreaths gracing barbed-wire fences. The other night she had even seen a tractor decorated with flashing lights.

With her heavy workload, Ellie hadn't had much time to enjoy it. She hadn't even gone Christmas shopping for Dylan. If she didn't hurry, there would be nothing left in any of the stores.

Still, she couldn't regret the last-minute rush. For the first time since she and Dylan had moved to Wyoming, she was beginning to feel like she had a chance at succeeding here, at making a life for the two of them.

Word had spread quickly after Thanksgiving about how she had saved Mystic's unborn foal and how Matt Harte had hired her to treat the rest of his champion horses.

She wasn't exactly sure how everyone had learned about it. She hadn't said a word to anyone, and Matt certainly didn't seem the type to blab his business all over town. But somehow the news had leaked out.

The Monday after the holiday, she'd barely been in the office ten minutes before her phone started ringing with other horse owners interested in knowing more about her methods and scheduling appointments for their animals.

She couldn't exactly say business was booming, but she was more busy than she ever expected to be a month ago. Ellie couldn't believe how rewarding she was finding it. It was everything she had always dreamed of—doing exactly what she loved.

"So how are the carnival plans going?"

She jerked her attention to SueAnn. "Good. We've got a really great crew working with us now. Barb Smith, Sandy Nielson, Terry McKay and Marni Clawson."

"That *is* a good committee. They'll take care of all the dirty work for you. And how's our favorite sexy rancher?"

She frowned at SueAnn's sly grin. "If you're talking about Matt Harte, I wouldn't know," she said brusquely. "I haven't seen much of him."

She wasn't disappointed, she told herself. Honestly, she wasn't. "He missed the last meeting, and every time I've gone out to treat his horses, he's had one of his ranch hands help me."

She'd only caught fleeting glimpses of him out at the Diamond Harte. If she didn't know better, she'd think he was avoiding her after their heated kiss in the barn. But he didn't strike her as the kind of man to run away from a little awkwardness.

"Well, you'll see him tonight. He can't very well miss a meeting when it's at his own house."

Ellie didn't even want to think about this wary anticipation curling through her at the thought.

After SueAnn left, Ellie tried to concentrate once more, but the words on the computer screen in front of her blurred together.

It was all SueAnn's fault for bringing up Matt. Ellie had tried for two weeks to keep him out of her mind, but the blasted man just kept popping in at all hours. She couldn't seem to stop thinking about his smile or his blue eyes or the way he teased Lucy and Dylan.

Boy, she had it bad. One kiss and she completely lost all perspective. It had become increasingly difficult to remember all the reasons that kiss was a lousy idea and why it would never happen again.

She blew out a breath. No sense wasting her time sitting here when she wasn't accomplishing anything. She might as well head out early to the ranch. Maybe she could have a few minutes to talk to Matt and work this crazy longing out of her system.

After putting on her coat and locking up the clinic, she walked to her beat-up old truck, relishing the cold, invigorating air. With the winter solstice just around the corner, night came early to this corner of the world. Already, dozens of stars peppered the night sky like spangles on blue velvet. She paused for a moment, hands curled into her pockets against the cold and her breath puffing out in clouds as she craned her neck at the vast, glittering expanse above her.

The moon was full, pearly and bright. It glowed on the snowy landscape, turning everything pale.

She loved it here. The quiet pace, the wild mountains, the decent, hardworking people. Moving here had been just what she and Dylan had needed.

Humming off-key to the Garth Brooks Christmas CD SueAnn had been playing before she left, Ellie reached her truck. She didn't bother fishing for her keys, confident she'd left it unlocked. It had taken a while to break herself of the habit of locking the battered truck, but now she felt just like one of the locals.

Next thing she knew, she'd be calling everyone darlin' and wearing pearl-button shirts.

Laughing at herself, she swung open the door, then froze, her hand on the cracked vinyl of the handle.

Something was different. Very, very wrong.

Through the moonlight and the dim glow from the overhead dome, she saw something odd on the passenger seat, something that didn't quite belong here.

It took her a moment to realize what it was—the carcass of a cat, head lolled back in a death grimace and legs stiff with rigor mortis.

Icy cold knifed through her, and her pulse sounded loud and scattered in her ears. As if that wasn't horrifying enough to find in the cab of her truck, she could see a note stuck to the poor animal's side—fastened firmly into place with one of her acupuncture needles.

Her hands trembled like leaves in a hard wind as she reached for the slip of white paper and pulled it carefully away, needle and all, so she could hold it up to the dome light.

It was printed on plain computer paper and contained only five words in block capital letters, but they were enough to snatch away her breath and send shock and fear coiling through her stomach.

WE DON'T WANT YOU HERE.

Chapter 9

If somebody told him a month ago he would be hosting a gaggle of women chattering about decorations and refreshments and publicity, he probably would have decked them.

Matt sat in the corner of his dining room, afraid his eyes were going to glaze over any minute now. The only streamers he even wanted to *think* about were on the end of a fly rod.

The things he did for his kid! He only hoped when she was stretching her wings in rebellious teenagedom and thinking her dad was the most uncool person on the planet, she would look back on this whole carnival thing and appreciate the depth of his sacrifice for her.

At the far end of the big table, Ellie reached for her water glass, sipped at it quickly, then set it down hard enough that water sloshed over the top and splattered the legal pad in front of her.

For a moment, she didn't react, just stared at the spreading water stain. Finally he cleared his throat and handed down one of the napkins Cassie had set out to go with her walnut brownies before she took off to see a movie in town.

Ellie jolted when Terry McKay passed her the napkin. Her gaze flew up and collided with his. Heat soaked her cheeks, then she quickly turned her attention to sopping up the spill.

The only consolation Matt could find in the whole evening was that she seemed to feel just as out of place as he did, at least judging by her jumpy, distracted mood.

He supposed it was pretty petty of him to feel such glee at her obvious discomfort. But he liked knowing he wasn't the only one who didn't want to be stuck here.

Only half-listening to the conversation—centering on the crucial question of whether to sell tickets at the door or at each booth—he finally allowed himself the guilty pleasure of really looking at Ellie for the first time all evening.

She looked bright and pretty with her hair in some kind of a twisty style and a subtle shade of lipstick defining her mouth.

That mouth. Full and lush and enticing. He hadn't been able to stop thinking about it for two frustrating weeks. The way it had softened under his. The way those lips had opened for him, welcoming him into the hot, slick depths of her mouth. The way her tongue had ventured out tentatively to greet his.

Today it had been worse, much worse, knowing she would be coming to the ranch for this meeting. His concentration had been shot all to hell. In the middle of stringing a fence line, he'd let go of the barbed wire and ended up taking a nasty gash out of his cheek.

Tonight wasn't much better. He couldn't concentrate on the meeting for the life of him. All he could think about was how she had felt in his arms. With an inward, resigned sigh, he tried to turn his attention to the conversation.

"I hope I have this kid before the carnival so I can help," Marni Clawson, wife of one of his high school buddies, was saying. "I would really hate to miss it."

"How much longer?" Sandy Nielson asked her with that goggly-eyed look women get when the talk centers on babies.

Marni smiled softly. "Three weeks. I'll tell you, I'm ready right now. I just want to get this over with. Speaking of which, you're all going to have to excuse me for a minute. These days my bladder's about the size of a teaspoon. I think I need to pee about every half hour."

Information he didn't need to know, thanks very much. All the women except Ellie laughed in sympathy. As heat crawled over his face, Matt felt as out of place as the town drunk in the middle of a church picnic.

Marni must have spotted his discomfort. She gave him an apologetic look. "Sorry, Matt."

"No problem," he said gruffly, praying the night would end soon.

As Marni slid back her chair, it squeaked loudly along the wood floor. Ellie jumped as if the sound had been a gunshot. She clutched the napkin in her hand so tightly her knuckles whitened.

He straightened in his chair, his gaze sharpening. What the hell? He could see that what he had mistaken for simple restlessness was something more. Something edgier, darker.

She looked frightened.

Sensing his scrutiny again, she lifted her eyes from the papers in front of her. They stared at each other across the table for several seconds, his gaze probing and hers rimmed with more vulnerability than he'd ever seen there, then her lashes fluttered down and she veiled her green eyes from his view once more.

What happened? Who hurt you?

He almost blurted out the questions, then reined in the words. Not now, not here. He would wait until everyone else left, then force her to tell him what was going on.

He spent the rest of the evening tense and worried, amazed and more disconcerted than he wanted to admit at the powerful need coursing through him to protect her. To take care of her.

He didn't like the feeling. Not one bit. It reminded him painfully of all the emotions Melanie had stirred up in him the first time he met her, when they'd bumped into each other at a dingy little diner.

She'd had a black eye and had been running scared from a nasty boyfriend who had followed her to Denver from L.A. She'd needed rescuing and for some reason decided the hick cowboy from Wyoming was just the man to save her.

Matt flinched when he thought about how eagerly he'd stepped forward to do it, sucked under by a beautiful woman with a hard-luck story and helplessness in her eyes.

He didn't know if there really had been a nasty boyfriend at all or if it had been another of her lies. But

Melanie had needed rescuing anyway, from herself more than anything.

Unfortunately, he'd failed, and his marriage had failed, too.

He pushed the thought away and focused on Ellie and that stark fear in her eyes.

Finally, when he wasn't sure he could stand the tension another moment, the meeting began to wrap up, and one by one the committee members walked into the cold, clear night, leaving him and Ellie alone in the dining room.

She rose and began clearing the napkins and glasses from the table with quick, jerky movements. "We've made a lot of headway tonight, don't you agree? I don't think we should have to meet again until February, right before the carnival."

She continued chattering about the meeting until he finally reached out and grabbed her arm. "Doc, stop."

She froze, and her gaze flashed to his once more. The raw emotions there made him swear.

"What's going on?"

She looked at the table, but not before he saw her mouth wobble, then she compressed it into a tight, uncompromising line. "I don't know what you're talking about."

"Come on, Ellie. Something's wrong. I can see it in your eyes."

"It's nothing. I'm just tired, that's all. It's been a hectic couple of weeks." She pasted on a smile that fell miles short of being genuine. "Thank you, by the way. I don't know how you did it, but you've single-handedly managed to convince people to give me a chance around here. I appreciate it, more than I can tell you."

"I didn't do anything other than let a few people know I'm now using you to treat my horses."

"You obviously have enough influence to make people think that what's okay for the Diamond Harte is okay for them."

He was arrogant enough to know what she said was true. That's why he'd tried to spread the word, whenever he had the chance, that he had contracted for Ellie's veterinary services, so business would pick up for her. It sounded like it had worked.

She picked up the dishes and headed for the kitchen with them, and he followed a moment after her.

"Shall I wash these?" she asked.

"No. I'll throw them in the dishwasher in a while."

"Okay. In that case, I'd better grab Dylan and head home." She looked about as thrilled by the idea as a calf on its way to be castrated.

"You could stay." His offer seemed to shock her as much as it did him. On reflection, though, he warmed to the idea. He didn't like thinking about her going home to her empty house, especially not when she was so obviously upset about something.

"It's late and bound to be icy out there," he said gruffly. "We have plenty of room—you and Dylan could both stay the night in one of the guest rooms and go home in the morning."

How could he have known that the idea of walking into her dark, empty house had been filling her with dread all night? What if she found another charming little warning there, as well? It would be so much worse with Dylan along when she discovered it.

Matt couldn't possibly know what was going on. He

was picking up on her nervousness, on the anxiety she knew she had been unable to conceal.

For a moment she was tempted to confide in him. He knew the valley and its inhabitants far better than she did. Maybe he would know who might be capable of delivering such a macabre message.

It would be such a relief to share the burden with someone else, especially someone solid and reassuring like Matt, to let those strong shoulders take the weight of her worry....

She reined in the thought. She wasn't her mother. She wasn't the kind of woman to fall apart at the first hint of crisis, to act helpless and weak so that everyone else would have to take care of her. This was her problem, and she would deal with it.

"I appreciate the offer," she said abruptly, "but we'll be fine. My truck has four-wheel drive."

"Are you sure?"

"Positive."

He sighed heavily. "You are one stubborn woman. Did anybody ever tell you that?"

"A few times." She forced a smile.

"More than a few, I'd bet," he grumbled under his breath. "Since you're not going to budge, I guess we'd better round up Dylan so you two can hit the road."

He led the way up the stairs, then rapped softly on the door of Lucy's bedroom. Ellie couldn't hear any sound from inside. After a moment, Matt swung open the door. They found both girls tucked under a quilt at opposite ends of Lucy's ruffly pink bed, with their eyes closed and their breathing slow and even, apparently sound asleep.

It was oddly intimate standing shoulder-to-shoulder

in the doorway watching over their respective children. She'd never done this with a man before and she found it enormously disconcerting.

She could feel the heat emanating from him and smell the leathery scent of his aftershave, and it made her more nervous than a hundred threatening letters.

"Do you think they're faking it?" Matt whispered.

"I wouldn't put it past them," she whispered back, trying to ignore the way his low voice set her stomach quivering. "I think they'd try anything for an extra sleepover."

She stepped forward, grateful for even that foot of space between them. "Dylan?" she called softly. "Come on, bug. Time to go home."

Neither girl so much as twitched an eyelid.

"At least let Dylan stay the night," Matt murmured. "It seems like a pretty dirty trick to wake the kid out of a good sleep just to drag her out in the cold."

"She's always sleeping over. I swear, she spends more time here than she does in her own bed."

"We don't mind. She's good for Lucy. I've got to run into town in the morning, and it would be no big deal for me to drop her back home on the way."

If she hadn't been so nervous about Dylan stumbling onto another grisly discovery like the one she had found in the truck earlier, she would have argued with him. She was dreading the idea of going home alone, but at least this way she wouldn't have to worry about Dylan, too.

"Are you sure?"

"Don't worry about it, Doc. She'll be fine."

With one more suspicious look to see if any fingers

twitched or eyelids peeked open, Ellie backed out of the room and joined him in the hall.

"I can't shake the feeling that we're being conned," she said.

"So what? If this is an act, they're pretty good at it and deserve a reward. Wouldn't hurt them to have a sleepover."

"So you want to encourage your daughter's fraudulence?"

He smiled. "I'm just glad to see her doing normal kid things for a change. Lucy's always been too serious for her own good. Dylan's done wonders for her. She's a great kid."

She smiled, genuinely this time. "What mother doesn't want to hear that her child is great? I think she's pretty cool, too."

Their gazes locked, and suddenly his eyes kindled with something deeper that she didn't dare analyze. She dropped her gaze and felt her cheeks heat as she vividly remembered those stolen moments in his horse barn.

"I should be going," she said, her voice hoarse.

"I'll walk you out."

"That's not necessary," she began.

"I know. But I'm going to do it anyway."

How did a woman go up against a man who was about as intractable as the Salt River Range? With a sigh, she followed him down the stairs and to the great room for her coat.

"Here. Let me carry that for you," he said gruffly, and pointed to her bulky leather backpack that held everything from her planner to basic medical supplies.

She opened her mouth to argue that she carried it around by herself all the time, but she closed it at the defiant look on his face, like he was daring her to say something about it.

"Thank you," she murmured instead, handing it to him. She had to admit she found it kind of sweet, actually. Like when Joey Spiloza offered to carry her books home from school in the first grade.

She hadn't let him, of course, completely panicked at the idea of anyone at school knowing what a trash heap she lived in. Or worse, what if her mom wandered out to the sagging porch in her bathrobe, bleary-eyed and stinking like gin?

She pushed the memory away and walked into the cold, clear Wyoming night with Matt. He was silent and seemed distracted as they crunched through the snow, even after his little brindle Australian shepherd sidled up to him for some attention.

At her truck, he opened the door and she climbed inside.

"Well, thanks for everything," she said. "I guess I'll see you tomorrow when you drop off Dylan."

"Right. Be careful on the roads." He stood at the open truck door studying her out of those blue eyes that seemed to glow in the moonlight. His shoulders leaned forward slightly, and for one crazy moment, she thought he would kiss her again.

At the last moment, he jerked back. "Oh. Don't forget your bag."

She stopped breathing completely when he reached across her to set the backpack on the passenger side, and his arm brushed the curve of her breast. He probably didn't realize it since she was swaddled in a thick winter coat, but she did, in every single cell. To her horror, she could feel her hormones immediately snap to attention and her nipple bud to life.

Even leaning back until her spine pressed against the seat wasn't enough to escape him or the first physical contact between them since that heated kiss on Thanksgiving.

She could vaguely hear the crackling of paper under the backpack as he set it down on the seat. "Sorry. I set it on something." He shoved the pack toward the other door, leaning into her even more. "Is it important?"

She blinked, feeling slightly feverish. "What?"

"Whatever I tossed this onto. Here. Let me see."

She looked down and saw what he was reaching for, that damned note with the needle still stuck through it.

"What's this?"

"It's nothing." She made a futile grab for it, but he held it out of her reach and up to the dome light. When he lowered the note, his expression burned with anger.

"Where did you find this?"

"I told you, it's nothing."

"Dammit, Doc. Where did this come from?"

She took one more look at his face, then blew out a breath. Somehow she didn't think he was going to rest until he bullied the truth out of her. "Someone left it in my truck. I found it when I left the office before driving out here tonight. It was, um, impaled in the carcass of a cat."

His expression darkened even more, and he let out a long string of swearwords. "Who would do such a thing?"

"Obviously not the Salt River Welcome Wagon."

"Did you call Jess to report it?"

She shook her head. "It's just a stupid prank, Matt. I didn't see the need to call in the police."

"This is more than a prank. Anybody who would leave this for you to find must have a sick and twisted mind. I'll call Jesse and have him come out to the ranch to get the details from you. There's no question now of you going home. You'll stay the night."

She bristled at his high-handedness. "That's not necessary. I appreciate your concern but I'm fine. Honestly. I was a little shaky before but now I'm just mad. I'll call the police in the morning and deal with it then."

"Doc, I'm not letting you go home alone tonight. Not after this. A person sick enough to torment you with something as warped as this could be capable of anything. Think about what's best for Dylan if you won't think about yourself."

He picked up her backpack as if the matter were settled, and Ellie pursed her lips. She had two choices, as she saw it. She could start the truck and make a run for it or she could follow him inside the house.

After his brother arrived, she would have backup. He'd have a tough time keeping her there against her will with a cop on the premises, even if the cop happened to be his brother.

Inside, he took off her coat and settled her into a chair as if she were too fragile to take care of herself.

"Tell me what happened. Could you tell if your truck had been broken into?"

She flinched. In the city this never would have happened. This is what she deserved for trying so hard to fit in. "No," she mumbled. "I left it unlocked."

"And you saw the dead cat when you opened the door?"

She nodded. "It was a little hard to miss there on the passenger's seat, with the note pinned between the third and forth ribs on the left side."

Storm clouds gathered on his features again, making him look hard and mad and dangerous. "Where's the cat now?"

"I took it inside the clinic. I'll autopsy it in the morning to try to figure out cause of death. From an initial exam, it looked like it was a feral cat that died of natural causes, but I'll know more tomorrow after I've had a chance to take a closer look."

He took a moment to digest the information, then frowned again. "Who would do this? Do you have any enemies?"

"Believe me, I've racked my brain all evening trying to figure it out. I honestly don't know."

"You been in any fights lately?"

"Yeah," she said dryly. "Didn't you hear? I went four rounds with Stone Cold Steve Austin in the produce aisle of the supermarket just last week."

"Seriously. Can't you think of anyone who might have done this?"

She shrugged. "I've had a few little disagreements with ranchers over treatment of their animals. It's part of the territory. Just business as usual for a vet."

"What kind of disagreements?"

"Well, for one thing, you'd be amazed at some of the conditions people think are perfectly okay for their animals. I'd like to see some of them try to stay healthy when they're living knee-deep in manure. And then they think it's their vet's fault if their animals don't thrive."

"How heated did these little disagreements get?"

"Not hot enough for something like this."

"Well, I still think you better come up with a few names for Jess to check out. Some of these old-timers are set in their ways and don't like an outsider coming in and telling them how to take care of their animals."

Outsider. The word stung like vinegar poured on a cut. How long would it take before she was no longer considered a foreigner in Star Valley? Would that day ever come?

She didn't bother to point out the obvious to Matt—that, for the most part, he still had the exact same attitude. Before she could come up with a nonconfrontational answer, they heard a car door slam.

"That will be Jess," Matt said, a few seconds before his brother burst into the kitchen.

"It's about damn time," Matt snapped. "Where have you been?"

The police chief snorted. "Give me a break. You couldn't have called more than ten minutes ago. What do you want from me? The department's Bronco only goes up to a hundred twenty."

Before Matt could growl out a rejoinder, Ellie rose, stepping forward in an instinctive effort to keep the peace between the brothers. "Thank you for coming out, Jesse, although it's really not necessary. I told your brother we could have done this in the morning."

Jesse immediately shifted his attention to her. To her complete shock, he reached both arms out and folded her into a comforting hug as if they'd been friends for years. "I'm so sorry you had to go through something like this. How are you holding up, sweetheart?"

She stepped away, flustered and touched at once, in time to catch Matt glare at his brother and Jesse return it with a raised eyebrow and a look she could only call speculative.

"Fine," she said quickly. "As I tried repeatedly to tell your brother, I'm really okay. He won't listen to me."

"Matt's a hardheaded son of a gun. Always has been." Jesse grinned at her, then removed his hat and coat and hung them on the rack by the door before making a detour to the fridge.

"I'm starving. Been on since noon. Anything I can eat while Ellie gives her statement?" he asked his older brother.

Matt scowled. "This is serious. Feed your face on your own time."

Jesse ignored him and pulled out a plastic-wrap-covered plate. "Here we go. Cassie's incredible fried chicken. The woman's an angel."

He set the plate on the table, straddled a chair, then nodded to Ellie. "Okay. I'm ready. Why don't you tell me what's been going on? Start at the beginning."

Her mind felt as scattered as dandelion fluff on a windy day, and for a moment she gazed at the two brothers as she tried to collect her thoughts. That didn't help at all. The two of them together in such close proximity were nothing short of breathtaking.

She'd never considered herself a particularly giddy kind of female, but any woman who said her pulse didn't beat a little harder around the Harte brothers—with their dark good looks and those dangerous eyes—would have to be lying.

Matt was definitely the more solemn of the two. There was a hardness about him his younger brother lacked. Jess certainly smiled more often, but she thought she had seen old pain flash a few times in his eyes, like at the dinner table the other day when the talk had turned to their parents.

"Anytime here, Doc."

She pursed her lips at Matt's impatience, but quickly filled the police chief in on what had happened, only pausing a few times to glare at his brother for interrupting.

"I still think it's a prank, nothing more," she finished. "Just a really ghoulish one."

"Hmm. I don't know." Jesse wiped his mouth with a napkin. "The only thing I can do at this point is check out these names you've given me and maybe something will shake out. In the meantime—"

The radio clipped to his belt suddenly squawked static. With an oath, Jesse pulled it out and pressed a button. Then Ellie heard a disembodied voice advising of a rollover accident on U.S. 89 with multiple injuries.

Jesse rose with surprising speed from the chair. "Shoot. I've got to run out to that. We're shorthanded, and the only other officer on patrol is J. B. Nesmith. He won't be able to handle this one on his own. Sorry, Ellie. I was going to tell you to be extra cautious at home and at the clinic. I'll try to have my officers keep an eye on both places whenever they can while the investigation is ongoing."

He shrugged into his coat and shoved on his hat. "Promise you'll call right away if anything else unusual happens. Anything at all." He gave her another quick hug, then rushed out, snagging a leftover brownie as he went.

Chapter 10

The subtle tension simmering between her and Matt had eased somewhat while Jesse was there. After he walked out of the kitchen and left them alone once more, her nerves started humming again like power lines in the wind.

She blew out a quick breath and picked up her backpack from the table. "I think I'll just head home now, too."

Matt's frown creased the weathered corners of his mouth. "I thought we agreed it would be best for you to stay here tonight."

"*We* didn't agree on anything." She stared him down. "You made a proclamation and expected me to simply abide by your word."

He gave her a disgusted look. "I swear, you are the stubbornest damn woman I have ever met."

"That's why you like me so much." She smiled sweetly.

For one sizzling moment he studied her, a strange, glittery light in his eyes. "Oh, is that why?" he finally murmured.

Heat skimmed through her, and she gripped her bag more tightly. She found it completely unfair that he could disarm her with a look, that he could make her insides go all soft and gooey without even trying.

"Please stay, Doc. Just for tonight. You know, if you went home I'd spend the whole night worrying about you, and I've got a horse to train in the morning. You wouldn't want me to make some dumb mistake and ruin her just because I didn't get any sleep, would you?"

"Nice try, cowboy."

He flashed a quick smile that sent her heartbeat into overdrive. "Humor me. It would make me feel a whole lot better knowing you're not at that house by yourself after what happened tonight."

She gave a disgruntled sigh. How could she continue to argue with him when he was being so sweet and protective?

On the other hand, she thoroughly despised this insidious need curling through her to crawl right into his arms and let him take all her worry and stress onto those wide, powerful shoulders.

She could take care of herself. Hadn't she spent most of her life proving it? She wasn't her mother. She didn't need a man to make her feel whole, to smooth the jagged edges of her life.

She could do that all by herself.

"Come on." He rose and headed for the door. "I'll show you to one of the guest rooms."

She looked at the stubborn set of his jaw and sighed. Like water on sandstone, he wasn't going to give up until he totally wore her down. Either that or he would probably insist on following her home and inspecting every single inch of her house for imaginary bogeymen before he could be satisfied it was safe.

The idea of him invading her home—her personal space—with all that masculine intensity was far more disturbing to her peace of mind than spending the night in his guest room.

"This isn't necessary," she grumbled.

"It is for me." He didn't bother to turn around.

She huffed out a disgruntled breath. She would spend this one night in his guest room and then she was going to do her best to stay as far away from Matt Harte as she possibly could, given the facts that Salt River had only five thousand residents, that she was contracted to treat his animals and that they had to plan a carnival together.

He was as dangerous to her heart as his outlaw namesake to an unprotected pile of gold.

The blasted woman wouldn't leave him alone.

Matt jerked the chute up with much more force than necessary. No matter how much he tried to stay away from her, to thrust her from his mind, she somehow managed to work herself right into his thoughts anyway. He couldn't shake her loose to save his life.

Ever since the week before when she had stayed at the ranch, his mind had been filled with the scent of her and the way she had looked in the morning at the kitchen table eating breakfast and laughing with Cassie and the girls. Fresh and clean and so pretty he had stood in the doorway staring at her for what felt like hours.

She haunted his thoughts all day long—and the

nights were worse. Try as he might, he couldn't stop thinking about the taste of her mouth and the way she had melted in his arms.

This, though. This was getting ridiculous. He damn well ought to be able to find a little peace from the woman while he was in the middle of checking the prenatal conditions of his pregnant cows.

But here was Steve Nichols bringing her up while he had one hand inside a bawling heifer. "You hear what happened to Ellie last week?" he asked over his shoulder.

Matt scowled at her name and at the reminder of the grisly offering left in her truck. "Yeah. I heard."

Nichols's blond mustache twitched with his frown. "Your brother have any leads?"

"Not yet. Ellie thinks it's just a prank."

The vet looked at him. "But you don't?"

He shrugged. "I think whoever is capable of doing something like that is one sick son of a bitch."

But a canny one, Matt acknowledged. One who knew how to lay low. Nothing out of the ordinary had happened in the week since she'd found the dead cat in her truck—a stray that, she learned during an autopsy, had indeed died of a natural cause, feline leukemia.

To be cautious, Ellie had installed an extra lock at her house and had hired Junior Zabrinzki's security company to check on the clinic during the night. So far, everything had been quiet, although she still claimed that she sometimes had the eerie feeling someone was watching over her shoulder.

He didn't know any of this firsthand. He'd only seen Ellie once since she had stayed at the ranch, the day before, when she'd come out to treat some of his horses.

Despite his best efforts to pry information out of her, somehow the contrary woman managed to steer every single conversation back to his animals.

Good thing his little brother was the chief of police. If he hadn't forced Jesse to give him regular progress reports on the investigation, he would have been a whole lot more annoyed at Ellie.

Progress was far too optimistic a word, though, from the reports he'd been getting. Jess was still as stumped by the threat as he'd been that first night, and Matt was getting pretty impatient about it.

"You talk to a lot of ranchers around here," he said suddenly to Nichols. "You have any ideas who might be angry enough at Ellie to threaten her like that?"

Steve shook his head, regret in his eyes. "I wish I did, but I'm as baffled as anybody else. I know she's had a rough time of it with some of the old-timers. Ellie's not exactly afraid to speak her mind when she sees things she doesn't like and, I have to admit, some of her ideas are a little out there. But I really thought things had been better for her in the last month or so."

He had to give Nichols credit for not showing any sign that he minded Ellie's presence in Star Valley. He wasn't sure he would have been so gracious in the same circumstances if a rival suddenly moved in to his business turf.

"I'd sure like to find out who it is, though," Steve said, his voice tight and his movements jerky. "It kills me to think about her finding something as sick as that. Of being so frightened. Ellie's a good vet and a wonderful person. She didn't deserve that."

Matt sent the other man a swift look, surprised by his vehemence. Maybe it was just professional respect, but somehow he didn't think so. Nichols acted more like a man with a personal stake in her business.

Did the two of them have a thing going? The thought left a taste in his mouth about as pleasant as rotten crab apples, and he had a sudden, savage urge to pound something.

But what business was it of his if she was seeing Steve? He had no claim on her, none at all. They were friends, nothing more. And not even very good friends at that.

Did she kiss Nichols with the same fiery passion she'd shown him? he wondered, then instantly regretted it.

"The investigation is still open," he said tersely. "Sooner or later Jess will get to the bottom of it."

"I hope so. I really hope so."

They turned to the cows and were running the last heifer through the chute when Hector Aguella hurried into the pens, his dark, weathered face taut with worry. "Boss, I think we got a problem."

"What's up?"

"Some of the horses, they're acting real strange. Like they got into some bad feed or something. I don't know. They're all shaking and got ugly stuff coming out their noses."

"How many?"

"Six, maybe. You better take a look."

"I'll come with you," Nichols said.

The noonday sun glared off the snow as he and Steve headed toward the horse pasture. When they were close enough to see what was happening, Matt growled an oath.

Even from here, it was obvious the horses were sick.

They stood in listless little groups, noses running and tremors shaking their bodies.

"Call Doc Webster and get her out here fast," he ordered Hector, breaking into a run. "And send Jim and Monte over to help me separate the healthy animals from the sick ones. If this is some kind of epidemic, I don't want to lose the whole damn herd."

"Do you want me to examine them?" Nichols called after him.

He hesitated for only a moment. Technically, the horses were Ellie's territory, but it seemed idiotic to refuse the other vet's offer of help when it could be an hour or more before she arrived at the ranch. "Yeah. Thanks."

With the help of the ranch hands, they quickly moved the animals who weren't showing any sign of sickness to a different pasture, then Steve began taking temperatures and doing quick physical exams.

"What do you think they've got?" Matt asked after the vet had looked at the last sick horse.

Steve scratched his head where thinning hair met scalp. "I've never seen anything like this. It looks like some kind of staph infection. They've all got the same big, oozing abscess."

"What kind?"

"I don't know. Whatever it is, it's hit them all the same. They've all got fevers, runny noses and chills. We'll have to run a culture to find out for sure. Whatever it is, it's damn scary if it can cause these symptoms to come on so fast. You said they were fine yesterday, right?"

"Yeah. I didn't notice anything unusual. So you're thinking a bacterial infection? Not something they ate?"

"That's what it looks like. I'm concerned about the abscess."

"How could something like that have hit them all at the same time?"

"I don't know." Steve paused. "When I was in vet school I heard about a herd getting something similar to this. Same symptoms, anyway."

"What was the cause there?"

"If I remember right, it was traced to unsanitary syringes used for vaccinations. Ellie hasn't given them any shots lately, has she?"

"She was out yesterday, but all she did was that acupuncture stuff on some of the mares to ease some of their pregnancy discomfort." He stopped, an ugly suspicion taking root.

Yesterday. Ellie had been here yesterday with her needles. Could she have done something that caused the animals to become deathly ill? Could she have used bad needles or something?

He couldn't believe it—didn't *want* to believe it. But it was one hell of a coincidence. He pushed the thought away. Now wasn't the time for accusations and blame. Not when his horses needed treatment. "So what can we do?"

"Push high dosages of penicillin and wait and see. That's about all we can do for the time being."

"You got any antibiotics with you?"

"Not much but enough, I think. It's in my truck over by the chutes. Let's hope it's the right one. I'll run a culture as soon as I can so we'll know better what we're dealing with."

He was only gone a few moments when Ellie's rattletrap of a pickup pulled up, and she emerged from it flushed and breathless.

"What's happening? Hector said you've got an emergency but he didn't say what. Is it Mystic? Is she threatening to lose the foal again?"

Before he could answer, her gaze landed on the horses, still shuddering with chills, and all color leached from her face. "Holy cow. What happened to them?"

"You tell me," Matt growled.

She sent him a startled look. "I... I can't know that without a thorough examination. How long have they been like this?"

Faster than a wildfire consuming dry brush, anger scorched through him—at her and at himself. He should have known better, dammit, than to let a pretty face convince him to go against his own judgment.

He should never have let her touch his stock with her wacky California ideas. He wouldn't have, except she had somehow beguiled him with her soft eyes and her stubborn chin and her hair that smelled like spring.

And now his horses were going to pay the price for his gullibility.

"What did you do to them?" He bit the words out.

She paled at the fury in his voice and stepped back half a pace. "What do you mean?"

"They were fine yesterday until you came out messing around with your New Age Chinese bull. What did you do?"

"Nothing I haven't done before. Just what you hired me to do, treat your horses."

She narrowed her green eyes at him suddenly. "Wait a minute. Are you blaming me for this? You think *I* caused whatever is making them sick?"

"Nichols says he thinks it's some kind of virulent bacterial infection. Maybe even—"

She interrupted him. "What does Steve have to do with this?"

"We were giving prenatal exams to the cows," he said impatiently. "He was with me when Hector came to tell us about the horses."

"And he thinks *I* infected these horses?"

"He said he's seen a similar case caused by infected syringes. The only needles these animals have seen in a month have been yours, Doc. You and your acupuncture baloney."

He refused to let himself be affected by the way her face paled and her eyes suddenly looked haunted. "You...you can't believe that's what caused this."

"You have any other ideas? Because from where I'm sitting, you're the most logical source."

She looked bewildered and lost and hurt, and he had to turn away to keep from reaching for her, to fold her into his arms and tell her everything would be okay.

"You can leave now," he said harshly, angry at himself for the impulse. "Steve is handling things from now on."

He had to hand it to her. She didn't back down, just tilted that chin of hers, all ready to take another one on the jaw. "We have a contract for another two months."

"Consider it void. You'll get your money, every penny of it, but I don't want you touching my horses again."

He drew a deep breath, trying to contain the fury prowling through him like a caged beast. It wasn't just the horses. He could deal with her making a mistake, especially since the tiny corner of his brain that could still think rationally was convinced she would never willfully hurt his animals.

But he had trusted her. Had let himself begin to care for her. He had given her a chance despite his instincts to the contrary, and she had violated that trust by passing on a potentially deadly illness to six of his animals.

He refused to look at her, knowing he would weaken when he saw the hurt in her eyes. He was a fool when it came to women. An absolute idiot. First Melanie with her needy eyes and her lying tongue and now Ellie with her sweet-faced innocence.

She had suckered him into completely forgetting his responsibilities—that the ranch came first, not pretty red-haired veterinarians. He was thirty-six years old and he damn well should have known better.

"That's your decision, of course," she said quietly after a moment, her voice as thin and brittle as old glass. "I certainly understand. You have to do what you think is right for your animals. Goodbye, Matt."

She walked out of the barn, her shoulders stiffen with dignity. He watched her go for only a moment, then turned to his horses.

What was she doing?

Hours later, Ellie navigated the winding road to the Diamond Harte while the wipers struggled to keep the windshield clear of the thick, wet snow sloshing steadily down.

She should be home in bed on a snowy night like tonight, curled into herself and weeping for the loss of a reputation she had spent five months trying to establish in Salt River. A reputation that had crumbled like dry leaves in one miserable afternoon.

That's what she wanted to be doing, wallowing in a good, old-fashioned pity party. Instead, here she was at nearly midnight, her stomach a ball of nerves and the steering wheel slipping through her sweat-slicked hands.

Matt would be furious if he found her sneaking onto the Diamond Harte in the middle of the night. The way he had spoken to her earlier, she wouldn't be surprised if he called his brother to haul her off to jail.

But despite his order to stay away, she knew she needed to do this. Cassie had tried to reassure her that the horses' conditions had improved when Ellie called earlier in the evening, but it wasn't good enough. She would never be able to sleep until she could be sure the animals would pull through.

She couldn't believe this was happening, that in a single afternoon her whole world could shatter apart like a rickety fence in a strong wind.

Matt's horses had only been the first to fall ill. By mid-afternoon, she'd received calls from the three other ranches she'd visited the day before reporting that all the horses she had seen in the last forty-eight hours had come down with the same mysterious symptoms.

She'd done her best for the afflicted animals, treating them with high dosages of penicillin while she struggled exhaustively to convince the ranchers to continue allowing her to treat their stock.

And to convince herself this couldn't be her fault.

The evidence was mounting, though. And damning. It did indeed look like staph infection, centered near the entry marks where she had treated each horse with acupuncture the day before.

How could this be happening? She was so careful.

Washing her hands twice as long as recommended, using only sterile needles from a reputable supplier.

Maybe she'd gotten a bad batch somehow, but she couldn't imagine how that was possible. Each needle came wrapped in a sterile package and was used only once.

The same questions had been racing themselves around and around in her head until she was dizzy from them, but she was no closer to figuring out how such a nightmare could have occurred.

Hard to believe the day before she'd felt on top of the world, had finally begun to think she had actually found a place she could belong here in Salt River.

All her dreams of making a stable, safe, fulfilling life for Dylan and for herself were falling apart. When this was over, she was very much afraid she would be lucky to find a job selling dog food, let alone continue practicing veterinary medicine anywhere in western Wyoming.

Every time she thought about the future, all she could focus on was this sick, greasy fear that she would have to sell the practice at a huge loss and go back to California and face all the smug people who would be so ready with I-told-you-so's.

She would have to leave the people she had come to care about here. SueAnn. Sarah McKenzie. Cassie Harte.

Matt.

Her chest hurt whenever she thought about him, about the way he had looked at her earlier in the day. With contempt and repugnance, like she was something messy and disgusting stuck to the heel of his boot.

He shouldn't have had the power to wound her so

deeply with only a look, and it scared her to death that he could. How had she come to care for him—for his opinion of her—so much?

He should mean nothing more to her than the rest of her clients. Only another rancher paying her to keep his horses healthy, that's all. So why couldn't she convince her heart?

The pickup's old tires slid suddenly on a patch of black ice hidden beneath the few inches of snow covering the road, and panic skittered through her for the few seconds it took the truck to find traction again. When it did, she blew out a breath and pushed away thoughts of Matt Harte and his chilling contempt for her. She needed to concentrate on the road, not on the disaster her life had turned into.

At the ranch, she pulled to the back of the horse barn, grateful it was far enough from the house that she could sneak in undetected. She climbed out of the truck on bones that felt brittle and achy and crunched through the ankle-deep snow to the door.

Inside, the horse barn was dark except for a low light burning near the far end where, she supposed, the sick mares were being kept. She made her way down the long row of stalls and was about halfway there when a broad-shouldered figure stepped out of the darkness and into the small circle of light.

Chapter 11

Matt.

Her heart stuttered in her chest, and for a moment she forgot to breathe, caught between a wild urge to turn around and run for the door in disgrace and a stubborn determination to stand her ground.

His little brindle-colored cow dog gave one sharp bark, then jumped up to greet her, tail wagging cheerfully. Ellie reached down and gave her a little pat, grateful at least somebody was happy to see her.

"Zoe, heel," he ordered.

With a sympathetic look in her brown eyes, the dog obeyed, slinking back to curl up at his feet once more.

"What are you doing here?" he asked.

Maybe it was wishful thinking on her part, but she could almost believe he sounded more resigned than angry to find her sneaking into his barn. At least he didn't sound quite ready to call the cops on her. That gave her enough courage to creep a few steps closer to that welcoming circle of light.

Behind him, she caught sight of a canvas cot and a rumpled sleeping bag. Matt had surrendered the comfort of his warm bed to stay the night in a musty old barn where he could be near his ailing horses.

The hard, painful casing around her heart began to crack a little, and she pressed a hand to her chest, inexplicably moved by this further evidence of what a good, caring man he was.

"Doc?" he prompted. "What are you doing here?"

She drew in a shaky breath. "I know you told me to stay away, but I couldn't. I… I just wanted to check on them."

"Cass said you called. Didn't you believe her when she told you the antibiotics seemed to be working?"

Heat crawled up her cheeks despite the chill of the barn. "I did. I just had to see for myself. I'm sorry. I know I have no right to be here. Not anymore. I won't touch them, I swear. Just look."

His jaw flexed but he didn't say anything and she took that as tacit permission. Turning her back on him, she slowly walked the way she had come, down the long line of stalls, giving each animal a visual exam.

As Cassie had reported, the infection seemed to have run its course. At least their symptoms seemed to have improved. Relief gushed over her, and she had to swallow hard against the choking tears that threatened.

"Delilah seems to have been hit the worst," Matt said just behind her, so close his breath rippled across her cheek. "She's still running a fever but it's dropped quite a bit from earlier."

Trying fiercely to ignore the prickles of awareness

as he invaded her space, she followed the direction of his gaze to the dappled gray. "What are you putting on that abscess on her flank?"

He told her and she nodded. "Good. That should take care of it."

"Now that you mention it, it's probably time for another application." He picked up a small container of salve from the top rail of the fence and entered the stall.

Speaking softly to the horse, he rubbed the mixture onto the painful-looking sore, and Ellie watched, feeling useless. She hated this, being sidelined into the role of observer instead of being able to *do* something. It went against her nature to simply stand here and watch.

He finished quickly and crossed to the sink to wash his hands. An awkward silence descended between them, broken only by the soft rustling of hay. Matt was the first to break it. "How are all the other horses faring?" he asked.

"You know about the others?" Why did she feel this deep, ugly shame when she knew in her heart none of this could be her fault?

He nodded. "Nichols told me. Three other ranches, a dozen horses in all including my six."

She had to fight the urge to press her hand against her roiling stomach at the stark statistics. "Just call me Typhoid Mary."

To her surprise, instead of the disdain she expected to see, his eyes darkened with sympathy. "So how are they?" he asked.

"I lost one." Her voice strained as she tried to sound brisk and unaffected. "One of Bob Meyers's quarter horses. She was old and sickly anyway from an upper respiratory illness and just wasn't strong enough to fight off the infection, even after antibiotics."

Despite her best efforts, she could feel her chin wobble a little and she tightened her lips together to make it stop.

The blasted man never did as she expected. Instead of showing her scorn, he reached a hand out to give her shoulder a comforting squeeze, making her chin quiver even more.

"I'm sorry," he murmured.

She let herself lean into his strength for just a moment then subtly eased away. "I don't know what happened, Matt. I am so careful. Obsessively so. I always double scrub. Maybe I got a bad shipment of needles or something. I just don't know."

"It's eating you up inside, isn't it?"

"I became a vet to heal. And look what I've done!"

His fingers brushed her shoulder again. "You can't beat yourself up about it for the rest of your life."

He was silent for a moment, then sent her a sidelong glance. "I said some pretty nasty things to you earlier. Treated you a lot worse than you deserved. I'm sorry for that."

His brusquely worded apology fired straight to her heart. "You were worried about your horses."

"I was, but I still shouldn't have lashed out at you like that. I apologize."

"You have nothing to be sorry about. You had every right to be upset—I would have been if they were my horses. I understand completely that you want to bring Steve back on-board. He seems to have handled the situation exactly right."

He shrugged. "Well, they all seem to be doing okay

now. Mystic was the one I was most worried about, but she was eating fine tonight, and neither she or her foal seem to be suffering any ill effects."

Something in what he said briefly caught her attention, like a wrong note in a piano concerto. Before she could isolate it, he continued. "As for the others, I think we're out of the danger zone."

"But you decided to stay the night out here anyway."

He shrugged. It might have been a trick of the low lighting, but she could swear she saw color climbing up his cheeks. "It seemed like a good idea, just to be on the safe side."

"Well, I'm sorry I woke you."

"You didn't. I was just reading."

She looked over his shoulder and saw a well-worn copy of Owen Wister's *The Virginian* lying spine up on the army-green blanket covering the cot. "Apparently your father was not the only one interested in the Old West."

A wry smile touched his lips. "It's a classic, what can I say? The father of all Westerns."

She could drown in that smile, the way it creased at the edges of his mouth and softened his eyes and made him look years younger. She could stay here forever, just gazing at it....

"Wait a minute." The jarring note from before pounded louder in her head. "Wait a minute. Did you say Mystic was sick, too?"

He nodded and pointed to the stall behind them. Dust motes floated on the air, tiny gold flakes in the low light. Through them she could see the little mare asleep in the stall.

The implications exploded through her, and she

rushed to the stall for a better look. "I didn't treat her yesterday!" she exclaimed. "Don't you remember? I was going to. She was on my schedule. But I ran out of time and planned to come back later when I could spend more time with her."

"What does that have to do with anything?"

"Don't you get it? If Mystic came down with the same thing the others had, it can't be because of me, because of any staph infection I might have introduced through unsanitary needles, like Steve implied. I didn't even touch her yesterday!"

He frowned. "You did a few weeks ago."

"So why didn't she show symptoms of illness much earlier than yesterday, when all the other horses became sick?"

"Maybe it was some delayed reaction on her part. Just took it longer to hit her."

"No. That doesn't make sense. I've been through at least two boxes of needles since then. They couldn't have all been bad, or every single one of my patients would have the same illness. Don't you see? Something else caused this, not me!"

She wasn't thinking, caught up only in the exhilaration—this vast, consuming relief to realize she hadn't unknowingly released some deadly plague on her patients. If her brain had been functioning like it should have been, she certainly would never have thrown her arms around Matt in jubilation.

She only hugged him for a moment. As soon as reality intruded—when she felt the soft caress of his chamois shirt against her cheek and smelled the clean, male scent of him—she froze, mortified at her impulsiveness. Awareness began as a flutter in her stomach, a hitch in her breathing.

"Sorry," she mumbled and pulled away.

He stood awkwardly, arms still stiff at his sides, then moved to rest his elbows on the top rail of Mystic's stall to keep from reaching for her again. "We've still got twelve sick animals here, then. Any ideas why?"

"No. Nothing." She frowned. "Steve's right, it has all the signs of a bacterial infection, but it's like no other I've ever seen before. And how could it spread from your ranch to the rest that have been hit, unless by something I did? I seem to be the only common link."

"Maybe you tracked something on your boots some- how."

"I don't know of anything that could be this viru- lent in that kind of trace amount. And what about the abscesses?"

He had no more answers than she did, so he remained silent. After a long moment, she sighed. "The grim re- ality is, we might never know. I'll get some blood work done and send the rest of the needles from the same box to the lab and see what turns up. Who knows. We might get lucky and they can identify something we haven't even thought about. Something that's not even related to me."

"I hope so," he said gruffly.

He wasn't sure when the anger that had driven him all afternoon had begun to mellow, but eventually his common sense had won out. Even if she had spread the infection, he had no doubt it was accidental, something beyond her control.

She was a good vet who cared about her patients. She would never knowingly cause them harm.

"I really hope for your sake everything turns up clean," he said quietly.

She flashed him another one of those watery smiles that hid a wealth of emotions. This had to be killing her. It would be tough on any vet, but especially for one as passionate and dedicated as Ellie.

"Thanks." After a moment, she let out a deep breath. "It's late. I should go so you can get back to your book."

She didn't look very thrilled at the idea. Truth be told, she didn't look at all eager to walk out into the mucky snow. She looked lonely.

"Where's Dylan tonight?" he asked.

"At SueAnn's. I was afraid I'd get called out in the middle of the night to one of the other ranches and would have to leave her home alone. I really hate doing that, so Sue offered to take her for the night."

"You have no reason to rush off, then?"

She blinked. "No. Why?"

"You could stay. Keep me company."

Where the hell did that come from? He wanted to swallow the words as soon as they left his mouth, but it was too late now. She was already looking at him, as astounded as if he'd just offered to give her a makeover or something.

"You…you really want my company after today?"

The doubt in her voice just about did him in. He was such a pushover for a woman in distress. She only had to look at him out of those big, wounded eyes and he was lost, consumed with the need to take care of her— to relieve that tension from her shoulders, to tease a laugh or two out of her, to make her forget her troubles for a moment.

"Yeah," he said gruffly. "Come on. Sit down."

Still looking as wary as if she had just crawled in to a wolverine's den, she unzipped her coat and shrugged out of it. Underneath, she wore a daisy-yellow turtleneck covered by a fluffy navy polar fleece vest.

She looked young and fresh and sweet, and he suddenly realized what a disastrous error in judgment he had just committed. Why hadn't he shoved her out the door when he had the chance?

His control around her was shaky at the best of times. Here, alone in a dimly lit barn with only the soft murmur of animals and rustling of hay surrounding them, he hoped like hell he would be able to keep his hands off her.

She perched on the edge of his cot while he rounded up the old slat-backed wooden chair that probably dated back to his grandfather's day. He finally found it near the sink under a pile of old cattle magazines and carried it to the circle of light near the cot.

She was leafing through *The Virginian*, he saw after he sat down. Her smile was slow, almost shy. "I read this in high school English class. I remember how it made me want to cry. I think that's when I first decided I wanted to move to Wyoming. I'll have to see if the library in town has a copy I could read again."

"You can borrow that one when I'm finished if you want."

This time her smile came more quickly. "Thanks."

"It was one of my dad's favorites. He loved them all. Louis L'Amour, Zane Grey, Max Brand. All the good ones. During roundup when we were kids, he always kept a book tucked in his saddlebags to read to us by the glow of the campfire. We ate it up."

"You miss him, don't you?"

He thought of the gaping hole his parents' deaths had left in his life. "Yeah," he finally said. "We didn't always get along but he was a good man. Always willing to do anything for anyone. I'd be happy if I could die with people thinking I was half the man he was."

"Why didn't you get along?"

Zoe shoved her nose against his knee, and he gave her an obligatory pat, trying to form his answer. "Mom always said we were so much alike we brought out the worst in each other. I don't know. I thought he should have done more with the ranch. Expanded the operation, bid on more grazing rights so we could take on a bigger herd. I thought he didn't have any ambition. Took me a long time to realize he might not have seemed ambitious to his cocky eighteen-year-old son, but only because he didn't have to be. He didn't see the need to strive for more when he already had everything he wanted from life."

"Do you?"

His hand stilled on Zoe's ruff. "What?"

"Have everything you want?"

He used to think so. A month ago he would have said yes without hesitating. He had the ranch and Lucy and his family, and it should have been enough for him. Lately, though, he'd been restless for more. Hungry. He prowled around the house at night, edgy inside his skin.

A month ago he had kissed her just a few feet from here.

He pushed the memory away. That had nothing to do with it. Absolutely nothing.

"I'd like somebody to invent a horse that never needs shoes. But other than that, yeah. I guess I'm content."

It wasn't really a lie. Right now, at least, he was more relaxed than he'd been in a long time. He refused to dwell on exactly why that might be the case and whether it had anything to do with Ellie.

"I'd still like to expand the operation a little more, especially the cutting horse side of it. I guess you could say that's where my heart is, in training the horses. The cattle are the lifeblood for the ranch but for me, nothing compares to turning a green-broke horse into a savvy, competition-quality cutter."

He paused, waiting for her to respond. When she didn't, he peered through the dim light and realized he'd been baring his soul to the horses. Ellie was asleep, her head propped against the rough plank wall and her sable-tipped lashes fanned out over her cheeks.

He watched her sleep for several moments, struck again by how beautiful she was. In sleep, she couldn't hang on to that tough, take-it-on-the-chin facade she tried to show the world. Instead, she looked small and fragile, all luminous skin and delicate bones.

For just a moment, he had a wild, fierce wish that things could be different. That he was free to slide beside her on the cot and press his mouth to that fluttering pulse at the base of her neck. That he could waken her with slow, languid kisses then spend the rest of the night making love to her in the hushed secrecy of the barn.

As tempting as the idea was—and it had him shifting in the hard slat chair as blood surged to his groin— he knew it was impossible. In the first place, she likely wouldn't be too thrilled to wake up and find him slobbering all over her.

In the second, even if she didn't push him away, even if by some miracle she opened her arms to him, welcomed him with her mouth and her hands and her body, what the hell good would it do? It wouldn't change anything.

Now that she was asleep, he could admit to himself that she was the cause of this restlessness prowling inside his skin. But even if he were free to kiss her again, it couldn't change the indisputable fact that he had nothing to give her but a few heated moments of pleasure.

For a woman like Ellie, that would never be enough. He knew it instinctively, just as he suddenly feared making love with her once would only whet his hunger, leave him starving for more. Like a little kid who was only allowed one quick lick of a delectable ice-cream cone.

She was soft and gutsy and spirited, and if he wasn't damn careful, he could lose his heart to her. The thought scared him worse than being in the rodeo ring with a dozen angry bulls.

He'd been in that position once. He had loved Melanie in the beginning—or thought he did, anyway—and it had nearly destroyed him.

Here in the silent barn, he could see his ex-wife as clearly as if she were sitting beside him. Dark, curling hair, haunted gray eyes, features delicate as a porcelain doll.

She had been so unhappy from the very beginning. Nothing he did had been enough for her. If he brought her roses, she wanted orchids. If he took her to dinner, she would make some small, wistful comment about how much she enjoyed quiet evenings at home.

Everything had always been hot or cold with her. Either she was on fire for him and couldn't get enough or she wouldn't let him touch her, would screech at him to keep his rough, working hands to himself.

In retrospect, he could see all the signs of bipolar disorder, but he'd been too young and too damn stubborn to admit then that she needed professional help. It had taken him years to realize he couldn't have saved her, that her unhappiness had been as much a part of her as her gray eyes.

When he couldn't fill the empty spot inside her, when he finally gave up trying, she had turned to other men, throwing her many conquests in his face at every opportunity. The first one had eaten him up inside, and he'd gone to the Renegade to beat the hell out of the unlucky cowhand. By the fourth or fifth affair, he told himself he didn't care.

He could still remember his cold fury when he found out she was pregnant, the bitter, hateful words they had flung at each other like sharp heavy stones.

At first he'd been afraid Lucy had been the product of one of her other relationships. The first time he held her, though, it had ceased to matter. He'd completely lost his heart to the chubby little girl with the big gray eyes, and he would have fought to the death if someone tried to take her from him.

But now, as Lucy grew into her looks, it became obvious she was a Harte through and through, from that dimple in her chin to her high cheekbones to her Cupid's bow of a mouth. She looked exactly like pictures of his mother at that age.

Something snapped inside Melanie after Lucy was born. It might have been postpartum depression, he didn't know, but everything she did had taken on a desperate edge. She'd spent every night haunting the Renegade in town, looking for trouble, trying to find some way out of Salt River, Wyoming. She'd found both in Zack Slater.

He blew out a breath. Why was he even thinking about this, about her? Maybe because Melanie was the reason he could never let another woman inside him. Why he would always be quick to fury and start throwing blame around, like he'd done with Ellie earlier that day.

He was afraid the wounds Melanie had carved in his soul would always make doubt and suspicion lurk just below the surface.

Ellie didn't deserve that. She deserved a man who could give her everything, especially the safe, secure home she'd never had as a kid. A man who could love her completely with a heart still whole and unscarred.

Whoa. Where did love fit in the picture? He didn't love her. No way. He was attracted to her and he admired certain qualities about her. Her resilience, her stubborn determination to succeed in the face of overwhelming adversity, her passion for her work. The same qualities that most irritated him, he admitted ruefully.

And he was fiercely attracted to her, no doubt about that.

But love? No way.

He shifted, trying to find a more comfortable spot on the unforgiving wood chair. He didn't want to think about this. He couldn't give her what she deserved so he had to settle for giving her nothing.

He knew it, had known it since he met her. So why did the realization make him so damned miserable?

He pushed away the thoughts. They weren't doing

him any good. Instead, he turned his mind to the puzzle of the sick horses. What was the connection between them?

Ellie.

He wished he could be as convinced as she appeared to be that she had nothing to do with the sick horses. But what other link could there be? Like she'd said, the ranches that had been hit were miles apart and didn't appear to share anything else in common but their veterinarian.

Or at least they *had* shared Ellie. He had a feeling she would have a hard time keeping any clients unless she could prove without a doubt she wasn't to blame for the epidemic.

He would contract with her again to treat his horses. He had to. She would be devastated if she lost the practice. That and her kid were everything to her.

If someone wanted to destroy her practice, they had hit on the perfect method—shattering her reputation.

The thought had him sitting up straighter as he remembered the grisly message left in her truck. Someone out there didn't want her in Star Valley. If he was twisted enough to leave a dead cat in her truck, wouldn't he be capable of anything? Even something as sick and warped as harming a dozen innocent animals in order to implicate Ellie? To force her to leave by driving away her patients?

No. He couldn't believe it. Who would do such a thing? And how would anyone possibly manage it? Some of the animals might have been pastured near enough to roads or in distant enough corrals for someone to slip them something—maybe give them a shot without anyone noticing—but sneaking onto the Diamond Harte would be damn near impossible.

Still, it wouldn't hurt to mention the theory to Jess. If there was a connection between the sick horses and the warning note, his little brother would find it.

Ellie made a little sound in her sleep, drawing his attention again. She'd be a whole lot more comfortable under the blanket with her head on his pillow instead of sitting up like that.

Of course, then he'd be forced to find another place to sleep for the night.

He sighed and rose to his feet, then gently eased her to the cot, knowing he didn't have a choice. She didn't stir at all when he drew the heavy blanket over her shoulders and tucked it under her chin.

He returned to the hard wooden chair, leaned his head against the rough plank wall and watched her sleep for a long time.

Chapter 12

Ellie wasn't sure what awakened her. One moment she was dreaming of lying beside Matt Harte on a white-sand beach somewhere while a trade wind rustled the leaves on the palm trees around her and water lapped against the shore, and the next her senses were filled with the musty-sweet smell of hay and the soft, furtive rustling of the horses in their stalls.

She blinked for a moment, stuck in that hazy world between sleep and consciousness, and tried to remember why she wearing her clothes and curled up on a hard cot in someone's barn. Her back was stiff, her neck ached from sleeping in an odd position and she felt rumpled and uncomfortable in her Ropers and jeans.

She sat up, running a hand through tangled hair. As she did, her gaze landed on Matt across the dim, dusty barn, and the events of the night before came rushing back like the tide.

This was *his* barn. She was curled up in *his* make-shift bed.

Ellie winced and hit the light on her watch. Four a.m. She must have been sleeping for hours. The last time she remembered checking her watch had been midnight, when Matt had been talking about his horses.

Embarrassed guilt flooded through her. Not only had she been rude enough to drift off in the middle of their conversation, but she had fallen asleep in the man's bed, forcing him to sleep in that torturous hard-backed chair.

He couldn't possibly be comfortable, with his neck twisted and his head propped against the wall like that. But he was definitely asleep. His eyes didn't so much as flutter, and his chest moved evenly with each slow, deep breath.

She watched for a moment, hypnotized by the cotton rippling over his hard chest with the soft rise and fall of his breathing, then her gaze climbed higher, over the tanned column of his neck to roam across the rugged planes and angles of his face. The strong blade of a nose, the full, sensuous lips, the spike of his dark eyelashes.

He was sinfully gorgeous and completely one in his surroundings, like something out of a Charles Russell painting.

Had he watched *her* this way after she drifted off? The thought unnerved her, made her insides feel hot and liquid, but wasn't enough to compel her to turn away. Even though it was probably an invasion of his privacy, watching him like this was a temptation she couldn't resist.

In sleep, Matt lost the hard edges that made him seem so tough and formidable. He looked younger, more relaxed, as if only in sleep was he free to shake the mantle of responsibility that had settled on his strong, capable shoulders so young.

What must it have been like for him after his parents died? She tried to imagine and couldn't. He had been twenty-two and suddenly responsible for a huge ranch and two troublesome, grieving younger siblings.

No wonder he seemed so remote and detached sometimes. He had grown up and become an adult at a time when many other young men were still having fraternity parties and taking trips to Fort Lauderdale for spring break. Instead of raising hell, Matt had raised his younger brother and sister.

And yet he had another side. She thought of the teasing grin he reserved for his daughter, the soft, soothing voice he used to calm a fractious horse, the woofs of a contented cow dog being stroked by his gentle hands.

He was so different from the perceptions she had formed about him that first day in Ms. McKenzie's classroom. Before then, even. She had thought him narrow-minded and humorless. Stuffy and set in his ways. But in the weeks since, she'd come to appreciate the many layers beneath that tough exterior. Hardworking rancher, devoted family man. Honest and well-respected member of the community. He was all those things and more.

It wouldn't take much for her to fall headlong in love with him.

The thought bulleted into her brain and completely staggered her. She paled, reaching for the edge of the cot to steady herself as a grim realization settled in her heart.

She was already more than halfway there.

She shivered, suddenly chilled to the bone despite the blanket he must have thrown across her knees.

How had she let things go so far? After her disastrous relationship with Kurt, she had been so diligent. So fiercely careful not to let anyone into her heart.

She didn't need anyone else—she and Dylan managed just fine, dammit.

Emotions like love were messy and complicated. They made a woman needy and vulnerable and stupid. Like her mother had been, like she had been with Kurt.

Besides, she had enough on her plate right now, trying to keep the practice alive and food in her daughter's mouth. She didn't have room in her life for a man, especially one like Matt Harte who would demand everything and more from her. He wasn't the kind of man who would be content to stay put in a neat little compartment of her life until she had time for him. He would want it all.

She could try to convince herself until she was blue in the face but it wouldn't change the fact that he had somehow managed to sneak into her heart when she wasn't looking.

Was it possible to be only a little in love with someone? If so, maybe she could stop things right now before she sunk completely over her head. It would be hard but not impossible to rebuild the protective walls around her heart, especially if she kept her distance for a while.

She could do it. She had to try. The alternative was just too awful to contemplate.

She would start by leaving this cozy little corner of the barn and going back to her own house where she belonged. Soundlessly, she pushed away the blanket and planted her boots on the ground, wincing a little as stiff muscles complained at being treated so callously.

If she was this sore, she imagined Matt would be much worse when he awoke.

She thought about waking him up so he could take the cot and even went so far as to reach a hand out to shake him from his slumber, then yanked it back. No. Better to sneak out and avoid any more awkwardness between them.

She shrugged into her coat and headed for the door. As she passed Mystic's stall, the little mare nickered softly in greeting, and Ellie stopped, jerking her head around to see if Matt woke up. He was still propped against the wall like one of those old-time wooden dime-store Indians, and she let her breath out in relief.

It wouldn't hurt to take a look at the horse while she was here, she decided. She could do it quietly enough that it didn't disturb Matt. Straw whispered underfoot as she made her way to the little mare's stall. The door squeaked when she opened it, but Matt slept on.

"You're a pretty girl, aren't you?" She pitched her voice low, running her hands over the horse's abdomen to feel for the foal's position. "Yes, you are. And you'll be a wonderful mama in just a few more months. The time will go so fast and before you know it your little one will be dancing circles around you and tumbling into trouble."

The mare made a noise that sounded remarkably like a resigned sigh, and Ellie laughed softly again. "Don't start complaining now. It's your own fault. You should have thought about what you might be in for when you cuddled up to that big handsome stud who got you this way. You had your fun and now you have to pay the piper."

Mystic blew out a disgusted puff of air through her

nose and lipped at her shoulder, and Ellie nodded in agreement. "I know. Men. But what's a girl to do? They look at you out of those gorgeous blue eyes and it's all you can do to remember to breathe, let alone keep your heart out of harm's way."

"You carry on heart-to-heart chats with all your patients?"

She jerked her head up at the rough, amused voice behind her and found Matt leaning his forearms on the top rail of the stall, his hair mussed a little from sleep and a day's growth stubbling his cheeks.

As predictable as the sunrise, she forgot to breathe again. "Hi," she said after a moment, her voice high and strained.

"Going somewhere?" He gestured to her coat.

"Home. I've stayed long enough. I only wanted to check Mystic one more time before I go. I hope that's okay."

He didn't answer, just continued watching her out of solemn blue eyes, and her stomach started a long, slow tremble.

"I'm sorry I took your bed. I didn't mean to. I must have just drifted off. Yesterday was a pretty rough day all around, and I guess all that stress took its toll on me." She was babbling but couldn't seem to help herself. "Anyway, you should have booted me out and sent me home. You must be one big bundle of aches right now."

"I ache," he finally said, his low voice vibrating in the cool predawn air. "I definitely ache."

She was suddenly positive he wasn't talking about a stiff neck. The trembling in her stomach rippled to her knees, to her shoulders, to her fingers. She shoved her hands into the deep pockets of the fleece vest, praying he wouldn't notice, but she couldn't do anything about the rest except take a shaky breath and hope her knees would wait to collapse until she made it out of the barn.

"Well, I, um, I should be going," she mumbled.

Nerves scrambling, she patted Mystic one last time, then walked out of the stall. She managed to avoid looking at him until she had carefully closed the door behind her.

When she did—when she finally lifted her gaze to his—she was stunned by the raw hunger blazing in his eyes.

She must have made some sound—his name, maybe— and then he ate up the distance between them in two huge strides, and she was in his arms.

His mouth descended to hers, hot and hungry and needy.

He devoured her, like he'd just spent days in the saddle crossing the Forty-Mile Desert and she was a long, cool drink of water on the other side. His hands yanked her against him, held her fast.

Not that she was complaining. She was too busy kissing him back, meeting him nip for nip, taste for taste.

Somewhere in a dim and dusty corner of her mind, her subconscious warned her this was a lousy idea. If her grand plan was to stay away from him until she had her unruly emotions under control, she could probably do a better job than this.

She didn't care. Not now, when her senses spun with the taste and scent and feel of this man she was coming to care for entirely too much.

With a groan, he framed her face with his work-rough hands and pressed her back against the wood stall as he had the first time he'd kissed her. She felt his arousal press against her hip, and her body responded instantly, leaning in to him, desperate to be closer.

She almost cried out in protest when he slid his mouth away, but the sound swelling in her throat shifted to something different, something earthy and aroused, when his lips trailed across the curve of her cheekbone to nip at her ear. His ragged breathing sent liquid heat bubbling through her.

"I think about you all the time," he growled softly into her ear, and her heart gave a couple of good, hard kicks in her chest.

"No matter what I'm doing, you're there with me. I hate it," he went on in that same disgruntled tone. "Why won't you get out of my head?"

"Sorry." Her voice was breathless, aroused. "I'll try harder."

His low, strained laugh vibrated along her nerve endings. "You do that, Doc. You do that."

He dipped his head and captured her mouth again in another of those mind-bending kisses. She wasn't aware they had moved from Mystic's stall until the edge of the cot pressed behind her knees, and then he lowered her onto it, the hard length of him burning into her everywhere their bodies touched.

"I hope this thing holds both of us," he murmured against her mouth, and she laughed softly, a quick mental picture flitting through her mind of them tumbling to the ground.

Before she could answer, his mouth swept over hers, his tongue slipping inside her parted lips. She lost track of time, lost in the wonder of Matt, of being in his arms again. She wanted to hold him close and never let go,

to cradle that dark head against her breast, to share a
thousand moments like this with him.

She wanted him.

The knowledge terrified her. She wanted Matt Harte
the way she'd never wanted anyone—never *allowed*
herself to want anyone.

She was supposed to be so independent. So strong
and self-sufficient. How could she know she had this
powerful need inside her to be held like this, to feel
fragile and feminine and *cherished*?

There it was, though, scaring the hell out of her.

But not scaring her enough to make her pull away.
She needed more. She needed to feel his skin under her
fingertips. He must have untucked his shirt before he
fell asleep, and she found it an easy matter to slip her
hands underneath, to glide across the smooth, hot skin
of his back, loving the play of hard muscle bunching
under her hands.

She was so enthralled with his steely strength that
she was only vaguely aware of his busy, clever fingers
unzipping her fleece vest until he caressed the curve of
one breast through the knit of her shirt. Desire flooded
through her, and she felt as if she were swimming
through some wildly colorful coral reef without nearly
enough air in her lungs.

She went completely under when his fingers slipped
beneath her shirt and began to slowly trace the skin
just below her bra. For once, she was impatient with
his careful, measured movements. *All right, already*,
she wanted to shout, suddenly sure she would die if he
didn't put those hands on her.

Finally, when she didn't know if she could stand the
sensual torture another instant, she felt his hands work-

ing the front clasp of her bra, then the raw shock of his fingers skimming over her breasts.

She closed her eyes against the overwhelming sensations pouring through her one after another.

"You are so beautiful," he murmured, his voice rough with desire. "The first time I saw you, you made me think of a sunset on a stormy August evening, all fire and color and glory."

To a woman who had spent her whole life feeling like an ugly, scrawny red-haired duckling, his words caressed her more intimately than his fingers. No one had ever called her beautiful before, and she had no defenses against his soft words.

This time she kissed him, lost to everything but this man, this hard, gorgeous cowboy. She arched against his fingers, begging for more of those slow, sensuous touches. He pulled away from her mouth, but before she could protest he slid down her body, pushing her shirt aside so his mouth could close over one taut nipple.

A wild yearning clawed to life inside her, and she closed her eyes and clasped him to her, her fingers tangled in his silky dark hair. He shoved one of his muscled legs between her thighs, and the hard pressure was unbearably arousing. While his mouth teased and tasted her, she arched against him, desperate for more.

He slid a hand between their bodies, working the snaps of her jeans, and her breath caught in her throat as she waited for him to touch her, to caress her *there*. Just before he reached the last snap of her jeans, though, he froze, his breathing ragged.

He pressed his forehead to hers and groaned softly. "Stop. Dammit. We have to stop."

She didn't want to listen to him, lost to everything

but this wild, urgent need pouring through her. With her hands still tangled in his hair, it was an easy matter to angle his mouth so she could kiss him again in another of those long, drugging kisses.

He cooperated for a moment, his tongue dancing with hers, then he groaned again. "Ellie, I mean it. We have to stop."

"Why?"

He pulled away from her, and she shivered as cold air rushed to fill the space he had been in, to dance across her exposed skin with icy fingers.

Matt raked a hand through his hair. "A hundred reasons. Hell, a thousand. The most urgent one being I don't have any protection."

Her mind still felt fuzzy, and for a moment she didn't know what he was talking about. "You…you don't?"

"Sorry," he said wryly. "It's not something I generally stock in my barn." She flushed, suddenly jerked to reality, to the grim fact that she was less than a scruple away from making love to Matt Harte on a hard canvas cot. In his barn, no less, with a dozen horses as witnesses, where any of his ranch hands could stumble upon them any minute.

Dear heavens. What had she been *thinking*?

She hadn't been. She had been so desperately hungry for him that she hadn't been thinking at all, had completely ignored the warning voice yelling in her head.

What had she done? This was absolutely *not* the right way to go about yanking him out of her heart. She was supposed to be grabbing hold of a branch to keep herself from falling any further in love with him, doing her best to hoist herself to safe ground, to sanity. She wasn't supposed to gleefully fling herself over the edge like this.

She was too late.

The realization shuddered through her. She had been so stupid to think she could stop things in mid-step. She was already in love with him.

"I have to go. I really have to go." She stood up and frantically began putting her clothes in order, snapping and tucking and zipping.

He saw her fingers tremble as she tried to set to rights what his hands had undone, and he had to shove his fingers into his pockets to keep from reaching for her again.

She was mortified.

He could see it in her eyes, even though she wouldn't look directly at him, just around and over him as if he didn't exist, as if he weren't standing here in front of her, frustrated and aroused.

He didn't know what to say to make it right, to ease her awkwardness. There was probably nothing he *could* say.

All he knew was that he still wanted her, that his blood pulsed thick and heavy through his veins just looking at her, all tousled and sexy from his hands and his mouth.

As awkward as things were, he had to stop it. He had no choice. They would make love—he suddenly knew that without a doubt—but this wasn't the right time, the right place. She deserved better than a quick tussle in a dusty old horse barn. She deserved flowers and candles and romance, things he suddenly wanted fiercely to give her.

She jerked on her coat and started for the door, but he reached a hand out to stop her. "Ellie—"

"I hope everything turns out all right with your horses," she said quickly. "As soon as I hear from the lab on the test results, I'll let you know."

He sighed. He was still hard enough to split bricks, and she was going on about test results. A vast, terrifying tenderness welled inside him. As much as it scared him, he knew he couldn't walk away from it. And he couldn't let her walk away, either.

She was in his system and had been since she'd first blown into town. Trying to ignore it had only heightened his attraction for her, made him more hungry than ever. It was the mystery of her, he told himself. The fact that she was off-limits. Like that kid he was thinking about before who had been denied a scrumptious ice-cream cone, suddenly that was the only thing he could think about.

Maybe giving in to it, spending more time with her, might help work her out of his system so he could have things back the way they were before she whirled into his life.

"Are you busy tonight?"

In the process of slipping on her boots, she blinked at him suspiciously. "What?"

"Have dinner with me. I know this great place in Jackson Hole that's not usually too overrun with tourists this time of year. I'm sure I could arrange it with Cassidy to watch the girls. Or we could take them with us, if you'd rather."

"Dinner?"

"Yeah. Or we could go to a movie, if that appeals to you more. If you don't want to go to the show in town, there are a couple of theaters in Jackson or we could drive over to Idaho Falls. I'm sure we could find something we'd both enjoy."

She narrowed her gaze suspiciously. "Are you asking me out on a date, Harte?"

"I think so. At least that's the way things used to be done. I'm a little rusty at the whole dating thing."

"Why?" she asked, her voice blunt.

He shrugged. "I just haven't done it in a while. But don't worry, I'm sure it will all come back to me."

She gave him an impatient glare. "No. I meant, why are you asking me out?"

"The usual reasons people go out on a date." He cleared his throat and looked away. "I'm, uh, attracted to you. I guess you probably figured that out. And I'm not a real good judge of these things, but I think you'd be lying if you said you were immune to me. I think we should get to know each other, since it's pretty clear where we're heading with this thing between us."

Everything about her seemed to freeze. Even the vein pulsing in her neck seemed to stop. "To bed? Is that where you think we're heading?"

He shifted, suddenly feeling as if he were walking barefoot across a pasture full of cow pies. "Uh, it sure looked that way five minutes ago."

"Yeah? Well, that was five minutes ago. Things change." She started toward the door again.

He plodded valiantly forward. "So you're saying no to dinner?"

"Right. No to dinner or to a movie or to any friendly little roll in the hay."

By the time she reached the door, his temper had flared, and he stalked after her. "What the hell did I do that's got you acting like a wet hen all of a sudden? All I did was ask you out on a date, for crying out loud."

She stopped at the door, her back to him, then she turned slowly, green eyes shadowed. "You're right. I'm sorry, Matt. You didn't do anything. This is just a bad

ʼidea for me right now. Yes, I'm attracted to you, but I don't want to be."

"Yeah, well, join the club," he growled. "I'm not too thrilled about it, either."

"Exactly my point. Neither of us wants this. I can't be interested in any relationship with you right now beyond vet and client, and now we don't even have that."

"I already told you last night I was sorry for the way I jumped down your throat yesterday. I'd still like to keep you on as my equine vet."

"Despite everything that's happened?"

"Yeah. Despite all of it. Mistakes happen. Whatever you did to the horses, it wasn't intentional. Consider yourself rehired."

She went stiff all over again, and he knew he'd screwed up. Before he could figure out how—let alone do anything to make it right—she drew in a deep breath and shielded her eyes from his view with her lashes, studying the tips of her Ropers. "You don't get it, do you?"

"What?"

"Never mind." Her voice sounded sad suddenly. Like she'd just lost something precious. "I think you'd be better off with Steve as your vet. You don't have time to constantly stand over my shoulder to make sure I don't mess up again. And I don't think I could work that way."

"What about the rest of it? About what happened a few minutes ago?"

She swung open the door and stood framed in the pearly predawn light. "I'm sure if we try really hard, we can both forget that ever happened."

Without another look at him, she walked out into the cold.

Chapter 13

"I don't understand," Dylan moaned into the phone. "Why isn't this working?"

"Maybe they just don't like each other as much as we thought they would." Lucy sounded as discouraged as Dylan, her voice wobbling like she wanted to cry.

Dylan lay on her bed and stared out the window at the black night, thoughts whizzing around in her head like angry bees. It was two days after Christmas, and she should have been happy. She didn't have to go back to school for another week, she got the new CD player and cross-country skis she'd been hinting about for Christmas, and she and Lucy were going to be having a mini New Year's Eve sleepover at the ranch in just a few days.

But the one thing she wanted more than anything else—having a dad and a sister and living happily ever after on the Diamond Harte—seemed as distant as those stars out there.

Things were not going right. Her mom and Mr. Harte didn't seem any closer to falling in love than they had when she and Lucy first came up with the plan.

In fact, they didn't seem to be getting along at all. Every time she brought up his name, her mom's face went all squishy and funny like she just stepped on a bug.

Right before Christmas she asked her mom to drive her out to the ranch so she could take Lucy her present. It had all been carefully arranged for a time when Lucy's dad would be at the ranch house, but then her mom ruined everything. She wouldn't go into the house, just said she'd rather stay out in the truck while Dylan dropped her gift off. She wouldn't even go in to say hello.

She knew her mom was really worried about work ever since a bunch of animals got sick, and Dylan felt a little selfish worrying about herself and what she wanted when her mom had so much big stuff on her mind.

But she just wanted her to be happy. She and Lucy's dad were perfect for each other. Even though he was old, he was super nice and treated his animals well and he always gave Lucy a big, squeezy hug whenever he saw her.

Why couldn't her mom just cooperate and fall in love with him?

"Dylan? Are you still there?"

She cleared the lump out of her throat so Lucy wouldn't hear how upset she was. How small and jealous those squeezy hugs always made her feel. "Yeah. I'm still here. I was just thinking."

"Do you have any ideas?"

She sighed. "I know they like each other. We just have to make them admit it to each other."

"How?"

"I think we're going to have to do something drastic."

"Like what?" Lucy sounded nervous.

"I read a book once about a girl whose parents were in the middle of a big divorce. She was all mad at them and ran away from home and while they were out looking for her, her mom and dad realized they still loved each other and didn't want to get a divorce after all. It was really mushy and kind of stupid, but maybe we could try that."

Lucy was quiet for a moment. "I don't *want* to run away, do you?" she finally asked. "It's almost January and it's cold outside. We'll freeze to death."

"We could just pretend to run away and hide out somewhere on the ranch or something. Or we don't even have to pretend to run away. We could just pretend we got lost. They'd still have to look for us."

"It doesn't seem very nice to trick them like that. Wouldn't they be awfully mad when they figured it out?"

"I'm doing the best I can," Dylan snapped. "I don't see you coming up with any great ideas." Frustration sharpened her voice, made her sound mean. "I'm starting to think maybe you don't want this to work. Maybe you don't really want to be sisters as much as I do."

Lucy's gasp sounded loud and outraged in her ear. For a minute, Dylan thought she was going to cry. "That's not fair," Lucy said in a low, hurt voice. "I've worked just as hard as you to push them together. It's not my fault nothing has worked."

The hot ball of emotions in her stomach expanded to include shame. "You're right. I'm really sorry, Luce. I'm just worried. I heard Mom on the phone to SueAnn tonight, and she sounded really depressed. I'm afraid if we don't come up with something fast to bring them together, we're going to end up having to move back to California."

"Your mom's having a tough time, isn't she?" Lucy asked quietly.

"Yeah," Dylan said, her voice glum. "I think things are really bad at work. Nobody wants her to treat their animals after what happened to your dad's horses and the others."

Lucy was quiet for a moment. "If you want to run away, I'll do it with you. We can pack warm clothes and even saddle a couple of horses if you want. It will be okay."

"No. I think you're right. I don't think it would work. It was a dumb idea. When they found us, they'd both be really mad."

"What else can we do, then?"

"I don't know. You think about it and I'll think about it and maybe we can come up with something brilliant between now and Friday, when I'm staying over."

After she finally said goodbye and hung up the phone, Dylan lay on her horse-print quilt for a long time, staring out the window at the stars and worrying.

"Okay. Stand back and watch the master at work." With his greased fingers held up like a surgeon's sterile gloves on the way to the operating table, Matt approached the ball of pizza dough on the counter.

"This is so cool," Lucy said to Dylan. "He twirls it

around just like you see guys do on TV." The two of them sat on the edge of the kitchen table, eyes wide with expectation.

"That's right." He lowered his voice dramatically. "You're about to witness a sight many have attempted but few have perfected."

"You're about to see a big show-off." Cassie rolled her eyes from across the kitchen, where she was chopping, slicing and shredding toppings for the annual Diamond Harte New Year's Eve Pizza Extravaganza.

"You're just jealous because this is one thing in the kitchen I can do better than you."

"The only thing," she muttered, and he grinned.

He picked up the dough and started tossing it back and forth between his hands, working the ball until it was round and flat. He finished off with a crowd-pleasing toss in the air that earned him two wide-eyed gasps, then caught it handily and transferred it to the pizza peel Cass had sprinkled with cornmeal.

He presented it to the girls with a flourish. "Here you go. Put whatever you want on it."

"That was awesome," Dylan said. "Do it again!"

"Sure thing, after we get that one in the oven."

The girls took the peel to the other counter where Cass had laid out a whole buffet of toppings from sausage to olives to the artichoke hearts he loved.

With them out of earshot, he finally had a chance to corner his sister. "So why didn't you go to the mayor's party?" he asked sternly. "I thought that was the plan."

She pressed her lips together. "I decided I wasn't in the mood for a big, noisy party after all. I'd much rather be here with the girls."

"I can handle the girls. It's not too late. You've still

got time to get all dressed up and drive over to the Gar-
retts'. A couple of the ranch hands are going, and they
said there'd be a live band and champagne and crab
cakes flown in all the way from Seattle."

"I'd rather stay here and have pizza and root beer
and watch the ball drop in Times Square." She smiled,
but there was that restless edge to it again that filled
him with worry.

She was so distant lately. Distracted, somber. No
matter how hard he tried to find out why, she kept as-
suring him everything was fine.

He sighed, knowing he had to try again.

"Cass—" he began, but she cut him off.

"Don't start with me, Matt. I didn't want to go, okay?
I enjoy a good party as much as anyone, but I just wasn't
in the mood tonight."

"That's just what my mom said. She didn't want to
go anywhere, either." Dylan spoke from behind them.

He turned at the mention of the woman who was
always at the edge of his brain. He hadn't seen Ellie
since that morning in the barn three weeks earlier, but
he hadn't stopped thinking about her, wondering about
her. Brooding about her.

Questions raced through his mind. How was she?
What had she been doing since he saw her last? Why
wouldn't she answer his calls? Did she have a date for
New Year's Eve? He almost asked, then clamped his
teeth together so hard they clicked.

As much as he wanted to know, it wasn't right to in-
terrogate her kid. To his vast relief, Cassie did it for him.

"What's your mom doing tonight?" his sister asked,
and he wanted to kiss her.

"Nothing. She said she was just going to stay home and have a quiet night to herself."

Cass frowned. "That's too bad. I wish I'd known. We could have invited her to have pizza with us."

"I'm not sure if she would have come." Dylan paused, giving him a weird look under her lashes. "She's pretty sad lately."

He stiffened. No way would she have told her kid what went on between them in the barn. So why was Dylan looking at him like the news should mean something to him? Was Ellie upset because of him?

"Why is she sad?" he asked, trying to pretend he wasn't desperate to hear the answer.

Dylan cast another one of those weird looks to Lucy, who quickly looked at the pizza. "I think it's because we're moving back to California," she finally said.

"You're *what*?"

Dylan winced. "Don't tell my mom I told you. I don't think she wants anybody else to know."

He felt as if he'd been punched in the stomach. As if the whole damn world had suddenly gone crazy. "When?"

"I don't know. Nothing's definite yet. Anyway, I don't think she's in the mood for a party, either. That's why she told the mayor's wife she wouldn't be able to go to their house tonight."

It was none of his business, he reminded himself. She'd made that crystal clear the other week in the barn. If she wanted to pack up her kid and head for Timbuktu, he didn't have a damn thing to say about it.

Still, that didn't stop him from pounding his frustration on the second hapless ball of pizza dough. By the time he was done, anger had begun to replace the shock.

Finally he couldn't stand it anymore. He whipped off the apron Lucy gave him for Father's Day the year before and turned to Cassie.

"Can you handle the girls on your own for a while?"

"Sure." She looked at him curiously. "Where are you going?"

The last thing he wanted to do was tell his little sister he planned to go have a few hard words with Ellie Webster. He could just imagine the speculative look she'd give him. "I just need to, uh, run an errand."

She studied him for a moment, then smiled broadly. "Sure. No problem. And while you're there, why don't you ask Ellie if she wants to come out for pizza? I'm sure there'll be plenty left."

"Who said anything about Ellie?" he asked stiffly.

Cass grinned. "Nobody. Nobody at all. What was I thinking? Wherever you're going, drive carefully. You know what kind of idiots take to the road on New Year's Eve."

Still grumbling to himself about little sisters who thought they knew everything—and usually did—Matt bundled into his coat and cowboy hat and went out into the cold.

Well, this was a fine New Year's Eve, sitting alone and eating a frozen dinner. How pathetic could she get?

Quit complaining, Ellie chided herself. *You had offers.*

Several of them, in fact. SueAnn wanted her to go to Idaho Falls to dinner and a show with her and Jerry. Ginny Garrett, whose pet collie she'd fixed a few months ago, had invited her to what she deduced was the big social gala of the year in Salt River, the party she and her husband were throwing. And Lucy and Dylan had invited her out to the ranch to share home-made pizza and a video.

Of the three, the girls' party sounded like the most fun. Unfortunately, it was also the invitation she was least likely to accept. She couldn't imagine anything more grueling than spending the evening with Matt, trying to pretend they were only casual friends, that she hadn't come a heartbeat away from making love with him just a few weeks ago.

Despite putting plenty of energy into it, she hadn't been able to stop thinking about him since that morning. About the way his eyes had darkened with desire, the way his rough hands caressed her skin, the soft words that had completely demolished her defenses.

The way his lack of faith in her had broken her heart.

She'd been right to turn him down, to put this distance between them. She wasn't having much luck falling out of love with him, but at least she couldn't go down any deeper when she didn't have anything to do with him.

Anyway, spending New Year's Eve alone wasn't so bad. With the exception of the frozen dinner, the evening looked promising. She had already taken a nice long soak in the tub using the new strawberry-scented bath beads Dylan had given her for Christmas and put on the comfortable new thermal silk pajamas she'd treated herself to. She'd been lucky enough to find a station on the radio playing sultry jazz and big band music, she was going to pop a big batch of buttered pop-corn later, and she had a good mystery to curl up with.

What else did a woman need?

She turned up the gas fireplace so that flames licked

and danced cozily, then watched the fake logs for a moment with only a little regret for the real thing. Although she might have preferred a cheery little apple-wood blaze, with the crackle and hiss and heavenly aroma, she certainly didn't mind forgoing the mess and work of chopping, splitting and hauling wood.

After a moment, she settled onto the couch, tucking her feet under her. She'd just turned the page when the doorbell rang right in the middle of Glenn Miller's "Moonlight Serenade."

Marking her place, she went to the door, then felt her jaw sag at the man she found on the front porch.

"Matt! What are you doing here? Shouldn't you be digging in to a big slab of pizza right about now?"

"I came to talk some sense into you," he growled.

She stared at him, noting for the first time the firm set of his jaw and the steely glitter in his eyes. "Excuse me?"

"You heard me. Can we do this inside? It's freezing out here."

Without waiting for her answer—or for her to ask what it was, exactly, he wanted to *do* inside—he thrust past her into the house, where he loomed in the small living room like a tomcat trapped in a dollhouse, getting ready to pounce.

She closed the door carefully behind him, shutting out the icy blast of air, then turned to face him. He was obviously furious about something, but she couldn't for the life of her figure out what she might have done this time to set him off.

His glower deepened. "I can't believe you're just going to run away. I thought you had more grit than that."

She opened her mouth, but he didn't wait for her answer. "Isn't that just like a city girl?" he went on angrily. "At the first sign of trouble, you take off running and leave the mess behind for everybody else to clean up. Dammit, you can't leave. You've got obligations here. A life. Your kid deserves better than to be shuttled around like some kind of nomad just because you don't have the gumption to see things through."

She stiffened and returned his glare. "In the first place, don't you tell me what my daughter deserves. In the second, do you mind telling me what in blazes you're talking about?"

For the first time since he'd stomped into her house, he looked a little unsure. "About you leaving. Dylan said you're moving back to California."

"Dylan has a big mouth," she muttered.

"Are you?"

"I don't know. Maybe."

She was seriously considering it. Not that she wanted to—the very idea made her stomach hurt, her heart weep. But she couldn't keep her practice open without any patients. "I haven't made a firm decision yet and I probably won't for a few months yet. But even if I were leaving tomorrow, what business would it be of yours?"

He shifted his weight. "I just don't want you to make a big mistake. I know how much your practice means to you," he went on. "It wouldn't be right for you to give it up without a fight."

"Without a fight?" She hissed out a breath. "I feel as if I've been doing nothing *but* fighting for six months. Each time I treat an animal I wonder if it's the last one. Every time I pay a bill, I wonder if I'll be able to pay it the next month. At some point, I have to face the fact that I can't keep waging a losing battle."

"Things will get better. You've just had a few set-backs."

"Right. I believe that's what Custer said to his men halfway through the battle of Little Big Horn."

"Is this because of the outbreak?"

"Partly. Funny thing," she said pointedly, "but the rest of the ranchers around here don't seem as convinced as I am that I wasn't responsible."

He looked uncomfortable, and she regretted sounding so bitchy. "As I said," she went on before he could respond, "although I'm considering leaving, I haven't made any final decision yet. I don't know why Dylan would have told you otherwise."

"I think she's worried about you. She said you were sad."

A child shouldn't have to worry about anything more earthshaking than whether she'd finished her home-work. She hated that Dylan had spent even a moment fretting about her mother, about the future.

For that reason, if nothing else, maybe she needed to give up this selfish desire for autonomy and take her daughter back to California, where she could make a safe and secure living, even if she found it suffocating.

She also hated that Dylan had blabbed to Matt about her melancholy. She didn't want to talk about any of it, so she turned the subject to him.

"I can't figure you out."

"What's to figure out?"

"Why would you pass up homemade pizza on New Year's Eve to come give me a lecture about perseverance? You don't even like me."

"That's not true. I like you plenty. Too much," he muttered under his breath.

Before she could figure out how to answer that growled admission, he went on. "I care about you. When Dylan told me you were moving to California, I was furious."

His gaze locked with hers, his blue eyes burning with emotions she couldn't even begin to decipher, and he reached for her fingers. "All I could think about was how much I would miss you if you left."

She drew in a shaky breath. "Matt—"

"I know, it's crazy. I don't understand it myself. But I haven't been able to think about anything else except how right, how completely *perfect*, you felt in my arms. And how I want you there again."

She closed her eyes, helpless against the tumble of emotions cascading through her. Listening to this big, gruff man speak words of such sweetness, words she knew would not come easily for him, affected her more than a hundred love songs, a thousand poems.

How could she ever have been stupid enough to think she could lock her heart against him? She had no defenses against a man like Matt Harte. He might seem arrogant and authoritative most of the time, but he cared enough about her to drive out on a snowy night to try to prevent her from making what he considered a grave mistake.

Why was she still fighting against him when she ached to be with him more than she had ever wanted anything in her life?

She loved him.

The sweetness of it seeped through her like hard rain on thirsty earth, collecting in all the crevasses life had carved into her soul. She loved this man, with his rough hands and his slow smile and his soft heart.

When she opened her eyes, she found him watching her warily, as if he expected her to kick him out of her house any minute.

"I've thought of it, too," she answered, barely above a whisper.

"So what are we going to do about it?"

"What else can we do?"

With a deep breath for courage, she stepped forward, wrapped her arms around his neck and lifted her mouth for his kiss.

For just a moment after she stepped forward and lifted her mouth to his, Matt couldn't move, frozen with shock and a fast, thorny spike of desire.

He never expected this. Never. She made it pretty damn clear the other day that she didn't want any kind of relationship with him. He hadn't liked it, but what could he do when she wouldn't give him much room for any kind of argument?

If he'd been thinking at all when he rushed over here after Dylan's little announcement—if he'd been able to focus on anything but his anger that she planned to leave Star Valley—he might have expected Ellie to throw him out the door after he finished giving her a piece of his mind.

Not this. He definitely wouldn't have predicted this soft, searching kiss that was curling through his insides like grapevines on a fence or her arms wrapping around his neck to hold him close.

Just when he was beginning to wonder if he'd ever be able to move again, he felt the whisper-soft touch of her tongue at the corner of his mouth. That's all it took, one tiny lick, and he was lost.

Need exploded through him like a shotgun blast. With a ragged groan, he yanked her against him and devoured her mouth. She smelled like strawberry shortcake and tasted like heaven, and he couldn't get enough.

He'd missed her these few weeks. Missed her laugh and her sweet smile and her smart mouth. He'd wanted to call her a hundred times and had even dialed the number a few times, but had always hung up before the call could go through.

She told him she didn't want a relationship and had obviously been going out of her way to avoid him. And he had too much bitter experience with rejection to push her.

He should have, though. Should have pushed them both. If he'd known she would greet him like this, that she would welcome him into her arms so eagerly, he damn well would have been knocking down her door to get here.

In the background, Miles Davis played some kind of sexy muted trumpet solo. Matt's subconscious registered it with appreciation, but all he could focus on was Ellie and her sweet mouth.

Her hands were busy pulling off his coat, which she tossed on the floor. His hat went sailing after it, then she raked her fingers through his hair, playing at the sensitive spot at the nape of his neck.

He wanted to have her right now, to tangle his fingers in her silky clothes and rip them away, then thrust himself inside her until neither one of them could move.

"I'm not stopping this time," he warned. He would

somehow find the strength to walk away if she asked it of him, but he wasn't about to tell her that.

To his vast relief, she didn't argue. "Good," she breathed against his mouth. "I don't want you to stop. In fact, I'd be really disappointed if you did."

He had to close his eyes, awed at the gift she was offering him. On the heels of his amazement came niggling worry. He hadn't done this in a while, and his body wasn't in any kind of mood to take things slow. It throbbed and ached, eager for hot, steamy passion. Writhing bodies. Heated explorations. Feverish, sloppy kisses that lasted forever.

But Ellie deserved to be wooed, and woo her he would, even if it killed him.

"You smell divine," he murmured, trying fiercely to get a little control over himself.

"Strawberry bath beads." She sounded breathless, aroused. "I just got out of the tub right before you showed up."

He had a quick mental picture of her lithe little body slipping naked into hot, bubbly water—and then climbing back out—and groaned as his hard-fought control slipped another notch.

She would smell like strawberries everywhere, and he suddenly wanted to taste every single inch.

While she was busy working the buttons of his shirt, he trailed his mouth down the elegant line of her throat to whisper kisses just under the silky neckline of her shirt. Her hands stilled, and she arched her throat, unknowingly exposing a tiny amount of cleavage.

He took ruthless advantage of it and pressed his mouth to the sweetly scented hollow, licking and tasting while his hands worked their way under her shirt.

She had nothing on under her thermal silk, he realized, and heat scorched him as his fingers encountered soft, unbound curves.

Her breath hissed in sharply when his thumb danced over a tight nipple, and she seemed to sag bonelessly against him. He lowered her to the soft, thick carpet in front of the fireplace, and she responded by tightening her arms around him, by pressing her soft curves against him.

She had somehow managed to unbutton his shirt, and her hands splayed across his abdomen, branding him with her heat. His stomach muscles contracted, and she smiled and shoved his shirt down over his shoulders.

While the music on the stereo shifted to a honey-voiced woman singing about old lovers and new chances, they undressed each other, stopping only for more of those slow, drugging kisses.

As he removed the last of their clothes, he leaned back on an elbow and stared at her, her skin burnished by flickering firelight. She looked like some kind of wild-haired goddess, and his heartbeat pulsed as equal parts desire and that terrifying tenderness surged over him.

He hadn't wanted this in his life, had done his best to push her away and pretend he wasn't coming to care for her. The scars Melanie had left him with still ached sometimes, made him leery to risk anything of himself.

But Ellie wasn't anything like his ex-wife. He knew it, had known it from the beginning. He just hadn't wanted to face the truth. It was much easier to focus on the few inconsequential things the two women had in common than the hundred of important things separating them. That way he could use the ugliness of his past as a shield against Ellie and her courage and her generous spirit.

Somehow this woman had sneaked into his heart. Now that she was firmly entrenched there, he wondered how he'd ever survived so long without her.

He wanted to take care of her. It sounded macho and stupid, and he knew his fiercely independent Ellie would probably smack him upside the head if he said it aloud, so he tucked the words into his heart along with her.

He wouldn't say them. He would just do everything he could to show her she needed him.

Why was he looking at her like that? Ellie squirmed, wishing his expression wasn't so hard to read sometimes. She felt vulnerable and exposed lying before him with her hair curling wildly around her. At the same time, she had to admit she found it oddly erotic having him watch her with those blue eyes blazing.

Finally she couldn't stand the conflicting emotions anymore. She reached out and pulled him to her, nearly shuddering apart as his hard, taut muscles met her softness.

This was right. Any lingering doubts she might have been harboring floated away into the night as his body covered hers, as his calloused hands skimmed over her, as his mouth devoured her.

She wanted to curl up against him, wanted to let his strength surround her.

"I've thought about this since that first time we kissed in the barn." His voice was low, throaty. "Why have we both been fighting this so hard?"

"Because we're crazy." She smiled a little and pressed a kiss to the throbbing pulse at the base of his throat.

"If I'm crazy, I know exactly who to blame. I haven't had a coherent thought in my head since a certain unnamed little red-haired vet moved into town."

He tugged gently on the hair in question so their gazes could meet. His words and the undisguised hunger in his eyes made her feel fragile and powerful at the same time, beautiful and feminine and *wanted*.

Fresh desire pulsed through her, liquid heat, and she drew in a ragged breath and reached for him.

Their kisses became more urgent, their caresses more demanding. The jazz on the stereo shifted to something haunting, sultry, as he teased her breasts, as his fingers slid across her stomach to the aching heat centered between her thighs, and she shuddered, lost to his touch, to the music weaving sinuously around them.

He pushed one long finger inside her, readying her for him, and she gasped his name and arched against him eagerly.

"You're killing me, Ellie," he growled. "I can't handle much more of this."

"You're the one taking his dear sweet time."

His low laugh sounded raw, strained. "I was trying to go slow for you."

She shivered again as his finger touched on a particularly sensitive spot, and she thought she would die if he didn't come inside her. "Don't do me any favors, Harte," she gasped.

His low laugh slid over her like a caress. "Wouldn't dream of it, Doc."

He reached for something in his jeans—his wallet, she realized—then pulled out a foil-wrapped package.

A moment later, he knelt between her thighs. His gaze met hers, and the fierce emotion there settled right into her heart, and then an instant later his mouth tangled with hers again as he entered her.

Love for this man—this strong, wonderful man—expanded in her heart then flowed out, seeping through every cell. She wrapped her arms tightly around him, wishing she had the words to tell him her feelings for him—or that she had the courage to give him the words, even if she managed to find them.

His movements started out slow, but she wasn't having any of it. She arched against him, begging for more, for fire and thunder and out-of-her-head passion.

He drew back, his breathing ragged. "Slow down. I don't want to hurt you," he growled.

"You won't. I'm not fragile, Matt."

With a harsh groan he drove into her, deep and powerful and demanding, and she shivered even as she met him thrust for thrust. He must have held himself under amazing control, she thought. Now that she'd given him permission to treat her like a woman instead of a china doll, he devoured her, kissing and stroking and inflaming her senses.

He reached for her hands and yanked their entwined fingers above her head so that only their bodies touched, skin to skin, heat to heat.

She never would have expected this wildness from him, the fierce desire that blazed out of him in wave after hot wave until she thought she would scorch away into cinders from it.

A wild, answering need spiraled up inside her, climbing higher and higher with each passing second. She had never known anything like this, this frantic ache.

She gasped his name, suddenly frightened by how close she was to losing control, to losing herself.

He groaned in answer and kissed her deeply, tongue tangling with hers, demanding everything from her, then reached between their bodies to touch her intimately. Just that small caress, the heat of his fingers on the place where she already burned, and she shattered into a thousand quivering pieces.

"I can't get enough of you," he growled before she could come back together again.

He kissed her fiercely, branding her as his, then with one more powerful thrust, he found his own release.

Afterward, she trembled more from reaction than the cold, but Matt reached up to the couch behind them and pulled down the knit throw there. He spread it over them both and pulled her against him.

She snuggled close. "And here I thought I was in for another boring New Year's Eve."

His low laugh tickled the skin at the back of her neck. "Boring is not a word I would ever dare use in the same sentence as you, Doc."

She lifted her gaze to his. "Are you complaining?"

"Hell, no. Even if I had any strength left to complain, I wouldn't dare."

She smiled and settled against his hard chest. He held her tightly with one hand while the other stroked through her hair.

"I used to tell myself I was happy with boring," he said after a few moments. "That's what I thought I wanted. A nice, safe, uneventful life. Then you blew into my life, and I discovered I'd been fooling myself all these years. Safe and uneventful are just other words for lonely."

His low words slid over her, stirring up all kinds of terrifying emotions, and she tensed. Not knowing how to answer—and not at all comfortable with this yearning inside her to stay curled up against him forever— she chose to change the subject. "Cassie and the girls will be wondering where you ran off to."

He studied her, and she had the awful suspicion he knew exactly how uneasy his words made her, then he shrugged. "I doubt it. At least Cass won't. Apparently my little sister knows a lot more about me than I'd like to think she does. More than I know myself. She asked me to invite you out to the ranch for the rest of the pizza party, if the girls haven't eaten it all by now."

"Oh. That was very kind of her."

"You could stay over in the guest room."

She thought about spending the evening not being able to touch him and she sighed. "I'd better pass."

"Why?"

"We have to tread carefully here, Matt. Really carefully. Think about the girls."

"What about them?"

"They can't know about…about any of this. How would they react?"

She saw understanding dawn in his eyes, and he winced. "Right."

"This can't affect them. I don't want either of them hurt."

Dylan would build this into a happily-ever-after kind of thing, something Ellie knew was impossible. She knew perfectly well that her daughter pined for a father, and she'd be over the moon imagining Matt in that role. Ellie didn't want to see her heart get broken.

"What are you suggesting?" he asked quietly. "If

you're going to tell me some bull about how you think this was a mistake that won't happen again, I might have to get mean."

If she were stronger, that's exactly what she *would* say. Letting this go any further would only end in heartache. For all she knew, she'd be moving back to California in the next few months. How much worse was it going to be to say goodbye now that she knew the wonder of being in his arms?

Still, she couldn't seem to find the words to push him away. "We just have to be careful," she said instead. "That's all I'm saying."

They stayed that way together on the floor for a long time, wrapped around each other while the soft music flowed around them. She couldn't touch him enough. His rough hands, his hard chest, the ridged muscles of his stomach. Eventually their caresses grew bold again, and she gasped when he picked her up as if she were no heavier than a runty calf and carried her to her bedroom.

There he made love to her again—slower this time, as if he planned to spend the whole new year touching her just so, kissing her exactly right, then he entered her and each slow, deep thrust seemed to steal a little more of her soul.

Afterward, she lay limp and boneless in his arms, content to listen to his heart and feel his arms around her. If the house caught fire just then, she wasn't sure she could summon the energy to crawl out of bed.

"I don't want you to leave," he said against her hair.

"This is my house." She was wonderfully, sinfully exhausted. "If anyone leaves, I'm guessing it will be you."

"You know what I mean. I'm talking about you going back to California." He was quiet for a moment, then he pressed another kiss to her hair. "You know, if your practice is really struggling that much, I could give you the money to keep it going."

In an instant, the world seemed to grind to a halt, like an amusement park ride that had abruptly lost power. The sleepy, satisfied glow surrounding her popped, leaving her feeling chilled to the bone.

She wrenched away from him and sat up, clutching the quilt to her breasts. "You what?"

"I could give you the money. Just to tide you over until things start looking up."

The roaring in her ears sounded exactly like the sea during a violent storm. "Let me get this straight. You want to ride in like some kind of knight in shining armor and give me the money to save my practice."

He shrugged, looking faintly embarrassed. "Something like that."

Fury and hurt and shame vied for the upper hand as she jumped from the bed and yanked on her robe.

"What's the matter?"

She didn't even spare him a glance. "Your timing stinks, Harte."

"What?" He sounded genuinely befuddled.

He didn't have a clue. She drew in a deep breath. "Let me give you a little advice. Next time, don't offer a woman money when her body is still warm from having you inside her unless the two of you have agreed on a price beforehand."

She thought of her mother, of the faceless, nameless strangers who had skulked in and out of her bed after her father left. The squeak of the rusty screen door as another of Sheila's "friends" dropped by, the low, suggestive laughter in the kitchen, the heavy footsteps down the hall toward her mother's filthy bedroom.

Hiding in her room with a pillow over her head so she wouldn't have to hear what came after.

Even then, at seven years old, she'd known what they were doing, had felt sick, dirty. And she'd known that in the morning, Sheila would have enough money for another bottle of oblivion.

That Matt would offer this, would put her in the same category as her mother, brought all those feelings rushing back.

"You know that's not what I meant." Anger roughened his voice. "I can't believe that kind of cheap thought would ever enter your head. It's demeaning to me and to you. Dammit, Ellie. I care about you. I want to help you. And why shouldn't I, when I have the means? What's wrong with that?"

"I don't want your help. I never asked for it."

"You'd rather have to give up the practice you love? The life you love? You'd rather go back to California and leave everything here behind?"

"If I have to, yes."

She stormed out of the bedroom, desperate to put space between them, but of course he stalked after her, fastening the buttons of his jeans and shrugging into his shirt as he followed.

"That's the stupidest thing I've ever heard you say. Why are you so upset about this? Just call it a loan. You can pay me back when business picks up."

"What if it doesn't? How will I pay you back then? By sleeping with you? Should I start keeping a little ledger by my bed? Mark a few dollars off every time you

come over? Tell me, Matt, since I don't have any idea—
what's the going hourly rate for prostitutes these days?"

He went still, and she knew her jab had struck home.
"That's not fair," he said quietly.

It wasn't. She knew it even as the bitter words flowed
out of her like bile. He didn't deserve this, but she
couldn't seem to stop, lost in the awful past.

All he did was offer his help. He couldn't be blamed
because she found herself in the terrible position of
needing it.

"I'm sorry," she said stiffly. "You're right. Thank you
for your kind offer but I'm not quite desperate enough
yet that I'd take money from you."

He glared at her. "Is that supposed to be an apology?
Because it sure as hell didn't sound like one from here."

"It's whatever you want it to be."

He was quiet, his face a stony mask. "You don't want
to take anything from anyone, do you?"

"Not if I can help it."

"And if you can't? What are you going to do then?"

She hated the coldness in his voice, the distance, even
though she knew she'd put both things there. Regret was
a heavy ache in her heart. A few moments ago they had
shared amazing tenderness and intimacy, and now they
were acting like angry strangers with each other. It was
her fault, she knew it. This was a stupid argument, but
it was also symptomatic of the greater barriers to any
relationship between them.

She had been fooling herself to think they could ever
have anything but this one magical night.

"I'll figure that out if that day ever comes," she finally said. "Go home, Matt. It's New Year's Eve, you

should be with your family. If you hurry, you'll make it home before the clock strikes midnight."

He stood there glaring at her, looking big and gorgeous and furious, then without another word he yanked on his coat, grabbed his hat and slammed out the door.

Chapter 14

Three weeks into the new year, the temperature spiked in western Wyoming in what the locals called the annual January thaw.

Though the temperature barely hovered above forty degrees and genuinely warm weather was still months away, the mountain air smelled almost like spring. Snow melted from every building in steady drips, kids put away their sleds and took out their bikes instead, and a few overachieving range cows decided to drop their calves a few weeks early.

She was far from busy, but Ellie was grateful to at least have a few patients to occupy her time.

She'd spent most of the day trying to ease a new Guernsey calf into the world for one of her few remaining clients. She still had the warm glow of satisfaction from seeing that wobbly little calf tottering around the pasture.

In the excitement of watching new life, she had almost been able to forget the clouds hanging over her head, this terrible fear that her time here amid these mountains she had come to love so dearly was drawing to a close.

Her choices were becoming increasingly limited. Fight as she may against the truth, she knew she couldn't keep hanging on by her fingernails much longer.

She drew in a deep breath. Maybe she ought to just forget about trying to go it alone and join forces with Steve Nichols. At least then she could stay in Salt River.

He might not be willing anymore, though. He hadn't asked her about it for weeks, and lately he'd been cool and distracted every time they talked, making her wonder and worry what she had done. Maybe he, like everyone else in town, had lost all respect for her.

She could always take out a loan from Matt.

The thought, sinuous and seductive, whispered into her mind, but she pushed it away. Never. She couldn't do something that extreme, no matter what desperate straits she found herself in.

Despite her resolve, she knew she owed him an apology for her overreaction on New Year's Eve. Remorse burned in her stomach whenever she thought about how she had lashed out at him.

She hadn't seen him since the night he had come to her house. The previous evening, the committee for the Valentine's carnival had met for the last time before the big event, and she'd spent all day with her nerves in an uproar over seeing him again.

It had all been for nothing, though. He'd sent a message with Sandy Nielson that a ranch emergency came up at the last minute and he wouldn't be able to make it.

She was relieved, she tried to tell herself. The last thing she needed to deal with right now was the inevitable awkwardness between them.

She sighed as she drove through town. Who was she kidding? She missed him. Missed his sexy drawl and the way his eyes crinkled at the edges and the way he could make her toes curl with just a look.

The sun was sliding behind the mountains in a brilliant display of pink and lavender that reflected in wide puddles of melting snow as she drove into the clinic's parking lot. She pulled the truck into the slot next to SueAnn's Suburban and climbed out, determined that she would do her best not to think about the blasted man for at least the next ten minutes.

SueAnn popped up from her desk like a prairie dog out of her hole when Ellie walked in.

"How did it go?" she asked.

Ellie forced a smile. "Not bad. Mama and calf are doing well. I was afraid for a while we'd lose them both but we finally managed to pull the calf and everything turned out okay."

"I'm sure that's a big relief to Darla. She loves that little milk cow."

Ellie nodded. "She says hello, by the way, and she'll see you tomorrow night at the library board meeting. Any messages?"

SueAnn handed her a small pink pile. "None of these were urgent. Mostly carnival committee members needing your input on last-minute details. Oh, but Jeb Thacker's having trouble with Cleo again. He wondered when he could bring her in tomorrow. I told him anytime. And here's the mail. Bills, mostly."

Ellie took it, wondering what she was going to do

when she left Star Valley without SueAnn to screen her mail for her.

"Oh, I almost forgot. The lab finally sent the results for that tox screen you ordered."

Ellie froze in the process of thumbing through the messages. The culture results on the animals that had fallen ill before Christmas. "Where is it?"

"Here." SueAnn handed over a thin manila envelope, and Ellie immediately ripped it open and perused the contents.

"What does it say?"

"It looks like the samples all were infected with an unusual strain of bacteria, just like Steve suspected. That's why it took so long for the results. The lab had never seen it in horses before."

"Could it have been spread by your needles?"

"Maybe." It wasn't outside the realm of possibility that the needles had been contaminated, although she would never believe that had been the cause. Damn. She had hoped for answers, for something that could definitively absolve her of responsibility.

SueAnn touched her arm. "I'm sorry it wasn't better news."

She forced a smile as the weight of failure pressed down hard on her shoulders. "Thanks."

"You have anything left for me to do today?" SueAnn asked. "It's almost six, and Jerry's got a touch of the flu. Last time he stayed home sick from work, he maxed out three credit cards on the home shopping channel."

"You'd better hurry, then, or you'll get home and find he bought a dozen cans of spray-on hair replacement."

As SueAnn switched off her computer and turned on the answering machine, Ellie unfolded from the edge of the desk. "Where's Dylan? Is she in the back doing her homework?"

SueAnn froze in the process of pulling her purse out of her bottom desk drawer. "I haven't seen her. She never came in after school." Anxiousness crept into her voice. "I… I just assumed she went home with Lucy. You didn't mention it before you went out to Darla's, but I figured it must have slipped your mind."

Unease bloomed to life inside Ellie like a noxious weed. "I don't remember her telling me anything about riding the school bus to the ranch today."

"Maybe it was a spur of the moment thing."

"Maybe." If she went to the ranch without leaving a message, Dylan was in serious trouble. Ellie's one strict, inarguable rule was that Dylan had to leave her where-abouts with her mother or with SueAnn at all times.

A hundred terrible scenarios flashed through her mind in the space of a few seconds until she reined in her thoughts. No. This was Star Valley, Wyoming. Things like that didn't happen here.

"I'll just call the ranch. You're probably right. I'm sure that's where she is." She dialed the number then twisted the cord around her fingers while she waited for Matt or Cassie to answer. No one picked up after fifteen rings, and her stomach knotted with worry.

"I am so sorry, El." SueAnn looked sick. "I should have called you when she didn't show up just to make sure everything was cool."

"Let's not panic until we have reason. She and Lucy are probably just playing outside in this warm weather, or maybe she went home with one of her other friends."

"Do you want me to run out to the ranch and see if she's there?"

"No. You go on home to Jerry. I'll just check at the house and buzz by the school. If I don't find her at either of those places, I'll drive out to the ranch."

She would find her daughter safe and sound. She *had* to. She absolutely refused to consider any alternative.

It had been one hell of a week.

The tractor bounced and growled as Matt drove through foot-deep muck on the way to the barn after delivering the evening feed to the winter pasture. Cows had been dropping calves like crazy with all this warm weather, the ranch was a muddy mess, and to make matters worse, two of his ranch hands quit on the same day.

He hadn't had a good night's sleep in longer than he could remember, every muscle in his body ached, and his shoulder hurt where he'd been kicked by an ornery horse that caught him off guard.

Days like this, he wondered if it was all worth it. All he wanted was dinner and his bed, and at this point he was even willing to forget about the dinner.

At the barn, he switched off the tractor, making a mental note that the engine seemed a little wompy and would need to be checked before planting season. He climbed out and shut the door behind him when he saw Ellie's battered pickup pull up to the house.

Of all the people he would have expected to show up at the ranch, she would just about come in last on the list. He hadn't been able to forget the bitter words she'd flung at him, the way she had thrown his offer of help back in his face.

He could see now that she'd been right, his timing could have been a whole lot better. But his intentions had been good.

A moment later, she swung open her truck door and hopped out. She was small and compact and, despite his lingering anger, heat rushed to his groin just remembering how that lithe little body had felt under him, around him.

She walked up the porch steps to ring the doorbell, and he made a face. Cassie wasn't home, and he was a little tempted to let her stand there ringing away in vain. He immediately felt spiteful for entertaining the idea even for an instant and headed toward the house.

As soon as he was close enough to catch a glimpse of the worry in her expression, he was heartily relieved he hadn't obeyed the petty impulse.

"What's the matter, Doc?"

She whirled, and relief spread over her face when she saw him. "Matt! I was afraid nobody was home. Did Dylan come home on the bus with Lucy today?"

He frowned. "Lucy didn't take the bus today. Cass picked her up after school so they could go shopping in Idaho Falls for something to wear to the Valentine's carnival. They're not back yet. She didn't come home?"

Ellie shook her head, her green eyes murky and troubled. "I don't know where she is. She usually walks to the clinic after school. When she didn't show up today, SueAnn thought she must have come home with Lucy."

"I suppose there's a chance she might have gone with them on the shopping trip, although I think she would have cleared it with you first. She's a good kid. Just taking off like that doesn't seem like something she'd do."

"No. You're right."

She looked helpless and frightened. As he saw her mouth tremble, his remaining anger slid away. He hurried up the steps and pulled her into his arms.

"We'll go in and call Cass on the cell phone. If she's not with them, maybe Lucy will know something. It'll be okay, Ellie."

She must be out of her mind with worry or she never would have let him lead her into the house and settle her into one of the kitchen chairs while he crossed to the phone hanging on the wall. He was just dialing the number when he heard another vehicle pull up outside.

"That's probably them now."

The words were barely out of his mouth when Ellie jumped up and headed toward the door. He followed close on her heels and saw her shoulders sag with disappointment when only Cassie and Lucy climbed out of his sister's Cherokee.

Cassie's eyes widened when she saw Ellie. "Everything okay?" she asked, instantly concerned.

In the circle of light on the porch, Ellie looked small and lost, her expression bordering on panic. A mother suddenly living her worst nightmare. Sensing she was on the verge of losing control, Matt grabbed her arm and guided her up the steps to the door and into the warmth of the house.

"Come on inside," he said over his shoulder to his sister. "I'll explain everything."

By the time they made it into the kitchen, Ellie had once more gained control of her emotions, although her eyes still looked haunted.

"Lucy," she began. "Dylan didn't go to the clinic after school today. Do you know anything about where she might have gone?"

For a moment, his daughter just stared, then color leached from her face and she looked like she was choking on something. She pressed her lips together and suddenly seemed extremely interested in the green-checkered tablecloth.

"Lucy?" he said sternly. "What do you know about this?"

"Nothing." She wouldn't look him in the eye and clamped both hands over her mouth, as if she were afraid something would slip out.

"Did she say anything to you after school about where she might be going? Can you think of any other friends she might have gone home with?" Ellie asked, her voice thin, pleading.

"No," Lucy said through her fingers in barely a whisper. Her chin wobbled, and she looked like she was going to cry any minute now. Once she started, they'd never get anything out of her, he realized.

Instead of obeying his first impulse to ride her hard about it until she told them what was going on, he knelt to her level and pulled her into his arms.

"Lucy, sweetheart, this is important. Her mom is really worried about her, just like I would be if you were missing. I know Dylan is your friend and you don't want to get her in trouble, but if you know anything about where she might be, you have to tell us."

She looked at the floor for a moment, and a tear slipped out of the corner of her eye and dripped down her nose. "She said she wasn't going to do it. She said it wouldn't *work*," she wailed.

"What? What did she say wouldn't work?" Ellie asked urgently.

Lucy clamped her lips together, then expelled the words in a rush of air. "We were gonna run away."

"Run away?" Ellie again looked lost and bewildered.

"Why? What was so terrible that she thought she had to run away?"

"We weren't really gonna run away. Just pretend." Lucy sniffled. "Dylan thought if the two of you had to look for us together, you guys would finally see how much you liked each other and you would get married and we could be sisters for real."

Thunderstruck, Matt looked from his daughter to Ellie. At Lucy's admission, color flooded Ellie's face, and her horrified eyes flashed to his then focused on the same tablecloth Lucy had found so interesting.

Oblivious to their reaction, his rascal of a kid plodded on. "We decided it wouldn't work and that you'd be too mad when you found out what we did. We were trying to come up with a better plan but I guess maybe she decided to do it by herself anyway. I can't believe she didn't tell me what she was going to do," she finished in a betrayed-sounding voice.

"But where would she go?" Ellie exclaimed. "It's January. It's cold and dark out there."

"I don't know." Lucy started to sniffle again. "We were gonna hide out in one of the ranch buildings."

"She wouldn't have been able to walk all the way out here." Cassie frowned. "She must have gone somewhere in town."

Matt headed for the door. "I'll send the ranch hands out looking around for her just in case. Cassie, call Jess and let him know what's going on. Meanwhile, Ellie, you and I can run back to town and see if she might have turned up at your house or at the clinic. Who knows, maybe her teacher has some clue where she might have gone."

* * *

Grateful to have a concrete plan instead of this mindless panic, she nodded and followed him out to his truck.

On the six-mile ride to town, she was silent and tense, her mind racing with terrible possibilities. While Matt drove, he compensated for her reticence by keeping up a running commentary about everything and nothing, more words than she'd ever heard from him.

He was doing it to keep her from dwelling too long on all those awful scenarios. She knew it and was touched by his effort but she still couldn't get past her worry to carry on a real conversation with him.

The trip from the ranch to town had never seemed so long. "Let's stop at your house first," Matt said when they finally passed the wooden city limit sign. "It's on the way and that seems the logical place for her to go."

When she didn't answer, he reached a hand across the seat to cover hers. "Hang in there, Doc. She's probably sitting at home waiting for you to get there and wondering if she'll still be grounded by the time she graduates from college."

She managed a shaky smile and turned her hand over to clasp his fingers. Reassured by the heat and strength there, she clung to his hand the rest of the way. When she saw her little brick bungalow was still dark and silent, her fingers tightened in his.

Matt pulled in to the driveway and turned off the pickup's rumbling engine. He gave her hand a comforting squeeze. "Okay, she's not here. But maybe she left a message for you."

Trying to keep the panic at bay, Ellie climbed from the truck and unlocked the side door leading to the kitchen. When she saw no blinking light on the answering machine, she almost sobbed. She probably would have if Matt hadn't followed her inside.

Instead, she flipped on every light in the kitchen, even the one over the stove. It seemed desperately important suddenly, as if she could fight the darkness inside her.

That done, she moved through the house urgently, only vaguely aware of Matt shadowing her while she turned on the lights in every single room until the house blazed like a Christmas tree.

The porch light. She should turn that on, too, so her little girl could find her way home.

She went to the front door and flipped the switch. Just as she turned away, something jarring, out of place, caught the edge of her vision through the small beveled window in the door.

She pushed aside the lace curtain for a better look, then felt the blood leave her face and a horrified scream well up in her throat. What came out was a pathetic little whimper like a distressed kitten's, but it was enough for Matt to grab her and shove her aside so he could look.

He bit out a string of oaths and yanked the door open. "What the hell is that?"

Her hands began to shake, and she was afraid she was going to be sick. "I… I think it's a calf fetus."

The yellow porch light sent a harsh glare on the poor little creature, still covered with the messy fluids of birth. She forced herself to walk toward it and saw at once that it was malformed and had probably been born dead.

Matt crouched beside the animal. "Dammit. Why can't Jesse find whoever is doing this to you?"

It had to be connected to the cat left in her truck. She

could see that another note had been impaled to the side of the calf with an acupuncture needle.

She didn't want to look at it. She would rather shove the needle through her own tongue, would rather have a hundred needles jammed into every inch of her body than have to face the idea that there could be some link between this gory offering and her baby.

But there had to be. She knew it as sure as death.

"He's got her," she said raggedly.

Matt stared. "Who?"

"Whoever left this has Dylan. I know it."

She couldn't breathe suddenly, couldn't think. Could only watch numbly while he ripped the note away to read it, then uttered a long string of oaths.

"What does it say?"

Wordlessly, he handed her the note. Her stomach heaved after she read it, and she had to press a hand to her mouth as bile choked her throat.

"If you don't want your kid to end up like this," the note said in that same ominous black type that had been used for the note left in her truck, "you're going to have to prove it."

Chapter 15

Prove it? Prove it how?

Ellie stared at the note in her hand, afraid that if she looked away from those sinister words she would find the whole world had collapsed around her. This couldn't be happening. Salt River, Wyoming, was a slice of America. Soccer games, PTA meetings, decent, hardworking people. She would never suspect someone here could be capable of such hideous evil.

Her baby.

Someone had her little girl.

She thought of Dylan, helpless and scared and wondering where her mother was, and she felt herself sway as every drop of blood rushed from her head.

Instantly, Matt was there, folding her into his arms. "Hang on, sweetheart. Stay with me."

"I have to find her. He has her."

"Shh. I know. I'll call Jess. He'll know what to do."

The phone in the kitchen jangled suddenly, sounding obscenely loud in the quiet house. She stared at it, then her heart began to pound. It was him. She knew it without a shadow of doubt.

She raced into the other room and grabbed the phone before it could ring again. "Where is she, you sick son of a bitch?" she snarled.

An electronically disguised voice laughed roughly in her ear. "You'll find out. If you do what you're told."

"What do you want?"

"You're still here. I thought I told you to leave. You obviously didn't learn your lesson."

"I'll go. I'll leave now, tonight. Please, just bring back my little girl." She hated the pleading in her voice but she would have groveled to the devil himself if it would have kept her baby safe.

A bitter laugh rang in her ear. "I won't make it that easy on you anymore. You had your chance. Now you have to cough up a hundred grand before you kiss Star Valley goodbye."

"I don't have that kind of money!" Sheer astonishment raised her voice at least an octave.

"You'd better find it by tomorrow noon. I'll let you know the drop-off site."

Before she could answer, could beg to at least talk to her daughter and make sure she was safe, the line went dead.

For several seconds, she stood in the harsh lights of her kitchen holding the phone while the dial tone buzzed in her ear. Then she carefully replaced it onto the base, collapsed into the nearest chair and buried her face in her hands.

* * *

Matt found her there when he returned to the kitchen after hanging up the extension in the bedroom. Everything in him screamed out to comfort her, but he knew he had to deal with necessities first. He called Jesse's emergency number, then quickly and succinctly laid out for his brother what had happened.

That done, he finally could turn his attention to Ellie. He knelt by her side and pulled her trembling form into his arms. "We'll get her back, Doc. Jesse's a good man to have on your side. He'll find her."

Her breathing was fast and uneven, and she seemed as fragile as a snowflake in his arms. "Where am I going to come up with a hundred thousand dollars in cash by noon tomorrow?"

"Me."

She stared at him, eyes dazed like a shell-shocked accident victim. "You?"

"I'll call the bank right now and get started on the paperwork." The ranch had a line of credit more than twice what the kidnapper was asking—plenty of credit and enough influence that he shouldn't have any problem rushing things through.

"It's almost seven-thirty," she said numbly. "The bank closed hours ago."

"The bank manager played football with me in high school. I'll call him at home. When Rick hears the story, I know he'll want to help, even if he has to work all night putting the ransom together."

He could almost see the objections gather like storm clouds in her eyes. Damn stubborn woman was going to put up a fuss even now. Sure enough, she shook her head. "No. I can't take your money. I'll... I'll figure something else out."

"Like what? Sell a kidney?"

That little chin of hers tilted toward the ceiling. "I don't know. But this is my problem, and I'll find a way."

It took everything in him not to reach out and shake her until her teeth rattled. This was for real. Didn't she realize that? He didn't have either the time or the patience to work at wearing down that brick wall of independence she insisted on building around herself.

"Look," he snapped, "I'm going to help you, whether you want me to or not, so just deal with it."

"This is serious money, Matt."

"Chances are the bastard won't get far enough away to spend even a few dollars of it before Jess finds him. I mean it, you don't have a choice, Ellie. For once, just accept my help gracefully."

She studied him, her green eyes murky with fear and frustration, then she crossed to the phone and ripped off a piece of paper from a pad next to it, scribbled on it for a moment, then handed it to him.

"These are my terms."

He read it quickly, then scowled. "What the hell is this?"

"I'll let you help with the ransom only if I can deed over the clinic and this house to you. It's probably not binding just handwritten like that, but I'll have official papers drawn up as soon as I can. You have my word on it."

"No way. Then what will you do without a clinic?"

"I'll be leaving anyway," she said tonelessly. "I won't be needing it."

He refused to think about how the idea of her leaving sliced into him like a jagged blade. "What am I supposed to do with an animal hospital? I'm a rancher, not a vet."

"Sell it and take the profits. It won't begin to cover what you're loaning me, but it will be a start. I'll have to figure out a way to pay back the rest as soon as I can."

He wanted to crumple it up and throw it in her face, but now wasn't the time for his temper to flare. If this was the only way she would take his help, he would let her think he was agreeing to her terms. Then he would shred the blasted thing into tiny little pieces and mail them to her.

As he pocketed the paper, a bleak resignation settled in his gut.

She was leaving, and there wasn't a damn thing he could do about it.

Her mom was gonna be so mad.

Dylan tried to keep from shivering, but it was really hard, not only because it was cool and damp on the straw-covered cement floor but also from the fear that was like a big mean dog chewing away inside her.

She didn't have a clue where she was or who had put her here. But she did know she was in serious trouble.

This was all her fault for disobeying. Her mom told her she was always supposed to walk right to the clinic after school, and she usually did. Today, though, she'd decided to take the long way.

Cheyenne Ostermiller said her dad was going to sell her pony since she got a new horse for her birthday and that if Dylan wanted to buy it, she could probably get a good deal.

She wanted that pony so bad.

It was all she had been able to think about since lunch, when Cheyenne told her about it. All afternoon, during math and music and writer's workshop, she hadn't been able to do anything but daydream about having her own horse. Taking care of it, feeding it, riding anytime she wanted.

Since it didn't look like her mom was going to marry Mr. Harte any time soon, she at least ought to be able to get a horse of her very own. It was only fair.

All she planned to do was walk by Cheyenne's house and take a look at the paint in the pasture. Maybe make friends with him, if he'd let her. It was pretty far out of the way on the edge of town, but she figured if she hurried she'd only be a little late to the clinic and SueAnn wouldn't even notice.

The pony had been perfect. Sweet and well-mannered and beautiful. She'd been standing there petting him and trying to figure out how she could convince her mom to buy him when she heard a truck pull up.

She hadn't paid much attention, thinking it was probably Cheyenne's mom or dad. Next thing she knew, somebody had grabbed her from behind and stuffed a rag that tasted like medicine into her mouth. It must have been something to put her to sleep because the next thing she knew, she woke up lying on the straw in this windowless cement room that reminded her of the quarantine room at the clinic.

She shivered again and pulled her parka closer around her. If only it were the clinic. Then she could bang on the door and bring SueAnn or her mom running.

This was newer than her mom's clinic, though. And instead of being clean and nice, this room had an icky smell, and the straw on the cement floor didn't seem very fresh.

Where could she be? And who would want to kidnap her?

If she weren't so scared, she might have been able to look on this whole thing as a big adventure, something to tell Lucy and the other kids at school about. But she couldn't help thinking about her mom and how worried she probably was and how mad she was gonna be when she found out Dylan hadn't gone straight home after school.

Tears started burning in her throat, and she sniffled a few times, but then she made herself stop. She couldn't be a crybaby. Not now. Crying didn't help anything, that's what her mom always said.

Her mom never cried. But she figured even her mom would have been a little scared a few moments later when there was a funny noise by the door then the knob started to turn.

She huddled as far into the corner as she could, her heart pounding a mile a minute, as a man walked through the door wearing a stupid-looking clown mask with scraggly yellow hair.

"You're awake." The voice from inside the mask sounded hollow and distorted, like when you talked into a paper cup, only a whole lot spookier.

She was afraid she was gonna pee in her pants and she was breathing as hard as she did when Mrs. Anderson made them run a mile in gym class, but she tried to stay calm, just like her mom would have done.

"Keep your hands off me. I know karate," she lied. "I'll kick you so hard in the you-know-where, you'll wish you were dead."

Through the round holes for eyes in the plastic clown mask, she could see pale blue eyes widen, and the alarm in them gave her confidence to sit up a little straighter.

"No. You've got this all wrong. That's disgusting! I'm not going to touch you. Look, I just brought you a couple of blankets and a pillow. It's cold in here. I'm sorry, but I didn't have any place else to put you."

She stuck her jaw in the air defiantly. "How about my house?"

The kidnapper made a sound that might have been a laugh. "Nice try. But I'm afraid that's not possible right now. You're stuck with me for a while, kid."

He handed the blankets and a small pillow to her but she refused to reach for them, just continued watching him warily.

"Nobody's going to hurt you," he said impatiently. "Just don't make any trouble and you'll be back with your mom by lunchtime tomorrow, I promise."

"Why should I believe you?"

"Believe what you want. Makes no difference to me. I have to go out for a while. Are you hungry? I can pick up some dinner for you on the way back, if you want. How about a nice hamburger and some French fries from the drive-up?"

Despite her fear, her mouth watered, since she'd been too busy talking about Cheyenne's pony to eat much of the cafeteria's chicken surprise at lunchtime. She wasn't about to tell him that, though, so she kept her lips stubbornly zipped.

The clown mask wobbled a little as the man sighed. "I'll take that as a yes. I'll be back in a little while. Maybe later, I can bring a TV in for you if that will help pass the time."

After he left, she wanted to throw a pillow at the door. What a jerk, if he really thought he could make everything all better by bringing her a hamburger and a TV.

She wanted to go home and hug her mom and tell her she was sorry. She wanted to sleep in her own bed, not in some stinky cement room with moldy straw on the floor.

There had to be some way to get out of here. But how?

She spread one blanket on the floor, then sat down and crossed her legs and wrapped the other one around her. She could figure this out. She just had to put her mind to it.

After a minute of thinking hard, a smile suddenly crept over her face, and she knew exactly what she was going to do.

See, she had this plan....

Matt stood in the doorway between Ellie's living room and kitchen feeling about as useful as a milk bucket under a bull.

His brother had taken over as soon as he arrived, and now Jess was on the couch holding both of Ellie's hands while he briefed her on what was happening. "The FBI handles kidnapping cases but they can't get agents here from Salt Lake City for at least an hour or two," Jess was saying.

"That long?" Her voice sounded small, tight, not at all like the confident, self-assured woman he'd come to care about so much.

"I'm sorry, Ellie. It takes time to mobilize a team and send them up here by chopper. In the meantime, I have every one of my officers and as many deputies as the sheriff could spare out interviewing anybody who might have seen her after school. They'll keep in constant contact and let us know if anything breaks."

She drew in a ragged-sounding breath, and Jesse squeezed her hands. "Dispatch is getting call after call from people wanting to help look for her. Your buddy Steve Nichols has offered to head up the volunteer search effort and he's getting plenty of support. Nobody in town wants to believe something like this could happen in Star Valley."

"Thank you so much for everything you're doing," she said softly.

Jess's mouth twisted into a reassuring smile. "We'll find her, El. I promise."

Given the circumstances, Matt was ashamed of himself for the powerful urge raging through him to yank his little brother off the couch and shove him out the door.

It really chapped his hide that she could sit there looking all grateful to Jess for what he was doing to help find Dylan and still go all prickly at Matt's offer to help.

She wouldn't grab Matt's hand if she were drowning, yet she seemed to think Jess hung the damn moon.

All this time, he thought she just had a hard time letting anyone help her. Now he realized it was only *him* whose help she didn't want. Why? Was it only his brother's badge that made the difference?

He cared about her a whole hell of a lot more than Jess did. They had a relationship, as stormy as it had been. So why did she continue to push him away?

"You've been so kind," she said to his brother, and Matt decided he'd taken just about all he could.

"I'm going to call Rick about getting started on the

ransom," he said abruptly, daring either of them to argue with him. Her kid was a lot more important than his hurt feelings, and he needed to keep that uppermost in his mind. "I'll use my cell phone so I don't tie up your line here."

He stalked outside and noticed the temperature had dropped. A cold wind howled out of the south, promising an end to the January thaw. He barely felt it sneaking through his coat as he made his way to his truck, ashamed of himself for letting his temper get the better of him.

Inside the truck, he quickly dialed Rick Marquez's number. The bank manager answered on the second ring, and Matt quickly filled him in on Dylan's kidnapping.

"I just heard," Rick said, his voice tight with shock. "MaryBeth just got off the phone with Janie Montgomery, whose niece works over at the police station. Any leads on what kind of an SOB would do such a terrible thing?"

"Jess is working on it."

"How's Dr. Webster holding up?"

"Pretty shook up. Who wouldn't be?"

"It's a real shame. Nice woman like that. Anything I can do?"

"Matter of fact, Rick, there is. I need to borrow some money from my line of credit." He cleared his throat. "Um, a hundred thousand dollars. Think you could round up that much cash by tomorrow morning?"

There was a long, pregnant pause on the other end of the phone. Even though he was the meanest linebacker Star Valley High had ever seen and had fooled many an opponent into thinking he was just another dumb jock,

Rick was as smart as a bunkhouse rat. "You're giving Ellie the money for the ransom?"

The speculation in his friend's voice made him bristle. Would everybody in town have the same prurient reaction? Probably, if word got out. He blew out a breath, suddenly realizing at least one of the reasons Ellie objected to his help. People were going to read far more into it than just one friend helping out another.

"Yeah," he said gruffly. "Yeah, I am. You got a problem with that?"

"You sure that's a good idea, Matt?"

He had no choice. Even though she would probably choke on her own tongue rather than admit it, she needed his help. And he was damn well going to give it.

"Can you get the money or not?" he asked, impatience sharpening his tone.

"It will take a lot of wrangling tonight, but I think I should be able to get my hands on that much."

"Good. Let me know as soon as the papers are ready and I'll come sign them."

After a moment, Rick ventured into risky waters again. "Is there something going on between you and Ellie Webster I should know about?"

Other than I'm crazy in love with her? The thought rocketed into his head, and he stared out the windshield as the wind rattled the skeletal branches of her sugar maple tree.

Love? No way. He didn't love her. He couldn't. He just didn't have that in him anymore. Not after Melanie.

On the other hand, what else could he call it when he suddenly couldn't imagine a life without her?

Yeah. He had it bad. He was only shocked it took him this long to figure it out.

"Matt?" Rick's voice yanked him back to the conversation.

"We're friends," he finally said.

"Pretty darn good friends if you're willing to cough up a hundred Gs for her."

"Look, I don't need a lecture. Her kid's been kidnapped, and I'm only trying to do what I can to make sure she comes back safely. Just get the money, okay?"

"I hope you know what you're doing."

He clamped his teeth together. It would have been easier to hold up a damn train. "I'll call you later to find out how it's going," he snapped.

He was getting ready to hang up when a thought occurred to him. "Wait a minute," he said to Rick. "You have your finger on the financial pulse of the whole valley, right? You probably have a pretty good idea who might be in need of a little cash, don't you?"

"Some." Rick drew the word out slowly, warily.

"So you could maybe point out a couple of people who might have a financial incentive to do something like this."

"I could. Of course, then I'd lose my job for handing out confidential bank information. I'm sorry, but I happen to like my job, Matt."

"A couple of names. That's all I'm looking for."

"No."

"What I can't figure out is why somebody would want her to leave town so badly they'd be desperate enough to risk fifteen to life on a federal offense like kidnapping. We're talking some major time here."

"Leave town?"

"Yeah. That's one of the conditions of him returning Dylan. Seems to me that was just as important to the kidnapper as the money. More, maybe. So who would benefit with Ellie out of the picture?"

"Even if I had any ideas, I couldn't tell you. You're not even a cop!"

"I can have Jess on the line in two seconds. Or better yet, why don't I call back and tell MaryBeth all about that little blond buckle bunny who followed you clear down from Bozeman after the college rodeo finals?"

"Hey, that was way before I got married." Despite it, Matt could hear the panic in his old friend's voice.

He pushed his advantage. "As I recall, you and Mary-Beth were almost engaged. Man, that blonde was one hot little number, wasn't she?"

There was a long, drawn-out pause, then Rick sighed heavily. "I don't know what you're looking for. But I can maybe give you one name of somebody who might have a motive."

"Go ahead. I'm listening."

As soon as Rick mentioned the name, his heart started to pound. This was it. He knew it in his bones.

Chapter 16

Ellie sat at the kitchen table drinking the glass of water Jess had forced on her.

This had to be a nightmare. But if it was, it was a pretty surreal one. Matt's brother sat beside her barking orders into the phone while the doorbell rang again with yet another concerned neighbor bearing food.

The Salt River grapevine worked fast. She'd received the ransom call less than forty-five minutes ago, and already she had at least four casseroles in the fridge and a half-dozen plates of cookie bars.

How did people whip these things up so fast? And did anyone really think tuna noodle bake with crushed potato chips on top was going to make everything okay?

Food seemed to be the panacea for every trouble in Star Valley. She wondered if there was some secret cookbook spelling out the best way to handle every situation. *Betty Crocker's Crisis Cuisine?*

Your neighbor's kid gets busted for growing pot? Take over banana nut bread. Your best friend's husband walks out on her for some secretary he met over the Internet? A nice beef pie ought to do the trick.

Your veterinarian's little girl is kidnapped walking home from school? Pick your poison. Anything was apparently appropriate, from soup to nuts.

Fortunately SueAnn had rushed right over to run interference at the door. There was nothing left for Ellie to do but sit here obsessing about what kind of monster would steal a nine-year-old girl.

She couldn't think about it. If she did, she would go crazy imagining Dylan's terror. Her mind prowled with terrible possibilities. Every time she started to think about it, she wanted to fall apart, to disintegrate into a mindless heap, but somehow she managed to hold herself together.

Still, when Matt burst into the kitchen a few moments later she had to fight with everything in her not to jump up and burrow against that strong chest.

She'd been so horrible to him, it was a wonder he would even stand to be in the same room with her. She had seen the hurt in his eyes when she pushed him away, when she rejected the comfort he wanted to give. She hated herself for it, but she couldn't seem to bend on this.

The need to lean on him, to let him take this terrible burden from her, was so powerful it terrified her. She couldn't, though. This was her burden and hers alone.

She had to be strong for her little girl.

Once she started down that slippery slope and let herself need him, it would be so easy to tumble all the way to full dependence. She was afraid she would lose herself in the process. And then what good would she be for Dylan?

Matt spared her one quick glance, then turned to his brother. "I think I know where she is. Come on, let's go get her."

Jess stared at him like he'd just grown an extra couple of appendages. "Lou, I'm gonna have to call you back," he said into the phone. "Yeah. Let me know as soon as you hear from the Feds."

He hung up the phone and frowned at his brother. "Are you completely nuts?"

"I just got a lead I think you'll be interested in. Did you know Steve Nichols is delinquent on payments to the Salt River bank to the tune of about ninety-five thou? He's up to his eyeballs in debt and is just a few weeks away from foreclosure on that fancy new clinic he just built."

Ellie stared at him, trying to process the information. "Steve? You think *Steve* took Dylan?" She wouldn't have been more shocked if he'd accused Reverend Whitaker.

"It makes sense, doesn't it? Somebody's been trying real hard to run you out of town. Who would benefit more if you left Star Valley than your main competition?"

"I hardly have a practice anymore! I'm not much of a threat to him."

"If he's only breaking even by the skin of his teeth, maybe you're what stands between survival and failure."

"But…but we're friends. He even offered to head up the search effort for Dylan."

"Think about it, Doc. Whoever left those notes for

you had access to two things—dead animals and needles. Doesn't it make sense that it might be another vet?"

She couldn't believe it. Not Steve. He had welcomed her into town, had treated her as a respected colleague and a friend.

"That's not enough for an interview, let alone a search warrant," Jess snapped.

Matt stared him down. "I'm not a cop, little brother. I don't need a warrant."

Jess glared for a moment, a muscle working in his jaw, then he picked up the phone again. "Lou, patch me through to Steve Nichols, will you?"

A minute later, he growled into the phone. "What do you mean, he's not there? I thought he was coordinating the civilian searchers."

After another pause, he hung up. "Lou says he had to take care of some business at his clinic. She said he told her he'd be back in an hour or so."

"Then that's probably where he took Dylan, to his clinic."

"You don't know that. It doesn't mean a damn thing."

Matt shoved on his Stetson. "I'm going, Jess. You can come along or you can sit here on your duff and forget we ever had this conversation. Your choice."

"I think you're crazier than a duck in a desert," Jess growled. "But I'm not about to let you head over there by yourself in this kind of mood."

"I'm going, too." Ellie jumped up from her chair.

Both of them looked at her with the exact same glower. "Forget it," Matt said. "It could be dangerous."

She glowered right back. "This is my child we're talking about. I'm going with you."

"You'll stay in the truck, then."

Not likely. She pressed her lips together, and Matt finally sighed. "Come on, then."

They took Jesse's big department Bronco so he could radio for backup if necessary, but he drove without sirens or lights.

Steve's clinic was a low-slung, modern facility on the other side of town. Ellie had always thought it looked more like some kind of fancy assisted living center than a country vet's office, with a porte cochere and that long row of high, gleaming windows.

The blinds were closed, but she could see the yellow glow of lights inside. If Dylan wasn't there—and Ellie wasn't nearly as convinced as Matt seemed to be that she was—Steve would be hurt and outraged when they barged in and accused him of kidnapping her.

She couldn't let it bother her, she decided. In the scheme of things, when it came to her daughter, the possibility of hurting Steve's feelings didn't matter at all.

"Let me do the talking," Jesse said after he drove under the porte cochere and turned off the Bronco.

"Sure, as long as you're getting answers."

Jess rolled his eyes at his brother, and Ellie felt like doing the same thing when Matt turned to her and ordered her to stay put.

She thought about obeying for all of ten seconds, then waited until they were at the front door of the clinic before she climbed out of the vehicle and followed them.

Matt scowled when he saw her but said nothing. As they walked inside, she thought she saw just the slightest movement behind the long, low wall separating the reception desk from the waiting area.

Before she could react, the men both tensed and moved

together, their shoulders touching so they created a solid, impenetrable protective barrier in front of her.

Jesse's hand went to his sidearm. "Nichols? Is that you?"

Time seemed to slow to a crawl, and the only sound in the room was their breathing. She couldn't see what was happening over their broad shoulders, so she stood on tiptoe for a better look as a small, frightened face peeked over the wall.

Ellie didn't know who moved first, her or Dylan, but an instant later she had shoved her way past the men and gathered her daughter into her arms.

Sobs of overwhelming relief welled in her throat as she held the small, warm weight. She forced them down, knowing she would have time later to give in to them. Right now her daughter needed her to be strong.

Dylan held tightly to her mother. "I'm so glad you're here! I was just calling nine-one-one when I heard a car outside. I thought maybe someone else was helping Dr. Nichols and I got really scared and tried to hide under the desk, then I heard Lucy's uncle. How did you know where I was?"

She couldn't seem to hold her daughter close enough. "It doesn't matter, honey. Are you okay? What happened? Where's Steve?"

A shudder racked her little frame. "In the back, in a quarantine room just like you have. That's where he kept me." She nibbled her bottom lip nervously. "Um, he might need an ambulance. He hit his head on the cement floor pretty hard."

Matt started to take a step toward the hallway, his face blazing with fury, but Jess reached a hand out to stop him. "No way am I letting you go back there right now. That's all I need is a murder investigation on my hands in addition to the kidnapping case. I'll handle this. You stay here with the ladies."

Despite everything, Ellie had to fight a smile when Dylan preened a little at being called a lady.

"Oh. The door's locked," she said suddenly. "I have the key."

She fished around in the pocket of her parka then pulled it out and held it out to the police chief. "Are… are you gonna shoot him?"

Jesse crouched and took her small hand, key and all, and folded it into his. "You want me to, sweetheart?"

"No," she said seriously. "He didn't hurt me. Just scared me a little."

"Sounds like you scared him right back."

Dylan gave a watery giggle then handed over the key, and Jesse disappeared down the hall.

After he was gone, Dylan's smile slid away and she looked nervously at her mother. "This is all my fault, Mom. I'm really sorry. I should have gone right to the clinic after school and I didn't. I just went to see Cheyenne's horse but I'll never do it again, I promise. Don't be mad. Please?"

"Oh, honey. I'm not mad. You're not to blame for this." She was, for not keeping her daughter safe. Just another thing she would have to deal with later. "What happened? How did you get away?"

"I tried to stay calm and use my brain, just like you always tell me to do. I didn't think he'd hurt me, but I still wanted to go home. The first time he came in, I saw he left the key in the lock and it gave me an idea. When he brought me dinner, I tripped him and he fell over and hit his head. I didn't know it was Dr. Nichols until he fell and his mask fell off but as soon as he did, I ran out and locked the door."

How on earth had she managed to raise such an amazing daughter? Ellie hugged her tightly again. "It sounds like you did exactly the right thing."

"You're about the bravest kid I've ever met." Matt's voice was rough, and he reached a hand out and squeezed Dylan's shoulders.

Dylan blushed at his approval and looked at him with an expression of such naked longing in her eyes that Ellie suddenly remembered Lucy's confession earlier in the evening, about how the two girls had connived and schemed to throw her and Matt together.

Dylan wanted a daddy, and she had obviously picked Matt for the role. *Oh, sweetheart.* Her heart ached knowing her daughter was destined for disappointment. She would give Dylan the world, but she could never give her this.

She pushed the thought away. She couldn't worry about how she would ever ease the pain of futile hopes and unrealized dreams. For now, all she could do was hold on to her daughter and whisper a prayer of gratitude that she had her back.

Hours later, Ellie sat in her darkened living room watching the gas logs and their endless flame.

Dylan was finally asleep, lulled only by the grudging promise that, yes, she could go to school the next day and tell everyone of her harrowing adventure and how she had single-handedly rescued herself.

Ellie had held her hand until she'd drifted off. Even long after her daughter was lost to dreamland, she hadn't been able to make herself move, had just sat on the edge of that narrow bed feeling each small breath and thanking Whoever looked over mothers for delivering her baby back safely.

Eventually she'd wandered here. Hard to believe that just a short time ago, the old house had been a frenzy of activity with people coming and going, the phone ringing, all the lights blazing. Now the air was still, with only the low whir of the artificial fire to keep her company.

She didn't mind. In truth, she was grateful for the chance to finally catch hold of her fluttering thoughts and sift through the amazing events of the day.

Every time she thought of Steve and what he had done, her stomach burned and she wanted to break something. He had tried to destroy her in every conceivable way. Financially, professionally, emotionally. She'd never before been the subject of such undiluted hostility, and it frightened her as much as it shocked her, especially because she had been so completely blind to it.

When Steve regained consciousness and found Jess and six other officers surrounding him, he had first tried to bluff his way out of the situation. Faced with the overwhelming evidence against him, though, he'd finally blurted out everything.

He had been desperate and had come to blame all his problems on her for scheming to take his uncle's clinic away from him. It should have come to him, Steve said. He'd spent years working there, even as a kid, cleaning cages and doing miserable grunt work, all with the expectation that someday the practice would be his and he could reap the benefits of his uncle's reputation in the community.

Then Ben had ruined everything by refusing to sell

the clinic to him, instead bringing in an outsider with wacky California ideas that didn't mesh at all with the conservative Star Valley mind-set.

Left with no other choice, Steve had been forced to build his own clinic and had ended up getting in over his head.

He told Jess he realized too late that the community wasn't big enough to support two veterinary clinics so he tried to persuade Ellie to go into business with him to cut down overhead. When she refused, he knew he had to find another way to make her leave, especially after she started to eat into his patient load.

He was the one who had left the warning in her truck. And, he confessed, he'd broken into her truck and read her planner. It hadn't been difficult to study her treatment log and inject specific horses with a virulent bacteria to make it look as if her shoddy care had spread disease.

When that didn't work, he knew he had to take drastic measures, so he'd come up with the twisted kidnapping plan.

She could forgive him the rest. Although it would take time and effort, she could rebuild her reputation, her practice.

But she would never be able to forgive him for terrorizing her little girl.

She'd been a fool not to see it before. No. She hadn't *wanted* to see it, the ugly bitterness he hid so well behind a veneer of friendship. It had been much easier to take Steve at face value, to see what she wanted to see.

SueAnn had seen it, had tried to warn her about him, but she hadn't listened. She had trusted him, and her daughter had ultimately paid the price for her mistake.

She wrapped her arms around her knees and gazed at the flickering flames. How had she forgotten the lessons she'd learned so early in life? Depend only on yourself and you won't ever have to know the cruel sting of disappointment.

A soft knock at the front door disturbed the silence of the house. She felt an instant's fear and then she remembered all was well. Her daughter was safe at home, where she belonged.

She pulled aside the lacy curtain at the door and felt only a small quiver of surprise to find Matt standing on the other side. He wore that shearling-lined ranch coat again, leather collar turned up against the cold night, and his chiseled features were solemn, unsmiling.

He looked strong and solid, and she wanted nothing more than to fall into his arms and weep after the emotional upheaval of the day.

She couldn't, though, and she knew it. Instead, she opened the door and ushered him inside. "Matt! What are you doing here? I thought you went back to the ranch hours ago."

"I did. But I couldn't stay away." He stood just inside the door watching her, a strange light in his blue eyes that suddenly made her as nervous as a mouse in the middle of a catfight.

She cleared her throat and seized on the only benign topic she could think of. Food. "Would you like something to eat? I've got enough here to feed most of the town. I haven't tried any of it, but SueAnn said Ginny Garrett's cinnamon sugar cookies were to die for."

To her intense relief, he shielded that strange light from her with his lashes. "Ginny does make one fine cookie," he said after a moment. "You sure you don't mind?"

"Eat as many as you want." She led the way to the kitchen, where the table practically bowed from the weight of all the plates of goodies covering it. "I've got enough stuff here to have a bake sale."

She peeled back the plastic wrap covering the plate the mayor's wife brought over, and Matt took one cookie and bit into it. "It's comfort food," he said after he'd swallowed. "Sometimes people don't know how else they can help."

"I know. Everyone has been so kind. I've just been trying to figure out how I'm going to find room in my freezer for everything. Maybe you should take some home to your ranch hands."

He leaned a hip against her counter. "Sure."

Grateful for something to do with her hands, she found some paper plates in the back of a cupboard and started loading them up with fudge and lemon bars and chocolate chip cookies.

"So how are you?" he asked solemnly while she worked.

She flashed him a quick look. "Okay. A little shaky still."

"Yeah. Me, too. I keep thinking, what if it had been Lucy? I wouldn't have handled it with nearly the guts you did."

A bitter laugh scored her throat. "I didn't handle anything. I completely fell apart."

He studied her solemnly out of those blue eyes, and for a terrible moment she feared he was going to cross the space between them and pull her into his arms. And then she really *would* fall apart, would give in to the tears of relief and hurt and remembered terror that choked her.

She turned to the table, ashamed that she couldn't control her emotions better, and after a moment of silence, he spoke again. "Almost forgot. One of the reasons I dropped by was to give you this."

Out of the corner of her gaze, she saw him hold out a wrinkled paper. It took her a few seconds to realize what it was, and then her face burned. It was the note deeding the practice over to him in exchange for the money to have her child returned.

She made no move to reach for it, mortified again that she had needed his help, that she had failed her daughter once more.

"Here. Take it. I don't want it," he growled.

As reluctantly as if it were covered in razor blades, she reached for it. A thousand unspoken words hovered between them. She would have preferred to leave them all that way—unspoken—but she knew she had to say something.

"I... Thank you for what you were going to do. I can't say I understand why you would be willing to do such a thing, but it meant a lot to me anyway."

"Did it?"

The hardness of his voice shocked her. "Yes! Of course!"

He didn't say anything, just continued to study her out of those blue eyes, and she flushed under his scrutiny.

"I said I appreciated it. I don't know what more you want from me."

"Why is it so hard for you?"

"What?"

"Accepting help from me. Admitting you're not some kind of superwoman and can't handle every rotten curve life throws at you by yourself."

She tensed. "I don't know what you're talking about." The lie burned her tongue, scorched her heart.

"No matter how hard I try, you keep pushing me away."

Better to hurt him by pushing him away than the alternative. He would leave her shattered if she let him. Would make her weak and needy and *vulnerable*, and she could never allow it, especially after tonight. She was all Dylan had, and she needed to remember that.

She said nothing, knowing there was nothing she *could* say. After a moment, he spoke again, his voice low and expressionless.

"It makes loving you pretty damn hard when you won't let anybody inside."

His words sucked the air from her lungs, every thought from her head. He didn't say he loved her. He *couldn't* have. It was a mistake. A terrible, cruel mistake.

Terror flapped through her on greasy bat wings. How could he say such a thing? Didn't he realize that she didn't want his love, that she couldn't handle it?

Her breath started coming in deep, heaving gulps. What was she going to do? She didn't want to hurt him, but she couldn't let him destroy her like her father had destroyed her mother.

"Aren't you going to say anything?" he finally asked.

I love you. Heaven help me, I love you. Even though I know you would leave me broken and bloody, I want to curl up against you, inside you, around you, and never, ever let go.

Instead, she made her voice tight, toneless, and hated herself for it. "What do you want me to say, Matt?"

He gazed at her, and she nearly sobbed at the hurt in his eyes, then those blue depths hardened. "How about the truth? That you love me, too. That you push me away because you're afraid."

He knew. Shame coursed through her. How could he say he loved her when he knew what a terrible coward she was?

"I'm sorry," she said, curling her hands into fists at her sides. "I can't tell you what you want to hear."

"You mean you won't."

"That, too." Her hands were trembling, and she didn't know if they would ever, ever stop.

"Dammit, Ellie. You don't think loving you, needing you, scares the ever-living hell out of me, too? It's the absolute last thing I ever wanted or expected."

She dared a look at him and found his eyes fierce with emotion.

"My wife walked out on me, Ellie. Before that, she screwed around with just about every guy in town. I told myself I didn't care, that I'd stopped loving her long before she took off, but Melanie still left me with deep scars covering every inch of my heart. I thought they'd be there forever, and I'd even learned to live with them."

He reached for her then, picked up one fisted hand and brought it to his lips. "But then you blew into town with your smart mouth and your compassion and your courage. And one day I realized I couldn't even feel those scars anymore. You healed them, Doc. I don't know how, but while you were treating my horses, you were working your magic on me, too."

This time a sob did escape her mouth, and she

yanked her hand back to press it against her mouth so the rest didn't follow.

"I love you, Ellie," he went on. "I want you in my life, forever if you'll have me. Up until now, you've shown more courage than any woman I've ever met. Don't let your fear win now."

For one wonderful, terrible moment, she let herself believe in fairy tales. In knights on white horses and orange blossoms and a happily ever after filled with laughter and love and joy.

And then the glowing picture faded.

In its place was a ramshackle trailer and a solemn-eyed little girl watching a woman who drank too much and sold her body and sobbed every night for a man who would never come back.

"I'm sorry," she whispered, and blood seeped from her heart.

"I won't ask again." His terse warning was edged with infinite sadness.

She hitched in a ragged breath. "I know. I... Good-bye, Matt."

With one last, searching look, he shoved on his Stetson and walked out into the night.

Only after he closed the door quietly behind him did her knees buckle, and she slid to the hard linoleum floor of her kitchen and wept.

Chapter 17

He never would have believed it.

Matt stood in the gymnasium of the elementary school on Valentine's Day, completely amazed at what creativity and a little elbow grease could achieve.

Instead of a dingy old room that smelled like a cross between canned peas and dirty socks, the gym had been completely transformed into a magical place.

Thousands of little twinkling white lights had been strung across the ceiling like stars in the night sky and wrapped around the branches of a couple dozen small trees temporarily commandeered from Jerry Clayton's greenhouse in town. A city skyline painted by the elementary school art classes graced the stage, covered by even more tiny white lights so it looked as if the windows of the buildings really glowed.

With the lights dimmed and the high school's jazz

band playing old dance numbers, this was the crowning jewel of the library fund-raiser—which by all accounts looked to be a smashing success.

It had been Ellie's idea to try to provide something for everyone at the fair. The little kids were still running from classroom to classroom using the tickets their parents had purchased for fishponds and beanbag tosses and cakewalks. Their older siblings were busy in the auditorium watching a PG-rated scary movie. And judging by the crowd already out on the dance floor, their parents and grandparents were obviously enjoying the romantic escape the committee had created.

He thought he would feel pretty weird about having his name listed on the program as one of the organizers, but as he watched couples dancing cheek-to-cheek under the starry lights, he had to admit to a fair amount of pride.

All evening, people had been telling him what a great job the committee had done. It seemed bitterly ironic that he'd been even a little instrumental in helping everyone else celebrate this holiday for romance, especially when things with Ellie had ended so badly.

She was here somewhere, but he hadn't caught more than a fleeting glimpse of her all night as she ran from crisis to crisis.

Even those brief, painful glimpses were better than what he had endured the last three weeks. Before today, he hadn't seen her since the terrible night he'd gone to her house, told her his feelings and had them thrown back in his face.

He wanted to be angry at her. He had been for a day or two, and the thunder and fury had been much easier to deal with than this constant, aching sadness that settled in his bones and weighed down his heart.

Why was she being so stubborn about this? He knew she loved him. She never would have given herself to him so sweetly, passionately, if she didn't. He couldn't make her admit it, though. Not when she so obviously wanted to deny her feelings, to him and to herself.

A couple of giggles sounded behind him, distracting him from the grimness of his thoughts, and he turned to find Lucy and Dylan being teased by Jess. The girls both wore dresses for a change and had put their hair up, and they looked entirely too grown up for his peace of mind.

"Hey, big brother." Jess grinned. "I think we need to escort these lovely ladies out on the dance floor. What do you say?"

The girls giggled again, and he summoned a smile for their benefit. "I think we'd be stupid not to grab the two prettiest girls here while we have the chance."

Jess had already snagged Lucy so Matt obligingly held his arm out to Dylan, who took it with a blush that reminded him painfully of her mother. Out on the dance floor, she stumbled around awkwardly for a moment then quickly lost her shyness and started jabbering away about her favorite subject, horses.

"My mom says maybe I can get a horse in the summer, when I'd have more time to take care of him and learn to ride him. That would be so cool. Then I could ride with Lucy around the ranch without anybody having to worry about us getting into trouble."

Like that day would ever come. The two of them invented the word. "I'll believe that when I see it," he teased.

Ellie's daughter giggled again. "Well, we wouldn't get into trouble because I don't know how to ride, anyway."

He smiled and twirled her around. Dylan was a great kid, despite her mischievous streak. Full of spunk and fire, just like her mother. He thought of the night she had spent frightened and alone in a concrete room because of that bastard Nichols and saw red again. Good thing the man was in the county jail awaiting sentencing after his guilty plea. Maybe by the time he was released, Matt might have cooled down enough to keep from beating the hell out of him.

"Oh, look," Dylan said suddenly. "There's my mom."

She pulled her hand from his arm and started waving vigorously to someone behind him, and he turned and found Ellie standing alone on the edge of the dance floor.

In the low, shimmering light, her green eyes looked huge. Haunted.

"Doesn't she look pretty?" Dylan asked innocently, and he dared another look. Like her daughter, Ellie wore a dress—a soft, sapphire-blue clingy thing that flared and bunched in all the right places.

He cleared his throat, but his voice still came out gruff. "Very," he said.

"I told her she'd be a lot prettier if she'd smile once in a while," Dylan said, sounding like a middle-aged, nagging mother instead of a nine-year-old, "but she hasn't been doing much of that lately."

"No?" He tried to sound casual and disinterested, even though the little scamp had his full attention, and she probably knew it.

"She's been really sad," Dylan said. "She even cries

at night sometimes after I'm in bed, so I know something must be really wrong. My mom never cries."

His heart stuttered in his chest at the thought of Ellie crying alone in her house.

Damn stubborn woman. If she was hurting, it was her own fault. Didn't she know how absolutely right they were for each other? He needed her to bring lightness and laughter into his life, to keep him from taking himself too seriously.

And she needed him to show her nobody expected her to bear the whole weight of the world by herself.

"Maybe you could talk to her, or ask her to dance, even. You're friends, aren't you? That might make her feel better."

Dylan's green eyes shone with hope, and he hated to douse it, but he was pretty sure he was the last person on earth Ellie wanted to talk to right about now.

On second thought, maybe that's just what he needed to do. He'd told her he wouldn't grovel. But just trying to talk some sense into her wasn't really the same, was it?

He had to try. Even if he looked like a lovesick fool, he had to try. Much more of this heartache was going to destroy both of them.

As soon as the dance was over, he would grab her, he decided, yank her into a dark corner and kiss her until she came to her senses.

But when the music ended and he walked Dylan back to Lucy and Jess, Ellie was nowhere to be found.

She couldn't do this.

Ellie stood outside the side door of the school breathing the February night air and praying the bitter cold would turn her heart to ice, would take away this pain.

She pressed a palm to her chest, breathing hard with the effort it took to regain control of her emotions. Seeing Matt tonight—looking so strong and gorgeous in his black dress jeans and Western-cut shirt—had been bad enough. Watching him spin around the dance floor while Dylan smiled at him like he'd just handed her the stars had been excruciating.

They looked like they belonged together—like they *all* belonged together—and she knew she had to escape.

What a fool she had been to think she could handle seeing him tonight without falling apart. She had spent three weeks trying to get through each day without thinking about him more than once every five minutes. Of course the shock of seeing him would be an assault to her senses, especially surrounded by all the trappings of the most romantic day of the year.

How was she going to get through this? They lived in a small, tight-knit community and were bound to bump into each other occasionally. Would it get easier in time or would her heart continue to pound out of her chest and her pulse rate skyrocket every time she saw him?

What could she do? She wasn't sure she had the strength to endure seeing him every week or even every month, not if it made her feel as if her heart were being sliced open again and again.

Yet she couldn't leave. She had a job here, a business that was booming now that people in town knew how Steve had tried to blacken her reputation. She and Dylan had a life now, and she couldn't walk away from that.

She blew out another breath. She could handle this. She was a strong and capable woman who could do anything she set her mind to.

Except stop loving Matthew Harte.

The door at her back was suddenly thrust out, and for one terrible moment she was afraid he had followed her outside. To her vast relief, Sarah McKenzie peeked her pretty blond head out the door.

"Ellie! I was wondering where you ran off to."

"I just needed a little air." A vast understatement. If she'd been any more breathless watching Matt dance with her little girl, she would have needed to yank old Bessie Johnson's portable oxygen tank right out from under her and steal a few puffs.

Concern darkened the schoolteacher's brown eyes. "Everything okay?"

"Sure." Ellie managed a smile. "I've been running all night and I just needed a breather."

"That's why I came to find you. I had to tell you what a fantastic job you and Matt did organizing this evening. I've had so many comments from people telling me it's the best carnival they've ever attended, and they can't remember having such a good time."

"I'm glad people are enjoying themselves."

"And the bottom line is that we've already raised twice what we were expecting for tonight! The school library will have more books than shelf space now."

Ellie smiled. "Maybe next year you can raise enough money to build a whole new library."

"I hope you'll help us again next year. You and Matt both."

Sure. When monkeys fly out of my ears. "Let's get through tonight before we worry about next year."

"Well, I just wanted you to know how good you have been for Salt River. This town needed shaking up. I'm so glad you're staying—we would all miss you very much if you left."

After Sarah slipped inside the school, Ellie stood looking at the rugged mountains glowing in the pale moonlight and thinking about what she had said. If she had given anything to the town, she had received it all back and then some.

She thought of all the people she had come to care about in the months since she had come to Wyoming. Sarah. SueAnn. The rest of the friends she had made on the carnival committee, and the people—some perfect strangers—who had rallied around her after Dylan's kidnapping, bringing food and offers of help and comfort beyond measure.

Her life would have been so much poorer without all of them.

She stared at the mountains as the truth she had refused to see finally slammed into her.

She needed them. All of them.

How stupid she had been. She thought she was so damned independent, so self-sufficient. But she would have crumbled into nothing after Dylan was taken if not for the people of Salt River she had come to love.

She had been trying so hard to stand on her own two feet that she never realized she would have fallen over long ago if it hadn't been for the people around her providing quiet, unquestioning support.

The door pushed open behind her once more, and she thought it would be Sarah again or one of the other committee members. She turned with a teary smile that fell away instantly at the sight of Matt standing in the open doorway, looking strong and solid and wonderful.

Her heart began a painful fluttering in her chest when she thought of how she had wounded him by rejecting the incredible gift of his love.

He had been right. She had pushed him away because she was afraid of needing, of trusting. It had all been for nothing, though. She had needed him from the very beginning, his slow smile, his strength, his love. Especially his love.

She had just been too stubborn to admit it.

Tears choked her again and she suddenly knew, without a shadow of a doubt, that he would never hurt her. He would protect her heart like he had tried to protect her body that day in Steve's office, by placing himself in front of anything that threatened her.

"Hi," she whispered.

He continued to study her, his beautiful, hard face as still as the mountains, and for one terrible moment she was afraid that her epiphany had come too late. That she had lost any chance she might have had.

Then she saw his eyes.

They looked at her with hurt and hunger and a vast, aching tenderness, and she forgot to breathe.

"It's frigid out here," he finally said. "Come inside. Are you crazy?"

A tear slid down her nose, and she quickly swiped at it before it could freeze there. "Yeah. Yeah, I am. Completely crazy. I must be or I wouldn't be so miserable right now."

He said nothing, just continued watching her, and she gathered up that courage he seemed to think she had in spades and took a step forward. "I'm sorry, Matt. I'm so sorry."

He stared at her for several seconds, blue eyes wide with disbelief, then she was in his arms. Her heart exploded with joy as he kissed her, his mouth fierce and demanding.

"I have to say this," she said, when she could think straight again. She pulled away and wrapped her cold hands around the warmth of his fingers. "You were right the other night. I didn't want to let you help me, to let you inside. I think I knew even from the beginning that you would have the power to destroy me if I let you."

"I never would," he murmured.

"I know. I should have realized it then, but I'm afraid I don't have much experience with this whole love thing."

His eyes turned wary suddenly, and she realized she had never given him the words. "I love you, Matt," she said softly. "I love the way you smile at your daughter and the way you take care of your horses and the way you hold me like you never want to let me go. I love you fiercely and I hate so much that I hurt you."

Emotions blazed out of his blue eyes. "I'm tough. I'll survive. Just don't do it again, okay?"

Another tear slipped down her cheek. "I won't. I swear it."

His thumb traced the pathway of that lone tear. "Dylan says you never cry."

She sniffed. "See all the bad habits you're making me develop?"

A soft laugh rumbled out of him, then his face grew serious. "I want everything, Ellie," he warned. "Marriage, kids, the whole thing. I won't settle for less. Are you ready for that?"

She thought of a future with him, of making a home together among these mountains she loved, of raising their daughters together—and maybe adding a few sons along the way with their father's eyes and his strength and his smile.

She couldn't imagine anything more wonderful. In

answer, she lifted her mouth to his and wrapped her arms tightly around him.

His exultant laugh rang out through the cold February night. "Come on. Let's go inside where it's warm and tell the girls. Hell, let's tell the whole world."

She went still in his arms, suddenly horrified. "Oh, no. The girls."

He shrugged. "What's the problem? This is what they wanted all along. They figured out we belonged together months before we did."

"That's what I mean." She groaned again. "They are going to be completely insufferable when they find out how well their devious little plan worked."

He winced. "Good point. So what do we do about it?"

"I don't think there's anything we *can* do, just accept the fact that our nine-year-old daughters are smarter than either of us."

"That's a terrifying thought."

"Get used to it, Harte. I have a feeling the two of them are going to make our life extremely interesting."

His smile soaked through her, filling every empty corner of her heart with sweet, healing peace. "I can't wait," he murmured.

She smiled and took the hand he offered. "Neither can I, Matt. Neither can I."

* * * * *

Also by Linda Goodnight

Love Inspired

House of Hope

Redeeming the Past

Sundown Valley

To Protect His Children
Keeping Them Safe
The Cowboy's Journey Home
Her Secret Son
To Protect His Brother's Baby

Love Inspired Trade

Claiming Her Legacy

Canary Street Press

A Honey Ridge Novel

The Memory House
The Rain Sparrow
The Innkeeper's Sister

Visit her Author Profile page
at Harlequin.com for more titles!

TO PROTECT
HIS CHILDREN

Linda Goodnight

For the glory of my Lord and Savior, Jesus.
And in memory of my son, Travis.
Someday I'll see you both. Won't that be a grand day?

I will lift up mine eyes unto the hills, from whence
cometh my help. My help cometh from the Lord,
which made heaven and earth.
—*Psalms* 121:1–2

Chapter 1

Wade Trudeau was losing his mind. What was left of it, anyway.

He slammed the landline back on the charger, pressed the heels of his hands against his eyes and groaned.

"No news from the employment agency?"

Wade let his arms flop to the desktop and looked up as his cousin, best friend and business partner, Bowie Trudeau ambled into the home office of Sundown Ranch.

"The trouble is, Bowie, nobody wants to take on three babies, especially in an area as remote as Sundown Ranch."

"We're only ten miles from town."

"Might as well be a thousand the way these town folks behave." No woman, including their own mother, seemed willing to care for three little babies.

"We were making it work until Miss Janey's brother got sick."

Miss Janey, a diamond in a gray ponytail.

"I can't fault Janey for putting her brother first. That's what family does." Wade's mouth twisted at the irony. His own family wasn't so adoring. "Or what they *should* do. And the two other housekeeper/nannies barely got unpacked before they were packing up again."

"No calls from those index cards you posted in town?"

The little mountain town of Sundown Valley was friendly like that. People stuck ads for yard work, babysitting, hay-hauling and whatever on community bulletin boards in cafés and grocery stores. Even in the pink Laundromat.

Last year, with a simple index card and a phone number, Wade had given away a litter of abandoned kittens.

Babies abandoned by their mother, apparently, were a different matter.

"None." Depressive air descended like morning fog over Jackfork Mountain.

Wade heard a familiar babble. One of the babies was awake. If he didn't hurry, the fifteen-month-old would elevate to an ear-splitting pitch that would wake the entire trio.

He loped toward the nursery, then tiptoed into the triplets' bedroom to scoop up the pajama-clad baby and quickly escape to the hallway.

"Good morning, nugget," he whispered.

He should have known the babbler was Abby. She'd been trying to talk since she was born.

Abby burrowed her face into the space between his neck and shoulder, a spot where his babies fit perfectly.

Wade's chest filled with pleasure. This was his baby girl. His daughter. A gift from God. No matter how difficult the journey, he was grateful for his babies.

Wade breathed in Abby's sleep-warmed scent. The hint of last night's bath marathon lingered in her hair. He probably hadn't rinsed well enough, a real challenge with a slick, wiggling toddler and two more waiting in the wings.

He was still learning, still adjusting to being both mom and dad. Two cowboys plus three babies equaled chaos.

He patted Abby's tiny back and headed for the kitchen for a fruit pouch to keep her happy while he rustled up breakfast.

Bowie had disappeared already, probably heading out to meet the vet. As if they didn't have enough to worry about, some of the cows in pasture three were coughing and bull five had a limp.

As he settled Abby into one of the trio of highchairs crowding the kitchen island, the doorbell rang.

Wade looked toward the baby, then toward the ringing bell and let out a beleaguered mutter.

He knew better than to leave a baby alone in a highchair, even for a minute. He'd learned the hard way.

Quickly unbuckling the safety straps, he pulled Abby onto one hip. She wasn't happy.

He pushed the fruit pouch against her lips and hurried to the door.

Then wished he'd ignored it.

"Keno," he said, wary.

A red-faced Bud Keno shoved a piece of paper into Wade's gut. Wade grabbed for it.

"What's this?"

"A bill for the four calves I didn't get out of my bull."

"How's that my fault?"

"Your bull busted through my fence, and now I got four calves that don't fit my breeding program."

Was that why bull five was limping? He'd been battling Keno's bulls? "If you'd keep your side of the fences repaired—"

Keno stuck a finger against Wade's nose. "Eight thousand or I'm suing."

While Wade tried to regain his breath and hold his temper, Keno marched to his truck and sped away.

Wade crumpled the bill in one hand.

"Starting out to be a real bad day." He sniffed at the baby. "And now, you stink."

He managed to change the dirty diaper before the next interruption.

The doorbell. Again.

"Lord," he said to the ceiling, "if that's Keno again I may have to act first and ask forgiveness afterward."

Storming through the house with his daughter on his hip and growing madder by the minute, Wade reached the door and yanked it open.

"What now?" he bellowed.

A startled young woman took two steps backward. "Have I come at a bad time?"

Was there anything other than a bad time lately?

"Sorry. It's been a rough morning." As if to prove his point, Abby slapped him upside the head with the fruit pouch. He felt a dribble down the side of his face and swiped a hand over it.

Nothing like first impressions.

"I'm looking for Wade Trudeau."

"That's me."

"I'm Kyra Mason." Eyes still wide and uncertain, she pointed. "You have a baby?"

He scowled. "You don't like kids."

She stiffened. "Of course I do. Everyone likes children."

His mouth twisted. "Apparently not."

Abby patted his whiskered face. So he hadn't shaved yet today. No wonder the woman—Kyra Mason—stared at him with something akin to suspicion. He probably looked like America's Most Wanted.

Had he even combed his hair this morning?

Wade glanced from the woman's wary hazel eyes to the driveway and the tiniest blue car he'd ever seen. Was she a…salesman, er, woman? "Is there something I can do for you?"

She hitched a large shoulder bag and handed him a familiar white index card. He recognized his own handwriting.

Oh.

Well, now.

This could be promising. Maybe his lousy day was taking a turn for the better.

Thank you, Lord. Please let her be the one. You know I'm sinking fast.

He'd prayed over this nanny situation at least a hundred times. Maybe God was finally showing him some mercy. Except Kyra Mason looked nothing like the sixty-year-old grandmother he had in mind.

After a quick glance at Keno's bill, now crumbled on the entry tile, Wade put on his nice face. If Kyra Mason was here about the nanny job, he didn't want to scare her to death.

"You're applying for the position?"

Her eyes went to the baby. "Maybe."

Wade bit back a growl. What was it with women these days? Weren't they supposed to be baby-adoring nurturers? Or was that only a TV fantasy created by a wishful-thinking male?

This woman said she liked kids, but the uncertainty in her expression made him wonder.

He wasn't sure he could take much more rejection, especially when it came to his triplets.

But he'd invite her in and ask. He was that desperate.

Stepping back from the door opening, he hitched his chin. "Office is the first room on the right. Come in."

He waited until she passed, then shut the front door and followed her into the ranch office.

The smell of her perfume trailed behind her, and Wade called himself seven kinds of idiot because he liked it. A woman's perfume was a dangerous thing.

Giving his head a shake as a reminder of what the last woman and her delicious perfume had done to him and their babies, he settled behind his desk with Abby on his lap.

Kyra chose one of the beige armchairs across from him. She let her purse slide from her shoulder to the floor, placed a manila file folder on her lap, sat up fence-post straight and clenched her hands atop the folder.

She was either nervous or a prissy little prig, her posture perfect, her lips tight, her nose tilted up just so. Granted, hers was a cute nose. So was the rest of her face. Not Hollywood gorgeous but fresh and wholesome, like a spring morning.

Perfectly groomed in an interview-worthy floral dress and sensible black shoes, she had smooth shoulder-length red hair, the kind that caught sunbeams.

Yeah, so he'd noticed the shiny stuff on some subconscious male level while he'd barked at her on the
front porch.

She was pretty, but he wasn't looking for beauty.
He'd had that. He wanted a woman willing to nurture
his babies while he worked. Period. End of subject. Cut.
Print. The end.

"Tell me about yourself, Kyra." There. Didn't he
sound businesslike?

The redhead whipped out a printed parchment résumé and placed it in his outstretched hand. Their fingers touched. Only a brush of skin, and then she sat
back, but not before Wade's nerve endings reacted. His
hands were hard and calloused. Hers were as soft as
Abby's.

Dropping the résumé on the desk as if it had suddenly burst into flames, he slid his hand beneath the
desk and scraped his fingertips across the rough denim
of his jeans. Rough. Not soft. Much better.

Abby made a dive for the pristine white paper. Re-
flexes always on the ready, especially since becoming
the only parent of three babies, Wade rescued the résumé from her grip and slid the wiggling child to the
floor.

She toddled off to explore. The house was baby-
proofed but he kept an eye on her anyway.

Babies, in his crash course of experience, had an uncanny way of finding things they shouldn't no matter
how a man tried. One person didn't have enough hands
or eyes. How mothers managed still mystified him.

He perused the slightly wrinkled résumé. "You're
a teacher."

His eyebrows lifted in surprise.

"I was. I'm considering a change."

"Teacher burnout already?" He softened the question with a slight smile. At least, he hoped it was a smile and not a grimace.

Kyra didn't return his feeble attempt. Instead, her lips formed a tight line, as if she didn't want to discuss the subject. "Something like that."

Okay, fair enough. He wouldn't pry. From the news and teacher friends, he had an idea of the pressures of dealing with twenty-five-plus kids in an enclosed space, half of those students without any home training. Teachers were leaving the profession in a stampede.

Still, a teaching education and her experience working with kids would be valuable when caring for toddlers. "Can you pass a drug test?"

She whipped out two more papers from her handy little folder. So organized.

"Most recent drug test and a background check. Standard procedure for educators." She pushed her folder across his desk. "References in there, too. I can get more if needed."

While he read the glowing references, Abby toddled toward the newcomer, chattering with every wobbly step. She patted the woman on the knee, smearing a dab of applesauce on the blue floral dress.

Wade watched from the corner of one eye. Kyra didn't react to the smudge, a major point in her favor. Babies were messy. Sticky. Smelly. Noisy.

He cast an ear toward the nursery. Why weren't the boys up? Not that he was complaining.

Abby reached up with chubby arms. As natural as could be, Kyra Mason lifted his baby girl against her shoulder for a messy hug. If the former teacher even noticed the smears and dribbles of pureed fruit soiling her nice clothes, she ignored them.

What kind of woman did that?

Wade clapped the folder shut. "Looks good to me. When can you start?"

To say she was startled by Wade Trudeau's sudden decision was a massive understatement. Kyra batted her eyes so many times in an attempt to get her bearings she lost focus.

"Wait. Wait. Mr. Trudeau."

"Wade."

"Right. Yes. Okay. Wade." She was stuttering. But she hadn't expected an immediate job offer. "I'm not sure yet if I *want* the position."

The handsome cowboy fell back in his chair. His voice became a despairing murmur. "Is it because of the applesauce?"

"What? Applesauce?" She followed his gaze to her sleeve. "I was a special needs teacher. I've had far worse things on my clothes than pureed fruit."

The cowboy tilted his head back against his office chair and closed his eyes for one long breath.

For a second, Kyra felt sorry for him. He looked tired. Frazzled. Beneath the uncombed brown hair and whiskery face, he was a good-looking cowboy, in a rugged Scott Eastwood kind of way.

The sleeves of his blue chambray shirt were rolled to the elbows over muscular forearms. Strong hands. Muscled chest. Broad shoulders.

Did ranch work keep all cowboys in such great shape?

Heat rose up the back of her neck.

This was a job interview, not a speed date.

To hide her foolish thoughts, she pressed her face against the baby's neck. She smelled like baby shampoo.

"Then what's the holdup?" he asked. "The job's open now. Today. I can pay you well." He named a satisfactory, though surprising sum, considering the nature of the job.

Which begged the question.

What exactly was she required to do to earn that amount of money?

"Stay long enough and I'll even put you on our medical."

"Mr. Trudeau. Wade. We haven't even discussed a job description. Your card said housekeeper. What exactly does this housekeeping position entail?"

"Well, uh—" He ran a finger beneath his shirt collar, a weird action because the top button was open on the casual shirt. "I might have left off the nanny part."

"*Nanny* part?"

This was supposed to be a job *without* children. In fact, bearing the responsibility of a child was the very thing she'd hoped to avoid.

Besides, what kind of parent hired a stranger on the spot to care for his child without even calling references?

Her opinion of the handsome cowboy, already questionable, hit rock bottom.

An hour ago, she'd driven away from a school parking lot too anxious to go inside to the scheduled interview for a teaching position. She'd thought she was ready to teach again. The cold sweats and shaky hands proved she wasn't.

At a coffee shop in the sleepy town of Sundown Valley, she'd seen Wade Trudeau's index card on a bulletin board advertising for a housekeeper at the Sundown Ranch. No mention of a child at all. On an impulse she still didn't understand other than her love for the Kiamichi Mountain area, Kyra had taken the card and driven to the ranch.

She needed a job. But did she want one with a child involved?

"Your card didn't mention a baby."

"Three." He held up three fingers, spearing her with a pair of tired blue eyes as if awaiting her reaction.

"Three what?"

"Babies."

Shock reverberated down Kyra's spine. *Three* babies? As in triplets?

She picked her chin up off the floor to consider exactly what she'd walked into.

Nanny to three children.

"Not a housekeeping job at all?" Had her voice squeaked a tad on the ending?

"Light housekeeping. We pick up after ourselves, but the triplets don't. Maybe a little cooking if you're willing, but if not, Bowie and I will go on handling KP duties."

"Who's Bowie?" She was starting to sound like a five-year-old, answering every statement with a question. But really, this man was so rattled, he was confusing her.

"Didn't I mention him? My cousin and business partner. He lives here, too."

Kyra raised her eyebrows. "Anyone else I should know about?"

And why didn't she put this cute baby down right now and head for the door? This obviously was not the job for her. Nothing, not one thing, was the way she'd imagined.

The cowboy's mouth gave a wry twist. "No one else at the moment. I have a wayward brother. Yates. But he hasn't been around in several years."

From the sad look in his eyes, the wayward brother was an issue he had yet to resolve. She couldn't think about that. She had issues of her own.

"So you're telling me, two men live in this house, but no women."

"Right. Plus three fifteen-month-old babies. We need a nanny in the worst way."

"Do you actually expect a woman to move in here, miles from the nearest town, with two strange men?"

That silenced him. His shoulders slumped. The frown, which seemed permanent, deepened.

Finally, he muttered, "Is that why no one wants the job?"

"It could be one reason."

"Do I look scary to you?" He touched his unshaven face, then held up a hand stop-sign style. "Don't answer that."

Kyra almost laughed. The poor guy was beside himself.

"Have you considered alternative lodging for your nanny?"

"Alternative…" His fingers scraped over the whiskery jaw as he considered. "Well, let's see. We have an old bunkhouse around back, but the place hasn't been used in years."

"Separate living quarters, I think, would help in your nanny search."

"Will you take the job if I fix it up?"

"What about time off?"

He looked thunderstruck. "Babies don't take time off."

"I wonder if that's another reason you're having a hard time finding a caregiver? Everyone needs some free time."

"I'm a rancher. I don't even know what free time looks like. But if you'll take the job, pick your days. Any days. Ranch work doesn't care. It keeps going. Like babies."

He sat up straighter, seemingly bolstered by what he thought was a great offer, as if normal days off would turn the tide in his favor.

It wouldn't, though she felt sorry for the three babies whose daddy seemed so eager to escape them.

"To be honest," Kyra said, "a nanny position wasn't what I was expecting. I'll have to say no. I don't think I'm interested."

She didn't know why she'd come here in the first place.

She started to put Abby on the floor.

"Wait. Hear me out. I'll pay a bonus." Wade's voice rose in anguish.

He leaned those fit forearms on the desk and stretched his hands toward her.

A plea. A pitiable, desperate plea.

"Why not take the job on a trial basis?" he was saying. "Three months. Until the end of summer. Three short months of sunshine and mountain air and country peace and quiet. School is out for the summer, anyway. If you choose to return to teaching in September, so be it. I'll pay you the fat bonus, anyway."

"For only three months?" She could definitely use the money. And she loved the idea of mountain solitude.

He nodded, solemn as a gravedigger. "Three months gives me time to look for someone else. Not that I hold out much hope. I've been searching for months."

"Have you considered a male nanny?"

"I want a woman."

When she tilted her head, he added, "What I mean is, I don't want a woman *personally*." He made a face. "Not ever. No thanks. The gain is not worth the pain."

He was certainly adamant. She'd be insulted for the entire female population if the man weren't desperately seeking a female nanny. "Then why not a male nanny?"

"Call me old-fashioned, but no. They have plenty of men in their lives. I want a woman. The balance thing. God's design."

Kyra understood where he was coming from. In her studies and in her classroom, she'd noted the importance of both a female and a male in a child's life. Thus, the value of mentoring organizations like Big Brothers and Big Sisters.

That Wade Trudeau needed her was evident, and she'd always been a soft touch, especially where kids were involved.

She wanted to help the babies. She really did. But a ranch with two men and three toddlers was out of her comfort zone.

"Have you considered a day-care center rather than a nanny?"

"Yes and no." He made a growling noise and pulled a face. "I've considered a day care and weighed the pros and cons. The answer is still no. Too far away and too expensive. Don't you get it? I want the triplets here, with me."

The sincerity in his voice went straight to Kyra's heart. Maybe he wasn't the jerk she'd assessed him to be.

He had a ranch to run. Having the triplets on site, in his house, allowed him to pop in from time to time to see them.

Was that his intent? Or was she reading her own emotions into the situation?

Poor little babies.

If she stayed in this office another minute, she might seriously be tempted to say yes.

"Let's do this," Kyra said, in a pity move as she reached for her folder. The baby squirmed at the pressure. Kyra sat her on the floor and took a pen from her purse. "Give me three character references I can contact. I'll check them and call you with my answer sometime tomorrow."

Saying no was easier over the phone.

Suddenly, loud cries erupted from somewhere in the house. Extremely loud, angry, frustrated someone-save-me squalls.

Kyra's head snapped in that direction.

The other two babies, apparently, had awakened.

Should she offer assistance? Or get out while she had a chance?

Wade bolted to his feet. His chair clattered backward on its rollers. "I missed the signals."

"What?"

"The babies babble first. Screaming comes after they're tired of waiting for me."

He raked his hand over his head. Messy brown hair shot straight up.

Abby toddled to him. He bent to pick her up.

Kyra took pity on him.

"Go," Kyra said. "I've got her."

The poor guy galloped away like a juiced-up race-horse.

Chapter 2

When Wade returned with the freshly diapered boys, each calmed with a fruit pouch, he found Kyra Mason sitting on the floor in her pretty floral dress, rolling a wadded ball of paper back and forth to Abby.

In a warm singsong voice, she said, "Throw, catch. Throw, catch. What a smart girl you are!"

She clapped her hands. Abby took this as the signal for patty cake.

With a chuckle, Kyra played the game, ending with a belly tickle. Abby cackled.

At that moment, Wade decided he'd do anything in his power to convince Kyra to become his nanny.

He was willing to beg.

And raise her salary.

And turn the bunkhouse into a castle.

Even if he had to sell a bull or two.

"Looks like you and Abby hit it off." *Please say yes.*

He lowered the boys onto the floor.

"This is Benjamin." He touched Ben's soft brown hair. "That one is Caden."

"They look identical." She lightly patted each boy's chubby leg and rose from the floor, leaving Abby to play with a snow globe he kept on his desk for that very purpose.

"They are. Abby is my outlier. Fact was, we didn't know she was in there until their birthday."

"Quite the surprise."

"Shock's more like it." Followed by the most over-whelming joy and responsibility, plus a tidal wave of other emotions that nearly brought him to his knees. Still did at times.

He'd been prepared for two rough-and-tumble boys. A sweet pink girl, not so much. Though now he couldn't imagine life without her.

"They were pretty small and had to be in newborn NICU for a while, so I'd stand at the window counting them, praying for them."

He didn't know why he'd told her that.

Kyra trailed a hand over the top of Benjamin's dark cap of hair. The baby looked up and grinned.

"May I ask about their mother?"

Wade's insides went on the defensive. The dark cloud of fury rose, tornadic in proportions. "They don't have a mother."

His words were terse. Harsh.

Kyra's face pinkened. She settled her gaze on the triplets and avoided looking at him.

An uncomfortable tension stretched between them, vibrating like a rattlesnake. His fault. He'd scared her with his bitterness.

He tried to keep the anger to himself, but one unexpected mention of Sabrina and the rage roared in to attack the closest person. Poor Bowie had taken the brunt of his hostility for a long time. The subject of Sabrina was taboo.

"I should go." Kyra reached down for her purse.

Oh, no. He'd messed up big-time. She was leaving. "Wait. My references."

Her mouth opened and closed before she nodded. "Right."

From the looks of her, she had no intention of calling any of them.

She hitched her purse onto her shoulder and looked toward the door. Eager to escape.

He found his cell phone under a pile of contracts and scrolled for names and phone numbers of responsible souls who thought he was a good guy. He jotted three contacts on a notepad.

She accepted the note, saying nothing.

Panic pressed in. She was going to leave and never look back. She wouldn't call, probably wouldn't answer if he called her.

Three babies crowded around him, one hanging on to each jean leg, while the other, Benjamin, managed to find a piece of something to stick in his mouth.

Wade scooped him up. "Give it to Daddy, big guy."

Of course, Ben had no intention of relinquishing his treasure, so Wade pried the paper from his mouth and tossed it in the trash can.

"Look," he said, leaning his face around the now-screaming baby. "I'm sorry about barking at you. Twice. My ex-wife is a touchy subject."

"So I gathered. And none of my business." Kyra started out of the office.

Wiping baby slobber on his jeans, Wade followed.

He opened the door for her. She started off the porch. Wade wanted to say something other than *you smell good* or *please stay*, but was at a loss.

He'd blown his one chance at hiring a nanny.

Abby, clinging to his leg like a wood tick, turned loose and began to follow the redhead out the door. When Wade caught her tiny shoulder and turned her around, Abby started to cry, straining toward a woman she'd met less than an hour ago.

Wade knew how she felt.

He hoisted his daughter onto his other hip, blocked Caden from tumbling out the door, while wrestling with the still-whining Ben who'd decided he wanted down.

In desperation, Wade yelled after the fleeing woman, "Three months, Kyra. That's all I'm asking. Three months."

Clearly, the man was desperate. He was also intense and cranky, even angry, though he undoubtedly loved his children. All three of them.

Triplets. My goodness.

Adorable, yes, but what a handful for any parent, especially a single man running a ranch far from town and a day care.

Kyra couldn't decide if she admired the guy for trying or thought he was a jerk with a bad attitude.

Either way, playing nanny to three babies, even for a summer, was more than she'd bargained for.

But she needed to work. Medical bills still flowed

in like the Arkansas River, not to mention the money she wanted to send to Tristan's family.

Tristan. The very thought of the bright little boy with the mischievous grin made her heart bleed.

She drove to the end of the long graveled driveway leading in and out of the Sundown Ranch and stopped, debating.

Should she go home to her Tulsa suburb and forget this whole idea of finding peace and healing in the gorgeous southeastern Oklahoma mountains?

Or drive into the picturesque town of Sundown Valley and inquire about other employment opportunities?

She closed her eyes. "Heavenly Father, I thought You were leading me to this area. What now?"

Opening her eyes, she stared to the left and then the right, finally choosing the winding country road leading away from town and toward the low ancient mountains surrounding Sundown Valley.

Five minutes of driving took her along a scenic byway, the kind of place her family had visited every summer when she was a kid. She parked at an overlook and exited the car, taking her water bottle with her to the metal railing.

Drawing a deep breath, Kyra exhaled, the tension seeping from her body. She shook out her arms, stretched her fingers.

Not another car passed on the rural road. The only sound was occasional birdsong and the breeze whispering through the sumac shrubs at her feet.

"I need direction, Lord."

Staring across the vast valley of pine and hardwood to the undulating bluish mountains on the other side was a respite for the soul.

Across the way, she recognized the Winding Stair Mountains near where she and her parents had often rented a cabin or, in their more adventurous days, had pitched a tent.

"You do such glorious work, Father."

The breeze told her He was listening. She believed that with all her heart. In the year since the tragedy, she'd felt God's presence in these quiet moments when the pain subsided, both mental and physical.

"'I will lift up mine eyes unto the hills, from whence cometh my help. My help cometh from the Lord which made heaven and earth.'" As a pastor's daughter, she'd memorized many scriptures and this psalm of David seemed fitting. "I trust You, Lord. Guide me."

She lifted her finger and traced the winding road that curved like a long brown snake up the opposite mountain. Even after her mother died, she and her dad had hiked miles into the wilderness from that road.

She could return to the Tulsa area and find a job there easily enough. Everyone seemed to be hiring these days.

Yet, home brought memories she couldn't face and people who were constant reminders. Everyone knew, and their well-meaning pity made things worse.

Three round innocent faces rose in her mind. Abby, Benjamin and Caden. ABC. Three precious babies with one very lost parent. Only one. *No mother*, he'd said, in a way that had made Kyra want to run.

Why would a woman leave her three babies? Was it the man? Was he such a difficult person that his wife had been compelled to escape? Why not take her beautiful children with her? Most mothers would. Wouldn't they?

Had Wade somehow wrestled custody from the triplets' mother?

Wade Trudeau and his triplets had left too many un-answered questions in her mind. She should have asked, but his overreaction had warned her off.

Why couldn't she get him and his babies out of her head?

Maybe because those babies needed her far more than the man did.

"Are You trying to tell me something, Lord?"

She sipped her bottled water, and then, taking out her cell phone, checked for a signal. Cell service was spotty in the Kiamichi.

"One bar." She might as well try calling Wade Trudeau's references. A single hint of negativity from anybody and her decision would be easy to make.

Ten minutes later, with the signal still holding, Kyra tapped her pastor-dad's photo.

The phone clicked.

"How'd the interview at Sundown Valley Elementary go?" That was Dad. Cut to the chase.

She pressed the speaker button and held the device below her chin. There was no one within miles to over-hear. "I backed out."

"You didn't go to the interview?"

"I canceled."

Her dad, the Reverend Jack Mason, was silent for a few seconds. Kyra imagined the slight pull of his blond eyebrows as he pondered her words and the deeper meaning behind a canceled interview.

"Are you okay?" he asked.

Sweet dad. Unlike her, he was more concerned about her well-being than the fact that she hadn't worked in over a year.

"I am, but I'm not ready to teach again. I want to be,

Dad, but I can't. I sat in the school parking lot for fifteen minutes trying to convince myself that the building was safe, that I could do this and that nothing terrible would happen."

"PTSD is a strange malady."

"When I realized I was shaky and in a cold sweat, I knew I couldn't go inside. I was on the verge of losing control."

She hadn't expected her triggers to follow her here, but the idea of stepping back into a classroom of kids overwhelmed her at the rural Sundown Valley school every bit as much as it had in the city.

She shuddered at the thought of experiencing a flashback in front of strangers during an interview.

"I'm sorry, Kyra. I'd hoped a change of location was the answer."

"So had I, but apparently any school building triggers the anxiety."

"So you're driving back home today?"

Home for most of the last year had been her father's spare bedroom in a suburb outside of Tulsa, the room she'd called her own as a child.

Dad had driven her to physical therapy, counseled her, cooked for her, prayed for her. All the things a loving parent should do for a broken, wounded child.

Now her body was healed. It was time to let her dad get back to his own very busy life.

"Actually, Dad, I'm considering another position down here."

"Something other than teaching?"

In the background of their call, she heard a door open and close, heard voices. A large church was a busy place, even during the week.

Was she really thinking of moving to a remote Kiamichi Mountain ranch for three months to care for a set of triplets? Seriously?

She glanced down into the lush green valley below. Maybe she was.

"The job is a nanny position, Dad. At a ranch outside of Sundown Valley. Sundown Ranch. The owner is a single man with triplets."

"Nannying? Where did that come from? This is the first I've heard of such a thing."

"I know, I know, but hear me out." Now she was sounding like Wade Trudeau.

She told her dad of finding the card on a community bulletin board and the basics of her interview with Wade Trudeau.

"Two men and three babies," her dad mused. "The set up sounds like an old Tom Selleck movie."

She chuckled. "At first, I was going to refuse, but then Mr. Trudeau asked me to consider taking the job just for the summer."

"Is this something that interests you? Living on a ranch in the country nearly three hours from all your friends and family, confined with three little ones 24/7?"

Now that he put it that way, she worried. Could she do it? Did she want to? Would her back hold up from toting around three toddlers?

"Not 24/7, Dad. I can choose my days off."

"That's something, at least."

While they talked, a cardinal landed on the guardrail a few feet away. She'd heard that a redbird was a love letter from God, a reminder of a deceased loved one, meant to bring comfort.

She didn't know if she believed in such things or not, but the thought was lovely, uplifting.

Watching birds, especially cardinals, from her hospital window had been a pastime when her body was too broken to do much else. The red birds never failed to cheer her, bringing thoughts of her mother. And of Tristan.

"I don't know if *interests* is the right word, Dad, but I have to work again. I *need* to work, if only to prove I can. A nanny job in the rural beauty and peace of the Kiamichi could be a way to ease in gradually and regain more of my strength. It might help reset my addled brain, too."

"I'm not trying to discourage you, honey. You have a gift with children."

She knew that much was true. Children were her calling. The tragedy had stolen too much from her already. She couldn't allow it to take any more.

"You said yourself I need a change of pace, a change of scenery. That's why we agreed for me to come to the mountains."

"You've always loved the Kiamichi. When your mom was alive and we'd spend vacations there, you were never happier."

"That's true. I love this area. Looking at the mountains, which I'm doing right now, and hiking in the quiet woods, makes me feel closer to God."

"And makes you poetic. Remember all the pretty poems you wrote when we were camping?"

"That was a long time ago." She hadn't felt like writing anything except lesson plans in years. Now, even those were in the past.

"Maybe you need to get back to that place. Writing can be cathartic."

"Are you telling me to take the job?"

"You know me better than that, Kyra. You're a grown woman. A brilliant, well-educated woman with a good head on your shoulders. You've been making your own decisions for years."

"Always with your wise counsel," she said.

"Except for Sean Allred."

"Dad, please. Don't mention *that* mistake. After the accident, he disappeared faster than evaporating mist."

She still ached at her boyfriend's reaction.

"The tragedy scared him."

"Yes, the coward." She and Sean had been edging toward forever, but after the tornado, he'd stopped calling, stopped coming to see her. "He was scared I'd be confined to a wheelchair, and he didn't want to deal with a disabled girlfriend. *Couldn't* deal with it, I guess."

While she was fighting to walk again, Sean had started dating someone else.

So much for true love.

"I hope you've forgiven him."

"Forgiven, yes, but any love that might have been developing between us left when he did."

"He hurt you. I understand that. I was pretty upset with him myself."

"Dad. Let it go. I have."

Romance was so far off her radar as to be nonexistent. For the last year, she'd been regaining her health. Maybe in the future she'd be interested in finding her special someone, but not now. Not anytime soon.

In this season of her life, her total focus and goal

was to get mentally and physically strong enough to teach again.

Her dad cleared his throat. "Back to our topic. Those little ones would be blessed to have you, but living in the same house with two strange men? I'm not comfortable with that. What do you know about them?"

She told him about the bunkhouse.

"Perhaps a change of occupations is what I need, Dad, at least for a while until the episodes go away for good."

Cold sweats, shaking and, the very worst, flashbacks to those horrific hours buried beneath a mountain of rubble.

"Have you had another one?"

"Not the flashbacks, no." The others she could handle. "Thank the merciful Lord, and you. I know you're praying for me."

"Daily. My entire congregation, as well. Healing of the mind often takes longer than healing of the body." He'd shifted to his counseling roll, something he'd done frequently over the last year. "Give yourself that time, Kyra."

"So you agree this might be God's answer for now?"

"The bigger question is, do you think it is?"

"Maybe. I called Wade Trudeau's references, including his pastor. They all said the same thing. He's had a hard time the last couple of years, but he's a Christian man as solid as the mountain."

He hadn't looked or acted too solid this morning. But she didn't tell her father that.

"Who's his pastor? I know a few down that way. Maybe we've met at a conference or retreat. We preachers run in a pretty small circle. I could give him a call, pastor-to-pastor."

Even though she'd already spoken to the man, her father knew the right questions to ask. And as he said, pastor-to-pastor was a special bond.

Kyra opened the note she'd folded in half. "I have it right here, Dad. Grab a pencil."

She heard her dad rummaging at his desk. This time of day, he worked in his office, taking care of a hundred duties no one knew lead pastors did.

"Go ahead when ready," he said.

She rattled off the name and phone number.

"Pastor Blake Cloud," he said. "The name sounds familiar. Let me give him a call and get back to you."

"Thanks, Daddy. I love you."

"You, too, honey."

They hung up, and Kyra climbed into the car, marveling that she'd gone from practically running away from Sundown Ranch to leaning toward living there for the next three months.

The attraction had to be the triplets. It certainly wasn't the man. Other than being pathetic, he had no charisma whatsoever.

Thank goodness.

Wade Trudeau was *so* not her type. She preferred smooth businessmen in suits, not wild, unshaven cowboys in dusty boots.

But those sweet little babies. She couldn't forget them.

Maybe Wade was doing his best, but he was trying to juggle childcare with ranching and the two didn't mix. Three active toddlers were a full-time job for any one person. Preferably two people.

She wondered how long Wade had cared for the triplets alone. Had his wife recently left? Or had he been
their sole caregiver since birth?

Okay, now she was feeling sorry for the man. But
more than that, she felt sorry for the triplets. They
needed time and attention Wade could not give them.
Not if he wanted to make a living on his ranch.

They needed a mother.

Within five minutes, her cell phone jangled.

Her dad was calling.

And Kyra's decision was made.

Chapter 3

"I blew it, Bowie."

Wade ripped off a giant, annoyed bite as if to punish the ham sandwich. While he chewed, he scooped Caden's sippy cup off the floor for the umpteenth time and thumped it onto the highchair.

Three sets of messy hands alternately shoved food into their mouths and slapped their high-chair trays containing said food. The floor, as usual, was a mess.

Maybe he should get a house dog. He could let Pudge inside to play clean-up duty. The blue heeler would love that, and a judicious swipe of the cow dog's tongue would save Wade or Bowie another sweep-and-mop job.

A win-win.

Not too sanitary but efficient.

"What happened?" Bowie put down his sandwich and reached for his tea glass.

"A woman showed up out of the blue to inquire about the nanny job."

"Sounds good so far."

"Except she'd gotten one of my cards from somewhere, and the ad asked for a housekeeper. Which we need. That wasn't a lie." He stared at the lettuce poking out of his sandwich and grimaced. "But I didn't exactly mention the nanny thing in the ad. Or the triplets."

He glanced up to see Bowie's reaction.

He didn't get much of one. That was Bowie's way.

Though plenty of women thought the Cajun cousin was a tall, dark and handsome dreamboat, Bowie seldom gave anyone a second look. He liked women. He was just quiet and reserved with a cautious streak a mile wide and ten miles long.

Wade knew the reasons for that caution, though, like Sabrina, the past wounds were seldom discussed. As in never.

His cousin took a long drink of sweet tea before asking, "Why not?"

"For obvious reasons, Sherlock." Bowie could be a little dense when it came to social cues, another reason he didn't date much. "The mention of three kids seems to terrify people."

"So she went running."

"Not at first. For a minute, I thought I had her on the hook."

Bowie crunched a chip, waiting for the punch line.

"She asked about their mother." He shot a look at his motherless babies. Women. They stole your heart and then crushed it. At least one woman. The woman he'd adored and treated like a queen.

Worst of all was what she'd done to their triplets.

Hurting him was one thing. He was a man, an adult. But how could he forgive what she'd done to his babies?

Another reason Bowie was women-shy. He'd lived through Wade's disaster.

"Uh-oh. Wrong turn."

"Yeah. I might have overreacted. Even though Kyra took my references, I'll never hear from her again."

Abby turned her cup upside down. Milk drip-dripped onto the high-chair tray.

Bowie calmly reached out and took the cup.

Abby howled.

Wade handed her a piece of cheese.

"So back to square one, Bowie. Looks like the ranch will be on you and Riley for a while longer." Wade didn't know how the dependable ranch hand and Bowie had managed by themselves since the triplets' birth. He, though part owner, had been pretty much useless on the ranch, and that had to change now that spring was here and the workload increased exponentially. "I'm gonna text Yates again, ask him one more time to come home and take his rightful place."

It wouldn't be the first time he'd tried to contact his wayward brother. More like the hundredth.

He whipped out his cell phone and scrolled to the number Yates had reluctantly given him three years ago.

"Think he'll answer?"

"Doubt it, but I have to try. Sundown Ranch is his, too. We need his help, especially now."

Yates had joined the military shortly after the accident that had cost their youngest brother his life. Yates blamed Wade for Trent's death, and he was right. Wade carried a load of guilt, along with the grief. But he'd already lost one brother. Losing Yates, too, was unthinkable.

He wouldn't give up until his maverick brother came home.

His thumbs raced across the digital keyboard, asking his brother to return and take his place on the ranch that was one-third his. Saying a prayer, Wade hit Send and then pocketed the device.

Bowie scraped his chair away from the table to retrieve a fallen or tossed sippy cup. Tossing the cup was a game all three babies found wildly entertaining.

"Teenagers look for work in summer," his cousin said as he plunked the sippy on Caden's tray. "Hire one of them to babysit."

Wade scowled. "I don't want a kid looking after the triplets!"

Bowie lifted an eyebrow, silent, then got up to fix himself another sandwich.

"All right." Wade waved his half-eaten sandwich. "I see your point. Beggars can't be choosers. But I'll hire a teenager only as a last resort. Someone we know from church. I'm holding out a while longer for an adult with experience. Like Kyra Mason."

"You keep talking about her." Bowie tilted away from the open refrigerator to look at him with those knowing black eyes. "Was she pretty?"

Wade's scowl grew deeper. The redhead's picture rose in his brain, all prim, proper and pretty. Fact of the business, he'd thought of her all morning. Of the sweet way she'd played with Abby. Of how good she smelled. Of her fresh, wholesome appearance and that glossy red hair.

He, who'd sworn off women for the rest of his life, couldn't get one small female out of his head.

Because she was the perfect candidate for the job. Not because he found her attractive.

"Doesn't matter. She's long gone. Probably high-tailed it back to Tulsa as fast as that itty-bitty car could take her."

"Tulsa?" Bowie slid a knife full of mayo across a slice of wheat bread. "Not a local?"

"I know what you're thinking. City girl. What was she doing down here in the bojacks, anyway?"

A city girl would never stick around. Just ask him. He knew from painful experience. You could take the girl out of the city, but you couldn't take the city out of the girl. The old saying was a cliché for a very good reason.

He grabbed for the wet wipes in the center of the table and ripped off a few for the yellow macaroni and cheese Benjamin had smeared on his baby-bird chest.

In return, Ben offered Wade a bite from his messy little fingers. Wade pretended to eat, making gobble-up noises like the Cookie Monster. All three babies chortled.

Man, they were awesome, his three cute nuggets, even if they kept him hopping day and night.

His cell phone chirped.

Wade fished the phone from his back pocket.

"Sundown Ranch. Wade speaking."

His pulse leaped. Then his hopes rose. He listened and then spoke for a moment before hanging up.

If his adrenaline jacked any higher, he'd be a helium balloon.

"Well?" Bowie asked, pointing the mayo knife. "Your face is red. Who was it?"

"Kyra Mason."

Bowie tilted his head as he screwed the lid onto the mayo jar. "The redhead who ran away?"

"Yes. She's on her way to look at the bunkhouse."

"For what? To live in?" Bowie stuck the condiment jar in the fridge.

"Yeah. I sort of made her an offer. A place to live away from the main house and us guys."

"You want her to live in the old rundown bunkhouse that nobody's used in forever? A city girl?" He whistled softly. "That's not good, cuz."

Wade slammed a hand through his hair, then realized he had macaroni and cheese on his fingers.

"Grab the cleaning supplies. I'll get the triplets. We've got work to do. Fast."

Kyra arrived at the Sundown Ranch to discover two cowboys motioning to her from the porch of a weathered, rustic building.

Was *that* the bunkhouse?

Rather than turn left from the long graveled driveway toward the ranch's main house, she turned right down a very short overgrown path and parked next to the sad-looking wooden structure.

For one very long moment, she questioned her decision to come back.

The hopeful expression on Wade Trudeau's face got her out of the car.

God had a plan, and that plan included a summer on the Sundown Ranch. After her phone call to accept the summer-only job, she'd driven home to Tulsa for some of her belongings.

"Did you have a safe trip?" Wade's tone was falsely jovial.

He must have seen her hesitation.

Kyra stepped up on the porch. A board was missing at one end, but otherwise the floor felt solid.

One positive thing.

Her gaze roamed over the tired building. Hopefully, the interior was better.

"Yes. Thank you. My car is loaded down."

One brown eyebrow jacked up. "Wouldn't take much."

Was he making fun of her cute car?

The three of them stood awkwardly while the building creaked and the wind ruffled the weeds growing around the steps. One lonely stray daffodil waved from the tangled mess.

The splash of yellow was exactly the impetus she needed.

"You must be Bowie," Kyra finally said, offering a hand to a tall, handsome man in a gray cowboy hat and dusty boots.

"Yes, ma'am." He wiped one hand down his jeans' leg before shaking hers.

He was obviously the cousin. The familial similarities to Wade were undeniable, though Bowie's coloring was darker. They were both tall and fit and bore the same sculpted jaw and strong cheekbones.

Handsome.

"I didn't think you'd come back," Wade said.

She smiled. "I guess I'm a surprise, then."

He let out a gusty breath. "A good one."

One of the triplets, she wasn't sure which one, toddled out the open door, dragging a baby blanket behind.

"Is this the bunkhouse?"

"Yes." Both men seemed to be guarding the doorway. "We're letting it air while we clean up some."

"May I see the inside?"

"Oh, sure. Yes. Sure." Wade's stuttering reply didn't reassure her.

He hoisted the advancing baby under the armpits and swung him or her through the doorway.

Kyra stepped inside behind the man and child. The other two babies, the identical boys, she saw now, played with a pile of toys in one corner of the long, narrow room.

Abby toddled to her brothers, chattering something only the three of them understood. Ben—or was it Caden?—offered the little girl a play cell phone. She held it to her ear and babbled.

Kyra let her gaze drift from the babies to the bunkhouse interior.

The place smelled musty. And dusty. So much so she coughed.

In one corner, directly inside the long rectangular room, sat a scarred wooden table and chairs for two. The other side was empty with swirls of dust on the flooring as if someone had recently moved out the furniture. A chair or couch, perhaps?

A few more steps into the space and two rows of heavy oak bunks bracketed the sides of the room.

Dust covered everything. Dirt daubers' red mud nests plastered the walls.

Were there mice? She shuddered. She hated mice.

Something in her expression must have warned him

because Wade said, "As I mentioned this morning, we haven't used the bunkhouse in a long time."

He wiped a finger across the end of a bunk. Dust motes swirled. "The place is a little dusty."

A little? Cobwebs hung from windows so dirty as to be opaque. The old curtains needed to be burned. Their color was indistinguishable.

An attempt had been made recently to sweep and mop the long wooden floor, a useless gesture given that the walls and ceilings needed to be cleaned and dirt daubers removed.

The mattresses on the double row of bunk beds, thankfully, were encased in plastic.

Could she live in this?

"We'll clean it up. Don't you worry." Wade sounded desperate.

Once again, Kyra felt sorry for him. Her tender heart was getting the best of her.

"I don't do mice," Kyra blurted.

"No signs of them. Nothing in here to attract them. Right, Bowie?"

Bowie nodded.

That was something, anyway.

"The bathroom and kitchenette are functional." Wade pointed toward the opposite end of the rectangular room where an alcove divided the space.

Kyra moved to the alcove, her footsteps thudding against the wood floor.

Wade followed. She could feel his anxiety.

Turning to the right of the alcove, she glanced inside a small bathroom, which didn't appear too disgusting. The window had been opened and fresh air flowed inside.

A full bottle of Lysol cleaner perched on the vanity next to a stack of cleaning rags.

The double vanity surprised her, but if several ranch hands had lived in the bunkhouse, two sinks probably hadn't been enough.

"Think this will work?" Wade asked, eager, hopeful, though the worry frown between his eyes expressed his real feelings. He was afraid she'd bolt.

So was she.

"Let's see the kitchenette."

She rounded the doorway to the left of the alcove.

A tiny kitchenette consisted of a greasy two-burner stove, no oven and a dorm-sized refrigerator bearing dirty handprints. She wondered how long they'd been there.

Above the appliances, a row of dusty shelves sat empty.

Toward the center of the space, beneath a window that overlooked a vast green field with mountains in the distance, was a small bar-sized sink. A rust stain ringed the drain. Underneath was a storage cabinet with a single drawer. Small but functional.

"You'll take most of your meals at the main house with us. If you want to," he hurried to add. "I could use your help feeding the triplets."

"Of course." Once cleaned, the kitchenette would serve adequately for snacks and morning coffee. "Is there a coffeepot? Or a microwave?"

"I'll get new ones. We tossed the others." He grimaced. "They were in pretty bad shape."

She could only imagine anything in worse shape than the stove.

"Bowie's good at mechanical things," he went on as

if pointing out the positives would convince her to stay. "He's checked out the appliances and bathroom fixtures. The AC is good. Fridge is working. Everything's a go."

No, everything was not a go. Making this building livable would take hours, maybe days.

"I—" Kyra considered turning down the offer, or at least postponing her start date until the bunkhouse was in better condition.

Without saying as much, she walked back into the bunk area.

If she lived here, she'd move the table to this end near the kitchenette. The light from the window on the east would be pleasant in the mornings.

And maybe she'd add an easy chair and a TV on the other side, a mini-living room of sorts.

A big area rug in the center of the room would brighten things up and make the room cozy. New curtains, too.

One of the triplets waddled over and offered her a touch-and-feel baby book. Kyra crouched low, took the book and the baby's finger, rubbing it across a wooly sheep.

"Sheep are soft."

So was her heart.

This baby needed her.

She read a few more pages, guiding the child to touch each one, then rose to her feet and faced Wade.

"Let's focus on this area and the bath for today. The kitchen and windows can wait. I'll help."

"You're staying?" Wade's blue eyes widened.

Bowie chuckled but didn't say anything. She'd noticed he didn't talk much.

"Once the place is clean, you promise to fix it up?

New curtains, rugs and anything else I deem necessary to make it livable."

"Anything you want. Anything."

"You might regret those words." She wasn't fancy or a germophobe. A special-needs teacher couldn't afford to be, but she wanted clean, organized and functional. "I'll take every weekend off and July Fourth."

"Agreed. Bowie and I can hold the fort."

"And I want new locks on the door and the only key to the bunkhouse."

If the demand offended him, he didn't react.

"Agreed, but you have my word that no one on this ranch will bother you. They try, and they answer to me."

"Thank you. I appreciate that." She also kept a baseball bat beside her bed, and she was not afraid to use it. In college, she'd been a pretty solid intramural softball hitter.

"So, it's a deal?" Wade asked. "You'll take the job? Move in here tonight?"

One of the babies, Benjamin, she thought, reached his arms toward her. How could she resist? She lifted his chubby body against her shoulder. He patted her hair.

He was such a precious lamb, even though his diaper sagged and his face was dirty.

"For the summer." She smoothed a hand over Benjamin's soft cap of hair, spotting what appeared to be a glob of yellow cheese.

"Three months." Three months she hoped she didn't regret. "Until school starts again."

She hoped and prayed that by late August she'd be ready to walk into a classroom full of children.

Wade looked at his hand, wiped it on his shirt and

held it out to her. Kyra put her fingers in his to shake on the deal.

His palm was calloused and rough and swallowed hers. She liked the feeling. And if tiny tingles played over her nerve endings, she blamed them on the back injury. She'd had plenty of tingles after the tragedy as feeling had slowly returned to her battered body.

The electric charges certainly couldn't be attraction.

She withdrew her hand. The tingles remained. "Let's get busy getting this bunkhouse clean. Otherwise, you're renting me a hotel room tonight."

Wade blinked several times.

Bowie laughed.

She gave them her sweetest smile, grabbed a bucket and headed for the bathroom.

Chapter 4

Wade pulled his pickup truck to a stop beside the bunkhouse and hopped out. He had a boatload of ranch work to do but his number one priority today, other than the triplets, was keeping the new nanny happy and in residence.

She'd stayed in the bunkhouse last night, though he had seen in her expression that she was less than impressed with his idea of appropriate nanny living quarters.

City girls had no comprehension of roughing it.

But he wouldn't complain. She'd taken the job. She was here. Best of all, she was doing okay with the triplets. So far. But it was early yet. Three toddlers was a lot for anyone. A woman without kids, even a teacher, couldn't know the challenges that lay ahead.

Which meant Wade had to make the bunkhouse as comfortable as possible, a refuge for Kyra to escape to each evening when he took charge of the babies. They mostly slept through the night now, anyway. He could handle the times they didn't. She, however, had to rise before six o'clock to take over while he headed out to work.

Only Caden had cried this morning when Wade left the house. Kyra had swooped in with a silly face, a tickle and a sippy cup, and the little guy had hushed up before Wade got to the back door.

He hoped her enthusiasm and energy didn't wane. It certainly had with the last two nannies. Fast.

He could not let that happen.

Wade pulled the handle of the tailgate and it fell open with a metal slam. The sound echoed in the spring sunshine, flushing a flock of blackbirds.

Pudge, his cow dog and loyal companion, leaped from the back of the truck to the ground, tongue lolling happily, looking at Wade as if to say, *What now, boss? Can I chase something? Got a cow that needs herding? Let me at 'em. Let me at 'em.*

That dog loved to herd cows and ride in the truck. "Soon, pal. We're vaccinating later today. You'll get to have your fun."

Three barns were within eyeshot beyond the house. Wade glanced toward them in search of help before recalling that his ranch hands were otherwise occupied.

Both Bowie and Riley were moving hay to the ranch's west forty acres and checking on the pregnant mamas. Wade didn't expect to see either one of them until evening.

Ah, well, no big deal. He'd get these bunkhouse items delivered and head for the barn to unload the rest. It wouldn't be the first time he'd worked alone. It was, however, the first time since Miss Janey left that he'd been able to work outside for any length of time.

Leaving the triplets for even a short period was not an option. Anything could happen. Bowie helped out in short spurts, but the babies were Wade's responsibility. He refused to impose on his easygoing cousin any more than necessary. Bowie loved the babies but he, an unconfirmed bachelor, knew less about kids than Wade did and wasn't eager to learn.

Hiring a nanny took a heavy weight off his shoulders, and it felt good to be back in the saddle, so to speak. Which he literally would be later today.

First, to make the nanny happy. Or at least happier.

Please, Lord, make her happy. I haven't been too successful in the make-a-woman-happy department.

Not that he was interested in making Kyra happy as in girlfriend happy. He only wanted her to be content and to fall so in love with his triplets that she couldn't leave them until they were a little older. Say maybe eighteen or twenty.

He snorted at the ridiculous thought.

The impossible dream.

Dragging the boxes toward the end of the truck bed, he hoisted the heaviest and started toward the bunkhouse.

The door stood open. He wasn't invading anyone's privacy.

He hoped.

He stepped inside and hollered, "Kyra? You in here?"

No reply, so he figured she and the littles were still in the main house. He'd left them in the kitchen this morning, having a breakfast he'd cooked before Kyra arrived.

She'd had to knock on the back door.

He needed to give her a house key.

With a groan, he recalled the new lock and key he'd promised for the bunkhouse.

Another trip to town. Maybe tomorrow. Not today. Too much catch-up work to do.

Toting the microwave to the kitchenette, Wade paused. The space still looked pathetic, particularly the cook stove. Better not set up anything until the place was clean.

With a sigh, he set the box on the scarred table in the main room, grabbed some rags and cleaner and got to work.

After running hot water in the tiny sink, he dumped in enough Lysol to make himself cough. The cleaner smelled great. It was just strong.

Using his considerable upper body strength, he started scrubbing grates while eliminating enough grease to lubricate his cab tractor.

Man, ranch hands were slobs.

A woman expected nice things. *Clean* things.

"I can do this, Wade."

At the soft female voice, Wade swung around. His belly did something weird. Sort of a jitterbug.

He ignored it. Mostly.

Kyra stood in the doorway. A baby on each hip, she held the other one by the hand. How did she manage that? It had taken him weeks to figure out the best way to herd/carry all three at once. He'd even considered training Pudge to help with the herding.

"I got your microwave." He nudged his chin in that direction.

"Thank you." She slid the babies to the floor, which he noticed looked a lot cleaner than it had last night. He and Bowie had swiped at the dust with a mop before she'd arrived, but now the floor looked shiny in the sunlight shooting in from the east window.

"Did you stay up half the night cleaning?"

Her grin was sheepish. "Maybe."

"Well, don't. I'll knock off early each evening until we get the place in shape. You shouldn't have to do this all yourself and watch the triplets, too."

"We cleared out the worst of the dirt and yuck last night, so I feel comfortable bringing the babies out here while I clean and organize." She ran a hand over the top of the microwave box. "If you're okay with me working out here with them present."

"Sure. Fine. Whatever you want to do." Yesterday, he'd worried about exposing the triplets to the dust, too, but a man did what a man had to do.

They'd been so dirty last night when he'd helped Kyra bathe them that they'd had to change the water between kids.

He was kind of embarrassed about that. He hoped she didn't think he was a negligent dad.

"I'm here," he said. "Might as well fumigate this stove."

She laughed and reached for a pair of rubber gloves he'd actually remembered to bring to the cabin last night. "It is bad, isn't it?"

"I should have bought a new one while I was in Sundown Valley." He'd been right there in the home store. He could have bought a stove, the lock, whatever. "You'll need to make a list for my next trip."

He hoped she didn't break the bank. So far, she'd not been demanding, but this was only day one. And she *was* a female.

Kyra cast a watchful glance at the triplets now toddling around the long mostly empty bunkhouse. His trio had a habit of getting into anything they shouldn't. Watching was duty numero uno.

A clothes basket of toys he'd never seen before was pushed against one wall. Abby headed toward them, babbling.

"No need for a new stove," she said. "This will do. It's only for three months."

His hopeful mood plummeted.

Oh. Yeah. Rats. Three lousy months.

In the confined space, she managed to take the two burners from him and dump them in the sink of water. "Let them soak. I'll use oven cleaner on them tonight."

He screwed up his face. "Do I have oven cleaner?"

She laughed. Which had been his intention. He sure liked the sound. Warm and light. And when she laughed, her eyes sparkled. He liked that, too.

"I don't know," she said. "Do you?"

"Probably not. Unless Janey, our previous house-keeper, left some in the kitchen."

"Don't worry about it. I'll look. I haven't had a chance to do much cleaning in the main house yet."

He stared at her, which wasn't a hardship. Her red hair was pulled back in a bouncy ponytail, which better displayed her apple cheekbones and slightly tilted nose.

Not that he was noticing. But he sure liked the color of her hair.

"You have your hands full here. For now, Bowie and I can shovel the house out if needed."

"What about dinner? Isn't cooking part of my job description, too?"

"We got it for now. Give yourself a few days to get settled with the bunkhouse and the triplets."

"I prefer to pull my weight, but that's thoughtful of you."

Thoughtful? No. Pure self-preservation.

He'd do about anything to keep her from jumping in that tiny blue car and running away to Tulsa.

They worked in silence for a few minutes. He wanted to say something but couldn't think of anything intelligent. The quiet was a little awkward.

Finally, he blurted, "I bought coffee."

Her back was turned to him as she scrubbed the shelves under the sink. She pivoted on a pair of tan canvas shoes that would be filthy by nightfall.

"What about a coffeepot?"

"That's what I meant. Coffeepot." His brain wasn't working properly. Likely because he'd actually slept most of last night. He wasn't accustomed to solid sleep.

"One of those pod coffee makers," he said, "and the coffee to go with it." He might have tossed in some tea and a few other pod drinks in case she preferred those.

She smiled up at him. "Perfect."

"It's in the truck. I'll get it." He started out the door, stopping to kiss each nugget on the head. Benjamin ended up following him onto the porch.

He grabbed the other boxes and, using his knee as an extra hand, guided his son back into the cabin.

Kyra met him halfway to the door. "I thought I'd lost him. They move fast."

"Truer words were never spoken." He hoped she understood how important every second was when it came to watching three little ones.

Though her references glowed, she'd worked with school-age kids, not babies. Besides, he didn't know her well enough yet to fully trust her with his most prized possessions.

He felt a little guilty about that, but he'd feel worse if something happened to one of the triplets.

After sliding the remaining boxes onto the only table in the place, he raked a hand through his hair, and said, "I'm sorry to abandon you."

"Go. You have work."

But he didn't want to go. He wanted to stay right here with her and those three babies.

It was probably that trust thing.

But something about Kyra…

Get a grip, Trudeau. City girl. Three months and she's gone. Don't be dumb. You've been dumb before. Don't be dumb again.

She might be pretty and personable. She might be kind to him and his children. That was what he wanted. That was the deal.

The *only* deal.

With a one-fingered salute, he backed away and loped to the truck. Pudge hopped into the bed and hung his happy canine head over the side while Wade slammed the tailgate and jumped into the truck.

Get back to work. And don't even think about the pretty nanny.

Kyra was nothing if not a good employee. That was the way her dad had raised her, and that was the way she'd always worked. A day's work for a day's pay, he'd said, and she agreed. Up until the back injury had sidelined her, she'd been the teacher who'd gone the extra mile, working before and after school and sometimes weekends.

Now, she was praying to make it through the first day.

Her back ached, and she longed to lie down and take a nap.

To make matters worse, she'd been awake half the night listening to the strange noises. That was why she'd been up cleaning. Not because she was a clean freak, even though she was, but because of the noises.

The coyote howls had been the worst. She didn't hear those in a Tulsa suburb. On camping trips, yes, but those days had been years ago when she was a kid with her family right beside her in the tent. She'd never even noticed the night sounds back then.

She wasn't afraid, but the howling had disturbed her sleep. Not to mention the strange bed in a strange building that barely passed as livable. And the odd mixture of cleaning products and dust annoying her nose. She had a powerful sense of smell.

Gritting her teeth against the ache in her back, Kyra hoisted two babies, took the other by the hand, and left the bunkhouse. She'd cleaned and rearranged all her body could take for now.

Nap time couldn't come fast enough. Not only for the babies. For herself.

Maybe she was trying to do too much too soon. Maybe her body wasn't ready for this much work. Or for dealing with small children.

Three toddlers were a lot for someone healing from a broken back. Then there was the unbearable thought that she might accidentally let down her guard and allow something to happen to one of them.

A memory flashed in her head. Screaming, whimpering voices, followed by the awful silence.

She'd been responsible that day, and she'd failed.

With a hard shudder, Kyra blocked the horror from her mind before the memory became reality, before the flashbacks hit her and she lost all sense of time and place.

Nothing would happen to the triplets. She must be vigilant, even if that required sitting beside their cribs while they slept and watching every step they took.

"Help me do this, Lord." She whispered a prayer she'd prayed numerous times in the last twenty-four hours. "Protect these children. Guard my heart and mind. Strengthen my body."

She'd come to Sundown Ranch to get her life back, to prove she could work again, that she could live a normal life. Most of all to prove that being with children wouldn't trigger the PTSD.

What if, while she was alone with the triplets, she suffered a flashback and lost touch with reality?

If Wade knew about the disaster that had brought her here, would he have hired her? Would he trust her with his babies?

She hadn't had an episode in months. But what if she did?

She shook her head to dispel the nagging worries.

Be careful for nothing; but in every thing by prayer and supplication with thanksgiving let your requests be made known unto God. And the peace of God, which passeth all understanding, shall keep your hearts and your minds in Christ Jesus.

As a kid, she'd grown weary of memorizing scripture. Now she was grateful when the exact words she needed flooded in.

The peace of God *would* guard her heart and mind.

"Thank you, Mom." For it had been her mother who

had assigned a memory verse per week. "Thank you, Lord, for the reminders."

Now, if she could only follow the very good scriptural advice. She'd prayed. Now to stop worrying and accept God's peace.

Benjamin the bold yanked from her grip to chase a butterfly. She let the other two wiggle worms slide to the ground, and they followed Ben, their chubby legs and arms pumping. Occasionally, one fell down, only to pop up and head out again.

Adorable.

A lot of work, but so, so cute.

She pulled her cell phone from her back jeans' pocket and snapped some photos to show Wade later.

A text box popped up. Amy, her best friend, checking on her, offering to commandeer some guys and a pickup truck if she wanted to bring any of her furniture from Tulsa.

Amy could always commandeer any number of guys. Kyra wondered what she'd think of two real cowboys?

Smiling, she dashed off a reply, then took a few more photos.

When the trio tired of the futile chase, Kyra herded them toward the back door of the main house. Herding distractible toddlers wasn't easy, but it gave her back a break.

How had Wade done this alone, for the most part, while still running a ranch and handling all the other chores a home and children required? Yes, his cousin lived here, but as he'd told her, the triplets were his children and his responsibility. He carried the load.

Her sympathy for him grew.

He wasn't a negligent dad. He had too much on his plate.

She planned to take some of those duties off his wide muscled shoulders.

That was what he was paying her for.

Never mind that she'd felt some tingly moments of attraction for the rancher. Watching a man gently diaper a baby shouldn't be such a turn-on.

She laughed at the ridiculous thought. All three toddlers looked up and grinned. Four teeth, two on top and two on bottom, showed in all three mouths.

Her heart squeezed.

Once inside the house, she settled the ABC trio on a questionably clean kitchen floor with a yogurt snack pouch.

With the babies momentarily occupied, she explored the kitchen cabinets, discovered a slow cooker and searched the freezer for something easy to prepare for dinner.

One less thing for Wade to handle.

She mentally patted herself on the back for the idea.

Even if Wade had promised to help, a meal that cooked itself would make life easier on all of them.

Though not an accomplished chef, she had a cell phone and could read a recipe.

After scrolling the internet, Kyra put together what she hoped would be a rancher-filling meal and plugged in the Crock-Pot. Would it be enough? She'd never cooked for three adults and three toddlers before.

By then, Abby was crying and rubbing her eyes. Caden needed a fresh diaper. And Ben pounded his empty pouch against the refrigerator, apparently demanding more food. At the top of his lungs.

Wade hadn't given her a schedule. Did he think an unexpected, unprepared nanny automatically knew what to feed toddlers? Or when to put them down for a nap?

She didn't, but she'd figure it out. Flexibility was the name of the game in the teaching profession.

She glanced at the food-prep mess on the counters, then at the needy toddlers. And there was this sticky floor to consider.

The back doorknob rattled. Kyra froze. The toddlers, on the other hand, amped up a few hundred decibels.

Their dad appeared in the doorway.

Kyra's stomach dipped, a car-over-a-high-hill dip. Not attraction. Definitely not. She'd been startled by his unexpected return to the house. That was all.

"How's it going?" he said over the cacophony.

Caden, the stinky one, rushed toward Wade, lost his balance and splatted against the tile. His howl rivaled last night's coyotes.

Wade went to his haunches to lift the boy into a hug. Abby took this as a good sign and joined them, consoling her crying brother with a pat or two on the face. Ben continued to yell from the fridge.

Over the din, Kyra wanted to answer Wade's question with one word. *Chaos.* She didn't. If Wade was already back in the house after his visit to the bunkhouse cabin, he was checking on her, making sure she could properly care for his children.

At the moment, she had her doubts.

"We're figuring things out," she said. "I could use a schedule."

He looked up. Her stomach did that dipping thing again.

He really was a good-looking man.

"For the babies?" he asked over Abby's skinny top-of-the-head ponytail. "Don't have one. If they're hungry, I feed them. If they're sleepy or cranky, I put them in their cribs."

"Oh." She was a schedule kind of person. A list-maker. A notetaker. Organization was the key to sanity. "I really need a schedule."

Wade rose from the floor, Caden in his arms. He patted the fussing child's back, his wide rancher's hand against the small cotton-clad body. Incongruous and sweet.

The baby sniffled and rubbed his wet face against the cowboy's blue shirt. Blue, a color that made Wade's eyes even more noticeable. Today, the pretty irises were less bloodshot, and the cowboy had shaved.

Not that she intended to notice.

But she did, and that bothered her a little.

Employee. Employer. Nothing else.

She wanted to keep this job all summer, not get fired. Wade had been more than clear about his attitude toward romance.

"We can make a schedule. Sure," he was saying, and Kyra mentally slapped her focus from the man's good looks to the toddlers. "Or you can make one to please yourself. Whatever works best for you."

What would work best for her was to stop noticing him so much. Here was a man with an ex-wife he obviously still loved or he wouldn't freak out when she was mentioned. And Kyra was a woman trying to get her life back on track. She couldn't chance adding another heartache to the mix.

"When do they usually nap?"

"Anytime after they eat lunch."

"They don't take bottles anymore? Right?"

He made a face. "No, thank the merciful Lord. Janey weaned them before she left. I'm not sure I could have managed that little trick on my own. All that crying and whining." He gave a fake shudder. And there Kyra went again, noticing those wide shoulders. "Brutal. Especially Ben. He's a demanding little critter."

Kyra smiled. "I noticed. Ben the bold. Abby the amiable talker and Caden the cuddler, maybe a little timid and tender."

"You nailed them." He looked pleased, which made her pleased, too.

Caden had now stopped crying. Kyra reached to take him from Wade. "He needs to be changed."

"Probably the others do, too." He hoisted the remaining two. "Let's do this."

"This is my job, Wade. You have the ranch."

He shrugged. "My babies."

He followed her to the nursery, and in no time, he'd changed his two while she was still wrestling to keep a naked but clean Caden in one place.

Suddenly, a hand appeared above Caden's face, rattling a set of plastic keys. The baby stilled, eyes watchful, and then latched onto them.

"You're a genius." Kyra quickly slid the diaper under Caden and secured the tabs.

"Practice. Lots and lots."

"How long have you done this by yourself?"

"This time? About three months. Since their first birthday. Janey, our nanny, left the next week. Her brother got sick."

Kyra wanted to ask how long the triplets' mother had been gone.

Lest she hit a nerve again, she chose her wording carefully. "Have you been on your own with them since birth?"

His face closed up. "Mostly." A new tension ebbed from him. He backed away from the changing table. "Gotta get to work."

"Wait. Wade." She lifted Caden into her arms, still zipping his onesie with the opposite hand. "I didn't mean to upset you."

He offered a tight, and most certainly fake, smile. "Not upset. Busy." He saluted in that charming way of his. One finger. "Later."

Abby ran after him, yelling something that sounded like, "Da-da-da-da-da."

Ben screamed and threw a stuffed monkey.

Caden snuggled into her shoulder and sucked his index finger.

Yes, indeed. For a long time, she'd refused to discuss Sean. So she knew the signs. Wade Trudeau still nursed a broken heart.

Chapter 5

Wade scooped another spoonful of the casserole Kyra had prepared for dinner. He'd not expected her to cook for them—not so soon, anyway. But, man, when he'd walked in the back door exhausted and smelled that food cooking, his mouth had watered and his belly had done a happy dance.

She'd set the dining room table, too. He couldn't remember the last time they'd used that room. Back when Sabrina had been in residence, he figured, though he didn't like remembering that very rocky time.

Usually, he, Bowie and the tots ate at the bar in the kitchen. Eating in the dining room again was kind of nice. Napkins and everything. And in the center of the square table, she'd set a pretty glass filled with Indian paintbrush. His mama had loved those red-orange wildflowers. Seeing them brought back good memories.

"Is the food okay?" Kyra asked anxiously, as if men who'd worked outside all day were particular. Especially men who'd been spared the task of cooking the meal. "I found the recipe on the blog of a rancher's wife, so I thought you might like it."

"Great," Wade said around a mouthful of ground beef, potatoes and cheese.

He squinted at his freshly filled fork. Were those chili beans? Or maybe kidney beans? Not too spicy for the toddlers. Tasty.

The trio of imps was making a royal mess of the food she'd put on each tray next to some sliced bell peppers. Even with plastic spoons in one hand, they mostly ate with their fingers.

She'd tried to make biscuits, which were as hard as his kneecap, but Wade gnawed through one anyway and shot a warning glance to Bowie to do the same. He didn't have the heart to tell her there was a bag of frozen biscuits and other quick items in the utility room Deepfreeze.

He snuck a look at the nanny, across from him, straight and proper in her chair, left hand in her lap unless she was feeding a baby. She'd positioned herself near the triplets and occasionally scooped bites into accepting mouths. Independent Ben shook his head and refused to let her feed him.

Wade knew he should be assisting, but Kyra appeared to be handling things. He wanted to watch her in action. Trusting a woman, especially a young pretty city woman, didn't come easy.

She'd filled him in on the triplets' afternoon and sounded as if they'd done okay. She even showed him some pictures she'd taken. He forgot to do that a lot, and they were growing so fast. She offered to text them to his phone and email.

She'd made a schedule, too, and started training the little ones to adhere to it. He wasn't sure about regimentation but figured a little organization wouldn't hurt them. Since Janey'd left, they were often up too late at night or slept too long in the afternoon because he was occupied with ranch work.

He frowned at his plate. Was he a lousy father? Did Kyra think that about him?

Bowie waved a fork to get his attention. "Bull five looks a little better after the vet was out yesterday."

Wade dragged his traitorous eyes from the pretty nanny. "What about that cow with the prolapse?"

"She's all right."

"Prolapse?" Kyra asked. "I've never heard that term."

He explained the condition. Her eyes widened, but she said nothing. She just turned to wipe Ben's messy face, a useless endeavor, Wade could tell her. There was no point in wiping up until they were finished.

Bowie reached for another rock-hard biscuit. He was either really hungry or really thoughtful. Or a little of both. "Her calf is trying to scour, though."

"Must not have gotten enough colostrum. Did you give it some electrolytes?"

"Yes, and moved him to barn three with his mama." Bowie poked another fork of meat and potatoes in his mouth.

"Think he'll make it?"

Bowie took a few seconds to chew and swallow. "Likely. He was still feisty. I'll check on him before bed."

"Do I dare ask the meaning of scour?" Kyra asked.

Both he and Bowie turned their heads to answer. "Diarrhea."

They went on talking about the cow and calf, then segued into mucking manure in barn four before the rains started and turned the lot into something neither of them wanted to consider. The stench was something akin to a dead coyote.

After a bit, Wade realized the new nanny was especially quiet. She'd started out the meal with pep and conversation, but now she'd gone silent and turned away, her side to him, her attention on the children. She'd barely touched her food.

"Everything okay, Kyra?"

Her head swiveled in his direction. "Fine."

She didn't look fine. "You look...green. Are you sick?"

Trying for a laugh, Kyra waved a hand. "I'm not accustomed to ranch talk. That's all."

Seriously? What had they said that could be the least bit upsetting?

Manure was a fact of life.

Realization moved through him.

Manure might be a fact of ranch life, but Kyra was a city girl.

And he'd do well to remember that.

Kyra chased Abby into the nursery, listening to her squeal with delight at what she clearly thought was a game of tag-and-tickle.

Rounding up all three for a bath proved to be a real challenge.

"Need some reinforcements?"

Kyra looked up into a pair of laughing blue eyes.

Wade leaned against the nursery door frame, watching her.

Watching, as if still deciding her value as a nanny.

During dinner, he'd lapsed into gloomy silence. She'd thought he was upset because she'd found his table conversation unappetizing.

Now, he was smiling again.

Puzzling man.

"When I get two in the bathroom," she said, ignoring thoughts of the man, "the other one races back into the nursery."

"Yeah, they think it's a game." He pushed away from the door and stepped inside.

"I noticed." She caught the little girl and carried her into the bathroom where Caden sat on a rug, naked as the day he was born, chatting to a yellow rubber ducky. "That's two. Guard the door and I'll go after Benjamin."

Wade laughed. "I've got them."

On his haunches, he braced himself in front of the bathroom opening while she chased down a squealing Ben.

Somehow, they secured the trio inside the small room and got them into the bathtub, along with several tub toys.

Both adults knelt by the tub, shoulder to shoulder. Though she wielded a sponge to wash a protesting Ben, Kyra was acutely aware of the man at her side. He smelled of the outdoors, not the disgusting things they'd discussed at dinner.

With a mental shake, Kyra focused her attention on bath time.

Noticing Wade was…discomfiting.

"How did you ever manage this alone?" She soaped

Abby's back and arms and dodged a splash from Ben. He chortled and splashed again.

"Bowie helped out," he said. "Sometimes. Once we get them in the tub, the rest is cake."

Abby grabbed for Caden's favorite ducky. Caden boo-hooed.

Wade rescued the situation by trading Abby a pink pig for the duck, all the while singing, "Rub-a-dub-dub, three kids in a tub."

"Cake for you," she said, bumping his side. "Rock-hard biscuits for me."

Wade's head turned. Twinkling blue eyes were so close she could see the yellow sunbursts around his pupils. "I didn't want to say anything."

"Kind of obvious, wasn't it?" She smiled into those eyes.

He smiled back.

She heard a *kerplunk* from somewhere. Hopefully, not from her heart. A baby must have dropped a toy in the water.

Managing to turn her attention to the task of shampooing Abby's hair, she considered the last two days. She'd definitely misjudged Wade Trudeau. But even if he was a nice man, a good guy, she did not intend to fall for him.

A week later, Wade rode his horse beside Bowie's as they checked for a gap in the east fence. Some of their new baby calves had been loose on the county road this morning.

"Didn't you and Riley ride this fence line last week?"

"Yes," Bowie replied. "No gaps."

Wade squinted toward the east where the Sundown

Ranch adjoined Keno land. "Think the Kenos had something to do with those calves getting out?"

"Maybe. But it's rained a lot this week, too."

Right. Rain sometimes washed gaps through the fences, especially near the creeks. Fence posts loosened in wet ground. "Let's ride the creek and check fence there."

They turned their horses in that direction. Moist earth squished beneath their horses' hooves. Green grass, thick and lush the way ranchers liked, had begun to spread across the pastures.

Pudge jogged alongside Wade's buckskin gelding, happy as a frog on a lily pad.

Bowie kept his countenance, quiet and watchful. The man could spot a deer two hundred yards away in tree-lined woods and could point out a squirrel thirty feet up in a sycamore.

Wade depended heavily on his cousin to find lost calves and cantankerous mama cows who wanted to hide their babies.

Bowie had an affinity with nature that Wade couldn't match. He was born to be a cowboy who spent his days in the great outdoors.

A hunter's eyes, that was what Dad had said about Bowie's uncanny abilities in the woods and fields.

Dad. Wade's heart pinched. He missed him, missed Mom and Trent. All gone too soon. Thoughts of Trent stabbed like an ice pick. His fault. His guilt to carry to his grave.

Would Yates ever forgive him and come home?

"There." Bowie pointed somewhere in the distance. "Fence down."

"Where?" Wade adjusted his hat against the sun and squinted. He saw nothing.

"Come on." Bowie clicked his tongue, and his bay mare picked up her pace.

Wade could do little else but follow.

They reached the five-strand barbed-wire fence they'd built across the creek to divide the Sundown Ranch from Keno property.

Bud Keno and his boys complained that the creek was completely on Keno land, though the abstract labeled the water source as belonging to the Sundown. To avoid trouble, Dad had built the fence right down the middle, dividing the wide creek in two, one section for each ranch.

Even that hadn't helped. Keno sabotaged the fence regularly. At least, Wade thought it was Keno. No one else had reason to.

As he dismounted, he growled low in his throat. This fence had been tight four days ago.

Bowie, on his haunches by the creek, looked up. "Could have been cut."

"Kenos." Wade reached in his saddlebag for fencing pliers and handed them to his cousin.

Could have been cut wasn't justification to ride over to the Keno house and cause trouble. Showing up on a doorstep with threats was Bud Keno's way of doing things, not his.

But he sure wanted to confront his less-than-friendly neighbors.

"Unless we know for certain a Keno is the culprit, nothing we can do."

Bowie nodded.

Butting heads with the Kenos was a full-time job

if anyone wanted it. Neither Trudeau did. They put up with a lot to keep the peace. He didn't want any more deaths on his conscience.

But he wasn't paying Keno eight grand for nothing, either.

Lord, I hate this neighbor trouble. Turning the other cheek hasn't accomplished a thing.

"You mind finishing up here?" he asked.

"Why? You said you're not going to see Keno."

"I'm not."

A grin split Bowie's face. "The nanny?"

A hot flush burned up the back of Wade's neck. He rubbed at the spot. "Going to see my kids. Make sure they're okay. Kyra's new to caring for three toddlers. I don't know her that well. I gotta keep an eye on them."

"Uh-huh." Bowie grinned again, bigger this time. "You're keeping an eye on the nanny, too. I saw how you bumped her out of the way this morning and fixed breakfast so she could sip her coffee."

For a man who didn't talk much, Bowie was sure mouthy today.

"She looked tired. We don't want to run her off by overworking her."

"Seems like she's trying to prove something."

"I noticed." The new nanny had taken exactly two days to settle in before she'd taken charge of the house, the cabin, the babies. "She's not afraid of hard work."

"You like her."

Wade hiked a shoulder. "She's the person caring for my kids. If I didn't like her, she'd be gone."

"No, I mean, you *like* her. She's pretty and interesting." Bowie gave the loose fence post a jerk to straighten it. "Smells nice, too."

Wade pointed. "Don't go there, Bowie. You know my thoughts on women, especially girlie city types."

"Seems like Kyra's doing all right for herself out here in the boonies. No complaints so far." He twisted two wires together. "Right?"

Right. She was.

"But she's still a city girl." And a woman who would hightail it back to Tulsa at summer's end. Another reason to steer clear of her.

Except he couldn't. Not as long as she was the nanny. Which he hoped was forever.

Disgruntled at the turn of conversation and his own troubling thoughts, he tossed a leg over the buckskin and gathered the reins. "Meet you at barn one. Riley's setting up to work yearlings later today."

"Tell the nanny I said hello."

Wade gave him the death stare.

His cousin grinned.

Pudge climbed out of the creek and shook water on Bowie.

Wade laughed and rode away.

The air was sweet this afternoon with the fragrance of spring blooms and fresh air. Sunshine heated the back of his shirt. He loved this land, loved riding fence and wrangling cattle. Ranching was hard work, but he wouldn't trade it for any other life.

If he had, would Sabrina still be his wife?

Probably not. He'd never understood what made Sabrina happy. It sure wasn't him or those three little babies she'd left behind.

Like Yates, she'd simply left.

He couldn't understand how his brother could have walked away. Yates was the best cowboy, best rancher of the family. He understood weather patterns, could smell dirt and know what minerals needed to be added. He could birth a calf or a colt as well as any vet. And no one could match him on a horse.

Yet, Yates had simply gotten up one morning, tossed his duffel bag in his truck and driven away. Not a word of warning. He'd simply left and never returned.

The hurt of that gnawed inside Wade all the time. His fault, he supposed. He'd driven his brother from the ranch he loved.

He was good at driving people away. Yates. Sabrina.

Wade wiped a hand across his eyes and mentally closed the door on his negative thoughts. God had blessed him with a beautiful spring day, a fine ranch and three children he would die for.

That should be enough.

Fifteen minutes later, he rode the path toward barn one, which put him in eyeshot of the house. He hadn't intended to stop. Not after Bowie's wise cracks.

His insides lifted at the sight on his back lawn.

On a quilt in the sunshine, Kyra played with the triplets.

The sun reflected the gold and copper in her hair. She wore it down today, tucked behind her ears, a curved sweep along her shoulders.

She had real pretty hair.

The triplets toddled around her, doing what toddlers do, which made no sense to an adult but was fun for them.

He slowed Doc to watch a minute. His babies were okay. No need to stop.

Then Kyra saw him and waved. She said something to the little ones and pointed toward him. She lifted Caden's hand in a baby wave that tickled Wade's chest. The other two joined forces with waves of their own, then started toward him, yelling at the top of their lungs.

He loved when they ran to him, as if he were the most important person on earth.

But Kyra caught them and dragged them back onto the quilt.

What could a man do? Riding past would be rude. His children would be disappointed.

Nudging Doc with his knees, he turned the horse from the trail. As he approached, Kyra's eyes widened. Caden sat in her lap, the constant cuddler, but she grabbed the other two and pulled them as close to her as she could, as if shielding them.

They looked real cute, a pile of babies and a pretty woman.

When he and Doc were ten feet from the edge of the quilt, she put out a stop-sign hand. "Don't come any closer."

He hadn't intended to, but there was anxiety in her voice.

City girl, he thought, recalling his conversation with Bowie. He wouldn't endanger his babies around a horse. Didn't she know that?

Wade pulled the buckskin to a stop and dismounted. Leaving Doc ground tied, he joined the foursome.

He eased down on the quilt. Benjamin whacked him with Caden's favorite rubber duck. Wade took the toy and danced it up Ben's belly until the baby grabbed for it and fell backward, chuckling.

"My favorite sound in the world," Kyra said.

His, too.

"How's your day going?" he asked, for lack of anything smarter to say.

"As you can see, so far so good. I managed to get all three of them fed, diapered and dressed without major incident. And—" she held up one finger "—finished two loads of laundry. I feel like a domestic princess."

She laughed, and so he did, too. All the while, he wondered why the idea of her laundering his shirts was so much more appealing than when Janey had done the wash.

They talked of mundane things. He told her about the cut fence and a little about their unfriendly neighbors. She told him about her pastor dad and talked about her best friend, Amy.

Wade worried she'd miss them too much and run back to Tulsa. He told her to invite them for a visit.

She smiled a lot, and he liked that about her. Her humor, her can-do attitude, her tenderness with the babies. There was a lot to appreciate about his nanny.

Maybe he was starting to trust her a little more than he'd let on to Bowie.

Truth was he liked the nanny. He liked her company. Having a woman on the ranch brightened up the days.

He didn't ponder the reasons.

Caden remained in her lap, soaking up her tender attention. Abby and Ben chased each other in circles, giggling. Occasionally, one of them ran to him or to Kyra. They'd taken to her as if she'd always been here.

Wade didn't want to think about her leaving them, breaking their little hearts.

As an adult, he could keep his emotions in check. They were innocent babies.

But what choice did he have? Kyra was here. He

needed her. The triplets needed her. Sundown Valley's employment service was still searching for a grand-motherly nanny to replace Kyra in September. So far, nothing.

"Why the frown?" Her soft voice pulled his gaze to her face.

"Aw, nothing." He plucked a weed and tickled Abby's cheek, tempted to tickle Kyra's sandaled foot, too.

He resisted. Barely.

The sunshine and the butterflies kissing the wild-flowers on his lawn made him lazy. A cardinal fluttered to the grass under a tall sycamore.

Wade pointed. "There's your bird."

She'd told him of her love for the scarlet birds, how they reminded her of her mother. Now, whenever he spotted a cardinal, he thought of his own lost loved ones.

Kyra, with Caden patting her leg with his ducky, watched the bird until it flew away, her expression tran-quil.

She carried that air of tranquility with her even in the chaos of triplets.

Wade peered toward the barn. From here, he could see clearly. Riley's truck wasn't there yet.

Five more minutes with his family wouldn't ruin his workday.

When Abby ran to him with a flower she'd plucked and was about to eat, he took the weed, and to stave off protests, lifted her high above his head and flew her like an airplane.

This activated both boys, who tackled him. He gladly fell onto his back on the quilt and gently wrestled the trio of delights.

"Oh, I forgot to tell you," Kyra said, as Abby poked him in the eye.

Kyra rescued him by pulling Abby slightly away. Her fingers brushed his shoulder. The touch buzzed through his veins, pleasant. Her soft perfume drifted around his head.

Lazily, he rotated his head toward her, enjoying the sound of her voice, the movement of her gloss-shined lips.

Attraction. He'd almost forgotten how good it could feel.

Not that he'd do anything except enjoy feeling human again.

"The area rug was delivered today," she was saying, "and it's perfect. The babies helped me put it down."

His mouth twitched. "I bet they did."

The large rectangular rug was the final thing she'd ordered for the bunkhouse. His wallet was glad the shopping was over.

"You'll have to come out to the cabin and see how everything looks when I get finished."

"Sure." Spend more time with Kyra after the triplets were in bed? Why not? The more he knew about her, the more comfortable he'd be with her as the triplets' nanny.

He was all about the babies. Being attracted to the nanny had nothing to do with it.

"I want to talk to you about something else, too." She sounded serious.

Wade's pulse thumped. He extricated himself from a trio of miniature bodies and sat up. "You're not quitting, are you?"

Caden toddled to Kyra and climbed into her lap. She kissed the top of his barely-there brown hair.

Oh, man. Her tenderness melted him.

"No, I'm not quitting. A deal is a deal, where I come from." She paused to wipe grass from Ben's outstretched hand. "I was thinking about going into Sundown Valley to shop for curtains and a few other items."

So much for his wallet. His shoulder jerked. "Go."

"Three car seats won't fit in my car."

He snorted, then staved off Ben's finger attack to his nostrils. "I doubt if even one sack of groceries will fit in that little toy you drive."

She wrinkled her nose at him. "I don't mind taking the triplets. Since you have a triple stroller, I might take them to a park to play. They're big enough to enjoy the kiddie toys."

The babies would love playing in the park. Not one of them had ever been on a slide or a swing. Was he neglectful for not taking them?

He glanced at the expansive backyard. Maybe he should buy a swing set. Were they big enough for such a thing?

"Take my truck." He motioned in the general direction of the garage. "The baby seats are already installed."

"Are you sure you don't mind?"

"You can drive a stick shift, can't you?"

Her face fell. "Your truck has a manual shifter?"

He laughed. "Naw. I was teasing. Just wanted to see your reaction." He poked her foot with the tip of his boot. "City girl."

She whacked his arm. He rubbed it, grinning. "You punch like a city girl, too."

She made that cute face again and he was tempted to hug her.

He hugged Ben instead. Ben wiggled free and bumped into Abby, who fell to her padded bottom and began to cry.

"Hey now, you're okay." Wade lifted Abby to her feet, distracting her with a toy.

Sound and movement came from the area near the barn. Riley had arrived.

"Break's over." Untangling himself from the kids, Wade stood to his feet. "Gotta go. The truck keys are hanging on the rack inside the garage door. Use it anytime."

"Thank you. That's thoughtful of you."

There she went again, telling him he was thoughtful. If she didn't stop, he'd start to believe her.

Sabrina had called him a self-centered jerk. He hadn't meant to be. He'd tried to please her. Had he succeeded for even one day?

Looking into Kyra's warm eyes, seeing her smile and her easy way with the triplets made him wonder if *she* was happy here on the ranch. She seemed content, didn't complain, but was she happy? Had he done enough to see to her comfort, to make her want to stay? Hopefully longer than September, though for now, he kept that wish to himself.

He took three steps toward Doc, then pivoted around. "Say, I was thinking. Other than the weekends, you don't get much free time. Would you like to ride with me sometime? The ranch is beautiful in the spring of the year. The mountains are in bloom, trees budding." She claimed to love the mountains. "Bowie could watch the triplets."

Her eyes widened. "Ride? As in, ride a horse?"

Her reaction, much like the moment when he'd ridden closer than she liked, gave him pause.

"You're not afraid of horses, are you? This is a ranch. You can't possibly be afraid of horses."

"Not afraid, exactly." She opened a zippy bag and handed Caden a blueberry. "I've never actually been around a horse. They're big. And intimidating."

The woman was afraid of horses. His life and livelihood were in the saddle. His triplets would learn to ride before their feet could reach the stirrups.

"What about cows? Do they scare you, too?"

"Well," she hedged, sheepish now, as she handed out more berries to the tots. "I once touched a baby cow at the Tulsa State Fair." Shoulders hunching, she pulled a cute face. "That was a long time ago."

A baby cow.

"A calf. You touched a calf." He shook his head and laughed. "You really are a city girl."

She laughed, too, that warm sparkly sound that made him think crazy thoughts. "Guilty to the tip of my pedicured toes."

She lifted a sandaled foot and wiggled those toes, the purple nail polish gleaming in the sun.

"I like animals, but I'm not accustomed to the big ones. I grew up with goldfish and small dogs."

As if Pudge understood the reference to his species, he rose from his spot in the shade along the back of the house and trotted over. Kyra rubbed a hand down his speckled back.

Ben toddled near to pat the affable dog's face. Pudge gave the baby's head a swipe of his pink tongue.

"Spending time with a good horse would get you used to their size," Wade said, "and all our horses are dead broke. They have to be to work a ranch. I'll teach you to ride if you're interested."

The more he thought about it, the better he liked the idea. She'd enjoy riding a horse once she learned. Then they could ride together, maybe go fishing or take a picnic. If he bought one of those safety carrier things, they could even take the babies. He wanted to teach his kids the pleasure of horses as soon as possible. He hadn't had the time or the help. Until now. Now would be the perfect beginning.

"Thank you, Wade, but I don't think I'll be here long enough for riding lessons."

His mood plummeted. What was he thinking? That if he taught her to ride a horse she'd suddenly love living two hours from the nearest city and want to stay on the Sundown beyond the summer?

Yes, that was exactly what he'd thought.

Dumb.

"Got it." With a single short nod, he headed for his horse and the barn.

When would he ever learn?

Chapter 6

The Sundown Valley Physician's Clinic boasted eight permanent doctors, a surgeon and several weekly specialists.

Kyra and Wade waited inside an exam room for Dr. Edgerton, the town's pediatrician, to examine the triplets. Today was their well-baby visit.

The fact that Wade had come along told Kyra one of two things. Either he was a great dad who wanted total involvement in the life of his children, or he didn't trust the nanny to do this by herself.

She opted to believe the first, having long since decided that Wade was a better father than she'd initially assumed.

"Nineteen pounds," the nurse declared as she lifted Abby into Kyra's waiting arms. "Here you go, Mommy."

"Oh, no, I'm not their mother." A blush rushed up Kyra's neck. "I'm their nanny."

The nurse looked from her to Wade. "Sorry. I'm new. I just assumed—"

Kyra waved off the apology. "That's okay."

Wade made no comment about the mistake, but something in his expression had darkened, as if the idea of a mother for his triplets gave him indigestion.

Was it because of his ex?

Without a glance at her, Wade rose to hold Benjamin on the scales while the nurse took the reading and then did the same with Caden.

Both boys outweighed their sister, but not by much.

"Is that normal for their ages?" Wade asked as Dr. Edgerton entered the room.

The doctor glanced at the notes the nurse jotted, her white coat swinging open to reveal a sunny yellow belted dress. "Normal for triplets."

She shook Wade's hand and then introduced herself to Kyra.

Blond, attractive and friendly, the young doctor exuded an easy, confident bedside manner that engendered trust. Kyra liked her right away.

"Let's have a look at these adorable little ones."

Kyra and Wade took turns holding a baby while the doctor executed a very thorough exam. She asked question after question. Eat and sleep habits, developmental milestones, behaviors and more.

Wade answered most questions, although Kyra knew a few things about the babies' latest food preferences, a fact that earned appreciative looks from the rancher dad.

She preened a little, pleased. Ben and Abby spoke a few comprehensible words, although someone who didn't know them probably wouldn't understand. Caden was the only who didn't seem ready to talk. He'd rather snuggle.

"Is Caden okay, Doc?" Worry creased Wade's forehead. "Shouldn't he be picking up a few words by now, too?"

Dr. Edgerton patted Caden's arm. "You're doing great, little man. No worries." To Wade, she said, "Every baby is different. He has plenty of time before we'd be concerned. From what I see, our man Caden is a listener, and that's perfectly normal, especially in multiples."

She studied her computer tablet. "Looks like today is another vaccine day. Time for a DTaP booster."

Kyra shot an uneasy glance toward Wade. "This is a first for me. I'm glad you're here."

Truthfully, she was glad for the rancher's company anytime. And not only because he helped her with the children.

Wade grimaced. "I have to admit I don't like this part, but I'm an old hand by now."

She raised her eyebrows. "Bet you'd rather vaccinate calves."

He pointed. "Got that right."

The babies proved to be troupers. Only Ben cried, and Wade walked the small space with him, patting and soothing. The sight splashed in the center of Kyra's heart, a drop of something as pure and precious as the love the cowboy had for his son.

When Abby's turn came, she puckered, her cute little lip quivering, but Kyra snuggled her close and pushed the button on a talking toy cell phone to distract her.

The doctor held Caden who was too occupied with the stethoscope around her neck to even notice when the skillful nurse slid the needle into his chubby thigh.

"All finished," the doctor said and placed Caden into the triple stroller before turning to Wade. "They're doing really well, Wade. Meeting milestones, catching up to their peers, very healthy triplets. I know this past year hasn't been easy for you, but whatever you're doing, keep it up."

Dr. Edgerton's veiled reference to his single-dad status inflamed Kyra's curiosity. What had happened to the babies' mother? Why had she left? And when? Had Wade been the only parent since birth? Did the doctor know?

The cowboy clearly had no intention of discussing his personal life in front of her.

Instead, he hitched his chin toward Kyra. "They have a good nanny."

At the compliment, Kyra's pulse fluttered, a silly reaction.

"I see that." The doctor smiled, her gaze moving between Wade and Kyra with a curious expression.

Did she think there was something personal going on between Kyra and Wade?

Did Kyra want there to be?

Her eyes slid toward the rancher. Yes, she liked him. Yes, he was handsome. And maybe she'd like to spend more time with him as a man and a woman, and not always as nanny and boss.

But he'd vehemently dealt with that complication before he'd hired her as nanny.

Wade had been burned. His full focus was the ranch and his family. Women were at the bottom of his favorites list.

Except they weren't. Not really. Even if he didn't

trust her much, he seemed to like her. He'd even offered to teach her horseback riding.

Fighting a blush, she tuned back to the pediatrician.

"Unless a problem arises," Dr. Edgerton was saying,
"I won't need to see them again until sometime around
their second birthday."

"Sounds good." Wade shook her extended hand.
"Sounds great, actually."

"A pleasure to meet you, Kyra. Take care of Wade
and these little ones. He's needed someone like you."
With that curious statement, the doctor left the exam
room.

Take care of Wade as well as the triplets? What exactly had the doctor meant by that?

While the implications rolled round and round in her
head, Kyra settled the triplets in the three-way stroller.
With Wade in front holding doors, Kyra rolled through
each one and headed toward the parking lot.

Wade snicked the truck locks and opened the back
door. "This calls for a celebration."

Kyra unbuckled the triplets and handed Abby to her
dad. "It does?"

"Certainly. We came out of shot duty relatively un-
scathed. Only one baby cried, and he didn't cry very
long. *I* cry longer than that!"

Kyra laughed at his silliness.

They completed the baby relay, and with the trio
settled and buckled, Kyra rounded the truck to the passenger side.

Wade followed.

She might be an independent woman, but she appreciated a man with manners.

He opened her door, but she didn't get inside. Instead,

she turned to face him. "So what do you suggest in the way of celebration?"

With the sun gleaming off the truck and the afternoon stretched out before them, he leaned his strong rancher's arm along the door frame, relaxed and easy and so close that she could feel the warmth of his body.

"How about ice cream?" His eyes glowed with something that made her pulse skitter. Again.

"Sounds perfect." The words came out soft, breathy. Kyra clamped down on her back molars.

What was wrong with her today?

"Great." Wade popped a hand against the side of the truck and stepped back.

Befuddled, Kyra climbed into the high cab, intensely aware of the rancher's fingers supporting her back.

Her muscles ached today as they did most days. Wade didn't know, but his touch felt nice. Really nice.

Some emotion, anticipation perhaps, though she didn't know what for, hovered in the cab as Wade drove to an ice cream shop at one end of Main Street. The Scoop, a cute place with inside seating and three sidewalk tables, was busy. Customers came and went with a variety of ice-cream delights or fountain drinks.

After getting their orders from a teenage clerk who obviously had a crush on the handsome rancher, they opted for a table in the pleasant sunshine.

Wade greeted several people he knew—a perk, she supposed, of small-town living. She received more than one speculative glance, though Wade identified her to each of his friends as nanny to the triplets.

The questioning looks stirred unwanted emotions in Kyra. Husband, babies, home. She desired those things.

Someday. In God's timing.

Kyra turned her focus to feeding the triplets. Three little bird mouths demanding ice cream took her mind off her attractive companion. A little.

Ignoring Wade wasn't easy.

He was fun and outgoing, not at all the rattled cowboy she'd first met.

During the well-baby visit and now a stop for ice cream, a family feeling had sprung up around Kyra like crabgrass. She needed to weed it out. So far, she hadn't.

"Wade Trudeau! You old hermit you." An attractive blonde in a turquoise sundress rushed to their table. "Where have you been hiding?"

The woman with her, a brunette in shorts and a T-shirt, went straight for the babies. "Oh, these adorable triplets. Wade, they're so cute."

"They're all going to have your gorgeous blue eyes, aren't they?" The blonde beamed at Wade with such obvious admiration Kyra had to close her eyes to keep from rolling them.

Wade appeared oblivious.

"Kyra," he said, "meet Shawna and Becky. They attend church at North Cross."

"Your church?" she asked.

"Yes."

"You should join us, Kyra." The brunette, Becky, tossed her long hair behind her back. Tall and strong-looking, with legs that went on forever, she had lovely brown skin and Native American features. "North Cross is a great church."

"Weekends are Kyra's time off," Wade said. "She's not here."

"I drive back to Tulsa on Friday night," Kyra explained. "My dad is a pastor there."

"What about our Bible study group that meets on Tuesday nights? We'd love to have you. Seven o'clock. Fellowship hall."

"I think I would enjoy that." Kyra figured if she was going to be in the Sundown Valley area for an entire summer, she'd like to make some friends outside the ranch. Though she and Amy talked or texted every day, Kyra missed the in-person interaction.

"Maybe you could arm-wrestle this guy into coming again." Shawna jerked a thumb toward Wade and winked, whether at him or her, Kyra didn't know. "At one time, he never missed."

"That was before I had three kids who are generally in bed by seven." Wade scooped a spoonful of ice cream into Ben's open mouth. The little guy pounded the stroller with both hands and drooled melted ice cream, his expression delighted.

"You never know. Something might work out. Your cousin, Bowie, rarely misses." Shawna waggled her eyebrows and waved a hand in front of her face. Apparently, she thought Bowie was a hottie, too.

Wade laughed. "My cousin's a catch, huh? I'll tell him you said so."

Shawna stuck a finger in his face. "Don't you dare, Wade Trudeau. He already avoids me."

"Probably because he thinks you're pretty."

"He does?" She perked up.

Becky gave her friend a gentle shove. "Shawna. Seriously. We have to go before you make a fool of yourself."

"Too late!" Shawna hunched her shoulders and giggled. "But we do have to go. Wade, are you bringing these adorables to the Spring Fling next Saturday?"

"Maybe. Depends on their mood and my workload."

"Try hard. And bring your cousin, too." Shawna turned toward Kyra. "See you at Bible study Tuesday night. Okay?"

"I'll plan on it. Thank you."

As the friendly pair departed, Kyra took out her phone and typed the Bible study information in the notes.

"Nice women." She stuck her phone in her pocket. Caden reached his arms toward her, indicating he wanted up.

Without a second thought, she unbuckled and lifted him from the stroller.

"Yeah." Wade didn't seem too enthused now that the women were gone.

"Is there something I should know about them? You look a little…put off. Should I avoid their friendship?"

"They're both terrific Christians. I've known them all my life."

"Then what's the hesitation?"

He didn't meet her gaze. Instead, he wiped Ben's face with a paper napkin and murmured, "None at all."

But she hadn't imagined the change in attitude. What was the deal?

Days later, Wade was still rehashing his negative reaction to Shawna and Becky inviting Kyra to Bible study. He felt like a jerk. They were great gals, which was exactly the problem. He didn't want his friends hurt again.

Frankly, after his ex-wife's behavior, he was amazed they'd reached out to Kyra at all.

In Sabrina's view, Shawna, Becky and the other Sundown Valley locals were backwoods hillbillies. She'd quickly cold-shouldered them, claiming they had nothing in common. Then she'd complained of loneliness and boredom.

He, as he'd discovered not long after their honeymoon to the Virgin Islands, was boring. Ranch life was boring. All he did was work. She needed action, fun, shopping!

Most days he wondered why she'd married him in the first place.

He also wondered if his bitterness toward Sabrina was clouding his judgment.

Kyra had given him no reason to suspect she was a snob.

But then neither had Sabrina at first. She'd wanted a cowboy. Trouble was, her idea of the cowboy life didn't include the hard truth that cowboys weren't only shiny belt buckles and Stetson hats. They worked outside with animals. They sweat. They got dirty. They tracked unmentionable things on the floors.

City folk didn't have a clue.

Kyra's soft voice dispelled his troubled thoughts. "They're going to love this, Wade."

He glanced up from the outdoor swing set they were putting together while the babies napped. The nanny looked cute sitting cross-legged on the grass in capris and sandals, the assembly diagram he hadn't bothered to read spread out before her. The baby monitor rested on the grass beside her.

Would Sabrina have read the directions aloud to him? Would she have patiently helped him sort the chunky plastic nuts and bolts and assemble the heavy-duty apparatus? He didn't think so.

Which elevated his opinion of this particular city girl.

"It's supposed to grow with them until they start kindergarten." He grimaced. "*If* I can get it put together before then."

She laughed, and her nose wrinkled in that cute way he always seemed to notice.

"We got this, Trudeau." She flexed a biceps. "Stay strong."

When she said things like that, he forgot all about his ex-wife.

"The slide goes on next."

He frowned at the structure. One side listed to the west, the other to the south. "You sure?"

"Let me look again." With a concentration frown tugging her eyebrows together, she caught her bottom lip between her teeth. "Yes. Now that the main frame is attached over the top, the slide connects to the end of that, then the ladder on the side and the swings last."

She rose from the grass and brought the paper instructions to him. "See?"

In his effort to do exactly that, he moved closer to peer over her shoulder. Kyra's upper arm grazed his chest. His chin hovered directly over her beautiful hair. Her perfume circled around them until he could barely focus on the diagram. Fact of the matter, his eyes might have crossed a little.

She put her finger on a drawing and tilted her face toward his. "Right there."

Wade stared down into her eyes. She stared back. Something flickered in her hazel irises. Something flickered inside him, too, as if a switch had turned on.

His chest tightened. Confusion muddled his brain.

He was a grown man with three kids and a big ranch

to run. Why did he suddenly lose the ability to reason whenever Kyra got too close? He wasn't a teenager. He most certainly knew better than to allow testosterone to override his common sense. Been there, done that and had plenty of scars and three motherless babies to show for it.

With the willpower that made him a successful rancher, he blinked and diverted his gaze to the diagram.

His heart, however, continued to ricochet against his rib cage.

Wade cleared his throat and, breaking the physical contact that was driving him a little crazy, he stepped back to the almost-completed swing set. "Got it. Slide first."

Obviously not as bothered by the strange moment as he'd been, Kyra pointed to something behind him. "Who's that?"

Wade pivoted. Dust rose over the long driveway leading into the Sundown. "You expecting anyone? Or any more deliveries?"

"No."

An irrational, hopeful thought shot adrenaline into his brain. Had Yates come home?

In moments, an older red pickup truck came into sight.

Wade's hopes crashed and died. Not only was the visitor not his long-lost brother, he was someone Wade would prefer never to see again.

The red truck braked to a gravel-grinding stop thirty yards from where Wade and Kyra stood.

A beefy red-faced man in a gray Stetson and dusty boots bolted from the truck and charged across the lawn like a mad bull. His tree-trunk legs chewed up the space between them faster than Wade thought possible.

Wade braced for the inevitable barrage of cursing, berating and threats.

With his eyes on the advancing man, he spoke quietly to Kyra. "Go in the house."

He felt her bristle, but she made no move to follow his directive.

He spun toward her and, between gritted teeth, growled the word, "Go!"

The last thing he wanted was for Kyra to witness Bud Keno's ugly behavior.

She sucked in a quick gasp and glared at him before stalking toward the back porch.

Wade whipped around to face his ever-angry neighbor. "What do you want now, Keno? Wasn't cutting our fence enough mischief for this month?"

"I don't know what you're talking about. You're the one up to no good, and me and my boys are sick of it. I come to collect my money."

"Then you've wasted your time and mine. We don't owe you a dime."

Keno let out a virulent streak of profanity. Wade whispered a silent prayer of thanks that Kyra had gone inside.

Keno leaned in, his eyes bulging. Sweat glistened on his red face. "You'll pay one way or the other, Trudeau. Better keep that in mind."

"Exactly what are you trying to say?" Wade's hands fisted at his sides. "Are you threatening me?"

"Call it what you want. I gave you fair warning weeks ago when I brought over the bill for all them calves you cost me. You ignored me then. You won't ignore me now."

Wade sucked in a deep breath and blew it out, praying for calm and for the right words to diffuse a volatile man who seemed intent on continuing an ancient family feud.

"Look, Bud, let's be reasonable and talk this out without swearing or accusations. I don't appreciate you using the Lord's name like that."

"The time for talk is over." Keno shoved an envelope into Wade's hands. "We're suing. And if you or any of your thieving bunch step foot on my land again, you better have your will up to date."

The warning was too clear and too dangerous to be ignored. Wade knew Kenos hated Trudeaus and had for generations, but this was taking things too far. "Don't be tossing out threats like that."

"No threat. Fact. I'll see you in court."

Keno spun on his boots and stomped back to his truck.

Wade shoved the envelope in his back pocket and rubbed both hands over his face. The action did nothing to dispel his burning frustration.

What had been a very nice afternoon erecting the babies' play set with Kyra had turned ugly.

The swing set would have to wait. He had to call a lawyer.

With a groan, Wade turned toward the house.

There on the back porch, her eyes wide and worried, stood Kyra.

Adrenaline, already at stratospheric levels, jacked a fresh dose into his blood stream.

"I told you to go inside!" Wade shouted as he stormed across the grass.

With every step, Keno's dratted envelope poked out of his pocket and into the small of his back, fueling his irritation.

"I'm a grown woman, Wade, and I did not appreciate your tone." She sounded calm and reasonable, something he wasn't.

His boots scraped as he stepped up on the porch. "My tone and my order to get in the house were for your protection."

"Your *order*?" She stretched to her full height, suddenly not so calm. "You may be my employer, *Mister* Trudeau, but this isn't the fifteenth century, and I resent being ordered to do anything."

Didn't she understand? He didn't want anyone hurt. Not again. Not on his watch. And Keno was far from stable.

If Wade had to make Kyra mad to shield her from Keno, he would. Fact of the business, he'd do whatever necessary to protect her and his triplets.

"Your job is to watch the babies. *They* need protecting even if you think you don't."

"I'm perfectly aware of that, and they are fine. Every single one of them is asleep." She shoved the monitor under his nose. "See for yourself."

Sure enough, all three of his dumplings, bottoms in the air, slept in their cribs. Two faces turned toward the camera. The third turned away.

Some of his aggravation seeped away. He groaned and let his head drop backward. "Right. Okay. Let it go. But steer clear of Bud Keno and his boys. You understand?"

Before she could shoot a retort guaranteed to burn his ears off, he pushed his hat down on his head and stalked off toward the barn.

Chapter 7

"What burr got under your saddle?"

At his cousin's calmly asked question, Wade dropped the mama cow's foot he'd been doctoring and gave her backside a shove to send her out of the chute.

This scalding afternoon, he, Bowie and Riley were working the cattle from pasture four. Riley rounded them into the holding pen, Bowie guided them down the narrow metal alley, inspecting each one as they moved, and Wade did the doctoring in the squeeze chute. The blue heeler did his part, too, chasing down strays and keeping mad mamas at bay.

"Bud Keno paid us a little uninvited visit."

"Ah." Bowie, with Pudge's assistance, guided the next animal into the squeeze chute. She mooed at him but accepted her lot in life when Wade lowered the head gate, trapping her inside.

"He's suing us."

"No way." Bowie shoved the brim of his hat back, blinking like a hoot owl. "What for?"

"A lot of money." Wade accepted the loaded applicator gun Bowie handed his way. The two of them had done this job for so long they anticipated the other's next move. "If Keno and his never-ending complaints aren't bad enough, Kyra's mad at me."

"What did you do?"

"Nothing." He'd never understand women. Never. "I told her to go in the house. She didn't. Then she was mad at me about it."

Bowie's soft laugh meandered above the sound of cattle banging against metal panels. A barn lot was a noisy place. Stinky, too, but the Trudeau boys were immune to the manure and muck stench.

"As little as I know about women, Wade, my man, I know better than that. Women don't like being bossed around."

Wade wrestled the cow's mouth open and injected the thick wormer paste. When she slung her head, fighting the head gate, he released the lever and let her run. She took off bucking and bawling into the hot afternoon. Dust swirled in her wake.

"Yeah," he admitted, "I might have been a little on the cranky side, too." Bud Keno could fire him up faster than a blowtorch on gasoline.

Bowie grunted as he pushed the next cow into place. "Not good, cuz."

"I was trying to get her away from Keno. The maniac came roaring up, loaded for bear, cussing a blue streak. Kyra's a nice woman, Bowie. Her daddy's a preacher! I can't allow her to hear the stuff that comes out of Bud Keno's nasty mouth."

"You can't allow it? Do you hear yourself, Wade?" A slow grin crept up his cousin's dark face. Black eyes sparkled. "You got it bad, son."

Wade grabbed for the next bovine head, wrestled its mouth open and filled its tongue with the pasty medication. "What are you talking about?"

"You. And the pretty nanny with the sweet nature who also happens to love your kids." Over his left chest, Bowie formed the fingers of both hands into a heart.

Wade turned a glare guaranteed to melt cement on his cousin.

"You've been out in the sun too long. You're going loco." But Wade's pulse took off faster than a racehorse in the Kentucky Derby.

Bowie smirked. The scoundrel actually smirked. "I call 'em as I see 'em."

"Huh. Better call the doc, get some glasses."

"You're saying I'm wrong?"

"That's right. You're wrong." He snarled at the tangled words. Words as tangled as his brain.

"Then you won't mind if I ask her out."

"Not happening, pal." Bowie might be joking, but the idea infuriated Wade. "I don't want a bunch of heathen cowhands scaring off my nanny. Including you."

Bowie's snicker was low and knowing. He had a way of saying a lot more with a look or a laugh than he did with words.

Today, he was full of talk. Talk that didn't make a lick of sense.

"Whatever you did wrong," the blabbermouth went on, "you'd better lope on in the house to kiss and make

up. We need her. She cooks good and smells nice." He
pointed a gloved finger. "And loves those babies. If Kyra
quits because of your bad moods, I'm quitting, too."

Wade scoffed. "You can't quit. You're a partner."

His cousin answered with a lifted shoulder.

Bowie was right about one thing, doggone it. They
needed Kyra in a bad way. They had neither the time
nor the energy to juggle ranch work and three little
ones again.

He'd have to find a way to smooth things over with
the nanny.

Mulling over the situation, Wade paid little attention to either Bowie or Riley as they worked and talked.
Rather, Riley talked and Bowie listened, laughing now
and then to keep the conversation flowing. Riley was
full of escapades and wild stories, most of them only
half-true.

Riley wasn't a liar. But he often saw things a lot bigger than most other people.

By the time the barn work was finished and Wade
had scrubbed his sweaty face and hands in the barn
sink, he had an idea.

While the other two men headed off on tractors to
separate pastures to cut hay, Wade decided to take a
little break and drop in on his munchkins. And Kyra.

He spent the time praying as he walked the short
distance across the open field toward the house. Praying had a way of setting his head straight.

A stand of wildflowers caught his eye, like the red-
orange of a sunset against the green grass. Kyra liked
sunsets. She liked flowers, too. The bunkhouse was
filled with pots and jars full of plants.

Bowie's teasing weighed on him. Both the ridiculous romantic talk and the worry that she might up and quit on them.

Wade couldn't let that happen. He tried not to contemplate his cousin's other remarks. Falling for the nanny was out of the question. He needed her too badly as an employee. If he gave any hint of finding her attractive, she might run for the hills.

But that was the trouble—Kyra *was* attractive. Even Bowie, who ignored women better than any man Wade had ever known, wanted to take her out.

Maybe he'd been kidding. But what if he hadn't been?

With all these worries rattling around his head, Wade's mind wandered. Thinking, praying, he turned his gaze to the magnificent purple hills. Kyra loved the hills and mountains around Sundown Ranch. Claimed she liked to hike and camp. She'd even quoted one of his favorite Bible verses to him. The one about looking to the mountains for help because God lived there.

Man, he liked the thought of that. God living right up on that big hilltop, watching out for him, never even taking a nap.

There was something incredibly reassuring in knowing an omniscient, omnipresent God was always there for him. Always.

Without the Lord Jesus this past year and a half, he'd have been a worse wreck than he'd been the day he hired Kyra.

She'd been God's answer to a desperate prayer.

Maybe he should take her hiking or on a wilderness picnic. Get her out of the house for a change, entertain her. Make sure she didn't get bored or restless.

Someday.

If she felt at home here on the Sundown, she might want to stay longer than the summer. The Kiamichi were beautiful in the fall and the destination of one of Oklahoma's best-kept secrets. Had she been here when the leaves changed and the mountains flamed with sunset colors?

Not knowing if the littles were napping, Wade entered the back door as quietly as possible. Kyra had created a schedule, but he didn't recall the babies' nap time.

The house was quiet. The only time that occurred was when the babies slept.

Taking off his boots, he grimaced at the muck he'd tracked in on what appeared to be freshly mopped tile. He should have shucked the footwear at the door.

Kyra was already mad. No use adding fuel to the flame. He grabbed a broom and dustpan and cleaned up his mess.

The house remained quiet. A beautiful sound.

Tiptoeing down the hall, he paused in the nursery's open doorway. Two babies still slept in their cribs. In the rocking chair, Kyra rocked Ben, his body angled across hers, his head on her shoulder.

Kyra didn't notice him at first, so Wade remained silent, observing for a bit as she stroked Benjamin's hair and made soft shushing sounds.

Wade no longer watched to be sure she was doing a good job. He watched because he was mesmerized.

The woman. The child. Madonna-like beauty.

A wave of tenderness moved through him, strong and mushy at the same time. This was the way things were supposed to be.

At times like these, when he watched Kyra with his triplets, he didn't see a nanny. He saw a loving mother.

And the thoughts scared him worse than being chased by a dozen Brahma bulls.

Kyra rocked and soothed the fussy baby, praying that the painful teething would soon subside. Baby drool pooled on the shoulder of her blouse. Benjamin was restless and miserable and only slept when she held him. The mood was uncharacteristic for bold, independent Ben. Her precious little Ben.

She'd fallen hard for these babies. Though they exhausted her every single day and left her with an aching back, she loved them.

She was growing fond of the men of Sundown Ranch, as well. Quiet Bowie with his pithy, wry humor had become a friend. He was a good listener, a gentle, artistic soul devoted to this ranch and his cousin. In his free time, he created gorgeous leatherwork in his shop.

Often in the evenings, he'd jump in his truck and leave the ranch. From Wade, she'd learned that Bowie was Sundown Valley's go-to guy. Anyone who needed a helping hand called on Bowie Trudeau and he rushed to the rescue.

She didn't see much of Riley, who drove to the ranch from Sundown Valley each day, but he was always willing to move a piece of furniture or unload boxes for her.

Then there was Wade. Her feelings were all over the place about that particular cowboy. He was not at all the person she'd first thought him to be. Intelligent and well-read, Wade was absolutely dedicated to his ranch and his little family. Most importantly, he loved the Lord.

She liked him. Most of the time, she enjoyed being with him.

Except for the fact that he made her pulse flutter. Not only when he came too close, but every time they crossed paths, or even when she smelled the faintest hint of his deep woodsy aftershave. She even liked his outdoor hay and leather scent.

She wasn't clueless. She knew she was attracted to him.

He was also her employer, a fact he'd made loud and clear.

Still, for now, she was content on the Sundown. After a few weeks, she'd begun to relax. Her body grew stronger, healthier. The nightmares came less frequently.

Most evenings, after the triplets were in bed, she'd walk through the hay meadows and fields until sundown, away from distractions to pray and absorb the calming effect of the surrounding Kiamichi.

Usually she'd spot a cardinal or two, and her thoughts turned to the nearness of God, the beauty of His creation.

Sunsets on Sundown Ranch took her breath away. Never had she felt so close to God as she did when she watched the sun drop behind the mountain, and the first shadowy veil of evening spread over the land.

Sometimes she lived through an entire day without remembering the tornado. A true gift.

"Hey." The quiet male murmur broke her thoughts and turned her face toward the doorway.

Her heart jittered. She continued to rock the child in her arms.

A sock-footed Wade, his brown hair mussed from his hat, eased into the nursery. He held a bouquet of Indian paintbrush in one hand.

"Truce?" he whispered, solemn and contrite.

Those rascally jitters got worse.

A smile lifted Kyra's lips. She nodded.

Rising, careful not to disturb the baby, she took Ben to his crib and eased him onto the cool sheet. When Benjamin raised his sweaty head and stared at her, she froze, waiting. Then, apparently satisfied, he flipped his face to the other side and lay down again. The teething pain must have subsided for now.

Thank You, Lord.

Wade moved silently to the crib and gazed down at his son. The heat and scent of the outdoors radiated off his body. His arm and right side connected with hers.

He looked from his son to her, his eyes holding hers for a long moment before he glanced down again.

Though the connection was innocent, it felt intimate, as if they were a couple.

She was acutely aware of his muscled arms, of *him*, of the tenderness flowing in the nursery. Maybe it was caused by her peaceful thoughts. Maybe it was Wade himself.

Maybe it was both of them and these little babies.

For a nanosecond, she imagined that this man and the triplets belonged to her. That she was more than the temporary nanny.

A mood floated through her. A yearning. She longed to put her hand on Wade's where it gripped the top rail of the baby bed. His attention remained on Ben, but she saw the movement of his throat as he swallowed. Was he feeling this, too?

Suddenly, he turned away from the crib and left the room.

Giving the sleeping triplets one final glance, Kyra followed.

Obviously, he'd not felt what she had.

But Wade had offered a truce. She was a peacemaker who disliked conflict.

The flowers were thoughtful, too.

She found him in the kitchen, pouring tea into a glass. When she entered, he tipped his head toward the pitcher. "Want some?"

"Sure." She got her own glass, filled it with ice from the front of the fridge and let him pour the tea for her. "What happened to our truce?"

"Still on." The wildflowers lay on the counter. He handed them to her. "I was mad at Keno this afternoon, not you."

Kyra lifted a shoulder. "You're my employer." Which was true, regardless of the strange, alluring mood in the nursery.

"You had every right to expect me to be with the triplets instead of standing on the back porch while you and that sumo wrestler in a cowboy hat argued."

His mouth quivered. "Sumo wrestler?"

Chuckling, she rolled her left shoulder and rubbed the stiffness in her arm where Ben had been sleeping.

Wade's gaze snapped to the spot. "Something wrong with your arm?"

"A little stiff from rocking Ben."

"How long?"

"An hour. Maybe more. His fifteen-month molar is trying to come through, and he couldn't get comfortable anywhere else."

"He's taken to you. All of them have."

She wanted to ask if he had, but that would be a dumb move.

Sundown Ranch was a respite, a summer job, a way

of easing back into the workforce with children. She had not come here to fall in love, certainly not with a man who still carried uncertain but volatile feelings for the mother of his triplets.

"I love them, Wade. Each of those babies is a unique and special little human being."

"You looked real good with him in your arms that way. It looked right."

Meaning what? That he was pleased with the job she was doing? Or something more?

And why was she reading so much into a simple compliment?

"What's the deal with Keno?" she asked to hush the voice in her head. "I couldn't hear all of the conversation, but he does not seem to be a nice man."

"That's an understatement." Wade took his tea to the bar, tossed a leg over a stool and gestured toward the opposite seat. "He's suing us, though our lawyer says he doesn't have a leg to stand on."

"That's good, isn't it?"

"Being in the right is good, but fighting him to prove it won't be cheap. Lawyers cost money. A lot of it."

She tickled the back of his hand with the Indian paintbrush. "Maybe you should take him some wildflowers."

He smiled at her joke. "If only flowers would do the trick. Peace offerings, which, believe me, I've tried, have no affect on Bud Keno or his boys. Kenos have hated Trudeaus for generations, and the current father and Bill, the eldest son, have taken the feud to new heights. The younger two are showing signs of feeling the same. No one in my family remembers why they hate us. Kenos probably don't, either, but they keep the feud going."

"I heard you and Bowie discussing a cut fence. Did a Keno do that?"

He nodded. "And that's not all. Untagged calves disappear, gates are mysteriously opened and more. Mischief mostly. Then they blame us if our bulls get in their pasture."

"I don't understand people like that. People who'd rather have trouble than peace." She circled the tea glass on the granite countertop. "My dad would say they can't stand to see others happy because they have a big empty spot inside where God should live."

"Your dad is a wise man."

"He'd also tell us to pray for them and for an opportunity to speak God's light to them." She flashed her eyes to his, not wanting to sound too preachy. "I'm sure you've done that."

"Maybe not enough. Talking to the Kenos in a peaceful manner isn't easy, especially now. The situation wasn't this bad until Yates left."

"Yates?"

"Yeah." He rubbed a hand over the back of his neck, expression pensive. "My prodigal brother. He and Keno had some kind of understanding. Keno was a little afraid of Yates, I guess." He spread his hands. "Or something."

A prodigal brother?

"Tell me about Yates." She was prying, but he seemed willing to talk, and she wanted to know him better. She didn't, however, want to consider the reasons.

"Not much to tell. Yates is my oldest brother. He left a long time ago and refuses to answer my calls or come home."

"Did something happen between the two of you?" When his face darkened, she put a hand on his sun-browned forearm. The muscles had gone tense. "I'm sorry. None of my business."

"No. It's okay. Not something I usually talk about." He took a long swig of tea and observed the condensation drizzling down the glass.

"We had a younger brother, Trent. He was four-teen. Yates and I were young adults. So was Bowie. His mother brought him to live with us when we were little, so Bowie's more of a brother than a cousin. Any-way, when my folks were killed in a plane crash, Yates, Bowie and I were pretty young, but old enough to take over the ranch and look after Trent."

"I'm sorry, Wade. I didn't know about your mother and dad." So very sorry. She knew how sudden trage-dies could change a person's entire life. "I can't imag-ine losing my parents. And in such a tragic manner."

He wagged his head, one finger tracing a single drop down the glass. "Wasn't easy. That's for sure. I still miss them. Always will."

"Is that why Yates wanted to leave? The shock?" The way she'd had to get away from Tulsa?

"Not at first. He loved this ranch. He's the best work-ing cowboy you'll ever meet. But then Trent died…"

His voice trailed off. He clamped down on his jaw, his mouth a hard line. His knuckles whitened against the tea glass.

More death. More heartache. He'd lost more, had seen more tragedy than any person should have to han-dle.

Yet, he'd soldiered on, even though it was clear his heartaches hadn't ended with his brother's death.

Her admiration for him elevated another few notches.

"Don't break the glass," she said softly as she lightly tapped his clenched grip.

Evidently, Trent and Yates presented a problem he didn't like to think about.

What could be worse than losing his parents and brother?

One by one, Wade noticeably relaxed his fingers.

When he didn't go on with the story, Kyra said, "We don't have to talk about this."

He gulped another long drink of tea and set the glass on the counter with a hard thud.

"Trent's death," he said at last, "was my fault. I killed my brother."

Kyra kept her gaze and voice steady. She understood guilt. He was a frequent companion of hers.

"I don't believe that. Whatever happened to your brother must have been an accident."

"Accident or not, I caused it. He's dead because of my negligence."

"Guilt is a hard thing to live with, Wade." Didn't she still hear Tristan's voice in her dreams, and sometimes when she was awake? "Have you talked with anyone about your feelings?"

"You mean like a counselor or a pastor?" He shook his head. "Pastor Blake offered, but what's the point? Trent is dead. Talking won't change a thing."

"Getting your feelings out in the open, though, might change you." She smiled, a little embarrassed. She was a preacher's kid. Offering advice and a listening ear was in her DNA. "I'm sounding like my dad. I'd apologize, except he's a great counselor."

He put a hand over hers and squeezed. "You are, too."

After two beats when he didn't move his hand, she let herself enjoy the contact. The pesky tingles started up.

"Will you tell me what happened?"

"Are you sure you want to hear it?"

"I do."

He pondered her face for a long moment as if he expected her to shy away. When she didn't, he took in a long breath, blew it out and began.

"I was supposed to be with him. With Trent. Yates had told me to go, but I had a hot date." He made a wry face. "Nineteen and crushing on a girl whose name I don't even remember now. You know how it goes. So I sent Trent to the bull pasture by himself."

Nothing about that sounded ominous. "Had he gone alone before?"

"A few times, but Yates was a worrier and preferred us to work in pairs around the bulls." Wade's voice grew small. "From what we later surmised, one of the young bulls went on a rampage and crushed Trent against his ATV. It was the worst thing I've ever seen in my life."

He closed his eyes as if reliving the horrific scene, his expression wreathed in grief.

A knot formed in Kyra's throat, hard and tight. "Oh, Wade, I'm sorry. That's horrible. But it wasn't your fault."

"Yates thought it was. Me, too. If I'd been there, Trent would still be alive."

"You can't be sure of any such thing. Being present isn't always enough." She'd been with Tristan, only a few feet away, but she'd been as helpless as he was. "Some things in this life—and everything in death—are out of our control."

She'd struggled with that hard truth for a long time.

Still did. Though her rational mind knew better, some part of her thought she should have been able to save Tristan's life.

She understood Wade's feelings far better than he could imagine.

"People make choices, Kyra. My dad used to tell us boys that all the time. God presents choices. It's up to us to make the right one. I didn't that day, and my selfish decision cost my little brother his life."

"You'll have to forgive me if I don't agree. The ultimate decision in life and death belongs to God."

He made a huffing sound. "I've wrestled with that, too."

So had she.

"Why Trent? Why not me? Why, after losing our parents, did my brother die, too? He was such a good kid." He tilted his head back, his chest rising and falling in a heavy sigh. "Man, I loved that boy. We all did. He was the baby, the favorite. You would've loved him."

The ache in his words tore at her tender heart. "What was he like?" Sometimes talking about the loved one soothed the wound of loss. Another of her dad-isms she'd found to be true.

"Athletic. Goofy in a fun kind of way." A tiny twitch of cheer creased the skin around Wade's eyes. "He always had this big cheesy grin on his face and you couldn't make him mad even if you tried."

Kyra nodded, feeling the mood lighten as he recalled the good things. "I never had a brother, but I know kids. You probably tried."

"Oh, sure. He was the baby, so Bowie and I tormented him, all in good fun, of course. Short-sheeted his bed, hid his boots, sent love notes to girls signed with his name. Trent never took offense. He'd laugh and laugh, and then he'd pay us back." Wade shook his head, finally allowing a nostalgic grin. "Don't even ask me about the plastic wrap across my toilet lid."

A giggle tickled its way up Kyra's throat. She pressed her fingers to her lips. "Sorry, but that's funny. You're right. He sounds like a great kid."

"He was. Yates, being the oldest, would sometimes tell Bowie and me to back off, leave the kid alone. So naturally, Trent thought Yates hung the moon."

"What about you?"

"Yeah. Me, too. Yates was the big brother everyone should have. Protective, smart, a strong leader." He pulled a hand down his face, effectively wiping away the pleasant nostalgia of moments before. "If he'd only come home…"

His voice trailed off, his thoughts lost in the brother who'd left him with a load of guilt and sorrow and loneliness.

"When did he leave?"

"Right after Trent's funeral. Packed up and left. No goodbyes. Just gone. Both of my brothers gone in a matter of days."

He turned her hand over and laced his fingers through hers. "Sorry for dumping this on you. You're a good listener. Maybe too good."

"Pastor's kid. I've also had a few counseling sessions from Dad over the years." Hours and hours since the tornado.

"Well, thanks. I hope you don't think less of your old boss now that I've spilled my guts all over you."

"No reason to. I loved hearing about Trent and Yates." She smiled, though the action held more sad tenderness toward the rancher than joy. "Thank you for trusting me enough to tell me."

"Yeah, well…" With a self-conscious chuckle, he untwined his fingers from hers. "Guess I should get back to work and let you do the same."

He pushed off the bar stool, reached for his hat, which lay upside down on the kitchen counter, and was gone before Kyra could wrap her head around his sudden departure.

Chapter 8

That night, after he and Kyra had put the triplets down for the night, Wade worked on the books for a while before hitting the shower.

He considered a trip to the bunkhouse to talk to Kyra some more.

Caution won out.

This afternoon, he'd felt closer to her than he had to anyone in a long time. He'd been mildly surprised to look down and discover he'd twisted his fingers with hers.

For those brief moments with Kyra in the kitchen, he'd remembered how much he enjoyed the differences between a woman and a man. Even the way she listened and encouraged was feminine. Sabrina had pounded all the good things about women out of his memory bank.

The feel of Kyra's smooth skin against his calluses lingered still, a reminder of what had been lost, drowned and swept away, in a sea of heartache and anger.

Bowie could be right. He might be attracted to Kyra. As in romantically attracted. Kiss face and all that feel-good but potentially trouble-causing business.

Considering the triplets' need for a nanny, he'd keep those crazy thoughts to himself.

When Kyra had thanked him for trusting her, he'd been shocked, bothered, shaken. He didn't trust her. He didn't trust any woman, no matter how attracted he might be.

His eyebrows tugged together.

Talking wasn't trusting. Was it?

Stretching out on his oversized king bed, Wade stacked his hands behind his head and watched the ceiling fan move lazily above him. Like his emotions, the fan went in circles and never got anywhere.

One thing for sure, trust or not, talking with Kyra about Yates and Trent had gotten his brain cells whirling. About his big brother, especially, and the close bond they'd once shared. About the discontent in Yates after Mom and Dad had passed. About how much Wade missed his brother and wished he could see him again. Most of all, he wished for Yates's forgiveness.

If he knew where Yates was, he'd jump in his truck and drive there right this minute, tonight, no matter how far he had to go.

What kind of family was so broken that a brother refused to come home or call or even reveal his location? Eight years, eight lousy years since he'd last seen his only living brother.

Wade's heart ached so much he could feel the squeeze beneath his rib cage.

Closing his eyes against the pain, he prayed for his prodigal brother.

The last time they'd spoken, Yates was running to catch a plane, deployed to military duty in some secret destination. No doubt a hot spot or danger zone. Wade didn't know exactly what his brother did for the military, but Yates was never one to shirk the most dangerous or grueling task.

Probably why Bud Keno had steered clear. Yates had a temper and could clean a man's plow at the drop of a hat. He could be tough and resolute where Wade tended toward mediation.

Since that last deployment more than three years prior, Wade had received a few terse replies to his texts but no answered calls. Since the triplets' birth, he'd heard nothing at all. Not even a congratulatory text.

Wade reached for his cell phone and scrolled through until he found the old photos he'd transferred to his phone. The four Trudeau boys, Wade, Yates, Bowie and Trent, hamming it up, unaware that life would soon tear them apart.

Nostalgia as thick as lemon pie and every bit as bittersweet settled in his bedroom like an old acquaintance.

Finding Yates's number in his contacts, he shot a text.

Call me.

Then, when he'd hopefully snagged his brother's attention, he pressed the call icon, praying that this time Yates would answer.

The *brrr* vibrated against his eardrum over and over until finally clicking into a generic voice mail message.

Disappointment moved in. It was always like this. He'd call, leave a message and Yates wouldn't respond.

When the beep sounded, he whispered, "Miss you, brother. I'm sorry."

Sighing, he pushed End and let the cell phone fall against his chest.

Kyra closed her devotional and put it aside.

Had she heard something?

She leaned forward in the easy chair to listen.

Living in the country was so different than the city.

Contrary to popular opinion—mostly from city dwellers like her—the country wasn't silent. It was calming, less hurried, but there were plenty of noises.

Were those footsteps she heard?

The hair rose on the back of her neck. She reached for her cell phone. Here in the cabin, she could receive decent service, thanks to a booster Wade had installed.

A light tapping sound came, as if someone hesitated to knock.

Eyebrows coming together, her thoughts went from fear to worry.

Had something happened to one of the triplets? Did Benjamin need her?

She leaped from the chair and hurried to the door. "Who is it?"

"Wade."

She opened the door a tiny crack.

Wade, looking freshly showered in a white T-shirt and faded jeans, his hair slightly damp and curling at the crown, lifted a bag of microwave popcorn and a DVD. "I couldn't sleep. I saw your light."

Kyra's heart executed a somersault worthy of the Olympics. He'd seen her light and come calling? Why?

"What about the babies? Who's watching them?" Undoing the security chain, she let him in.

"Asleep. Bowie's on duty."

"Everything's all right, then? How's Benjamin?" *And why are you here if nothing is wrong?*

He put a hand on her shoulder.

"They're great, Kyra. Stop fretting. Ben barely wiggled after you rocked him and put him down."

Some of her tension eased away. "Oh, good. Maybe the worst is over."

"For him. Not for us." With a wry twist of his lips, Wade lifted three fingers and then lowered one. "One down, two to go."

"Poor babies." She offered a one-shouldered shrug. "Such is life with three toddlers."

"Tell me about it. I had no idea how hard it would be to care for three kids at once."

"Me, either."

"Seriously? I couldn't tell. You have a natural, easy way with them."

He wouldn't say such nice things if he knew how anxious she was at times, worrying that something would happen to one of them or that she'd fail them the way she'd failed Tristan.

"That's because you help and in desperate moments, so does Bowie." She didn't know how else she would have managed.

"Desperate moments? You mean like when you're changing one baby and you hear the toilet flush, and the other two babies have disappeared, toting stuffed animals, which can wreak havoc on your plumbing?"

"Ah, the voice of experience." She chuckled. "And I'm not trying to run a ranch at the same time. A full-time nanny with help is much easier than one dad and three babies."

"Are you saying we make a good team?"

"I think we do." The ramifications of that statement were not lost on her.

And she was reading *way* too much into a simple conversational statement. They were a team, friends, employer and employee. That was all.

Looking a tad uncertain, Wade remained standing inside the bunkhouse door as if he might dash away at any second. He'd been inside before, mostly to help her carry something, but not in a while and never late at night.

Why had he crossed the driveway tonight?

Was this afternoon's conversation still weighing on his mind?

A current passed between them, the sizzle of attraction she felt every time they were together. He felt it, too. She could tell by his sharp intake of breath and the way his bewildered gaze settled on hers.

This sizzle thing was, indeed, bewildering.

"You can come into my *living room*." Kyra put the words in jaunty air quotes, determined to keep the mood light and friendly. "I've moved it closer to the kitchenette." She pumped her eyebrows. "Where the snacks are."

Wade pointed a finger at her. "Smart woman."

His boots made thudding noises, softened by the giant area rug she'd place in the center, as he followed her to a cozy corner with two easy chairs, a TV and a small coffee table.

"I like what you've done." He made a wry face. "But considering the alternative…"

Remembering, her lips curved. "We've come a long way since that first dust-covered day."

"Yes." His eyes smiled into hers. "I think we have. A very long way."

What exactly did he mean by that? Was she, once again, reading more into the statement than he'd intended?

Again, she wondered why he'd come knocking this late. Not that she wanted him to leave. She didn't.

Perhaps that was the issue.

"I doubt you came over tonight to compliment my decorating skills."

The uncertainty in his expression returned.

"If I'm bothering you. Or keeping you up too late—" he stabbed a thumb over one shoulder "—I can hightail it back to the house."

"No, no. Not at all. I wasn't sleepy yet." Truth was her energy had shot to double-espresso level the moment he'd walked in the door. She didn't know why he was here, but she was glad he'd stepped over the barriers he seemed determined to keep between them and crossed the driveway. "Was there something you wanted to talk about?"

That couldn't wait until morning?

A terrible thought hit her. Wade wasn't about to fire her, was he, because of their earlier disagreement? Not after he'd declared a truce and they'd had such a deep conversation.

Yet, after their heart-to-heart, he'd hurried out of the house as if he wished he'd said nothing at all.

While these worrisome thoughts flashed through her mind, Wade handed her a DVD. "I figured after our bar stool counseling session, I owe you a movie and popcorn. A thank-you or an apology, whichever it requires. What do you say? You, me and Denzel Washington?"

Relief rushed in, and she thought how silly she was. Wade needed her. The triplets needed her. He wasn't about to fire her. He was grateful, and unless her radar was completely messed up, Wade Trudeau liked her company. She liked his, too.

Flipping the DVD over, she glanced at the movie title. "This looks good, and I appreciate the gesture, but I don't have a DVD player."

Shoot. Now he'd leave. And she didn't want him to. The two of them rarely had time alone.

Wade opened his mouth, closed it, opened it again, stacked his hands on his hips and looked defeated. "So much for my great idea."

Exchanging looks, they both grinned. If their gazes held an extra beat or two, she wasn't complaining. A man with those kind of eyes was meant to be looked at.

"All is not lost," she said with more hope in her tone than she'd intended. "There's probably something amazingly bad on TV. Or if our timing's good, we might find a classic."

Kyra caught herself and stopped. She was behaving as if this were a date, and Wade had come over with the expressed intention to be in her company. He'd brought the movie as a thank-you, nothing more.

He hoisted the microwave bag. "Somebody's gotta eat this popcorn."

A smile lit her insides. "Absolutely."

With a satisfied grin, he tossed the DVD on the coffee table, picked up the remote and started channel surfing while she stuck the popcorn in the microwave.

In minutes, they'd settled in their respective chairs,

a bowl of buttery-scented popcorn serving as a buffer between them while they watched a corny old melodrama that was more funny than sad.

At one particularly maudlin part, Kyra faked a sniffle. Wade pretended to gag and then bopped her in the side of the head with a popcorn fluff.

"What?" She squinted at him in mock anger. "Aren't you finding this Oscar-worthy?"

"I'm pretty sure my IQ has fallen ten points in the last ten minutes."

"A point per minute. Whew! At that rate, you'll run out of brains by the movie's end. And then what?"

He hit her with another shot of popcorn.

"Hey!" She grabbed a handful and peppered him, one fluffy projectile at a time in rapid-fire sequence. Her softball skills, which she'd eschewed as worthless, were coming in handy.

Wade dipped and ducked, returning fire and laughing in a way she rarely heard from the overworked, harried cowboy daddy. Popcorn flew around the room, bouncing off the TV, the walls, each other.

Kyra laughed so hard, her throws lacked much velocity. When one shot fell a good two feet short, Wade pointed, smirking, his blue eyes sparkling with humor. "That all you got, noodle arm?"

"I'll have you know I was an ace second baseman. *Ace!*" She gave the next throw her all, beaning him between the shoulder blades as he twisted his anvil-shaped torso to one side.

Wade needed this. So did she. *A time to laugh*, like the Bible said. A time to play and forget their worries.

This playful Wade seemed more approachable, more real and, if such a thing were possible, more appealing.

When they'd emptied the bowl and popcorn lay strewn about the space, they fell back against their respective chairs, faces turned to grin at each other.

Kyra's pulse raced from the exertion. Her breath puffed, short and quick. So did Wade's.

Except for the television neither of them wanted to watch, the only sound was their breathing.

After a bit, she said, "That was fun."

"Yep. Movie's going off," he said. Though he never turned his head to look at the TV, his mouth twitched. "Thank goodness."

"No kidding. How's the IQ?"

Using the heel of his hand, Wade bopped the side of his head a couple of whacks. "Shaky as ever."

Kyra emitted a tired laugh.

"Want me to make more popcorn? I have some in the cabinet."

"Nah. There's plenty on the floor if I get hungry enough."

Kyra snorted.

Until now, she hadn't realized what a fun sense of humor Wade had. Which only made her like him more.

Another movie began, but neither of them paid it any mind. They began to talk, at first about the triplets and the ranch, steering clear of the afternoon's painful discussion of Wade's brothers.

The conversation veered into other topics. Movies they actually liked or wanted to see. Favorite music. College. He was an Oklahoma State Cowboy, naturally. She graduated from Oral Roberts University.

After they'd good-naturedly argued about which was best, they moved on to their faith, their favorite scriptures and when they'd come to know Jesus. He asked her opinion of the Sundown Valley Bible study she'd begun attending, and they discussed the topics and the friends she'd made there.

He seemed especially interested in her opinion of Becky, Shawna and the other women she'd met. When she admitted to enjoying their company enough to make a lunch date, he seemed oddly relieved.

When he asked about her work as a teacher, Kyra stumbled over her reply. Although she considered telling him about the devastating tornado, she didn't. Wade had enough tragedy in his life. He didn't need to carry her burden, as well.

"You miss teaching," he said after she'd waxed nostalgic about some of her students.

"I do, but my hands are full right now with the triplets." Her heart, too.

"You'll go back in September." His expression had grown solemn.

"Probably. Hopefully." She was healing. She could feel it. Other than an occasional bad dream, she'd not had one flashback episode. Her mind and spirit were more rested, more at peace, quieter these days. God was preparing her for a return to her former life in the classroom.

Wade stared at the flickering TV, silent, pensive.

"You'll find another nanny by September," she said, confident that his sudden withdrawal was concern for the triplets.

"Yeah." He didn't sound convinced, and for good reason, she supposed.

The older woman who'd cared for the triplets since birth was the only person who'd ever applied for the job. Miss Janey had only agreed because she'd been friends with Wade's late parents and attended the same church. The kind woman had felt sorry for a man whose wife had abandoned him and their infants.

Replacing her as nanny might not be easy.

"It's late." Wade stood, found a piece of popcorn in his chair and tossed it at her. "I should go."

"I'm glad you came over. This was fun."

"It was. Thanks." Yet, some of the energy had seeped out of him. Tired, probably.

She followed him to the door where they both paused.

"I have a doctor's appointment in Tulsa next Friday," she said. "Would you mind trading days with me, and I'll work the weekend in exchange?"

Alarm flashed in his expression. "Are you sick? Is something wrong?"

She held out a hand. "It's only a checkup."

"Sure. Take the day. Whatever you need." He rubbed a hand over the back of his neck and stretched his head from side to side as if the muscles had tensed. "Why don't we trade Friday for Sunday. That gives you two full days with your family. Then come back on Saturday night and attend church with us on Sunday. If you want to. No pressure."

Warmth spread through her. "I'd love to."

"Good. It takes an army to get the triplets ready and out the door on Sunday morning."

Right. The triplets. He'd invited her to church because of them, not because he wanted her company.

And he was right. She'd taken the dynamic trio into Sundown Valley to shop a few times. Traveling with three babies took the logistics ability of a field general.

She admired Wade for running the baby gauntlet

every Sunday. A lesser man would have used the triplets as an excuse to skip church.

His faith was real and deep, like hers.

Reaching around her, Wade opened the door and
stepped out on the wooden porch. Clean green-scented
night air, cooler than the June day, enveloped them.

"Look at that." His voice was hushed.

"What?" She stepped out with him.

To the right, the night spread over the land, dark as
ink. To the left, pale yellow security lights illuminated
the main house and nearby barns.

He pointed toward the darkness. Tiny points of light
flickered above the grass near a line of woods.

"Fireflies?"

"Lightning bugs, my brothers and I called them, but
fireflies is a cooler term."

Delight filled her. She clasped her hands together.
"We don't see them much in the city."

"No, I guess you wouldn't." He slid the flat of his
hands into his back jeans' pockets.

"Too much light, I'm sorry to say. Even the stars and
moon are brighter here on the ranch, in the country. The
sheer nearness of nature makes me feel closer to God.
All of this, the stars, the mountains, the woods, is his
design, his handiwork."

"Do I hear a poem stirring?"

Wade turned his head to smile down at her, and then
looked back toward the fireflies and the inky diamond-
laden night sky.

"Maybe." She'd told him about the poems she'd
begun writing again since moving into the bunkhouse.
His kind reaction encouraged her.

The moon had risen, a cantaloupe slice cradling a bright twinkling star.

"When I look at the night sky," she said, "and see the work of His hands, the moon and stars He set into place, what are mere humans that He should even consider us at all, much less that He should care for us?" She tilted her chin toward Wade's profile. "I didn't write that. It's too beautiful."

"Psalms?" The deep timber of his voice carried a smile.

Pleased, she nodded. "The Kyra paraphrase. Dad used to quote it every night when we camped in these woods and mountains. He taught us to see God in everything."

"Nowhere is He more visible than in nature and the ranching life." Wade pivoted slightly, angling his body closer to hers. So close that she whiffed his shower soap. "Ranchers live close to the land. My parents taught us not only to use the land as a livelihood, but to love it, respect it, care for it, and to remember that God ultimately controls everything. He's given us stewardship, but we're only borrowing it for a while."

"He's blessed you here on the Sundown."

"Yeah," Wade murmured as if he hadn't considered his blessings in a while. "Yes, I guess He has."

Not wanting him to leave or to disturb the peaceful aura that had settled over them, Kyra asked, "What's that pulsing noise? Frogs?"

"Tree frogs. Crickets. Katydids. They all have rhythmic mating songs. Summer sounds."

"They don't sing in the winter?" She'd never been to the mountains in winter. What would it be like here in chilly December or frigid January?

"Winter is real quiet out here," Wade said. "Coy-otes mostly."

Shivering a little at the thought of coyotes or wolves, she moved a half step closer.

He looked down at her, his face serious. "Scared?"

"No." She rubbed her upper arms. "Not really. I just don't want to be a meal for predators that howl in the dark."

He smiled.

"I won't let them get you." The gentle teasing timbre of his manly voice caused tingles on her skin.

"My knight in cowboy boots?" Her tone dropped low, hushed and tender.

In the dim shadows of the porch, Wade turned to face her. The tree frogs' song seemed to throb in Kyra's chest.

For a long, pulsating moment, she thought he might kiss her.

And she wasn't sure what she'd do if he did.

Her heart yearned toward him. But they were employee and employer, and she had a job to do here.

Yet, she could not deny that sizzle of attraction.

"Kyra," he started.

She tilted her head in question.

His fingertips grazed her cheeks. A delicious shiver raced down Kyra's spine. She liked his hands, the strength, the hard work she could feel in them.

When she started to lean into his touch, his hands fell away.

"Good night."

Then he stepped off the porch and faded into the darkness.

Chapter 9

Wade fumed as he, Bowie and Riley wrestled a pile of rocks and logs blocking the creek.

A half-dozen cows and calves meandered the bank, bawling and jostling for a drink of the normally spring-fed stream.

"No doubt who did this." Riley kicked at a log in frustration, his face dark with fury.

"Keno knows this section of the creek is the only water source for this particular pasture." Wade wiped a shirtsleeve across his sweating face. "If you hadn't been checking fence, these cows could have been in trouble fast."

"Yeah. And *he's* suing *us.* How does that make sense?" The usually mild-mannered Bowie glared at the obviously man-made dam holding back the water. The stream, with its origin in the mountains, was the purest, freshest water on the Sundown Ranch.

"It doesn't make sense. Not a lick. But like always, the Kenos are sneaky and we can't prove they did this." Wade had snapped photos of the dam to share with their lawyer, but he didn't expect them to make a difference in the lawsuit.

True to his threat, Keno was moving forward with the frivolous legal action.

Wade kicked a rock, an action he instantly regretted. The dull pain shot through his boot leather like a stubbed toe.

Today, his frustration was about more than Keno trouble.

Last night, he'd almost kissed the nanny.

She'd probably have slapped his face.

No. She wouldn't have.

There lay the trouble.

He liked her a lot, and he was pretty sure she liked him back.

"Riley," he said, more to get his mind off Kyra than anything, "you'd better ride the other fences. Most likely this is the only trouble area, but with the Kenos you never know."

"I could take the east fence," Bowie said.

"Weren't you going into town for more baling twine?"

"Yes, but—"

"—I got the fence. No problem." Riley removed a bandanna from his hip pocket and wiped sweat from his mustachioed face before mounting his horse and riding away.

After Riley's departure, Bowie said, "He likes riding fence."

"So do you."

"Yeah. Peaceful."

"Except for when it isn't." Wade wiped sweat again and glanced at the sky. "The humidity today is killing me."

"Might storm later."

"Maybe. Remind me to clean the storm shelter out."

Bowie waved him off. "I already did it. The babies and all. Didn't want to chance it with the new nanny."

Just like that, Kyra was back in Wade's head.

Before his brain could engage, his alligator mouth blurted, "I almost kissed her last night."

With a grunt, Bowie tossed a heavy rock onto the bank and then turned a mild gaze on his cousin.

"Told you."

"Don't be stupid. It was a mistake. I realized it at the last minute. I mean, it was dark outside and we were watching lightning bugs and stars and standing kind of close. The next thing I know this urge to kiss her rose up like a tidal wave."

"Watching lightning bugs? And stars? Together. Uh-huh. Kind of romantic."

"It wasn't supposed to be. I went over to thank her and next thing I know we're having a great time together. She's so easy to talk to, and she's pretty and sweet. And she's wonderful with the triplets."

"You're falling for her."

"I can't." Frustration building, he heaved the biggest rock he could find. He'd probably have a backache tomorrow.

Sometimes Kyra's back bothered her. He'd noticed how she pressed her hands to her lower vertebrae. She took ibuprofen nearly every day. He'd seen her do it. Were the triplets too heavy for her?

He heaved another rock, this one lighter.

"I hear you," Bowie said. "Too much like Sabrina."

She was. Except she wasn't.

During last night's conversation, she'd admitted how eager she was to leave the Sundown and head home to Tulsa as soon as her time here was up.

You can take the woman out of the city, he thought, but she'll go back. This was a vacation of sorts, a respite. Even though, when he'd hired her, she'd claimed to need a break from teaching, last night she'd revealed the truth. She was eager to return to the classroom.

But, his brain argued, she loved the mountains. Her family enjoyed nature, loved camping.

Most likely her dad had one of those fancy RVs that was more like a hotel than true camping. Somehow, he couldn't see a Tulsa girl roughing it in a tent.

There was a lot about the nanny he didn't know.

But he wanted to know everything.

Irritated with the direction of his thoughts, he insisted, "She's the nanny. She's here to care for the babies. That's all."

Bowie grunted. "Whatever you say."

"She won't be here on Friday. I'll have to take off work to watch the triplets."

"Scared her off last night, did you?"

Wade scowled his opinion of that statement. He hoped he hadn't scared her away.

"She has a doctor's appointment in Tulsa."

Bowie paused in their seemingly endless efforts to clear the stopped-up creek. "Is she sick?"

"That's what I asked her. She says no. Only a checkup. But her back bothers her a lot. She doesn't complain, but I noticed."

"You sure notice a lot about a woman who's only the nanny." His cousin gave him another of those mild looks that spoke volumes.

Wade was tempted to toss a rock at him.

The way he and Kyra had tossed popcorn at each other. Silly, but fun. When had he simply let himself go and had fun like that?

Not since Sabrina came into his life. No, even before that. Life had stopped being fun when Yates had disappeared.

Maybe Bowie was right.

He noticed everything about Kyra. The shine in her red hair, the changeable color of her hazel eyes, the way she smelled too good. Mostly, he noticed the way she mothered his babies.

Mothered.

Something Sabrina had never done.

Remembering his ex-wife's selfishness made his heart hurt. Her treatment of his babies made him angry, too, and solidified his reasons for not getting involved with another woman. Women could eviscerate a man and destroy the security of their children.

He wouldn't chance anyone hurting his kids again.

Kyra was an employee, not a relative. She got paid to care about his children. For three short months.

He'd best remember that, too.

On Friday morning, after her doctor's appointment, Kyra stopped by the pastor's office at the church where she'd grown up.

When she walked in, her dad pushed away the stack of correspondence he'd been reading and got straight to the point. "What did the doctor say?"

"They ran another MRI." She made a face. Lying in the tube with the top pressing in toward her face wasn't her favorite activity. Not being able to move reminded her too much of the hours beneath the tornado rubble. But she'd gotten through without a panic attack, something she hadn't managed in the early days of the injury. "Dr. Jacobson only saw the preliminary report, but he thought everything looked good. Great, even."

"Glad to hear it." His smile lit up his eyes. Eyes the same nondescript hazel color as hers, though his hair was fair where hers was red like her grandmother's. "How goes the nanny job?"

A picture rose in her head of Wade, his face in shadows, his fingers touching her cheek.

She felt a hint of a blush heating her neck. "The triplets are wonderful, Dad. Benjamin finally cut his molar, but now I think Caden's is trying to come through. And Abby is starting to say actual words. Yesterday, Wade walked into the house and she yelled, 'Dad!' It was so cute."

Those hazel eyes contemplated her face for a long moment as Dad leaned his elbows on his desk and clasped his hands together. "You're enjoying them."

"Yes, of course. You know how I feel about kids."

"But these are special. I hear it in your voice every time we talk."

Though they texted often, their real conversations came in person on weekends.

"They're precious, innocent babies who need all the love anyone can give them. They're adorable and funny and energetic and exhausting." She laughed. "Watching them explore the world is a gift. Yesterday, Benjamin shared his pancake with me, and that boy does not like to share."

Her insides warmed at the sweet, sticky memory.

"Are you getting too attached, honey, considering your plan to teach again in the fall?"

"It's hard not to, Dad. I worry how Wade will manage once I leave. He's trying to find another nanny, but Sundown Valley is a small town."

"So you're getting along well with the children's father, too? You feel safe there?"

"Very safe." She didn't mention the problems with the Kenos. "You should drive down sometime and meet Wade and spend the day with me. He's a good Christian man, Dad, a hard worker with a good head on his shoulders. He's wonderful with his babies, and I'm told he was very active with his church's youth before the triplets were born. I think you'll like him."

Her dad's gaze rested on her again, discerning. "Sounds like you are also getting attached to the babies' dad."

Kyra and her parents had always been close, but during her recovery, the relationship between her and her dad had deepened. Sharing her concerns with him was second nature.

"I'm not sure. Maybe. Probably. I like him a lot. And when we're together..." She shrugged, embarrassed not to be able to put her feelings into words.

"Your heart beats a little faster and you feel lighter and happier?"

"Yes." Might as well admit it.

"Does he feel the same?"

"I don't know that, either. Sometimes I think he does. Not that there's been anything romantic going on between us." Not really. The night on her porch had been an aberration, a moment out of time. They'd been tired, and emotions run amok when people are tired.

"Tread lightly and be wise. I'm your old dad, and I'm still concerned about you even though you're a grown woman."

"I'm cautious, Dad, especially after Sean." Smiling, she pointed a finger at him. "But remember what you taught me about worry."

"Practice what I preach, huh? Take my concerns to the Lord in prayer." His smile was amused.

"Exactly. And while you're praying for me—" she stopped to give him a knowing look "—if you would, please pray for Wade. He's had a lot of heartache in his life."

She told him about Trent and the estrangement from Wade's older brother. She kept Wade's overreaction to any mention of his ex-wife to herself. But she prayed about his anguish just the same.

The phone on her father's desk jangled. He held up one hand. "Excuse me a minute."

Accustomed to these interruptions, especially when they were in the church office, Kyra sat back and pretended not to listen.

Of course, she heard every word.

When he hung up the phone, her father looked a bit uncomfortable. "That was Lisa. I've asked her to join me for dinner on Sunday."

"Lisa Coleman?" Something in her father's expression warned her. "Are you and Lisa dating?"

Though she'd never thought about it, her dad was an attractive man and still plenty young enough to find love again.

When Mom was alive, Dad had fiercely guarded against being alone with a female parishioner, though several had been obvious in their pursuit of the handsome, eloquent pastor.

But the idea of him with a woman other than her mother stunned her.

"Would you mind?"

Did she?

And even if she did, what right did she have to deny her father a chance at finding love again?

"Of course not."

During the long year of her recovery, Dad had been at her side. Other than his pastoral duties, he'd had no social life. She'd never considered how lonely he must have been.

"Lisa is a lovely woman. A devoted Christian. And if she makes you happy, then I'm happy for you." Shocked and unsettled, perhaps, but truly glad for the man who'd sacrificed a great deal for his daughter.

Getting used to the idea of seeing him with another woman, though, would take some doing. And a lot of prayer.

Sunday morning, Wade walked into the white-framed church in Sundown Valley with Kyra at his side. They were early, as he tried to be, considering how long it took to get the triplets settled in the nursery.

Heads turned, and he could practically hear the wheels turning in nosy heads. His friends knew Kyra was the nanny. They knew she attended their age group's weekly Bible study. The other congregants, however, didn't know, and speculative glances rippled through the church.

Small towns loved to talk, and he and Kyra had given them new meat to chew on.

The Sundown Valley grapevine stretched all the way to the ranch. Now it would bear lots and lots of fruit.

Once the babies were in the nursery, he took Kyra's elbow and guided her to his usual spot four rows back from the altar. Regardless of gossip, Wade felt proud to have her at his side. She was beautiful. And she smelled great. Like sunshine and flowers.

He filled his lungs with her perfume as he shook hands and introduced her to those nearby.

The fortysomething pastor, Blake Cloud, came out of his study and stopped for a chat. "Kyra, it's a pleasure to see you again. How are you enjoying Bible study?"

"I love it. We've been discussing the book of Ephesians and I'd forgotten how rich and deep it is." She laughed. "I call my dad after every session to discuss it with him."

"How's your dad doing?"

"He's well. Thank you for asking."

They exchanged a few more pleasantries before someone called Blake's name and he turned away.

Kyra's eyes followed the Native American reverend. "He seems like a great pastor."

"He's been there for me, for all of us, anytime we've needed him." Through the loss of Trent and the abandonment of his brother and wife, Blake visited, texted, called and prayed with him so many times God surely felt sorry for them both. "Our church is thankful to have him."

The piano began to play, a reminder that service was about to begin. North Cross was a traditional church, different, Wade knew, from the more contemporary nondenominational services Kyra was accustomed to.

He handed her a songbook. She looked down at it and then back at him as if she'd never seen a hymnal in her life.

A sudden clutch grabbed Wade's throat.

Would Kyra appreciate the small-town church? Or turn up her nose at the old-fashioned hymns and traditionally structured service?

"What did you think?" Wade asked as they exited the church following the benediction.

Leading one toddler while Wade and Bowie each held hands with another, Kyra walked toward the pickup truck. "I loved it. 'Great is thy Faithfulness' is one of my favorite old hymns, and as soon as the singing started, I felt peace flood over me."

A late June sun already threatened to heat up the world, and she was glad for the cool, peach and cream dress she'd worn with beige sandals. The tea-length hem swirled around her calves, stirring the breeze.

"Good." Wade sounded relieved as if he'd expected her to criticize. "I'm glad."

Abby tugged her daddy to a halt and reached for a pebble on the pavement. Wade hoisted her into his arms. "Pastor Blake can get pretty wound up. I didn't want him to scare you off."

Kyra smiled in an effort to ease Wade's anxious expression. "My dad's style may be different, but anyone who preaches biblical truth is fine with me. The sermon was excellent. Hard to hear in places, but good for us. For me, anyway."

"I needed to hear it, too. For sure, we can't pick and

choose which parts of the Bible we like and leave out the hard parts."

"As Dad would say, truth isn't always easy to hear, but it's the key to resisting those temptations that might sound good at first, but that harm us in the long run." With a chuckle, Kyra shook her head. "Sorry. I always seem to be quoting my dad."

"Nothing to apologize for. He sounds like a great dad and pastor. He sure raised a fine daughter."

Kyra flashed a glance his way. Today he'd worn a turquoise dress shirt that made it impossible not to stare at his eyes. "I invited him to drive down for a visit sometime. If he does, I'd like for you to meet him."

The skin around those vibrant eyes crinkled. "I'd like that, too."

His reaction pleased her. Though their lifestyles differed, Kyra was confident Wade and Dad would hit it off.

A friendly relationship between the two men was starting to matter to her.

When they reached the truck, she and Wade took turns strapping the triplets into the rear baby seats. Once the babies were settled with a toy, and the back doors were secured, Wade turned to her and Bowie, who had tagged along to help with the babies.

"I'm starved and not in the mood to cook. Let's grab Sunday dinner at Dave's." To Kyra, he said, "Have you eaten at Dave's? It's a great family-friendly restaurant. Really good fried chicken and pot roast."

"I haven't, but eating out sounds terrific. I don't want to cook, either."

"Then it's decided. How about you, Bowie? You coming?"

"No." Without further explanation, the cousin looked at Wade, gave a small laugh and headed to his truck.

Kyra frowned after him.

What was that all about?

Dave's Restaurant was noisy with cheerful-sounding conversations and after-church diners. Families in their Sunday best and others in casual clothes gathered at square tables or in padded purple booths. The friendly atmosphere smelled wonderful—like yeasty hot rolls dripping in butter.

Guided by two servers carrying high chairs, they wound their way toward an open table.

Not surprisingly, the triplets drew lots of attention. During the meal, other diners, some who knew Wade and others who were simply attracted by a set of three dark-haired babies, paused at the table to chat.

She was glad she and Wade had dressed the tots for church with extra care so they looked as cute as pie. The boys wore matching knee-length khaki shorts with yellow golf shirts and sturdy walking shoes. Abby matched them in a sunny yellow dress and headband bow with the cutest little white sandals and lacy socks.

The trio were definitely attention grabbers, and Kyra's heart swelled every time someone stopped to exclaim about their adorableness. As if they were her babies. As if she had a right to receive the compliments.

Eventually, the visitors disbursed and the food was served.

"This looks amazing." She sniffed the steaming pot roast with mashed potatoes and brown gravy. "And the smell!"

Wade had ordered the same. With a pleased smile, he said, "They cook from scratch, the old-fashioned way."

"For which I am thankful."

"Speaking of thankful, let's pray." He bowed his head and murmured a short blessing.

Ben yelled in disgust at the delay in his dinner.

Wade put a hand on the child's arm and said, "Amen."

Abby grabbed for the hot rolls, but Kyra was too fast for her. "One at time, little miss cuteness."

She tore off a small portion and handed it to Abby and was rewarded with a bright, "Tank oo."

Kyra and Wade traded proud looks that held.

The family feeling that was never far away rose inside Kyra, tall and strong and flexing an ever-thickening muscle.

Warmth spread up her neck and over her cheeks when Wade continued to stare, the softest smile barely tipping his lips.

The attraction was like a cord stretching across the table, tethering their hearts together.

And she was being ridiculous.

Except her heart didn't think so.

To break the spell, Kyra blinked and turned away to offer Caden a green bean.

"No." Caden's head swung back and forth as he rocked away from Kyra's outstretched hand.

Both adults stared at the baby. Wade spoke first. "Did he say no?"

"He did." Excitement rose in her voice. She grabbed Wade's hands and squeezed. "Wade, that's his first word!"

Wade laughed, his pleasure real. "Leave it to my kid. Instead of Da-da, his first word is *no*."

With a fondly knowing gaze at Ben, Kyra said, "He probably learned it from his brother."

Wade's laughter deepened. Oh, how she loved his laugh. "Or from Abby. She likes that word, too. Especially at bedtime."

Aware that she still held his hands prisoner, Kyra released him and sat back in her chair. "So true."

She offered the rejected green bean to Ben, and he crammed it into his mouth, then stuck out his tongue and let the offending vegetable fall to his high-chair tray.

"Green beans are not garnering any fans today."

A server stopped to top off tea glasses and bring applesauce for the triplets. The pureed fruit was a hit with all three babies, although a messy hit.

Kyra whipped out a pack of wipes from the diaper bag and began cleaning faces as a well-dressed couple stopped at the table.

"Wade, I thought that was you. Your little ones are precious." The perfectly coifed woman wiggled Abby's reaching hand.

Kyra grimaced. Abby's hand was loaded with applesauce.

When the woman pulled back and looked at her soiled fingers, Kyra grimaced and offered her a wipe. "I'm sorry. Right now, they're a mess."

"Babies are messy, and dealing with so many of them at once. My goodness. I can't imagine."

The woman's words weren't intentionally snarky, but they raised Kyra's hackles just the same.

She didn't *deal* with the triplets. She loved them. Yes, they were a challenge at times. Yes, they were lots of exhausting work. But they were pure joy packed into three small bodies. This strange woman had no right to demean them.

Wade held a hand toward Kyra, and she slapped several wipes into his wide palm.

He must have felt her tension because he said, "Kyra Mason, meet Ted and Liz Cohen. Ted's my attorney."

His wife nudged the attorney's arm. "But you didn't stop to talk business, did you, Ted?"

"No, no. We can do that tomorrow. I'll give you a call." The lawyer reached inside his suit jacket. "Liz is committee chair for the July Fourth Independence Day celebration." He handed Wade several tickets. "We thought you and your girlfriend would enjoy taking the little ones to the carnival and petting zoo."

Kyra looked up from wiping Caden's chin. Again. "But, I'm not—"

Wade interrupted. "That's real nice of you, Liz. Thanks."

The couple said their goodbyes and moved on, but Kyra couldn't get their comment out of her thoughts. She wasn't a giddy teenager. Naturally, people assumed a man and a woman were a couple if they were dining together, especially when children were involved.

But her silly heart had leaped like a kangaroo at the mere mention of being labeled as Wade's girlfriend.

And he had not disabused them of the notion.

Wade tapped the tickets against the table edge. "What do you think?"

"They seem very nice."

"No. I mean, about Independence Day. Would you like to go with me? It's a big event for Sundown Valley. Carnival, rodeo, ball games, three-legged races, picnic, fireworks, you name it. Maybe take the triplets to the petting zoo?"

She'd love to. She'd love sharing the babies' delight. And she'd love being with Wade, though he was only asking her because the couple had brought up the topic. And because he'd need help with the triplets.

But should she? Should she allow herself to get any more involved on a personal level when she would be leaving at the end of summer?

What difference did leaving make? Tulsa wasn't that far away.

Too far, however, for a real relationship. Which they did not have.

Who was she kidding? Wade had been clear from the start. He still harbored deep feelings for his former wife. Kyra would be crazy to let herself fall in love with a man who pushed her away at every turn.

"I'm scheduled to be off work on the Fourth, remember?" If she stayed in town to attend the celebration, she'd be working, not on a date. It was best if she reminded herself, and him, of that fact.

"Oh. Yeah. I forgot." With slow deliberation, and what looked for all the world like disappointment, he slid the tickets into his shirt pocket and glanced at his watch. "Nearly nap time."

"For you or the babies?"

"Both." He smiled at her joke, but it was a sad smile that left her troubled.

As they gathered the triplets to leave, Kyra wondered. Had Wade invited her as a date and not as a nanny? Was he disappointed?

She certainly was. Which was totally senseless,

considering the mental counseling session she'd given herself.

Hoisting a triplet into each of his strong arms, Wade led the way to the door. As he used his body to open and hold it as she passed through with the diaper bag and Abby, he said, "I could have won you a teddy bear at the carnival."

Her pulse, that untamable rhythm, did a Snoopy dance.

Chapter 10

The triplets climbed and swung and raced around the small playground in Sundown Valley's municipal park, cackling and squealing with the pure joy of life.

"They're having such a good time, Shelby. Thank you for inviting us on this playdate."

"I'm glad you agreed. This gives you and me a chance to hang out and get better acquainted. We have so little time to visit at Bible study." Shelby, a short bubbly brunette, was married to one of the town's police officers and seemed to know everyone in Sundown Valley. "Besides, Austin loves playing with other kids, and being an only, he needs the socialization."

Shelby had been candid about her fertility issues. Austin was likely to be her only biological child.

An old worry niggled at the back of Kyra's brain. After she'd been crushed in the tornado, the docs warned that she might not be able to bear children. Since those early days, the subject hadn't come up again, but she still thought about it now and then.

First, though, she needed a husband.

Wade's handsome face flashed behind her eyes. Yes, she was falling for him. Falling hard.

A sniffling Caden toddled toward her, holding out a tiny palm covered in grass. He'd taken a tumble and appeared near tears.

"You're okay, baby sweetness." Kyra wiped away the grass and smacked a kiss right in the center of his little hand. "See? All fixed up."

The sad expression disappeared. Caden gurgled out a reply and hurried back to his pals.

"These babies adore you."

"I adore them in return."

The bag crinkled as Shelby withdrew a potato chip. "How are you and Wade getting along?"

"Fine."

Shelby, sitting beside her at the concrete picnic table, gave her an elbow nudge. "I mean, how are you *really* getting along? He's a good guy. Hard worker. Runs a successful ranching operation. He's no slouch in the looks department, either."

"Can't argue that."

"So, what gives?"

"I'm the nanny. He's my boss."

"Oh, brother." Shelby crunched another chip in disgust. "Seriously? I saw the two of you at church. You're so cute together, and you're telling me there are no sparks?"

"Sparks are overrated."

Shelby hooted. "Now you're talking."

Kyra held out a hand, stop-sign style. "There is nothing romantic between us, Shelby. For real. Wade's still hung up on his ex-wife."

Shelby rolled her green, green eyes. "That woman, don't get me started. Sabrina Myers is a piece of work. And yes, she went by Myers, even after they married. She's beautiful, but as shallow as a dry pond." She hitched both shoulders up close to her ears. "If I sound judgy, I am only judging her by the fruit she bore, and that's perfectly scriptural."

Kyra chuckled.

"Well, it is," Shelby said with a sniff. "Sabrina was a drama queen, self-centered and spoiled. She treated all of us in Sundown Valley like we were ticks on her favorite poodle."

Very descriptive. And sad. The citizens of Sundown Valley were, for the most part, good salt-of-the-earth people. "But Wade loved her. He married her."

"Men are blind sometimes, especially when a woman is as beautiful as Sabrina. We're talking high maintenance, movie-star gorgeous, tons of lush brown hair, huge violet eyes and long shapely legs up to the moon."

Which made Kyra feel as attractive as a dishrag. She wasn't even close to beautiful. Presentably pretty, but not gorgeous.

"She wasn't from this area?"

"Definitely not. I'm not sure where they met, but she was not a small-town country girl."

As Kyra pondered this bit of information, the wind picked up and sailed a napkin from the table. Kyra trotted after it. Ben considered this a game and toddled to help. She scooped him up for a kiss, letting him carry the napkin back to the table.

Shelby was frowning at the sky. "Teddy warned me that we might be in for a storm today. I should probably head home. He frets unless Austin and I are safe and sound if the siren blows."

"Siren?"

"Tornado warning. Don't worry, it only blows if a tornado is spotted in the area."

As if someone had poured ice water down her back, Kyra shivered. Not a storm. *Please, dear Jesus, not a storm.*

While they'd talked and the kids had played, thick dark clouds had rolled in. The sun had disappeared. The air felt hot and sticky.

Panic rose in her throat. She swallowed it. There was nothing to get upset over.

There hadn't been a tornado in Oklahoma in over a year. And she hadn't had a flashback in months. She was fine. The babies were fine.

Wade had a storm shelter.

She needed to get them home.

Quickly, she stuffed the remains of the picnic lunch into a bag, deposited trash in the nearby containers and called to Abby, Caden and Ben.

"You can come to our house until this blows over if you want," Shelby offered.

"We're okay. I'll head to the ranch."

A gust of wind whipped her hair back from her face.

"Call me when you get there."

"Will do." When another gust of wind pushed Abby onto her bottom, Kyra grabbed her and Caden and ran toward Wade's truck, put them inside and hurried back for Ben who was fighting the wind to keep up.

Fat droplets of rain struck the windshield as they drove away from the park.

"It's only rain," she said, more to herself than to the babies buckled into the back seat.

The wipers flapped a rhythm against the windshield, smearing dust and rain.

"It's only rain," she said again. "God is watering the flowers. We are safe."

Plenty of rain had fallen in the last year. She could handle rain.

But her heart pounded and her mouth had gone dry as baby powder from the moment Shelly mentioned the word *tornado.*

A jagged bolt of lightning split the sky in front of the car. She jumped. A tiny shriek slid between her lips.

Don't scare the babies. Take care of your charges. They are your responsibility.

Thunder rumbled, deep and loud. More lightning flashed. The dark clouds lit up, flickering like fireflies, only far more terrifying.

Help me, teacher.

Her chest hurt. Unwanted images of that terrible day pressed in. Flashing, like the lightning, until she wasn't sure where she was.

Clinging to reality, Kyra fought against the flashback.

"The babies. I have three babies. I have to get them home. Remain focused." She clenched her teeth together hard, struggling to remain in the present.

What would happen if she lost control? If she forgot where she was? Something terrible could happen to Wade's children. She must protect the children.

Teacher. Teacher!

Hands gripping the steering wheel, she prayed, "When I am afraid, I will put my trust in You. I trust You, Lord. I trust You. You are my strength and refuge, an ever-present help in time of trouble."

Rain pounded Wade's truck as she guided it the ten miles from town to the ranch, murmuring every scripture that rolled through her mind.

By God's grace and mercy, she made the drive in one piece.

As she turned into the driveway, her fingers trembled so badly she couldn't work the garage remote.

Suddenly, the door rose as if by mental telepathy.

Wade stood inside the structure, waiting.

She'd never been so thrilled to see anyone in her life.

"Thank you, Jesus." She pulled in, turned off the key and leaned her forehead on the steering wheel. They were safe. The babies were safe.

Wade opened the driver's-side door. "Are you okay?"

She lifted her face. "Is there a tornado? The babies. The babies. Hurry."

She must sound like a madwoman.

He put a reassuring hand on her arm. "No tornado, Kyra. Only a thunderstorm. A fierce one, but we'll weather it."

Tears sprang to Kyra's eyes. She batted them away. "Oh. Thank God."

"Hey, now. You're all right. Everything's all right."

He reached for her, and she fell into his arms, shaking so hard she thought she might fall to the concrete floor and dissolve into a hysterical puddle.

As if Wade sensed her fear, he pulled her shivering body close to his very warm, sturdy, chest. Solid. Safe. Caring.

"Storms scare you?" he whispered against her hair.

She nodded, unable yet to explain the reasons.

Wade stroked her back, murmuring reassurances, as tenderly as he did for the triplets.

She'd been afraid, and he'd instinctively embraced her.

But the touch of his lips against her ear was a different matter.

A reaction, surely. Nothing to ponder.

More importantly, she hadn't lost control. She'd fought off the flashback. She'd brought the triplets safely home.

Everything *was* all right.

Slowly, her heart rate settled and the shaking ceased, though she felt as weak as a newborn kitten.

After a bit, the storm inside abated. Kyra sucked in a long breath and on the exhale said, "We should get the babies inside. They must be scared."

"They're asleep." His quiet baritone rumbled above the rain pounding outside the garage.

"Asleep?" Reluctant to be out of Wade's strong, comforting arms, she turned only her head toward the back seat. Three sets of eyes were closed in peaceful rest. The triplets had slept while she panicked.

There was a lesson there somewhere. She'd think about it later.

She rested her cheek against Wade's chest, aware of his steady, confident heartbeat, and sighed in contentment.

She'd needed him, and he'd been here for her. No questions asked, no mockery. He'd simply pulled her into his arms and made her feel safe.

"I thought," she whispered, when the dryness freed

her tongue, "I was going to have a flashback. I was afraid of losing control and letting something happen to the triplets."

He eased her back a little to look into her face. "Flashback?"

"PTSD. I should have told you before you hired me, but I thought I was over the worst of it. I would never have intentionally endangered your children."

"PTSD?" His eyebrows slammed together. "From what? What happened, Kyra?"

The concern in his tone made her brave. She should have told him before. Now she did.

"A tornado warning came over the school intercom, but I couldn't move fast enough. Several of my students were in wheelchairs, others had limited ability to fully comprehend the danger. I got most of the children out with a paraprofessional, but then the tornado struck, loud and powerful. The whole world turned upside down. Boards and bricks and desks flew around us. The ceiling crashed in and—"

Kyra stopped. Her heart hammered wildly, as if the organ would escape her rib cage and fly away. Her throat had thickened, shutting off her air.

Now was not the time to flashback to that awful day.

Sensing her distress, Wade began the soothing back rubs again. "I've got you. You're okay. Safe and sound right here in the garage with me. I've got you."

Bless him. He'd instinctively reoriented her to the garage, understanding the danger of PTSD.

Kyra nodded, swallowing the thickness, taking a deep shaky breath.

"Tristan. He was eight. A second-grader." She bit her lip, fought the grief. "I heard him calling me. *Teacher,*

teacher! I could see him. But I couldn't reach him. Oh, Wade, I tried so hard."

Her words broke on a sob. She reined it in. Gulped. Started again.

"I dug and scratched." She looked down at her hands, curled against broad shoulders. "I didn't even notice my bloody fingers. They didn't matter. I had to save my kids. But I couldn't. I couldn't."

Tears leaked from her eyes. She hid her face against Wade's shirt, though this time she didn't fight off the emotion. Tristan was worth her tears.

"You tried, honey." Wade's deep voice choked with emotion. He snugged her closer, his heart as tumultuous as hers. "I know you tried."

"He was trapped upside down in his wheelchair, his face only inches from a floor rapidly filling with water." She closed her eyes against the memory, but it was there, waiting, like always. Haunting and guilt inducing. "A ton of debris and bricks covered me from the waist down. I could only move my arms."

She shuddered in a breath, leaking it out in a painful whisper. "After a while…he didn't call out anymore."

The memory of that terrible silence, broken only by the shifting bricks and the distant sirens, was forever etched on her soul.

She'd broken three fingers fighting to dig free in those last awful, silent moments before it was too late to save him. And she'd failed.

"He drowned. My sweet little Tristan with the biggest smile you've ever seen died because I couldn't reach him."

Wade tipped her chin upward with his strong fingers, blue eyes filled with compassion, sharing her grief.

"I'm sorry. So sorry. But I know you, Kyra. If it had been in your power to save that child, you would have. You were hurt, too."

His thumbs stroked her face, catching the tears she couldn't seem to stop.

"My back was broken in a couple of places. A few other injuries, too."

Wade shook his head, as if in disbelief.

"My strong, amazing Kyra." He kissed her then, a kiss of compassion, of comfort, as gentle as the ones he gave the triplets. A tender touch of lips.

Her foolish heart reacted as if they were a great romance for the ages.

When the too-short kiss ended, he studied her tear-stained face for several seconds before, embarrassed, she forced herself to pull away. "I'm okay now."

"You sure?" His long rancher's hands rested on her shoulders. Strong, dependable hands that could wrangle a bull or soothe a baby. Or a panicked woman.

"Yes. Thank you for…being kind." *For holding me. For kissing me.*

"Kind," he whispered as if to himself. "Yes. Kind."

A beat passed while the rain drilled the roof and Kyra longed to step back into his arms.

She didn't, though.

If she'd been confused about her feelings—and his—before, she was even more bewildered now.

The Sundown Valley Independence Day celebration was in full swing. And Wade wondered why he'd come at all.

Being a divorced dad instead of married or single

was no fun. He felt old and lonely, pushing a trio of tots around in a triple stroller all by himself.

Bowie was here somewhere, probably silently grinning at a girl or two who were trying to coerce him onto the Ferris wheel. He might ride the Ferris wheel or even go on a date, but the relationship would end there. Bowie never let anyone get too close.

Wade had watched him go through the cycle a dozen times. Bowie was a nice guy, a great friend, the man to call in a time of need, but his heart was as closed off as a top security military base.

He had a good notion why his cousin was so wary, but they never talked about Bowie's parents or the scars he carried deep inside. Maybe that was the problem with the Trudeau boys. They held too much inside, and it ate away at them like rust on an old '57 Chevy.

Pausing at the cotton-candy stand, Wade ordered a cone of the fluffy sugar. The girl who waited on him smiled at the triplets but barely noticed their dad.

Such was his life now.

He shoved a wad of spun sugar in his mouth. Normally, he'd find some friends and tag along. Today, he felt all out of whack and wouldn't be good company for anyone.

He and Bowie had come to the festivities in different trucks, so Wade was on his own with the triplets. As it should be. Bowie was single. He should be mingling with the ladies and his pals.

Later, there'd be a rodeo. Bowie and Riley wouldn't miss that. In the pre-dad days, Wade wouldn't have, either.

Not that he'd trade one hair on his babies' heads for all the rodeos in the world.

Still, he'd be lying if he said he didn't miss the old days on occasion.

In spite of the heat, the triplets were doing great. They'd watched their first parade from the shaded sidewalk, alternately clapping and staring, although Caden and Abby had cried when a clown came too close. They'd squealed with glee at the high school marching band, though.

After the parade, he'd pushed their stroller around the fairgrounds for a while, visited old friends, stopping at the petting zoo where he'd snapped photos to share with Kyra.

He missed her. So did the babies. Abby had asked more than once for Kee, her name for Kyra.

Since the thunderstorm episode in the garage, he'd tried to be more circumspect with the nanny, more thoughtful.

The story she'd shared had shaken him, twisted his guts. He'd give anything if he could erase the trauma from her life. Kyra was strong, though. She'd survived and thrived.

One of the things that kept playing in his head since that thunderstorm was the way she'd focused on the triplets. She'd fought off a panic attack to protect his three babies, to get them safely home to him. Her concern had been for them, not herself.

The same way she'd fought to save her students.

The story of her bloody fingers, her broken body, the awful tragedy had nearly done him in.

He'd wanted to absorb her grief and carry it for her.

Then he'd gone and done something crazy. He'd kissed her. And he'd wanted to go on kissing her for days and days.

He'd meant the kiss only as comfort, but it had become much more. He'd felt the impact clear to the toes of his Justin Ropers. But a man like him, a bitter country cowboy who'd been dumped by a city girl, had no business locking lips with another one. Not again. Not when he had three children to protect.

Kyra had protected them, too.

Wade shoved another wad of pink fluff into his mouth.

He couldn't deny his growing feelings for Kyra. But they'd laid out the ground rules from the beginning. Three months. He wouldn't risk his heart and those of his triplets. They'd had enough loss in their short lives.

He paused to rescue a dropped sippy cup and adjust the canopy over Abby. She babbled at him, Ben played with a whirly red, white and blue pinwheel, and Caden shouted, "Dad-dad-dad."

His chest expanded with love. They melted him, these three nuggets, and no matter how alone he felt at times, he thanked God for them.

A calliope pumped music from the area of the carnival, a small affair set up a distance from the bounce house, sack races and food vendors. From here, he spotted the Ferris wheel and heard shouts and laughter as feet dangled from rocking seats high above the crowd. He saw no sign of his cousin.

The luscious smells of the barbecue cook-off drifted through the air. His taste buds hummed.

The sun slid toward the western horizon, taking some of the heat with it.

He thought about skipping tonight's fireworks, grabbing a plate of barbecue, calling it a day and heading for the house. The loud firecracker noises would probably scare the babies, anyway.

Suddenly, a pair of cool hands covered his eyes from behind. Female hands. His heart jumped. Had Kyra changed her mind and returned to Sundown Valley?

"Guess who?" a voice said against his ear.

A voice that wasn't Kyra's.

Gently, he reached up and removed the hands, turning toward the speaker. Jessica Wallace, a woman who'd once shown considerable interest, stood before him in short shorts and a patriotic tank top smiling a little too brightly.

Apparently, her interest had returned.

He wished he could say the same.

"You all by yourself?" she asked.

"No." He lifted his eyebrows pointedly toward the stroller.

"Oh, silly, you know what I meant." She flapped a hand at him and giggled. "Are you here with someone other than your kids? A girl, maybe?"

His thoughts, those disobedient things, went straight to Kyra. "No."

"Great. Let's hang out."

He wasn't up for it. Not with Jessica, anyway. But instead of refusing, he tossed the ball in her court. "I could use some help taking the triplets on the carousel."

Jessica shrugged. "Sure. Okay. But didn't you know one of the churches has a childcare service going on? A local youth group is raising money for missions or some such thing."

"That's my church."

Her expression brightened. "Great. Let's drop off your kids and go have some real fun."

Wade bristled.

"My kids *are* fun, Jessica." Kyra thought so. "They're my life now."

Saying it out loud made him feel better. To prove the point, he led the way to the carousel. After the ride, Jessica made excuses and disappeared into the crowd.

He couldn't say he was sorry. He didn't mind leaving the babies for a few hours now and then, but any woman who considered his triplets a burden to be dumped somewhere wasn't a woman he wanted in his life.

Not like Kyra, who loved his kids and enjoyed every second with them.

Or at least, he thought she did.

Maybe it was an act. Maybe she was all about the fat check he gave her every two weeks.

Growing disgruntled, he started toward the truck. Home was the best place for him today.

Taking the most direct route through the carnival midway, he passed the workers hawking darts or balls for a chance to win a prize. Light bulbs dangled over the booths, lighting the ever-darkening way.

The sun would set soon. Kyra loved sunsets.

Suddenly, familiar laughter hit his ears. He stopped the stroller to stare through the milling crowd.

Was that Kyra?

Of course it was. He'd recognize that red hair anywhere. Today, she wore a ponytail that swung when she laughed.

And she was laughing up into the face of a man. Jay Fleming. The real-estate agent.

What was she doing with him?

They stood at the counter of a dart game. Jay hurled

darts like a madman while Kyra laughed and clapped her hands.

Why hadn't she called or texted if she was returning to Sundown Valley today?

Or had she been planning to attend the festivities all along with Jay? And hadn't wanted to share that bit of news with Wade. Had Kyra intentionally misled him?

Scowling, Wade pushed through the crowd, a knot in his belly and his jaw clenched.

The awful insecurity left by Sabrina swept in, a tidal wave. He had no right to feel angry or jealous or whatever this hideous feeling was that was ripping his insides.

Kyra didn't belong to him. They weren't a couple. She could date whomever she chose.

But he'd thought she cared about him enough to be honest. He desperately needed honesty after Sabrina's betrayal.

As he pushed the babies closer to the dart game, fighting emotional turmoil, Kyra turned slightly and spotted them. A bright smile broke over her face.

"Kee, Kee, Kee!" Abby bounced up and down in her seat. The boys reacted, too, with wildly gyrating arms and indecipherable language.

Wade slowed. Face alight, Kyra didn't look the least bit guilty.

She put a hand on Jay's arm and said something. Jay handed her a pink fuzzy boa and then waved toward Wade.

Wade's nod was short. The knot in his belly had moved to his throat. His chest hurt, too, as if a horse had kicked him in the sternum.

Draping the boa over her shoulders, Kyra said something else to Jay and then strode toward Wade.

He glared at her, wondering.

When she drew near, her smile faltered. A tiny frown pulled between her golden eyebrows. "I've been looking for you."

Sure she had. That was why she'd been laughing with another man, a man who'd won her a prize at the carnival.

"You could have texted."

"I wanted to surprise you."

"You succeeded." He turned the stroller and began walking toward the parking lot.

Kyra hustled to catch up. "Are you upset about something?"

"Why would I be?"

"I don't know. That's why I'm asking. Because I'm getting really strong vibes from you that you're angry at me about something."

"Why were you with Jay if you were looking for us?" There. As childish as he sounded, he'd spoken his thoughts.

She grabbed his arm and stopped his fast retreat. "We ran into each other at the dart game. I was trying to win a prize and failing miserably."

"So he offered to win one for you."

"That's right. He did." She wiggled the boa against his arm. The feathers tickled. "Now I am the proud owner of this lovely fake boa that's making my neck sweat."

At her jaunty, innocent teasing, some of Wade's steam seeped out.

Feeling suddenly stupid and childish, Wade paused

beneath a shade tree and stacked his hands on his hips. "I thought you'd lied to me."

Her head drew back. "About?"

"You said you were celebrating in Tulsa with friends and family."

She bent to kiss Ben's extended hand, declaring him delicious and yummy. The baby grabbed for the boa and slid it from her shoulders. She let him have it.

"I changed my mind."

He wondered why. But didn't ask. His insides still roiled.

He shouldn't be upset. He had no right, except maybe he wanted to have that right. Which scared him out of his mind.

After the number Sabrina had done on him, he didn't know if he'd ever trust another woman. He wanted to, but held out little hope of that ever happening, especially when a small incident like this one shot holes in his self-esteem and turned him into a suspicious jerk.

Another reason to ignore his growing feelings for the nanny.

If he couldn't trust himself, he sure couldn't trust someone else.

Chapter 11

The Fourth of July didn't go exactly the way Kyra had planned. Wade was in a terrible mood, for reasons she couldn't understand, and had left soon after she'd found him at the carnival.

He'd used the triplets as an excuse to go home to the ranch, but she strongly suspected his attitude had something to do with her.

Was he angry because she'd come back earlier than planned?

But that didn't make sense. Why would he care? She hadn't interrupted anything or interfered with him in any way.

So what was the deal?

After a cookout with friends and family in Tulsa, she'd decided to drive back to Sundown Valley for tonight's fireworks show. If she were honest, she'd hoped to watch them with Wade.

He clearly had other plans.

Like what? To sit at the ranch and stare at the TV while the triplets played or slept?

That didn't make sense, either.

With a sigh, she gave up worrying about Wade for now to look around the fairgrounds. She'd never attended a small-town function like this and decided to stroll the grounds and soak up the atmosphere. Even for someone alone, the event was fun, festive and safe.

Families with their children filled the place. Which made her think of Wade and the triplets again. If he'd stayed, they could have been enjoying a family outing together.

She shook her head in disgust. He and his kids were a family. She was the nanny. She had become way, way too attached to the Trudeau family.

Even if she toyed with the idea of being more than an employee, Wade sent up so many mixed signals she got a headache trying to sort them out.

As the sky darkened, the smell of smoked meat tempted her taste buds. She bought a barbecue sandwich and iced tea at a concession run by a local service club and sat down at one of the many awning-covered picnic tables found throughout the fairgrounds.

Attending a festival alone felt odd, but she saw people she knew, mostly from church, but some from businesses around town.

She bit into the spicy-sweet sandwich and watched two teenage boys try to impress their girlfriends at the strong-man game. Jockeying like peacocks, they took turns slamming a hammer onto a lever as they tried to ring a bell at the top of a tower.

"What are you smiling at?"

At the male voice, Kyra looked up to find Bowie at her table.

She hitched her chin toward the game. "Those boys. They're trying so hard to impress their girlfriends."

"A man thing." He looped a leg over the opposite bench and joined her. "I thought you were in Tulsa."

She was surprised some woman hadn't latched on to the quiet, gorgeous cowboy. "Was. My cookout and swim party was this afternoon, so I decided to come home for the fireworks."

Home. Was she really considering Sundown Valley as her home?

"Does Wade know you're here?"

"Yes." A hot wind stirred the air, and Kyra brushed a few stray wisps of hair from her face. "He wasn't in a great mood so he took the triplets home."

Bowie's shoulder jerked. "His loss. Want to watch the fireworks show? I'm meeting other friends, but you're welcome to join us."

"I'd like that. Thanks."

She finished her sandwich and, taking her cup of iced tea, walked with Bowie. They didn't talk much at first. She'd grown accustomed to his long silences.

Eventually, he asked, "What ruffled Wade's feathers?"

She tried to explain, although she wasn't sure herself. "He thought I lied to him."

The tall Cajun gave her one of his long thoughtful looks. "Sometimes my cousin is an idiot."

After that cryptic statement, they were swallowed up by a group of friends and Kyra had no further chance to ask exactly what Bowie had meant.

* * *

"You're an idiot."

Wade clicked off the TV and stared at his cousin. The mildly spoken sentence lingered in the living room like the smell of burned beans.

It was late. Bowie had just returned from the night's festivities. He'd walked into the house and, without preliminaries, had declared Wade an idiot.

He was probably right.

Unable to sleep, Wade had watched some of the fireworks from the backyard after the babies were in bed. With the ranch on a rise above the valley, the display was visible above the trees.

They'd reminded him of the night he and Kyra had looked at the stars together. And he'd started missing her all over again.

"Did you hear me?" Bowie planted his booted feet in front of Wade's recliner.

"Loud and clear."

"I sat with Kyra at the fireworks show."

He hadn't expected that. Wasn't sure he liked it, but who was he to object? "So?"

"You should have been there. She wanted you to be."

In another life, he would have been. But this was the life he had to lead. "Can't risk it."

Bowie tossed his hat onto the couch and sat down beside it. "Coward."

Wade took offense at that. He was a lot of things, but he was not, never had been, a coward. "I have three kids to consider."

His cousin sighed, long and loud and tired-sounding. "She's not Sabrina."

"No, she's the nanny. And she'll be leaving in less than two months."

"Look. I get that you're bitter. If anyone understands, it's me. I was there, remember? But sometimes a man has to close the door on the past and walk through the one that's opened right in front of him."

Bowie understood about leaving the past behind. His own life had been trampled by the very people who were supposed to care about him the most. Yet, somehow, he'd picked up the pieces at the tender age of ten and kept moving.

Not that he'd had much choice.

"Was Kyra okay?"

"Ask her yourself." Hands to his knees, Bowie pushed up from the couch and left Wade to stew in his own juice.

Such was his cousin. He didn't say a lot, but when he did, Wade knew to listen.

He picked up the remote. Tossed it down again.

After a few minutes, he went to the window that looked out toward the bunkhouse.

Her lights were still on.

Without letting himself think too much, he shoved his feet into his boots and exited the house.

The July night was sticky hot, but beautiful with a clear starry sky. In the distance, fireworks still boomed now and again, silencing the insect songs. Probably kids down on the lake, the place he and his brothers had gone as teens to show off and pop fireworks.

He stepped up on the bunkhouse porch.

What would he say to her? That he was a bitter man who'd never again trust a woman enough to have a relationship?

Maybe. Or maybe they'd just talk. He liked talking to Kyra.

She wouldn't get the wrong idea.

They were friends.

Yes, friends.

The little imp in his brain, which sounded a lot like Bowie, laughed.

Kyra had seen Wade's shadowy figure as he'd crossed the driveway beneath the security light. And she'd heard his boots thud against the wooden porch. But he hadn't yet knocked.

She waited another twenty seconds and then opened the door. "Are you going to stand on my porch all night like a Peeping Tom?"

"May I come in?"

"Sure." She pushed the door open farther and let him pass. "Want something to drink? A Coke maybe? It's hot tonight."

"Sounds good."

She fixed them both a soft drink while he settled at her tiny two-person table.

As she joined him, he said, "I'm sorry about today. I was a jerk."

"Yes, you were. And I still don't understand why."

"Me, either. Not really." He shook his head. "That's not true. But my lousy mood had nothing to do with you." He cleared his throat, took a swig of soda. "It's my ex-wife."

Kyra gulped the drink she'd taken, almost choking on it. This was the first time he'd mentioned his ex-wife without fury.

An unexpected frisson of unease skittered up her back. "Was she there? Did you hear from her?"

He scoffed. "No. Never."

"Not even to inquire about her babies?" She could hardly believe any woman would be that callous.

Wade's chin shot up. Blue eyes arced fire. "They're *my* babies, not hers. She signed over all rights. All they have is a daddy. Not a very good one, either."

"That's not true, Wade. You're a great dad. Being both mother and father is a task not many could handle, especially with three. But you do it."

The corner of his mouth curved. "You didn't always think that way."

"That was before we were friends. I know better now." Regardless of his long work hours, Wade found time to stop by the house or wherever she and the triplets were. He might be harried and tired, but his children came first. She hadn't seen his devotion at first. Now she did.

She also saw how badly his ex-wife had wounded him. "Want to talk about her?"

"No." He tipped his head to one side, his expression sad. "But maybe I need to so you won't hate me for being such a jerk."

As if that could ever happen.

"You must have loved her very much." Saying the words caused a pinch in her chest, but she was nothing if not a good friend.

"I did."

His admission hurt worse, so she reminded herself again that they were friends, and she was a summer employee.

It didn't help much.

"Sabrina was a head-turner," he said. "I fell like a boulder the first time I saw her. Thought she felt the same."

He rubbed a hand over his five o'clock shadow. The whiskers made soft scratchy sounds.

Kyra steeled herself against the surge of attraction. Scruff and blue eyes had a powerful effect on her.

"Everything seemed fine at first. Sabrina claimed to adore cowboys, wanted to live on a ranch and own horses. She loved showing me off to her city friends, like some kind of new toy." His laugh was bitter. "This cowboy was too dumb to see the truth. Her idea of ranch life was nothing more than a TV fantasy, a romantic notion. Glitz and glamour and doting cowboys. That's what she wanted. She got me instead."

Lucky girl.

Kyra stretched a hand across the small table. He twined his fingers with hers. They were cool and damp from the soda glass.

"I thought we could work things out. Thought she'd settle in and be happy. Right away, she got pregnant. I was thrilled. She was not."

The sadness in his eyes tore at Kyra. He was a man who'd dote on a pregnant wife and be proud of the babies—his babies—growing under her heart.

"What did she do?"

"Avoided me like the plague. And shopped. Retail therapy, she called it. Buying new clothes, decorating the nursery, ordering baby items. I didn't care."

"You just wanted her to be happy."

His head bobbed. "It didn't work. She stayed gone all hours, *shopping.*" He put the word in air quotes. "Sometimes overnight. Once for four days. I wanted to believe her, so I did. Anytime she was home, she was angry. At me, of course. I refused to see the truth. Blamed her moods on hormones. Stupid me."

"What happened?" Kyra kept her voice low, praying silently. Longing to understand this man better, to help him heal the wound his ex-wife had left behind.

He'd comforted her during the storm. She could do the same for him.

"Our marriage imploded. When she learned we were having twins, she had a fit, cried and screamed and blamed me for ruining her life." He looked toward his reflection in the darkened window, eyes glazed as if reliving the ugly moment. "If I thought she was going to be some barefoot, pregnant hillbilly stuck out in the sticks with a dozen snot-nosed kids, I was sadly mistaken."

Kyra sucked in a gasp. "That's horrible. I can't fathom anyone saying such a cruel thing."

"Such was her attitude about Sundown Valley and the Sundown Ranch. And me." In an aching voice, he said, "The next day she announced she was getting a divorce."

Kyra's sympathetic heart bled. For Wade. For the triplets. For a woman who did not know how to count her blessings.

"You must have been devastated." Sabrina had taken what should have been the most bonding time of their marriage and used it to emasculate her husband.

"Yeah. I was already reeling with the news that I was about to be a double daddy, and then my wife wants a divorce. I argued with her, reasoned with her, begged her to reconsider. For the sake of the babies."

He made a small cheerless sound of self-derision.

"Humiliating. But she finally agreed, after I offered her a lot of money, to stay until the pregnancy was over."

With a shudder, he reached for his Coke but didn't drink.

Kyra's gut twisted, aching for all he'd been through.

What kind of woman did that to the man she'd promised to love forever?

"Was she a Christian?" She knew the answer before he replied.

"That was my first mistake. I knew better, had been taught not to even date a nonbeliever. Sometimes a woman makes a man stupid. Anyway, I was."

"Not stupid. In love."

He patted her hand. "Thanks for that. But stupid fits better."

They exchanged a tiny smile, though his was sad.

"What happened when the babies were born? I guess she didn't change her mind?"

"Not hardly. They were delivered C-section, which infuriated her. Scars and stretch marks, you see. They were my fault. The babies were my fault. The C-section was my fault. Being stuck out here in the middle of nowhere was my fault. I'd ruined her life, and she wanted out."

Kyra squeezed his fingers, offering what little comfort she could.

"To add insult to what she viewed as a disaster," Wade went on, "we had three babies instead of two." He shook his head, his mouth drooping. "They were tiny and helpless and beautiful. I couldn't understand why she was angry."

"You loved them."

"Instantly. Fiercely."

Yes, fiercely. That's exactly how he loved them now. "And Sabrina?"

"I pray they never learn of her reaction." His shook his head, slow and disbelieving. "Refused to touch them. I practically had to drag her to the NICU window to look at them. Which only happened once. The doc said she was suffering from postpartum depression, but I never believed that…"

A sick feeling tightened Kyra's stomach. "You still loved her."

"She was my wife. I took my vows very seriously. I'd promised to always love and cherish her. Do you know how a man feels when a woman rejects everything he is, including their children?"

"I can't imagine." But she could hear his bitterness and heartache.

"I'm a Christian, or try to be." He tapped his temple. "In my head, I understand that my feelings toward her, toward women in general, are wrong, but I can't stop resenting what she did. Especially to our babies."

Toward all women. Toward her, too.

He made a harsh, self-derisive sound. "You should have seen me when I first brought the triplets home from the hospital. What a disaster."

"What about Sabrina?"

"She'd had a C-section, so I understood at first why she kept to herself and claimed to be resting. But after I brought the babies home, I thought things would be different. That she'd change her mind about the divorce. About the triplets. She didn't. She stayed on the phone, making plans for the divorce and her new life."

While the old life needed her more than ever.

"Having kids was my idea, she said, so I could very

well take care of them." Wade ran a hand over his face. "I still can't accept that she did that. How could she? But she did. So I moved into the nursery to look after the babies."

"How could you sleep?"

"I didn't. I was too worried about those tiny infants. Scared of doing the wrong thing, of hurting one of them. Sleep wasn't as important as watching them breathe." He huffed. "But then, I hadn't slept much since Sabrina made her divorce announcement."

"Alone with three newborns," she mused, barely able to take in how shattered and unnerved he must have been.

"Yes, scared out of my mind. They were needy and tiny, and I knew less about babies than I do astrophysics." He shook his head. "Bowie's great with horses, but babies scared him as much as they did me."

"So you hired Janey."

"Eventually. Thank the Lord for Janey." His mouth twisted. "The triplets should have had a mother to love them. Instead, I have to hire people to do what she should have done naturally. Turns out she'd reconnected with an old boyfriend during her so-called shopping trips, and he didn't want another man's kids."

Kyra would have done or said about anything just then to spare him the pain of her betrayal. No wonder he was bitter.

"Sabrina made a terrible choice that hurt you, hurt your children and hurt her, too, Wade, though, she may not realize it yet. She needs our prayers."

He extracted his hand from hers. She felt the disconnect as his anger returned. Nearly two years had passed, but Wade was far from over his ex-wife.

"She deserves to be hurt." He closed his eyes, head down. "That's wrong. I know it is. God forgive me."

"He will. But you have to forgive Sabrina, too."

"Not possible."

She reached for his hand again, hoping, praying he'd receive her touch as a compassionate friend. "Only God can heal wounds as deep as yours, and He will, if you'll let Him."

He lifted his head, looking at her from beneath hooded eyes. "Is that what your dad would say?"

Her lips tilted a tiny bit. "Yes. And he'd give me a dozen scriptures to go with his advice."

"Such as?"

"'Come unto Me, all ye that labor and are heavy laden, and I will give you rest' is a good one. I know it sounds like a trite platitude right now. It did for me at first, too."

"And now?"

"Now, I know He's the only way to ever be truly, fully healed and whole again. When I struggled with guilt over Tristan's death, His promises gave me comfort. And when I was afraid I'd never walk again, His peace settled over me like a hug. I can't explain it. But I know it's real."

She was still healing, both physically and emotionally, but she'd made great progress here in the quiet country with the mountains around her and with children to love.

Eyes widened, Wade tilted back in his chair. "They thought you wouldn't walk? That you'd be paralyzed? Why didn't you tell me that?"

Lots of reasons. One, he wouldn't have hired her to tote around his triplets. Two, it hurt to remember how terrified she'd been. Three, the long months of rehab were not cheerful dinner conversation.

"You have enough to worry about." She took a sip of Coke, the fizzy jolt burning her throat, washing down the memories.

"Uh-uh. No deal." He waved off her dismissal. "You listened to my pathetic tale, and you've lived through an even worse ordeal. Tell me."

Kyra inhaled a deep lungful of country air and put on a perky face. She was thankful to be alive. The year of recovery didn't matter anymore.

"I guess the worst part was not knowing the outcome. I'd lie in the hospital bed, put back together with plates and pins and super glue and wonder what it would be like to spend the rest of my life in a wheelchair." She widened her eyes at the joke, intentionally breaking the somber mood. "Maybe not super glue."

His eyes lit with humor. "It's pretty amazing stuff."

"That and duct tape." Again, an intentional joke, though a spot beneath her breastbone throbbed with painful remembrance.

She told the story quickly, hitting only the high spots. They'd had enough drama for one Fourth of July.

"All we could do was wait and see if my spine would heal. And that was up to God. Apparently, He was teaching me patience." She wrinkled her nose. "Waiting is not my forte."

"I had no idea. I'd never have guessed you'd been that badly injured." Blue eyes roamed over her appreciatively. "You look great. Really great."

Her neck warmed. To hide the flush of pleasure, she dipped her head and fluttered her eyelashes, teasing.

"Thank you, kind sir."

"I'm serious, Kyra. This paints an entirely new picture. Are you sure the triplets aren't too much for you?"

"Oh, no, no. I'm fine now. The physical therapy fixed me right up."

Physical therapy included painful months of regaining lost motor skills and learning to stand on her own two feet. Literally. But she wouldn't share the ugly details with Wade. Not tonight.

"Best of all, during that time, Jesus became my best friend. I learned to trust and lean on Him as never before."

"You do that well. You inspire me to be a better Christian."

Kyra let the comment slide by. Trusting Jesus was a daily walk, a need to grow in her relationship with Him. She'd begun the journey, but she had a long ways to go. She was no one's model Christian.

"With God's help, here I am. Well and healed and chasing triplets every day. God's been good to me."

His fingers squeezed hers. "Is the injury why you stopped teaching?"

He seemed determined to know all her secrets.

She sobered. Sighed. He might as well hear the rest.

"The long recovery period was part of the reason I stopped teaching, but also the PTSD. I've been afraid even of going into a school building. I had panic attacks at the thought of something happening to one of my students again." Her mouth twisted. "So much for trusting Jesus, huh?"

"Was that why you were reluctant to take the nanny job?"

She nodded. "But I strongly believed God was leading me here. At first, I thought it was because the babies needed me, that I could help you."

He gave a soft, derisive laugh. "You were right about that."

"Maybe, but this summer was for me, too. I've healed, mentally and physically, and I'm confident I can teach again in the fall."

She'd not had a single flashback, not even on the day of the storm when she'd been frightened for the triplets.

His nod was slow and serious, but something flickered in his eyes, a disturbance of some sorts. "Any school would be fortunate to have you in the classroom."

"I hope so. I've lived in limbo too long already."

A tick of time passed. Slowly Wade extracted his hand and rose from the table. "It's late. I've kept you up too long. I should go."

She didn't want him to leave, but she followed him to the door and stepped out onto the porch. Tonight they'd turned a corner by sharing their deepest wounds. She felt closer to him.

Did he feel the same?

He stopped at the porch's edge near a post and turned toward her. "Thanks for listening. Keep praying for me, and I'll do the same for you. Okay?"

She tipped her head to one side. "How do you know I do?"

"Because I know you. You're a good woman, Kyra. Special." He swallowed and the sound was loud in the country quiet. "Knowing you has been—" He didn't finish the thought. "I'm glad you chose to spend your summer with the Trudeau gang at the Sundown Ranch."

"Me, too." She tried to keep her voice light. And failed. "I've grown very fond of the Trudeau gang."

Very, very fond.

"Yeah?" He stepped closer, and in the next instant,

she was in his arms. Kyra wasn't sure who'd made the first move and she didn't care.

When she lifted her face, his lips found hers and she melted into him. The kiss was nothing like that first brief kiss of comfort.

This was real. A man and a woman, two hearts thudding against each other, a swarm of emotions.

Time stopped. The pulsating night beat around them. Somewhere in the distance, a Roman candle boomed, and it was as if the fireworks sparkled behind her eyes in a kaleidoscope of color.

With the summer smells and sounds and the faintest remnants of Wade's manly aftershave swirling through her senses, Kyra's knees trembled a smidgeon. Her pulse went all fluttery, like tiny butterfly wings beneath her skin.

Every sense heightened, Kyra was aware of each place they touched, of the beat of his heart against hers, of his strong, tender hands in her hair, against the sensitive flesh of her neck.

She focused on how soft Wade's mouth felt against hers, felt his controlled passion and adored him all the more for it.

He held her close, but respectfully, his hands moving with tenderness against her back.

She'd been kissed before, but this was different. This was magnificent. She felt cherished and beautiful.

And she never wanted it to end.

He had to stop this craziness. Kissing Kyra was not on the agenda.

Not five minutes ago, she'd reiterated her plan to return to Tulsa.

Oh, but holding her, kissing her felt so right. She fit in his arms as if she were the missing piece to his broken puzzle.

He didn't want to let her go.

Reluctantly, he ended the kiss with a sigh. Kyra laid her head against his chest, saying nothing, but not moving away.

She made him feel like a man again. Worthy. Desirable.

He hadn't felt that way since his disastrous honeymoon.

Maybe that was why she'd let him kiss her.

Kyra had a tender, compassionate heart. She pitied him.

He shouldn't take advantage of her kindness.

"I'm sorry," he muttered, though he didn't realize he'd spoken out loud until she stepped away from him. "I shouldn't have done that."

In the shadowy darkness, he couldn't read her expression. "It was only a kiss."

It hadn't felt that way to him. But when had he ever read a woman's signals correctly?

She'd casually brushed off the best kiss of his life as nothing. And her reaction hurt. Crushed him, to be honest. Which was about as dumb as kissing her had been.

But he'd felt so close to her. She'd listened, letting him unload his bitterness without judging or turning away.

He'd do anything to maintain that friendly, warm, accepting relationship, even if it meant never kissing her again.

"The employer-employee thing," he said. Such a lame,

untrue excuse. "I had no business stepping over that line."

She crossed her arms and turned her face up toward the sky.

He wanted her eyes back on him. Wanted her hands on his shoulders, in his hair. Wanted her in his arms.

Where she should *not* be.

"Don't worry about it, Wade. I'll see you in the morning."

She was dismissing him, sending him home. Rightfully so. If he stood on this porch two more minutes, he'd say something stupid. Like, I love you.

Which was impossible, given the length of time they'd known each other.

"Right. Okay. Good night, then."

Fearing he was about to make a fool of himself, Wade stepped off the porch and strode toward the main house without looking back.

Chapter 12

Several awkward days passed in which Kyra wasn't sure what to say to Wade, and he avoided her with the excuse that the ranch was super busy. When they had a spare moment, he was cordial, thoughtful, polite, but he seemed to regret their conversation and that spectacular kiss. She didn't mention it, either, though she wanted to.

Something brewed between them, too strong to deny, though Wade was doing a real good job of the denial thing.

Haying season, he claimed, kept him in the fields from dawn until after dark.

This, at least, was true, but she missed their conversations, the times of teasing and sharing their day over the supper table.

Finally, late one night, their camaraderie returned as suddenly as it had fled. She wished out loud for a bowl of chocolate ice cream, and as tired as he had to be from a long day in the hay field, he'd gotten into his truck and driven to town, returning with a half gallon.

They ate ice cream together at the kitchen bar while he shared the woes of equipment failure during haying season and she told him about the T-ball game she and the triplets had played.

All three babies could hit the ball with the plastic bat and run on short chubby legs around the yard, yelling at the top of their lungs. They'd tumble and fall and jump up and run to her for a hug or a kiss or a high five.

It was adorable.

Wade had beamed with pride, looking, more than once, at the photos and videos she'd made.

The conversation had segued to other topics—her hobbies of biking and writing poetry, his surprising love of history and books. When she'd told him about belonging to a tap-dancing troupe at one time, he'd insisted she demonstrate.

But though they were friends again, he behaved as if they'd never been in each other's arms while she yearned for the sweet intimacy again.

Days melted into weeks and as the dates changed on her cell phone, she wanted to push back time. As much as she desired to teach again, she loved these precious children and cared deeply for their dad.

If the *love* word lingered in her heart, she didn't fight it. To her way of thinking, loving another was a beautiful thing, whether he returned the feelings or not.

But, oh, if only he could let go and see where their relationship might take them.

She prayed for him, as she'd promised, wanting only the best for him. Praying that his broken heart would someday heal, and he'd be free to love someone again. Even if that someone wasn't her.

Most nights, he and Bowie would come in after dark, covered in dust and bits of hay, so weary they could barely put one foot in front of the other.

Kyra had never realized what hard work went into running a successful cattle ranch.

Bowie would eat his dinner from the microwave and disappear. Sometimes he'd drive into town. Sometimes he'd head to his workshop. Mostly, he'd retire to his end of the rambling ranch and not be seen again until morning.

Wade invariably went to the nursery and stood over the cribs for a while, watching his triplets sleep.

His devotion tugged her heartstrings.

Fierce love, he'd said.

Toward the end of July, Kyra updated her résumé and, with a reluctance that troubled her, filed applications with several choice schools in her Tulsa suburb. Classes began in August. She couldn't wait around forever to make a decision.

Wade hadn't asked her to stay on as nanny. She couldn't stay anyway, not when she fell more in love with him every day, and he didn't return the feelings. The situation would prove too awkward.

Wade had received a few nanny applications from the employment office. Mothers wanting a day job when their kids started back to school. Every time he brought up the subject, she tensed, afraid this applicant was the one.

So far, none suited him, but someone would soon.

Her summer in the Kiamichi was nearly over.

All these thoughts rolled through Kyra's head one

afternoon as she drove home from a quick milk-and-diaper run while Wade played with the triplets.

The day was scalding hot and bone dry, the sun relentless. Such was summer in Oklahoma, even here in the old rolling mountains she loved so dearly.

Dust rose in clouds from the graveled road, and a fat green grasshopper rode her unused wiper blades. Miles of wildflowers, yellow, orange and white, bloomed along the roadside.

She'd miss this. So much. But not as much as she'd miss the man and his babies.

Yet, this was the way things had to be. Her life was in Tulsa. His was here. City and country. He'd said as much at least a dozen times, letting her know his feelings in subtle ways.

She pulled off the road to pick Indian paintbrush and wild black-eyed Susans, the red and yellow color combination a cheer to her spirit and a pretty addition to tonight's dinner table. Butterflies flitted over the blossoms.

She drew in a breath of fresh-scented country air. Even in the heat, the air smelled good.

A splash of red caught her eye. She smiled at the cardinal and said a quiet "Thank You, Lord."

She'd seen them everywhere this summer, as if God wanted her to think of Him, of her mom, of Tristan.

Thinking of Tristan was bittersweet now, the sweet a new occurrence and evidence of her healing.

Back in the air-conditioned Spark, she turned up K-Love radio and headed home.

Home.

But not for much longer.

Rounding a curve near pasture four of the Sundown,

she spotted a red pickup parked at the gate. Attached to the truck was a stock trailer.

She didn't know much about ranching, but she knew no one except the Trudeaus had any business on Sundown land. Especially with a trailer backed to the fence.

Tensing, worry slithering along her nerve endings, Kyra slowed for a good look, recognizing the truck and the barrel-chested man. Bud Keno. The neighbor with the filthy mouth who was suing Wade.

What was he doing on Trudeau property? Why had he backed a stock trailer close to the gate?

Even a city girl suspected he was up to no good.

Without considering the danger, Kyra wheeled into the turnout next to Keno's truck.

"Excuse me, sir." She leaned out her window. "May I help you? This is private property."

The red-faced man looked up, smirked, then blatantly cut the lock and shoved the gate open.

Several cows mooed and ambled toward the opening.

Shocked, Kyra slammed the car in Park and hopped out. "What are you doing? You can't do that!"

He glared at her, one hand on the open gate. "Mind your own business."

Kyra's pulse kicked into overdrive. Was the man trying to steal Wade's cattle? "This is my business. It's Trudeau land. You're trespassing."

Keno shoved off the fence and stalked in her direction.

Kyra backed up a step, fumbling in her short's pocket for her cell phone. A shiver of fear replaced the indignant concern.

"You need to leave right now."

Her voice sounded squeaky and scared. Fear roared in her ears.

The man stomped closer, jaw set and eyes bulged. Sweat stained his shirt.

He grabbed her upper arms and squeezed hard. She jerked against his grip. Big and bulky, he didn't budge.

"You're fixing to get yourself hurt, lady." Teeth clenched, spittle gathered in the corners of his mouth. "Get gone before I forget my manners."

With a powerful shove, he sent her flying backward. She stumbled and fell, landing hard. Pain shot up her vertebrae. Gravel dug into her elbows.

Keno snorted a cruel laugh, the ugliest sound she'd ever heard.

"Jesus, I need You." Her breath short and shaky, the prayer came unbidden as Kyra scrambled to open the screen on her phone. Her fingers shook.

If the man was stealing cattle, Wade needed to know what was happening.

And she needed help. She needed it now.

Before she could complete the call, Keno yanked the device from her hand and flung it across the road.

Kyra crab-crawled backward, seeking purchase against the slick gravel to get on her feet. The man was a maniac.

Adrenaline stoked, she grabbed a fence post, lurched to a stand and rushed across the road to find her phone.

"I know who you are," she yelled back at him, waving the broken phone as if it would work. "You won't get away with this."

Unless he killed her.

"God is my refuge, my ever-present help in a time of trouble. In Jesus's name, leave!"

Keno cursed and shied away as though she'd hit him. Then, muttering under his breath, he stormed to the red truck and roared away. Loose gravel pinged Kyra's legs and arms.

Weak and trembling, she hurried to close the gate, shooing the cows away from the opening. The big bovines weren't nearly as intimidating as the man.

Reaction began to set in. The adrenaline crash turned her legs to jelly.

All she could think of was getting home to Wade.

"Wade. Wade!"

Wade heard the fear in Kyra's voice and nearly broke his big toe rushing toward the sound. He'd been barefoot, taking a brief siesta while the triplets napped and Kyra went into town.

They met head-on in the hallway. Her face was as white as paper.

She fell against him.

Heart lurching, he caught her by the shoulders.

Fear gleamed from her eyes.

"What's wrong? What happened? Did you have a wreck?"

"Keno."

The name elicited a visceral response. His gut twisted. His blood began to heat.

"Keno? What did he do?" Wade heard the danger in his voice. "Did he hurt you? Are you hurt?"

He pushed her away to see for himself.

"Just my elbows." She turned her arms for his appraisal. They were scratched and bloody. "I fell."

"He pushed you?"

She nodded.

Wade's jaw tightened. "He will pay for this. If he wants me, I'm here, but touching you crosses the line. This ends now."

She put a finger to his lips. That sweet, precious finger trembled, inciting his rage all the more.

"I'm all right, Wade. Keno scared me, pushed me down and broke my phone, but I'm okay now that I'm home. But your cows—"

Wade sliced a hand against the air. "Forget the cows. He *hurt* you!"

"Thank heaven the babies weren't with me."

Leave it to Kyra to think of the babies before herself. She even considered his cows first.

Incredible woman.

"What happened? Tell me. Start at the beginning."

She did, but when she got to the part about Keno grabbing her, Wade thought his head might explode.

"You shouldn't have stopped. You should have driven past and called me."

"I know that now, but at the time, I saw his trailer backed close to the gate getting ready to steal your livelihood. I thought if I stopped and said something, I could scare him away. I never imagined he'd attack me."

"Well, imagine next time. Don't take chances." He sounded mad, but he wasn't. Not at her, anyway. Keno, on the other hand, was in his crosshairs. "We need to get those scrapes cleaned up."

"I will." She touched a reassuring hand to his shoulder. He wanted to grab it and hold on, afraid to let her out of his sight.

"Wade, I am all right. Stop fretting."

"Are you sure you don't need a doctor?" The thought

of her injury, still healing, hit him like a brick. "Your back?"

"Jarred, sore, but ibuprofen should fix me up." She pointed toward the door. "Go see to your cattle."

She had to be kidding. "Keno's not stable, Kyra. Stay away from him at all costs. Next time, he might hurt you badly."

"Don't worry." Her head swung back and forth, one palm held outward. "I don't want another encounter with him."

"If anything would have happened to you, I don't know what I'd do. Something drastic probably." He was tired of turning the other cheek. He felt wild, dangerous, vengeful.

Kyra was a small, delicate lady, and no match for the burly rancher.

Her bravado scared him to pieces.

Giving in to an irrational need, he tugged her back into his arms. Every primal, overprotective cell in his body rushed to guard duty.

His lips grazed her soft flower-scented hair. She loved flowers.

"Are you sure you're okay?" The question was a whisper, spoken from a heart that had nearly shattered when she'd rushed into the house, calling his name.

"Yes."

He didn't want to leave her. She was hurt, regardless of her argument to the contrary. Her elbows leaked blood. Reminded him of her bloody fingers digging to save her students.

He shuddered.

"Thank God," Wade murmured over and over again,

as if to reassure her when actually he was reassuring himself.

Kyra's head moved in agreement against his chest.

A slight tremor shivered through her body.

Still, he held her. And she let him.

His rage burned against any man who'd put his hands on a woman. Not just any woman, but on Kyra. Keno would pay for this.

When her trembles finally subsided, and while Wade struggled not to say something stupid, he led her to the couch and sat next to her, close in case she needed him.

She kept hold of his hand.

He liked the feeling. The need to protect swelled his chest, flamed in his heart.

"You need to check that gate, Wade," she insisted, "and make sure he doesn't return. He had a trailer."

"And you need to clean up those scrapes and call your doctor."

Her smile was tentative. "I will if you'll stop fretting over me and go."

"I'm not leaving you. Bowie can handle the cattle." He pointed toward the bathroom. "Antiseptic in the cabinet."

"I know." Pushing off the couch, she left the room.

Of course she did. She tended his and Bowie's ranch scrapes and cuts, as well as those of the babies.

Tended. Nurtured. Loved. Such was his Kyra.

Keno's actions today were the final straw.

He was done. *Done.*

Stewing, jaw tight, still trying to control the need to drive to Keno's ranch and pound his head into the ground, Wade texted Bowie.

After another minute, he called the sheriff. This time he was pressing charges. Enough was enough.

That night, for the first time in weeks, Kyra suffered a nightmare. Trapped beneath rubble with rain pouring in, Tristan calling her name and the babies crying, she struggled to reach her cell phone. Bud Keno stomped on her back and then on the phone, laughing, mocking her distress. Helpless, she pleaded for mercy, but the man walked away and left them to die.

She awoke with a start and sat up in bed, disoriented. Her heart thundered. Anxiety jacked through her veins.

She flung back the covers. Her legs were free. Could she move? Could she walk?

Swinging her feet to the floor, Kyra stood, relief flooding in with the sunlight, reminding her where she was.

Safe. Not trapped. Not paralyzed, though her back ached.

She stretched, hoping against injury from the fall. She didn't want Wade to worry. He'd been angry enough as it was. If he thought Keno had reinjured her back, he might do something crazy.

At his insistence, she'd used the office landline to phone her doctor since her cell phone was broken. The neurologist had given instruction to resume her physical therapy protocols and call him in a few days if the discomfort continued.

Both Wade and Bowie had convinced her to press charges against Keno for assault, and the sheriff had taken things a step further by opening an investigation into Keno's cattle operations.

She prayed for a resolution to the trouble between the

two ranches. She prayed for quick healing of her back, too. Triplets taxed the healthiest body.

After dressing, Kyra crossed the dimly lit yard to start breakfast.

"Morning." Wade was already up, as usual, putting bacon in the skillet. The man did love his bacon. "Kids are still down."

"They're sleeping later now."

A cute little grin made spokes around his eyes. "Praise the Lord."

"Where's Bowie? Still in bed?"

"Long gone. Gotta finish the south hay meadow today."

"He has to eat."

"Put a plate in the microwave. He'll eat later." He looked her over. "You okay? How's the back?"

He would have to ask. "A little stiff."

"Why don't you take off today? Rest. Take care of those elbows. I'll stay home and wrestle the triplets. You shouldn't be lifting."

She waved him off, then opened the fridge and took out a carton of eggs. "It's haying season. You're needed in the fields."

He paused, a spatula aloft. "Well, aren't you sounding like a rancher this morning?"

Unshaven, Wade's dark beard framed the supple lips she couldn't forget and brought out the intensity of his blue eyes. The effect was a little dangerous, a lot manly and so handsome she nearly lost her breath.

But looking was such a pleasure. "Pancakes or eggs?"

His eyebrows lifted, hopefully. "Both?"

With a snicker, she gave him a shoulder push and took out the pancake mix. "Someday I'll learn to make flapjacks from scratch."

"You don't hear me complaining."

Come to think of it, he never complained about anything. He was easy to be with, a good man. "Men will eat shoe leather and not complain."

"Only if you put gravy on it."

She laughed. "What put you in such a good mood this morning?"

"I'm not sure. Maybe pressing charges against Keno did the trick."

Maybe. But from her way of thinking, pressing charges was like waving a red cape at a horned bull. He'd only get angrier.

Wade's good mood lasted all morning even after the baler broke down and he'd had to come in for repairs. Once the baler was up and running, he popped into the house for a break to see the triplets, and if he were honest, to see the nanny.

He worried about her, especially after yesterday.

What she'd done had shaken him to the core. But he also thought she was the bravest woman in the world. His petite little nanny going mano a mano with a bully like Keno to protect Trudeau property. *His* property.

He shook his head as he wandered through the rambling house in search of her.

She was still recovering from that horrific tornado, another incredible act of bravery on her part. The thought of her trapped beneath a school building with dying children nearly brought him to his knees.

More than a year's recovery. He couldn't fathom such strength, such courage in so small a woman.

Keno, blast his eyes, could have caused more injury, setting back her recovery for months.

This morning, Wade couldn't get that out of his mind. He fretted, wanting to be with her, to be sure she and the babies were okay.

Logically, he knew they were. The primal male in him had to verify.

He found them in the den. They were busy and didn't notice him at first, so he simply watched and enjoyed, his heart too full to speak.

Kyra sat in the middle of the floor surrounded by toys and toddlers. Behind her was a basket of folded clothes and a notebook. He'd noticed how she scribbled poems and milestones in her free time, such as it was.

Maybe he should give her more time off. To enjoy herself, preferably with him.

But who would watch the babies?

As he mulled the dilemma, kiddie songs played in the background. Abby and Ben stacked blocks and knocked them down, cackling with each destruction. Caden spun in circles, clapping his hands and singing gibberish to the music.

On one half-turn, Caden spotted Wade and yelled, "Dad!"

On chubby legs, his boy ran to him and stuck his head between Wade's grass-flecked knees. Chest filled with love, Wade flipped the baby upside down, relishing the gurgle of laughter.

The other two left their toys to get in on the game, and he spent the next few minutes flipping kids upside down, then slowly pulling them to his chest for an upside down hug and a loud smacking kiss.

Kyra remained where she was, a soft smile on her face. She was so pretty, so serene and calm with his babies. Most of all, she was loving. Could another nanny ever take her place?

In the midst of this controlled chaos, his phone rang. With a child clinging to each leg, he untangled himself. Kyra swooped in to distract the balls of energy while he stepped into the hallway to take the call.

Kyra could hear the low rumble of Wade's voice. He sounded serious. When he returned, he waded through the babies and said, "We need to talk."

A frown dented the space between his eyebrows.

"What's going on?"

"That was Keno's lawyer."

"Oh, no. What now?"

"He wants to make a deal. If we'll drop the assault charges, he'll drop his frivolous lawsuit."

"Then do it."

"He threatened you, Kyra. He shouldn't get away with that."

"Isn't dropping the silly lawsuit enough recompense?"

"Not in my book." He raked a hand through his hair. Already tousled from his hat, the light brown locks stood straight up. His lips formed a hard flat line. "But the decision isn't mine, Kyra. You're the injured party."

Kyra reached up and smoothed his hair. Standing close, he smelled of hay and outdoors with a hint of hardworking sweat. Strange how she could find manly sweat appealing.

"Make the deal, Wade." She spoke softly, her eyes on his blue, blue ones. "If you don't, he may get angrier and meaner than he already is. Dropping the charges could be the olive branch that brings peace between you two."

He stacked a fist on each hip and stared toward the toddlers who seemed to be everywhere at once.

"I don't like it."

"Have you prayed about it?"

"No. But I imagine you have." He exhaled a long frustrated breath. "Are you sure?"

"Positive. We have to try. Besides, you have enough on your plate without a frivolous lawsuit hanging over your head. I want that gone."

"Ah, Kyra." He reached out, cupped her face. "You're a special kind of woman."

"I want what's best for you, Wade. Always." The words were as close as she'd come to dumping her heart out on the family room floor.

"I want the same for you."

Though she didn't fully understand his meaning, her heart soared.

A beat of time, two thuds of her pulse, passed while they stared at each other. She longed for him to kiss her again, as he'd done weeks ago.

His gaze fell to her mouth, his tender rough palm still warm against her cheek.

He cared for her. She was convinced he did. Why couldn't he let go of the past and trust in love again?

Just when she thought he might, one of the babies howled and the moment was lost.

Aching, Kyra moved away from Wade's warm tempting person to stop Ben from whacking Abby with a block.

When she turned back, Wade had moved to the doorway. "Almost forgot something. Be right back."

He loped out of the room.

Running from his own emotions? Or running from her?

Probably both.

Flummoxed by his conflicting behavior, Kyra returned her attention to the babies, distracting Abby with a different toy. Ben was not about to give up his blocks.

Wade reentered the room. If the almost kiss was on his mind, he didn't show it.

"I had to run into town for a baler part and stopped at the cell phone store." He handed her a small box.

She opened it. Inside was a new smartphone.

"You didn't need to do this." But her heart sang with pleasure at his thoughtfulness.

He shrugged. "It's my fault yours is broken. You were protecting Trudeau property."

"Which was my choice."

He gave her a lopsided grin. "Come on, Kyra. Take the phone. The store clerk set it all up, imported your numbers and apps. You can change anything you like." He shrugged. "Or return it for a different kind. Whatever you want."

You. I want you.

Kyra didn't say that, of course.

She ran her fingers over the dark shiny glass. "I don't know what to say. This is beyond thoughtful and generous…" *And caring.*

"Consider it a bonus."

"Oh. Right. A bonus. Okay." A shadow passed over her good mood.

Wade had promised a bonus if she cared for the babies until school started.

The expensive gift wasn't personal. It was business, payment for a job well done.

Wade watched as various emotions moved over Kyra's face. Her reaction wasn't what he'd expected. He'd wanted her to be thrilled. Truth was, he'd kind of expected her to throw her arms around his neck and snuggle up close the way she'd done yesterday.

Instead, she stared at the phone, unsmiling, as if she were disappointed.

"If you want a different brand—"

She shook her head. "The phone is perfect, Wade. Thank you."

Then why wasn't she beaming with pleasure? Why did she look sad?

He'd never understand women.

Wade grabbed his hat from an end table. Boots shuffling like an awkward adolescent, he said, "Guess I'll get back to work."

Unless she asked him to stay.

When she didn't say a word, he turned on his boot heels, crammed his hat down on his hard head and walked out.

Chapter 13

An uneasy truce hovered over the ranch in the days following the incident and the dropped charges. No more gates left open or fences cut. No more creeks dammed up. No more threats and ugly phone calls.

Dare he hope the feud was over?

After generations of animosity, Wade wasn't counting on it.

But peace with the Keno bunch wasn't the only thing weighing on Wade's mind.

His real trouble was Kyra. He thought about her constantly, though he chalked this behavior up to concern about her well-being. He didn't trust Keno as far as he could toss a tractor.

He also felt responsible for her injury. She seemed fine. Her elbows healed, and she denied any further back pain. Thank the Lord. She'd had enough pain in her life.

Her odd behavior on the day he'd given her the phone still played in his head like a bad movie. He'd wanted to kiss her, to hold her, to make her happy, none of which made a lick of sense.

The fact that he texted her several times a day to be sure she and the babies were safe wasn't lost on him, nor on his cousin, Bowie. The quiet cowboy didn't say much with his words, but his looks spoke a whole dictionary.

Inside barn one, the scent of horse sweat and freshly mucked stalls rose with the day's heat.

Holding his smartphone in one gloved hand, Wade scowled at his cousin. "What?"

Bowie shrugged and went back to grooming his bay gelding.

"She can't even ride a horse," Wade said, certain he read Bowie's mind.

Bowie smirked. "Teach her."

He could ask again. Maybe, now that she knew him better, she'd trust him to teach her, to keep her from harm.

He stared at the phone screen for a full minute, awaiting her reply. When nothing happened, he shoved the device in his back pocket and said, "Call it a day. I'm going to the house."

Bowie's quiet laugh followed him all the way to the kitchen where Kyra, with the triplets spread around the floor like moving rugs, was stirring chicken and rice in the Crock-Pot.

The woman had more Crock-Pot recipes than he knew existed. He'd have to ask where she got them before she left.

Which he didn't like to think about.

He yanked his hat off. "Hey."

She turned away from the counter with a smile. "Hey yourself. You look hot."

Was that a blush he spotted? Did she think he was hot in the attraction department?

Yeah, he thought maybe she did. She wasn't the kind of woman to go around hugging and kissing guys without a real good reason. And that one spectacular kiss on the Fourth of July lingered in his mind, delicious and tempting.

Except she was the nanny.

"Want some tea? Freshly made."

He stared at her, contemplating the woman, recalling that kiss, considering all the ways she'd made his life easier. Better.

Without waiting for his answer, she filled a glass with ice and poured the amber liquid.

He loved iced tea, and she knew it. So did she. It was one of the many things they had in common. His was sweet. Hers unsweetened with lemon, and she always had a thermal cup by her side. Lidded, naturally. Otherwise, one of the kids would upend it.

"Thanks." He swallowed a cold drink and wiped his mouth with the back of his hand. "I was thinking. Weather's cooled off, but it won't last long. After dinner, let's take the babies for a stroll. I want to show you something."

She looked at him for a long moment as if gauging his intent. Well, he didn't know his intent. He only knew he wanted to spend more time with her.

Probably to make sure she was safe and happy.

Yeah, that.

She nodded. "Sounds fun."

Suddenly, his mood went from okay to terrific. He

grabbed a baby and two-stepped around the kitchen while Kyra smiled, and Wade wished she were the one in his arms.

"Baby kittens?" With the triplets secure in their triple stroller, Kyra fell to her knees on the soft hay inside barn one. "Oh, Wade, they're gorgeous."

When they'd started their evening stroll, a request that delighted her, Wade had taken them directly to the barn for a surprise.

"I thought you'd like them." His expression was pleased, his eyes sparkling with gentle humor. "Not big and scary like horses, huh?"

He knelt, too, and picked up a mewling orange kitten, handing it to Kyra. Barely opened eyes blinked at her.

The six kittens of all colors and patterns had round, full bellies. Each time one of them moved, the mama cat nudged her baby back into place and gave it a good lick.

"Horses and cows don't seem so scary anymore."

"No?" Wade's head swiveled toward her. "Think you might reconsider my offer of riding lessons?"

Smiling, Kyra snuggled the furry baby close to her face, but didn't respond to the invitation. She'd love to learn to ride with him, but unless something changed quickly, she wouldn't be here long enough to begin.

Especially after today's phone call. The trajectory of her life seemed to be taking a path away from Sundown Ranch and back to Tulsa.

She'd been praying for God's will. Was this it?

She should tell Wade about the call.

How would he react?

She snuggled the kitten closer, relishing the beauty of new life, new beginnings.

And yet, she didn't know if the next new beginning was the one she truly desired.

With a tenderness that belied his strength, Wade stroked between the mama cat's ears. "You're doing good, little mama."

The pretty calico blinked large yellow eyes, watchful but trusting of the man who fed and cared for her.

A man to trust. A man of integrity. A man with deep scars that held her at arm's length.

Except when he didn't.

So confusing.

The triplets, upon seeing the barn cats, began their usual demands to get out of the stroller.

"Not happening, kids," Wade said. "Kittens are delicate and you might accidentally hurt them. Daddy will help you hold one, but you have to be super gentle. Okay?"

Three heads nodded, eyes wide and fascinated.

"Are these their first kittens?"

"Yep."

Side by side, their shoulders touching, they showed the children how to stroke the kittens. Kyra used her quiet coaxing voice, and each child proved surprisingly gentle. Even Ben controlled his boisterous impulse.

"They're such good kids, Wade." On their first meeting, she'd never imagined how much the rancher had put into training and caring for his children. No wonder he'd been frazzled.

"You have a lot to do with that."

"So do you. Kids this age learn fast and want to please. Guiding them in the right direction isn't rocket science, but it takes time and thought. You obviously gave them that long before I came into the picture."

"Takes lots of patience and love, too." He placed

the kittens back with their mother and pulled Kyra to a stand. "You have both those in spades."

"Lying in a bed for months doesn't give a person much choice. Learn patience or be miserable."

"You chose patience."

"Trust me, it wasn't easy. I prayed a lot, and that's the only thing that kept me sane."

"Which is one of the things I find so admirable about you. Prayer first. I sometimes forget how crucial God is to every single day of my life. Of my children's lives."

His strong hands, gentle with the kittens, took hold of her bare upper arms with the same tenderness.

They stood facing one another, the triplets squirming and pounding their respective toys against the stroller, the kittens quietly mewing. In a nearby stall, a horse whickered, his hoof bumping the sheet iron wall.

It would be so easy to blurt out her feelings, to admit she'd fallen in love with him.

But what good would that do? He'd only feel guilty that he didn't feel the same. Affection, yes. Attraction, definitely. Even appreciation. But Wade was stuck in the past, and until he let go and forgave, he couldn't love again.

Because she cared, she wouldn't put him in an awkward position.

So she kept her thoughts to herself.

With a lightness of heart she didn't feel, she tiptoed up and kissed his cheek and took two steps back.

If she remained close, she might say something she shouldn't.

"Thank you for showing us the kittens." Kyra squeezed her hands together in front of her. "Now, I need to share something with you."

* * *

Wade blinked three times in an attempt to reorient. He'd been about to kiss the nanny. He'd decided the time was right and hoped maybe, just maybe, he could convince her to stay on long after the summer ended.

Which would happen any day now.

"Share something?" Her wording made him wary. "Are you okay? Your back?"

"My back is fine." She accepted an empty sippy cup from Caden and thanked him. The baby garbled, "Tank oo," and went back to the toys dangling from his section of the stroller.

"A school in Tulsa called me earlier today. We set up an interview."

Wade's heart stopped beating—he thought it had, anyway. An interview meant one thing. She was leaving. Soon.

He wasn't ready, and his reluctance had nothing to do with the fact that he had yet to approve a new nanny.

Tulsa might only be a few hours away, but it might as well be the moon. The babies were losing her. *He* was losing her.

He gulped back the cry of protest. Teaching was her dream, her calling. She'd told him as much from the start. He couldn't stand in her way.

If she wanted him and the babies, she'd say so.

Instead, she'd scheduled an interview.

"Is it a good school?" he managed. "A safe one?"

"Yes." She stepped behind the stroller and aimed it toward the outside. Baby legs kicked a pounding rhythm against the footrests. "Lincoln Elementary has a top-notch reputation and one of the best special-needs programs in the area. I'm fortunate to get an interview."

He held the barn door while she and the stroller passed through into the fading day.

"Don't sell yourself short. You're terrific. They'll snap you up like a dog on a cheeseburger."

How he could joke at a time like this amazed him. He wanted to fall in the dirt and kick like a disappointed child.

But he was a man. He'd been left behind before. He could do it again. At least, this time, the woman had been honest. They'd come into this with an agreement, and though his feelings had changed, hers hadn't. She liked him, loved his babies, but she would leave.

"To be honest, I'm nervous. I haven't been in a school building since the tornado."

Right. The tornado. Of course, it would be on her mind. "Worried about the flashbacks? You haven't had any, have you?"

"Just a bad dream one night, but I haven't been in a school building, either. I freaked out in the parking lot of Sundown Valley Elementary a few months ago and never went inside."

"You can do this now, Kyra." Somehow, with a prayer in his aching heart, Wade managed to say the words she needed to hear. "It's what you've worked toward for more than a year. The woman I've come to know is strong and resilient. God has not given you the spirit of fear, remember?"

Her lips curved. "Look at you tossing verses at me. And you're right, of course."

The stroller wheels crunched onto the gravel path surrounding the house and barns as casually as if this were an ordinary sunset stroll with the triplets.

As if they were two friends discussing the weather.

"God's words, not mine. Gotta be true." He winked, though his heart felt like it would come out of his chest.

Don't leave, don't leave, don't leave.

But she would. Returning to the classroom was her dream, her goal. He'd known that from the beginning.

She'd go back to Tulsa where she belonged.

He didn't want her to go. But he wanted her to be happy.

"Hey." He curved one hand over hers on the stroller bar, their sides bumping, their footsteps in sync. So much about them was in sync. All but the leaving.

"You can do this, Kyra. You're strong." *And beautiful and wonderful.* "You're ready. You know you are. But if you need moral support, let me go with you."

He'd die a little in the doing, but, if she needed him, he wouldn't let her face her fears alone.

"No. You're right. I can do this."

Fighting the urge to stop the stroller and beg her to stay, Wade accepted the truth. She didn't need him. She didn't want him. "When?"

"Next Tuesday. If you don't mind, I'll switch days and work on Sunday. I love going to church with you and the babies, anyway."

"Sure thing." He tried to sound pleased. "Whatever you want to do. If you change your mind about that moral support, I'll drive you up on Tuesday."

She gave him a long searching look, then turned her head to look at the blazing sunset.

Had her eyes looked glassy?

Nah, he was imagining things.

This was what she wanted.

So it was what he wanted for her.

Chapter 14

Pulse whacking her eardrums, Kyra smoothed her hair, straightened her summery white over-jacket and, with full skirt swirling around her knees, started the long walk up the sidewalk into Lincoln Elementary.

Dad's prayer moments before by phone bolstered her confidence. Her mind and body had healed. She could do this.

Inside the bag containing her document folder, her phone pinged a text message. Stepping under the shady, covered porch, she fished out the device.

I'm praying for you. You got this.

Kyra smiled through a sudden rush of moisture behind her eyes.

Wade. Thinking of her. Knowing the exact time she'd need his encouragement.

Her thumbs moved over the keyboard. I've arrived, about to go in the building. Feeling strong.

She sent the text, and a reply came almost immediately. You ARE strong. ABC send their love.

ABC, a shortcut for Abby, Ben and Caden.

The text closed with a silly strongman emoji intended to make her laugh.

With Wade's encouragement swirling in her thoughts, she pushed open the door and went inside.

The scent hit her first. The smell she'd always loved. Books and paper mingled with cleaner and the fresh paint of summertime updates. And that indefinable something that smelled like school.

She closed her eyes and fought off a sudden flash of memory, the sounds of falling bricks and ripping lumber. The cries of frightened, injured children.

Praying, seeking a place of peace, she paused in the hallway and focused on the entry bulletin boards, bright and colorful with welcome-back information.

Everything was intact. The building was secure.

There was nothing to fear.

She was firmly in reality.

As she made her way to the door marked Office, the jitters began to subside. Any residual anxiety was interview nerves, not PTSD.

Her palms were damp, her chest tight, but she was here, and, with God's help, she would be okay.

Drawing a deep cleansing breath, she turned the knob and stepped into the principal's office.

All through the interview with the principal and his selection team, Kyra's confidence grew. She fielded questions about the tragedy and her recovery, and even spoke of Tristan without breaking down.

She silently thanked Wade for that. He'd listened, letting her purge the ugly guilt and take a step closer to healing.

With every question and every answer, her thoughts strayed again and again to the Sundown Ranch, to Wade and his adorable triplets.

To the laughs they'd had, their shared pride in the babies' milestones, to the tender moments between them.

What a wonderful summer God had given her with Wade and his babies.

How could she bear to be away from them now that she loved them so?

Who would know about Abby's favorite blankie? Or Caden's need to be held and rocked before nap time? Who would have the patience to see past Ben's rambunctious nature to the kindhearted lovebug inside?

All these thoughts swirled while she answered a volley of questions and asked some of her own.

When the interview ended, she rose, clutching her folder. Like everything else, the folder reminded of her Wade, of their first meeting.

The principal stood, too, and as he did so, buttoned one button on his gray jacket. He was a friendly man, likely a fine principal. "Thank you for coming in today, Miss Mason."

"Thank you for the opportunity." Her gaze swept the other three people in the office. "I've enjoyed meeting you."

"You should know, we took the liberty of contacting references from your application before today. They are stellar." He smiled. "I think you'll be hearing from us soon."

She should be delighted, but all she could do was nod and say, "Thank you."

As Kyra exited the building and stepped into the August heat, waves of relief mixed with dread rolled through her.

She'd proven to herself that she could enter a school building, that she could teach again. "Thank you, Lord."

Now, she had to make a decision. What would be her answer if she was offered the position?

Wade checked his text messages a dozen times during the hour he knew Kyra was interviewing.

In between checking, he prayed for her, prayed to say all the right words, prayed to be an encouragement.

This was her dream, and he wanted it for her.

He re-pocketed the cell phone, replaced his work gloves and started shoveling again. They had a problem with the ranch's irrigation system, and the only way to find the stoppage was to dig.

Alfalfa without water wouldn't make much fodder.

Bowie tossed a shovelful of mud behind him. Sweat beaded his face. Scalding hot August was a lousy time to be digging anything. "If you love her, don't let her go."

"What am I supposed to do, kidnap her?"

Bowie's teeth gleamed in his dirty, sweaty face. "I knew it."

"Knew what?"

"You'd finally wake up and realize that Kyra and Sabrina are not the same. Growing up in the city doesn't mean she can't love the country. And the people in it."

Wade huffed and stabbed the shovel harder into the

ground. "You do remember that she has a job interview today, right? In Tulsa."

"Have you told her how you feel?"

Mud flew behind him. "She's bound to know."

Bowie made a rude noise. "I give up. Women aren't worth the trouble, anyway."

Wade glowered. "Kyra's worth about anything."

Shaking his head, his cousin laughed, and it was the kind of laugh that said Wade was being an idiot.

He stomped hard on the shovel, driving it deep.

Was he being an idiot? Should he talk to Kyra, tell her how he felt, ask her to stay?

He shook his head.

If he cared about her feelings, he'd keep quiet and do what was best for her.

Or was that the coward in him, the man who feared getting his heart stomped again?

"If she wants to leave, who am I to stand in the way?"

His cell phone tinged. He shucked his leather gloves and grappled for the device. The message was from Kyra.

Everything went great. Thank you for your encouragement and prayers.

As he read her next words his heart tumbled to the drainage ditch at his feet.

He looked up at his cousin. "They've already offered her the position."

Kyra drove straight to her dad's church, though she had to wait a few minutes to see him, something she'd grown accustomed to as a preacher's kid. He was in a premarital counseling session.

While she waited, she'd shot Wade a text, telling him about the job offer. Then she reread his texts. All of them.

The last one twisted her heart.

You did it. Proud of you. ABC send big love.

Big love. The kind she wanted from him.

The pastor's office door opened and a young man and woman exited, holding hands.

The tender sight pinched her heart.

Her dad appeared behind them, saw her and waved. "Next."

It was their usual joke.

Inside the office, Kyra settled into a chair, unsure where to begin.

Dad got straight to the point. "How'd it go?"

"Good. Great, in fact."

"No issues this time?" His tone was relieved.

"A bit of jitter, but once the interview began I was fine, and they must have liked what they heard because they took a vote as soon as I left."

"And?"

"They offered me the job with a significant pay raise. It's a wonderful opportunity."

Her dad studied her, his discerning eyes looking deep. "Why don't you look thrilled?"

"I am." She pressed her lips together, then sighed. "But I don't know if this is the right decision."

"Why wouldn't it be?" Elbows on his desk, he steepled his fingers the way she'd seen him do a hundred times when he was listening. She loved that about her pastor-dad. He truly listened. "You're a teacher. It's a position you've wanted. Tulsa is your home."

"That's my issue, Dad. I'm not sure this is home anymore."

"Ah." The steepled fingers tapped, tapped, tapped. "Wade Trudeau?"

She nodded. Dad knew her well, and his advice meant the world.

"I think I love him, Dad."

"I suspected as much when you invited me down to meet him. He seems to be a good man."

"He is. But I'm not sure he returns my feelings. That's the confusing part. One minute, I think he does, and the next, I'm sure he doesn't."

"He hasn't said anything to encourage you?"

"Sometimes I think he's afraid to, that he's afraid of getting hurt again." She'd told him about Wade's ex-wife.

"That's understandable, all things considered. Trust lost is hard to regain."

"But what if it's not fear? Maybe he doesn't care for me the same way I care for him."

He threw up his hands. "Then, the man's a moron."

She laughed. "Oh, Dad. You're such a dad."

"I take that as a compliment. Any man who doesn't see that my daughter is worth more than rubies, as Proverbs says, qualifies as a moron." He raised one finger. "However, I perceive Wade's problem is exactly what you said—fear. He has those little ones to consider. For that reason alone, he must be extremely wise in his choice of a mate."

"I never thought about that. He's devoted to those kids. Naturally, he'd want what's best for them."

"From what you've told me of his ex-wife, the man is bound to have a load of insecurities, especially about romantic relationships. He made a mistake once. He fears making another, painfully aware that another wrong choice would further harm his children."

"But I'm their nanny. He's watched me care for them."

"As an employee."

"When I'm with the babies, I don't feel like an employee."

"And yet, as evidenced by the interview today, and the fact that the two of you agreed to a summer-only work arrangement, Wade may see you as temporary in his life, another woman destined to leave him and his kids."

Could that be the reason for the push-pull in his behavior toward her? "That's true, I guess. When he hired me, I agreed to a summer only."

"Consider this. Take off another semester. Continue to work for Wade and see where God leads."

"I've thought about that. Wade hasn't found anyone to take my place. But the dream teaching job at Lincoln won't wait."

"Let me ask you one question. Perhaps your answer will tell you what to do."

"Okay."

"If you knew Wade was in love with you, and if he asked you to stay, which would you choose, Sundown Ranch or Lincoln Elementary?"

The answer was easy. "Love, Dad. You taught me that. Silver and gold and ambition fade away, but love never fails."

"Yet, the problem remains. You still don't know how Wade feels."

"Exactly."

He leaned back in his chair, steepled fingers tapping together beneath his chin.

"Don't you owe it to yourself to find out?"

Wade prayed off and on most of the day. He prayed for Kyra, for himself, for the crazy feelings he had for her. Most of all, he prayed to the do the right thing for everyone concerned.

His babies were at stake here. He couldn't foul up and make another major mess.

"Lord, I want Your perfect will. Show me the way," he'd prayed. "And help me forgive Sabrina."

He didn't want to, but Kyra had convinced him that forgiveness was freedom. Without releasing his ex-wife to God, he'd never experience real peace.

And now, as he perused the nanny application lying on his office desk, he wondered if God had sent an answer to at least one of his prayers, even if it wasn't the one Wade wanted.

Across from him, holding Caden on her lap, sat a grandmotherly woman with warm brown eyes and a kind face. Lena Craddock, a nanny by profession. A woman in search of a new crop of children.

Abby and Ben explored the small office space as if they'd not been inside a hundred times. Frequently, they stopped playing to stare at the stranger, and every time she'd pause the conversation to focus on them.

Everything about her seemed right for the position.

Except she was all wrong.

"You nannied for Mayor and Mrs. Reinholt for fifteen years?" He knew the answer. He'd already spoken with both, as well as with one of the children, now grown. They praised her highly.

"I did, but Mandy and Jacob are both in college now. They don't need my services any longer."

"I see." The woman was perfect on paper and in references. From what he could tell in a brief meeting, she'd do a great job.

He continued the interview, asking question after question, his hopes sinking with every strong reply.

When she left, he promised to call her in a day or two with his decision.

But he had a bad feeling that the decision was already made. Kyra had gotten her dream job, and a new nanny had arrived at the perfect time.

Might as well accept the inevitable.

God had answered his prayer.

Chapter 15

From the cool blue-and-white comfort of her old bedroom at Dad's house, Kyra propped on a fluffy mound of pillows and pondered the conversation with her father.

She owed it to herself and Wade to be open and honest about her feelings. Even if she ended up rejected and embarrassed, she'd leave knowing she'd tried, knowing that she left a legacy of love behind on Sundown Ranch.

But the ache of loss would remain a long time.

Taking her phone, she whispered a prayer and tapped Wade's number. When he didn't answer, she tried the ranch office.

On the third ring, Bowie answered.

"This is Kyra, Bowie. Is Wade home? I tried his cell."

"He's on the south pasture. No service out there."

She knew that. The mountains blocked cell signals on a large part of the ranch.

"Okay. I needed to talk to him about…something."
Boy, was that ever lame.

"I'll ride out and get him."

"No, no. No need to do that. We can talk when I get back tonight." Although a phone conversation would be easier than a face-to-face rejection.

"How'd the interview go?"

"Great."

"Wade said they offered you the job."

"They did."

Bowie, who was normally short and to the point if he spoke at all, seemed inclined to chat this afternoon.

"So, you're leaving us?"

"I don't know, Bowie…" Her voice trailed off. "I just don't know."

"Ah." That one word said he knew. "He feels the same."

Her heart leaped. She gripped the phone tighter. "You think?"

"Trust me. I know. I'm the one he's driving crazy. Kyra this. Kyra that. Kyra loves the triplets." His voice became a singsong. "Kyra's a great cook. She's a terrific listener, so caring and genuine. Kyra can calm the sea and walk on water."

She laughed at the last. "Then why hasn't he said anything?"

"You gotta understand something about Wade. Sabrina did a number on his confidence, his manhood." He made a growling noise. "Woman ought not do to a man what she did to him. And her own kids."

The usually quiet cowboy rarely said anything, much less anything negative about someone else. Sabrina must have been a disaster. "I know. He told me."

"Then you should understand. He thinks he's not enough to keep you here. Thinks you're eager to get back to your life in Tulsa, to teach again. He wants the best for you, Kyra, and he'll not stand in your way if Tulsa's what you want."

"It isn't." She laughed lightly. "And those are more words than I've heard you say all summer."

She could practically hear him shrug. "Needed saying."

"I hope you're right."

"Come home. Talk to him. Find out for yourself."

Go home. To Wade.

And pray that Bowie knew his cousin as well as he claimed.

Three chubby-legged toddlers ran toward Kyra, squealing and jabbering as if she'd been gone for years instead of one day.

Her emotions seized up. She fought off the tears pushing behind her eyelids. Love for these three flowed over her in a tsunami.

Going to her knees, she received all three at once, the impact rocking her backward. She laughed and hugged, kissing each one, admiring the toy Caden had shown her a dozen times.

She breathed in their scent, a mix of apple juice and baby soap, loving everything about them, their sweetness, their orneriness, their unconditional love.

A pair of dusty brown Justin Roper boots appeared in her line of vision.

Her pulse jumped. The moment was now. She'd prayed all the way from Tulsa, asking God to give her the strength to say what was in her heart, regardless of the outcome.

She looked up into Wade's eyes. A gentle smile hovered there.

"They missed you." His chest rose on an inhale. "So did I."

The jiggling pulse became a hammer in her heart. "I missed them, too. All of you. Can we talk?"

He nodded, serious now, as she untangled herself from the triplets and stood.

"I knew they'd love you," he said.

"The babies? Babies are easy." *What about you?*

He shook his head. "I meant Lincoln Elementary."

"Oh. That. Wade, I—"

He waved her off. "You don't have to explain or apologize. I understand. We had a deal. When will you move out?"

Was he asking her to leave?

Benjamin wrapped his arms around her knees. Holding her.

How could she leave him? How could she leave any of them?

Her dad's words, mingled with Bowie's, filtered through the uncertainty.

You owe it to both of you to find out.

With trepidation and longing, she raised her eyes to Wade's and said, "I didn't accept the position."

Hope flared in Wade like a Roman candle. He tamped it back. Just because she didn't take the job didn't mean she was remaining at Sundown Ranch.

Trying to give her an out, he asked the easy question. "The PTSD?"

"No." She took a step toward him. "The ABC and W."

"What?" Hope surged again and shot to the ceiling, hovering there, waiting, waiting.

Was she saying what he thought she was saying?

"I love these three nuggets of yours," she admitted, using his nickname for the triplets. "I can't leave them."

Hope, that fragile thing, lost all its air and tumbled down.

It was the babies she loved, not him. Kyra wanted to remain their caregiver.

"I've already found another nanny," he managed.

Make the break. Make it clean and quick before he lost his resolve, dissolved at her feet and begged her to stay. "I won't need your services."

"Oh, Wade," her voice ached. "I don't want to be their nanny. I want to be their mother."

Kyra's words hung in the air, changing everything. If Bowie had been wrong, she'd just made a fool of herself. Wade would be embarrassed, but he'd be kind in his rejection.

Heat rose in her cheeks. Her mouth went dry. Her heart pounded hard enough to break a rib.

She watched the play of emotion across the rancher's face. Shock. Amazement. Uncertainty.

It was the uncertainty that scared her.

"Aren't you going to say anything?" she asked.

Wade's Adam's apple bobbed. His eyes never left hers.

Suddenly, as if a dam broke inside him, he groaned, took the final two steps to reach her and yanked her against his chest. She could hear his heart thundering as loudly as hers.

Against her hair, he murmured, his voice fierce with emotion, "I thought you wanted to leave. I wanted you to be happy. Don't leave. Please don't leave."

"No." Her hair rustled against his shirt. "No."

He tilted her back, holding her face between his strong cowboy hands, his eyes searching. Searching as if he could not believe what he was hearing.

"You'd choose me over your dream job in your hometown?"

"Always."

He tipped his head toward the ceiling. His chest rose and fell. "Ah, Kyra, my amazing Kyra. I think I loved you the moment you walked into my life and let Abby smear applesauce on your pretty dress, but I was convinced you'd go back to Tulsa."

"Maybe I wanted to at first, but then I fell in love with you. So many times you seemed to push me away. I wasn't sure you cared until I spoke to Bowie earlier today."

"Bowie?" He shook his head in wonder. "*He* told you?"

Kyra widened her eyes, as amazed as he. "In his own succinct way, he said you loved me, but you thought I'd tire of the ranch life and leave the way Sabrina did."

"He's right. Exactly right."

"You weren't only safeguarding yourself. I understand that now. You were protecting the triplets. Your choices affect them, too."

With a relief in his expression that she'd never seen before, he nodded. "I don't want to tie you to something you'll despise in the long run. Your dreams are important."

"Yes, they are, and I'll teach again when I'm ready.

But I can teach here in Sundown Valley, in this place that brings me such peace and joy. This ranch, these babies, *you* are my dream now. If you want me."

"Want you?" He lifted her chin. Wonder brightened his face. "Letting you go was about the hardest thing I could imagine. You fill a place in me that I thought was dead and buried. You give me hope. You build my faith."

At the beautiful words, emotion clogged the back of her throat.

As if he could see the tears she held inside, Wade's thumbs brushed the skin beneath her eyelashes, then slid down to stroke the corners of her mouth.

Tingles shimmered through Kyra's nerve endings.

"I need you, Kyra. You've brought light back into my life. I know I've been a hardhead, holding on to bitterness, fighting God, and you, every step of the way. I asked Him to forgive me. Will you?"

Jubilation bubbled up inside Kyra, a fountain filled with certainty. "Of course, I will. I do. I love you."

"Then please stay. Forever."

"Forever," she said, her lips closing in on his. "I like the sound of that."

Epilogue

One year later

"Don't say anything to Wade or Kyra. No need to worry them on their wedding day. We can check it out on our own."

Wade's ears perked up at Bowie's warning to Riley. The two men must be right outside the door to his dressing room.

He was pretty sure they weren't discussing the Keno problems, which had resurfaced with a vengeance about six months ago. That is, unless Keno was here at the wedding, waiting to cause a scene.

Nah, Kyra had picked an outdoor rustic-chic venue a few miles from the ranch. The chance of any of the Kenos knowing the exact location was slim.

The fact that his bride-to-be loved the outdoors and nature as much as he did still impressed and amazed him. During the past year, they'd hiked and fished and ridden horseback in this wilderness. And picnicked.

His mouth curved. Ah, those romantic picnics.

He'd truly met his match in Kyra Mason. Soon to be Kyra Trudeau.

Man, he liked the sound of that.

Wade grinned at his reflection in the mirror and straightened his mint-colored tie one last time. Mint, a color he'd never heard of until Kyra had chosen it as one of their wedding colors. He didn't care. If she liked it, so did he.

Opening the door to the dressing room, he found Bowie and Riley, as he suspected, standing outside. Behind them, in the beautifully decorated lodge where they'd hold their reception, friends and relatives gathered in clutches, filling the space with cheerful noise. White fairy lights above white-and-mint-laden tables added a silvery glow.

"Looking spiffy, cousin," Bowie said, tugging the sides of Wade's jacket together as if to cover the conversation he'd overheard.

As members of the wedding party, Bowie and Riley wore matching boots, gray vests, white dress shirts, mint ties and dark blue jeans. A carnation fluffy with mint and silver ribbons decorated their vests. Only Wade wore a jacket.

Bowie and Riley looked good, Wade thought, for a couple of old rough-hided cowboys.

The ever-hovering ache of loss tightened in his gut. Bowie and Riley shouldn't be his only attendants. Yates should be here. His best man. His only surviving brother.

Though he'd texted and called and left messages, his

brother had, once again, shunned an important event in Wade's life.

It hurt.

Fighting off the sadness, he cut to the chase. "Tell me what's going on. Your voices came through the door."

"Nothing important. No big deal."

"Then tell me."

Bowie huffed, clearly unhappy that he'd overheard. "Some guy was lurking around near the edge of woods. When I spotted him, he ducked into the thick trees."

Wade stiffened. "Keno?"

Bowie shook his head. "Too thin to be Bill or Bud. Maybe one of the younger Kenos, but I don't think so."

His jaw tightened. "Describe him."

"Like I said, thin. About your height, maybe taller. Other than that, I don't know. He was too far away."

"Didn't you say he wore a ball cap pulled low?" Riley asked.

Bowie nodded. "Might have had a beard. He was in shadow so it's hard to say."

"Probably a vagrant hoping to score some free eats," Riley said, patting his flat belly. "I could smell that smoked meat all the way to my house."

Wade's lips twitched. They'd catered smoked ribs and chicken for the reception. "You're probably right. Nothing to worry about."

But he didn't like it.

Bowie put a hand on Wade's shoulder. "We'll keep our eyes peeled. You focus on marrying that fine woman of yours."

No use borrowing trouble. Whoever the guy was, he likely meant no harm. Marrying Kyra was the order of the day, not fretting over vagrants or Kenos.

His belly quivered with anticipation. He checked his watch. Today, he was taking a wife, the woman he should have waited for in the first place. Except he wouldn't have the ABCs, and those three toddlers were worth the pain of the past.

A clutch of Sundown Valley friends flooded into the lodge, including Becky and Shawna who would later serve the cake and punch. He couldn't be more pleased that Kyra had become close friends with the two women. Fact was she'd made so many friends in Sundown Valley their guest list was a mile long.

His friends spotted him with his groomsmen and came over to say hello.

After the usual congratulatory comments, the conversation moved to other topics.

At one point, Shawna, in her perky blond manner, said, "Did you hear the great news? Sage Walker is back in Sundown Valley. I don't know whether she's visiting or home to stay, but won't it be great to see her again?"

Beside him, Wade felt Bowie stiffen.

Wade slid a glance toward his cousin. The groomsman looked frozen in place, like a gray Popsicle in a mint tie. His jaw had gone rock-hard, his dark skin blanching. His mouth formed a straight line.

The conversation flowed on. No one else seemed to notice his cousin's odd reaction to the former resident's name, and Bowie didn't say anything, which wasn't unusual. But after that frozen moment, he pivoted abruptly and went inside the dressing room.

Wade frowned after him.

What was that all about?

He'd barely had time to wonder when Amy, Kyra's best friend and maid of honor, came his direction. Thick brown hair in long waves, she looked pretty in her gauzy, flowing mint dress.

"The bride wants to know if you're getting married today or want to wait until next October?"

Wade laughed. "Not a chance. Let's do this."

All thoughts of the mysterious stranger and Bowie's odd behavior fled as he thought of what would happen in the next few minutes.

The year they'd waited was finally over.

The time had been well spent, growing together in love and respect, counseling to put past wounds to rest once and for all. But now he was ready. And he thanked God Kyra was as anxious as he was to finally be his wife.

"I wish your mother were here today to see how beautiful you are."

Lace and tulle softly rustling, Kyra hugged her dad. He looked so handsome and dignified in his suit with his temples graying. And she felt like a fairy-tale princess in her long gown and flowing veil.

"Me, too, Dad. I miss her so much." Though something deep inside her believed her mother would be here, at least in spirit.

Amy, in drill-sergeant mode, swept past. "Time to start, y'all. Wade and the groomsmen are in place."

Kyra's stomach quivered.

She'd expected to be nervous. But she wasn't. Excited, yes, thrilled, absolutely, but calm and confident that God had ordained this marriage and that she and Wade were about to begin a wonderful life together.

She, Wade and their children.

"One minute." Careful not to step on her train, she

crouched before the triplets. Ben and Caden were dressed identical to the groomsmen and Abby wore a long mint dress with a flower garland in her brown baby-fine hair.

Kyra's heart surged with love. They, like their dad, were a gift from God.

Adjusting the boys' ties and tucking their shirts for the third time, Kyra smooched each one on the cheek. Abby twirled in circles, fascinated with the swirl and swish of her chiffon skirt. Kyra caught her in mid spin for a hug.

Then her aunts, Patty and Hannah, funneled the adorable trio out the door to a grassy path strewn with flower petals.

Kyra tucked her hand into her father's elbow and stepped into place.

The hired keyboardist and his musical trio struck the opening notes of the "Bridal Chorus."

The triplets trotted down the nature-made aisle, waving small banners that proclaimed, Here comes the bride!

Soft chuckles and wide smiles greeted the babies.

As she began her walk, Kyra looked up. Her breath caught.

Her handsome groom waited beneath a rose-and-chiffon-draped arch, watching her with love in his eyes.

Behind him, a multicolored carpet of God's glory spread over the hills and valleys beneath a sky so blue she could almost taste it. Fluffy clouds drifted above the rounded mountaintops.

The outdoor setting could not have been more perfect. But even nature's glory was eclipsed by the way her heart yearned toward the man waiting to be her forever.

When they reached the arch, her father gently placed her hand into Wade's and stepped into his role as officiant.

Wade tucked her fingers into his strong rancher's hand. Where she wanted to be. Where she belonged.

"Marriage," her dad began after the welcome and prayer, "is more than a legal contract and the exchange of a few words. It is a sacred, eternal bond between a man and a woman. God, Who created us from the beginning of time as male and female for this very purpose said, 'Therefore shall a man leave his father and mother and shall cleave only unto his wife, and they shall be one flesh.'

"Deuteronomy 7:9 states, 'Know therefore that the Lord thy God, He is God, the faithful God, which keepeth covenant with them that love Him and keep His commandments to a thousand generations.'

"A covenant is permanent and must not be entered into lightly. After much prayer and study, Wade and Kyra come before us today to commit to a covenant marriage, an unbreakable, eternal relationship of spirit, soul and body."

With her dad's words in her head, Kyra glanced at Wade and saw the reflection of her deep commitment to him and their life together.

Today, they'd enter forever. She was ready.

Wade's blood thundered in his temples as he listened to the pastor. No words could adequately convey the love and commitment he wanted to give to Kyra. In a thousand years, he'd never be able to love her as much as she deserved.

But he'd live the rest of his life trying.

The pastor continued, taking them through the traditional ceremony. They exchanged rings, and Wade was proud to wear this symbol of his covenant with Kyra. He treasured each word Kyra spoke and refused to be embarrassed when emotion moistened his eyes and threaded his own promises.

Kyra was worth his emotion.

At last, it came time to share the words they'd written for each other.

Wade cleared his throat, holding fast to both of his Kyra's silky hands. "Kyra, my love, my beautiful bride, I am overwhelmingly grateful and proud to commit my life and that of my children to you. I am a better man, a better Christian and a better father because you're in my life. You loved me and my children even when I didn't believe in love. I didn't know what I needed, but God did. And He sent you. So, I vow to love you as my own body, to cherish you even as the Lord cherishes the church and gave Himself for her. I promise to serve the Lord at your side and to be faithful to you every day of my life."

With trembling lips and teary eyes, Kyra received her groom's pledge. Then it was her turn.

"Wade, my love," she said, "God had a plan when He led me to the Sundown Ranch. I didn't understand it then. Now, I see. My body and mind needed to heal. Your heart needed mending. We needed each other, but God's plan was even better than simple need. He gave us love. He gave us family."

Thick emotion clogged her throat. She paused, fighting to continue.

Wade leaned close and whispered, "You're amazing."

Through tears, she smiled. "Is that supposed to help?"

They both laughed, as he'd known they would and, once composed, she continued.

"I choose you to be my forever. I commit to love you in word and action and to serve our Savior with you. I give you myself, all of me, and promise to be faithful, to respect and honor you and to proudly stand at your side as long as I live. With God as our guide, we'll weather any storms and come out stronger. I believe in you. I believe in us."

With hearts full, they lit a unity candle, and after the final words and prayer, the pastor said those lovely words. "I now pronounce you man and wife. Wade, son-in-law, you may kiss your bride."

Grinning, Wade leaned in to kiss his wife. Just then a commotion erupted on the front row. Laughter tittered through the guests.

In the front row, Benjamin broke loose from Aunt Hannah and rushed to Wade, arms stretched high. "Daddy, Daddy! I kiss. I kiss."

Laughing with their guests, Wade lifted his son for Kyra's smooch.

She motioned for the other two. Even in her gorgeous gown, Kyra wouldn't ignore his kids. *Her* kids, too, a blessing he'd never dreamed possible.

Together, they crouched to receive their little family with kisses and hugs all around.

The musicians continued to play the recessional, so he took the hint and pulled Kyra to her feet.

A single scarlet cardinal fluttered past. Kyra followed the flight with her head.

"Wade, look."

He turned toward the mountains to see the bird circle and land on the unity table.

She'd told him about her love of cardinals, of the way their bright color outside her hospital window had cheered her, of how they reminded her of her mother.

For the rest of his life, when he saw a cardinal, Wade would think of this day, of the day God had given him the treasure of Kyra.

From reluctant nanny to loving mother and wife, his city girl was his now and he was hers.

And together they were the family they'd both always wanted.

* * * * *